D0040747

ALSO BY ROBERT WESTALL
PUBLISHED BY FARRAR, STRAUS AND GIROUX

Demons and Shadows: The Ghostly Best Stories
The Stones of Muncaster Cathedral
Stormsearch
The Kingdom by the Sea
Echoes of War

Shades of Darkness

SHADES
of
DARKNESS

More of the Ghostly Best Stories of
ROBERT WESTALL

Farrar, Straus and Giroux
New York

Copyright © 1994 by the Estate of Robert Westall
All rights reserved
Published simultaneously in Canada by HarperCollinsCanadaLtd
Printed in the United States of America
Designed by Debbie Glasserman
First edition, 1994

Library of Congress Cataloging-in-Publication Data
Westall, Robert, 1929–1993.
Shades of darkness : more of the ghostly best stories of Robert Westall.—1st ed.
p.   cm.
1. Ghost stories, English. 2. Horror tales, English.
3. Children's stories, English. [1. Ghosts—Fiction. 2. Horror
stories. 3. Short stories.] I. Title.
PZ7.W51953Sh   1994   [Fic]—dc20   93-42229   CIP   AC

CONTENTS

Shades of Darkness

WOMAN AND HOME

THE HOUSE caught him, the first time he played truant from school.

Playing truant wasn't a habit. This was the first time. The trouble was, he was new at the school, and not fitting in. He'd come from a good county high school, and this was a city secondary. He had a posh accent he wasn't able to hide. Anyway, why should he? It was his voice.

He was bullied; but he didn't bully easy. He was tall and thin, but quick and not soft. When Brewster tried twisting his arm, he gave Brewster a very bloody nose. That should have finished it, especially as Brewster was far from heroic in defeat. It *would* have finished it, at his old high school.

But this was a city secondary, and not a well-run one. Brewster went to his Head of Year to complain, and it was the victim who got the telling off.

"We don't hold with physical violence in this school," said the Head. "We find talking things out peacefully is better."

He shook hands with Brewster in front of the Head. But afterwards Brewster was not inclined to talk things out peacefully; he summoned his gang. It never came to fists again. No, it was endless little things that weren't worth reporting. Like being tripped up in the corridor; or having your bag snatched from under your arm, and tipped out under the feet of the trampling herd. Or having "London Poof" scrawled on your locker door with lipstick, or having your trousers dumped under the shower if you weren't back first from games.

They never seemed to tire of it. And after a month came the morning he just couldn't face any more of it. He turned away back toward the city center.

He solved one problem, and immediately a lot of others landed on his head. Had any of his class seen him duck down the side street? They would certainly report *him* to the form master.

And here was one of them coming toward him up the side street now . . .

He ducked away like a rabbit, into an even more ramshackle side street, lined with rusty corrugated sheds in a sea of rosebay willowherb, and realized the city center wasn't for him today. It would be full of teachers nipping out to do a bit of shopping in their free period, board members who would recognize his school uniform, his mum's new friends and neighbors . . .

So he wandered the back streets, until it started to rain. Pretty heavily. Where on earth could he *go?* Mum only worked part time, and she would be home all day, doing the washing and ironing. They knew him at the library; the bowling alley was shut; there was no cinema matinee till two o'clock, and *they'd* just ring school, anyway.

The only place in the world was a derelict shed with the door hanging off its hinges. He slipped in like a thief. The floor was wet mud, a pattern of footprints filling with water from a big puddle in the middle. There were two big blue oil drums lying on their sides, and a heap of black-and-white ash, where somebody had tried setting fire to the end wall. Somebody else had scrawled, in huge letters of yellow chalk, BANANA LEGS IS A BUMMER.

"Banana legs" was what they called the head, because he braced his legs back tensely while waiting for something like silence to fall in assembly.

The evildoers had been here before him; this was where *they* came when they were playing truant and it rained.

He was one of them now. He was sure some kid would have reported him. The head would ring his mum. Trouble with Dad, who was already worried sick about his new job . . .

He wished he was back in school. School might be hell, but it was better than *this*. He looked at his watch: an age seemed to have passed, but it was only twenty past nine. Soon they'd be coming out of assembly. If he ran, could he slip in with them to first lesson?

But he knew even if he ran like mad he'd never make it. He'd arrive wet and sweating in the middle of the lesson, to face questions and jeers.

The rain fell heavier, making a noise like machine guns on the tin roof. What could he *do*?

First lesson was English. In a desperate attempt to be a law-abiding citizen, he got out his English book, sat on a blue oil drum, and tried to read. But it was too dark. And drops of water from the leaking roof began falling on his head.

The quality of the light changed. He looked up, to see a cat peering in the door. A cheerful-looking black cat with a white bib. It seemed a godsend . . . he was good at making friends with cats. He held out his hand, called gently to it.

It gave him a look of sheer contempt and vanished.

Even the cat didn't want him . . .

He packed up his books in a frenzy; as he did so, his English exercise book fell into the mud. Open. At the English essay he'd spent two hours on last night. A *good* essay, because he *liked* English.

He fastened his bag and ran out of that dreadful place like a mad thing—just wanting to get away. Anywhere.

That was when the house caught him.

IT WAS THE SUN shining on the wet back of his neck that brought him to his senses. He looked around in surprise. It had stopped raining; the sky was blue, with only a few little friendly fluffy clouds. And he was utterly lost. But still he was afraid somebody might drive past in a car and see him. They said the Heads of Year spent half their days driving around the town looking for truants out of school. He *must* get under cover.

There was a high, overgrown privet hedge. A giant, obscene privet hedge like a young forest, ten feet high. And a double white gate. Half the gate was open. It drooped into the gravel as if it hadn't been moved in years. The paint was peeling off, leaving the wood beneath dark and soggy. Beyond, a worn gravel drive wound around to the left. There were tall thin fronds of grass growing out of the drive, all over. Dry and dead, last year's grass. Nobody must have gone up that drive for ages. It was *inviting*. Well, at least the passing cars wouldn't see him . . .

Even Brewster might've warned him. But Brewster wasn't there.

IT WAS A FUNNY GARDEN. He helped Dad with the garden at home, so he soon spotted just how funny it was. Nobody had touched it for years, but it was O.K. It hadn't turned into a jungle. He could see where weeds had tried to grow: but the weeds had died. They lay like shriveled little pale corpses, though it was high summer. Whereas the garden plants and flowers were doing fine. Mind you, they needed pruning; the roses had put out branches ten feet high, waved in the warm breeze like crazy fishing rods. But they were doing O.K.

Perhaps that should've warned him, too. But he passed through the formal garden, suddenly happy and peaceful and feeling at home. Up the stone steps, between the mossy pair of urns, up to the statue and the lily pond, where the white flowers were just breaking the surface, and goldfish big as herring swam in the green depths. He wondered what the goldfish fed on . . .

He looked up, and saw the house.

HE HAD TO SQUINT at it, because the sun was above it, and the sun was also reflecting up from the dark water of the lily pond.

He couldn't make out if anyone was at home or not. There was no smoke coming from the white chimneys, but then it was summer.

There were no broken windows, or slates off the roof. There were curtains at the windows, and stuff inside.

On the other hand, there was a white veranda with wisteria growing up the pillars. Lumps of the wisteria had grown out uncontrolled, and been tugged free of their wires by the wind, and hung in great loose clumps, swaying, as nobody who loved plants would've allowed. Nobody in their right mind would've allowed. They swayed crazily, dangerously.

The other odd thing was the half-bricks lying on the paths between him and the house. Not many, but placed temptingly, tempting you to hurl them into the lily pond, or through the glass of the frail conservatory.

The temptation *annoyed* him; because he was not that sort of person. It wasn't that he was a goody-goody, or teacher's pet. It was because he *liked* lily ponds and conservatories and old houses . . . So he carefully picked the half-bricks from the paths, and tucked them away out of sight, before they tempted somebody else.

In the same way, when he reached the veranda, he couldn't help fastening back the wisteria inside its wires as best he could, and neatly pruning off the rest with his pocketknife. It seemed to *want* to be done, somehow . . .

And then a door banged, around the corner of the veranda. He stood, paralyzed with the knowledge that somebody lived here after all; blushing from head to foot with embarrassment that they must have been watching him, fiddling with their wisteria. Such enormous *cheek* . . . He waited, wild-eyed, trembling.

But the minutes passed, and nobody came. In the end, he moved, his legs stiff with tension. Around the corner . . .

There was a door. A double door, with glass panes in the top. One half was open. But as he watched, it swung closed in the wind, with the same bang. Then, in the next gust of wind, it swung open again.

And closed.

Then open again. The paint on the door was peeling off in great curls, like the paint on the gate. As the door slammed open and shut, great flakes fell off, to join flakes already lying on the veranda. It said quite clearly to him that nobody had lived there for ages. But if it was allowed to go on slamming in the wind, sooner or later the glass would break, the door would come off its hinges, the rain would get in.

He walked forward to shut the door safely.

And saw the huge heap of letters lying on the doormat inside. Like they'd found at home, when they came back from a fortnight's holiday. He peered down at them. The ones at the bottom were browning with age and rain and mingled with brown leaves that had blown in, but the ones on the top looked quite new. Again, it offended him: it was a breach in the sensible world. He leaned through and gathered them up, crouching on his heels and swaying dangerously, for he had a reluctance to put a foot inside. Then he retired to the fence of the veranda and sorted them into order by postmark. The oldest were over a year old, but some were only a week. Most of it was junk, addressed to "The Occupier" but there was one addressed to "Miss Nadine Marriner" in a small, mean, spidery hand. And somehow the name made him shudder, in spite of the warmth of the sun on his back. Miss Nadine Marriner—it had a thin spiteful sound, he thought.

There were a couple of elastic bands around some of the letters. He used them to make the whole thing into a neat bundle. But what to do with the bundle? He looked through the glass panes and saw a hall table, and a grandfather clock.

Well then, put them all on the hall table, slam the door shut properly, so it wouldn't blow open again, and that was *that*. Somehow, although he liked the garden a lot, he didn't like the house so much. It looked dark inside, after the sunny garden.

He stepped in and put the letters on the table. Looked at the grandfather clock. He sometimes went around the antique fairs with Dad. Dad liked to buy up old stopped clocks cheap, mend them, and sell them at a profit. Notes in your hand and not a word to the Inland Revenue.

This clock was stopped. But he could also see it was a

very good one, with a silvered brass face, and brass tops to the columns, and a little brass eagle on top. Even with the dead leaves gathered in a drift around its base, it looked what Dad called a two-thousand-pound clock . . . He opened the door in the base, and looked inside. The pendulum was properly hung, the weights in place, but run down right onto the floor. That was why the clock had stopped. He reached automatically for the shelf where keys were usually kept. The key was there. Unthinking, he put it into the winding holes, and wound up the heavy weights, and swung the pendulum.

Immediately the clock began to tick, a slow stately beat that was a comfort to the ear. It seemed gently to bring the whole house alive.

Then suddenly, without warning, it chimed. Loud and long, it struck ten, though the hands pointed to half-past two. He knew he shouldn't be alarmed. When clocks wound down, the chime sometimes got out of synch, as Dad said. But the chimes were so *loud* and triumphant: as if the clock was telling the whole house, the whole world, that he had come. He suddenly felt he had done something irrevocable. He turned to run . . .

He heard the door slam shut in the wind, behind him.

Oh, well: open, shut, open, shut.

But when he pulled at the brass handle, green with lack of polishing, he found the lock had really worked this time. The door really was shut. And, what's more, struggle as he might, he couldn't get it open again.

WELL, HE TOLD HIMSELF bravely, there will be other doors—or windows at a pinch, if they weren't painted up solid. He moved forward into the house, among the shadows. Outside, the sun had gone in . . .

He had a funny desire, every few paces, to stop and

listen for other footsteps. Especially footsteps upstairs.
That locked door made a difference. Before, one sound
and he could have taken to his heels, and been out of the
house and out of the garden in less than a minute. Now
he was . . .

A prisoner. No longer free. If somebody came, he would
have to do what they said . . .

The sooner he got out of here, the better.

He went into the first room with an open door. It seemed
less cheeky. Less dangerous than trying one of the closed
doors.

This was obviously the kitchen. Huge cold black kitchen
range, and a battered electric cooker that must have been
1950s. Stone-flagged floor, with beetles scurrying away
into the dark corners. The sink was full of dirty dishes,
onto which the cold tap dripped, its sound quarreling with
the ticking of the clock that had followed him in. Every
work surface was covered with an intricate clutter, like a
spiderweb to catch the eye. He got a feel of Miss Nadine
Marriner's mind, somehow. A muddled, devious, cluttered
mind. He didn't like it. His mum kept their kitchen spot-
lessly tidy.

But the huge pine table in the middle of the kitchen
held different kinds of things. A packet of cigarettes, with
one taken out, smoked, and left as a trampled-out stub on
the floor. A tin, with three crude rough-looking cigarettes
inside that smelled funny when he sniffed them. Reefers?

A bottle of whisky, half-empty. And a glass with a thin
damp brown stain on the bottom.

He sniffed without touching. Yes, it was whisky all right.

Again, he was tempted. But he'd tried whisky, and hated
the taste. And his first and only cigarette had made him
sick. Besides, he didn't know where they'd been.

He left them alone.

He looked under the table. There was a huge dirty bundle there: a sleeping bag wrapped around what looked like trousers and sweaters, with an enamel mug attached by a length of coarse white string.

A tramp's bundle. A man tramp, from the smell of it.

So now he had a tramp to worry about, as well. An old lady was one thing. But a tramp who probably stole whisky and reefers was a lot more scary.

C'mon, let's get out of here. Quick. He moved swiftly to the kitchen door. Undid the bolts, top and bottom. But it was locked as well, with a huge old-fashioned lock. And the key wasn't in it. He searched the cluttered work surface in vain, feeling he was wasting time he could ill afford.

Well, other rooms, then. With a veranda, there were bound to be french windows.

The next room did have french windows.

And a dog lying down next to them, asleep. Probably the tramp's dog. If he tried to get out through the french windows, it might wake up and bark, or even attack him. The tramp would come. From upstairs. He kept having this funny feeling there was somebody upstairs.

He studied the dog carefully. It didn't look dangerous. It was a small brown mongrel, with floppy ears. Oh, he could deal with that. He tiptoed forward, trying not to wake it. Reached the french windows, and twisted the handle.

The door didn't open. He saw with despair the empty keyhole. Almost felt the dog reaching to bite his ankle. It must have heard, must have wakened.

But it still lay there. It lay there, still. *Too* still. Its belly wasn't going up and down. It wasn't *breathing*.

It must be *dead*. He looked down at it in horror. It still looked just . . . asleep. Comfortably asleep. There was no smell or maggots or any kind of nastiness, like fur falling off. Not like the dogs you saw floating drowned in the river . . .

He *had* to touch it. He didn't want to, but he *had* to.

It moved dryly, all of a piece, like a statue.

It was a stuffed dog. A real dog, real skin and fur, that had died and been stuffed. Nothing to do with any tramp. This had cost a lot of money. It must have been Miss Nadine Marriner's pet that had died. She must have had it stuffed and gone on living with it.

What a crazy thing to do, living with a dead, stuffed pet!

Then he wished he hadn't thought that. It wasn't nice to think Miss Nadine Marriner was crazy. But it explained the open door, and the leaves blowing in on priceless antiques, and the pile of unopened letters. He listened. Listened especially for ceilings creaking, which would mean somebody moving, upstairs. But there was just silence, and the ticking of the clock.

He looked longingly outside, through the glass of the french windows. There, at the end of the garden, was the drooping white gate. Beyond, cars would be passing. Far off, his class would be having their break. He could break the glass, get out that way. The sun was shining out there again.

But it wouldn't mean just breaking one pane of glass. It would mean breaking the french windows.

And he couldn't do that.

Well, there were plenty more rooms. Get on with it. You're just being silly. This is Monday morning the 3rd of October, and Mum is at home doing the washing. What could possibly happen?

As he turned to go back to the door, he saw the rocking chair: a big American rocker with a green upholstered back and seat. The upholstery was old, worn, and greasy. And it seemed to bear the marks of a thin body, worn into it with time. There was a hooked rug beneath it, worn through to the canvas where two feet had pressed. There was a bag hanging on one arm of the chair, a cracked plastic bag, with a trail of tangled gray knitting dangling from it. On the other side of the chair, on the dusty carpet, was a cup and saucer, with a dry brown stain on the bottom.

He just knew this was where Miss Nadine Marriner had sat all day, knitting something the dullest gray color imaginable. She was so much *there* that he gave a little humble apologetic bob of his head, and said, absurdly, "I'm sorry. I'm just going. When I can find a way out."

The moment he spoke, he knew it was a mistake. Speaking to the chair made Miss Nadine Marriner more real in his mind. He could imagine her now. Very thin, with gold-rimmed spectacles and gray hair pulled back in a bun, and knobbled veined thin hands, knitting, knitting. He couldn't *move*, for looking at the chair. He couldn't make his legs work, standing facing the empty chair, with the stuffed dog at his back.

Then with a yell like a feeble war cry, he moved and leaped past the chair. As he passed it, he must have caught it with his sleeve. For when he glanced back from the doorway, it was rocking, rocking.

Frantic now, he tried other doors. All were locked. And he could tell from trying to force the handles that they were very solid old Victorian doors. And from under one came the foulest smell he had ever smelled. A smell of utter rottenness. Like the time they came back from holiday, and the freezer had broken down, and the smell of that joint of pork Mum had been keeping for their return . . .

But he consoled himself that that door was plain, and next to the kitchen. Must be the pantry door. Some meat must have been left, and gone rotten inside. He thought he heard the buzz of a bluebottle, through the thick woodwork.

But he could've been imagining it. He knew he was in a very odd mood, one he'd never been in before. His body was shaky, his mind all whirly. He was starting to be silly and imagine things. He must get a grip on himself.

He must go upstairs. Look for keys, he told himself. So he wouldn't have to start smashing his way out . . . But he knew he was kidding himself.

Upstairs was calling him. He didn't want to go up there; he didn't want the shock of opening any more doors, of walking into rooms where he didn't know what he might see. The tramp asleep, snoring. Suddenly opening his eyes. Or Miss Nadine Marriner, standing watching him. Or Miss Nadine Marriner dead in her bed.

He hovered piteously in the hall, looking out through the glass in the door at the sunlit garden. Again, he contemplated smashing the glass, knocking out every sharp edge and crawling through to freedom. But suppose somebody came, while he was doing it . . .

Finally he turned, and slowly began to climb the stairs. The stair carpet was thick, but old and gray and full of dust. The dust shot up in clouds from his feet, hung golden in the shafts of sunlight streaming down from the window on the landing above. The dust of Miss Nadine Marriner, creeping, sweet and sour, into his body through his nostrils, so he wanted to stop breathing.

And the sun was shining down the stairs so brightly he couldn't see if there was anybody standing at the top of the stairs, waiting for him.

But there wasn't. There was just the window. It was

clear in the middle (though very much spattered by dirty rain) but blue and red stained glass around the edges. Through it he could see what appeared to be the kitchen garden. Again, not much in the way of weeds, but cabbages sprouting to a great height with yellow strings of flowers. And beyond the garden, quite far off, a kind of summer-house with glass windows.

And the window in the door of it was broken.

And through the jagged hole he could see what looked like a flat bloated figure, half lying, half sitting inside. He might have thought it was a bundle of dark old clothes, except he could see the head, and a blurred sort of face, with dark holes for eyes, looking up at him in a rather pleading way. It gave him quite a turn, though it must have been fifty or sixty feet away, just sitting there, staring up at this window.

Then he realized it must be a made-up stuffed figure, a Guy Fawkes or a scarecrow, because the face was all weird colors, green and purple, and the eyes were just holes.

He had enough worries without scarecrows stored in summerhouses. Find a key, and get out!

The first three doors were locked. Again he smelled, more faintly, the smell of rotting pork; but he thought it must be drifting upstairs from the larder. For it was *very* much fainter.

The last door was half-open. But the room beyond was dim, as if the curtains were drawn. He hovered, listening. No sound at all, except the ticking of the clock, coming up the stairs behind. He sniffed. There was a very strong smell of old lady. Lavender and powder, old sweat and the sickly sweetness of age. He felt pulled forward, as the receding waves had tried to suck him out to sea last summer. But he fought against it now. As if he knew once he was sucked into that room, he would never come out again.

And then, downstairs, the clock struck eleven. The clang seemed to fill the whole house. And it was as if it was announcing his presence outside that door.

He was caught. He had to walk in.

There was a figure standing straight opposite him, in the gloom of the drawn curtains. A figure that watched him with eyes that glared out of a white face, standing stock-still.

It was no bigger than he himself. It made no move to attack, standing with its arms by its sides. It looked . . .

Hopeless, helpless, drowned in the green gloom.

He half raised an arm, to ward off the terrified glare.

The figure in turn raised its arm.

And then he saw it was himself: caught in the long mirror of a wardrobe. But lost, drowned, frozen as if under green ice.

He tried to force a laugh; it failed, making a weird mad sound in that dim silent room. But it released him to move.

He swung around to look behind the door, where the bed would be . . .

The bed was made, pulled flat and tight. Nothing to be afraid of there. He looked under the bed: nothing but the dim shine of a white chamber pot. He let his eyes pan to the left. A chair with a heap of old lady's dark clothes piled up on it. Another mirror, above a dressing table as cluttered as the kitchen work surfaces downstairs. Miss Nadine Marriner's, without a doubt. Then a tall dark chest of drawers, with half the drawers pulled open, and pale female things hanging out.

Then the big white marble fireplace, and above it . . .

Miss Nadine Marriner stared down at him.

Larger than life. Seated in the rocking chair from downstairs, with her knobbled veined hands clutching the wooden arms with a grip that said "Mine, mine, *mine!*" She looked exactly as he had imagined her, when he first saw the rocking chair. Tall, very bony, with gold-rimmed spectacles and her gray hair pulled back tight in a bun.

A portrait. A picture in oils, in a huge gilt frame. Just a huge oil painting. But how could he have known so exactly what she would look like, before he saw the portrait?

And why did the face stare at him so, the eyes seeming to burn right through him, as if she was alive? Why did it make him feel so small, so helpless, so . . . obedient? Why did her presence seem to fill the whole room, the whole house? And why did he stand so submissive, waiting for her to . . .

Speak. He was waiting for her to speak; to give him orders. To obey her every whim, even as he saw, without hope, the cruelty in her, the lack of any sort of kindness or mercy.

He waited.

And then he saw the picture was a little crooked; it sloped down a little to the right.

He must set it straight. Slowly he walked up to it, closer and closer to those claw hands, those piercing eyes.

He tried to straighten the picture by grasping the two bottom corners. But the picture wouldn't move; it seemed stuck to the wall. He tried to pull it away, toward him.

As it moved and straightened, something fell down from behind it, bounced on the marble top of the mantelpiece, and fell among the soot splashes that the rain had left on the green tiles of the hearth.

A thick brown letter.

Well, he couldn't just leave it there, getting dirty among

the soot. He picked it up and read the writing on the
envelope.

TO THE FINDER.

That was *him*. And he was in no state to disobey the tall,
spiky, spidery handwriting of Miss Nadine Marriner.

Inside was another envelope, and a note.

The note said: DELIVER THIS BY HAND TO THE ADDRESS
ON THE ENVELOPE.

The envelope was addressed to a firm of solicitors in
the city center. It was open, and he could not help being
curious. He looked up at the piercing eyes of Miss Nadine
Marriner, and, strangely, they did not forbid him.

He opened the envelope and unfolded the large stiff
piece of paper. It was headed, THE LAST WILL AND TESTA-
MENT OF NADINE MARRINER, DECEASED.

He shuddered a little, and read on.

*I am dead. Have no doubt about that. Do not look for my corpse.
You will never find it. I am in a very safe place.*

*But I leave my house, lands, and all I am possessed of to the
bearer of this letter. I have found him honest and trustworthy.
He will care for the house and my possessions now I am dead.
He gets it only on condition that he sells nothing, but lives in
this house, and keeps it as it is and in good repair as long as he
shall live.*

*As for the others who came, the thieves who tried to steal, the
vandals who came to smash and burn, find them where you may
and bury them where you will. They brought their deaths upon
themselves.*

There was more, and signatures at the bottom. Miss Nadine
Marriner and two others he couldn't read.

The phrases hammered through his head: "They

brought their deaths upon themselves . . . Find them
where you may and bury them where you will."

He remembered the bloated green-faced scarecrow who
had glared up at him so pleadingly from the broken glass
of the summerhouse. The awful smell in the room downstairs . . . The whole house was a *trap*. He remembered
the half-bricks he had been tempted to throw in the lily
pond, and at the frail conservatory. The whisky and the
cigarettes and the reefers on the kitchen table. How many
more traps?

And he knew she *was* still here. In the house. He had a
weird feeling she was behind that tomb-like marble fireplace, still sitting upright in her chair, her hands clutched
on the arms, saying, "Mine, mine, *mine*." The whole house
was full of her. It was as if she had moved out of her tall
frail body, into the bricks and mortar, the glass and wood,
the very soil itself, poisoning the intruding weeds . . . What
had the huge goldfish fed on, to stay alive all this time?

There was no way out. He was trapped, finished. He
must obey her, or he would never get out of here. And if
he obeyed her, he would be caught up with her in a
bargain, till the day he died . . .

And then he remembered the pile of letters on the
doormat. The postman must have walked up the path
nearly every day, and walked out again, untouched.

Because he was innocent. Because he was just delivering
letters, whistling to himself, thinking about something else.

It gave him a little bit of courage. Enough to put everything back in the big envelope, and to say firmly, "No
thanks," and to lift the portrait and tuck the letter back
where it had come from.

He was frightened it might fall out again: with a dreadful
insistence; as a dreadful warning.

But it stayed where it was. So he went while the going was good. Down the dust-laden stairs, to the front door. Through its glass he could see his schoolbag lying on the veranda, where he'd left it, what seemed like half a lifetime ago.

He put his hand on the dark green brass of the door handle and tried it.

It turned first time, and he grabbed his bag and was off the veranda, tearing past the goldfish pond, down the steps between the urns, and out through the white gate.

He was still running when he heard a voice bellow.

"HIGGINSON!"

He stopped because that was his name. He had a feeling that the voice had been bellowing it for some time.

He was in the city center, between the McDonald's and the video shop. He had no idea what streets he had run down, what streets he must have crossed, though he had a vague memory of car horns hooting.

"Higginson? Where the hell do you think you are going? What's got into you, lad?"

It was Toddser Todd, Head of Third Year, glaring at him through the wound-down window of his Ford Fiesta, his red face clashing horribly with his ginger hair.

He didn't like Toddser much; didn't trust him. Yet at that moment he felt like flinging his arms around his neck. But he only went over, and leaned against the car's bonnet, shaking.

"Get in," said Toddser. "You're in trouble, real trouble. This will have to go to the Head. You kids think you can get away with murder . . ."

He got in, and held his bag tight on his knee, so that Toddser wouldn't see how much his legs were shaking. But Toddser wasn't interested. He was still cruising the city center, peering down every side street they came to, looking for other truants, and at the same time mumbling the same old crap about order and discipline that he must mumble to all the kids he caught. But you could tell he was pleased to have caught somebody; you could tell he enjoyed the game.

"You're in *real* trouble," went on Toddser, like a tape recording. "You don't know what real trouble is like, till now . . ."

"I won't do it again, sir," he said, with a great deal of fervor. So that Toddser, halted at a traffic light, stared at him as if he was seeing him for the first time and said, "You sound as if you really mean it."

Then the lights changed, and Toddser drove back to school, and he closed his eyes and relaxed into the paradise of the real trouble to come. Knowing he could never find that white gate again. Even if he *tried*.

ST. AUSTIN FRIARS

THE CHURCH of St. Austin Friars stands in an inner suburb of Muncaster. It is huge for a parish church, beautiful in the Perpendicular style, and black as coal from the smoke of the city. It stands on a hill, amid its long-disused graveyard, and its only near companion is the Greek Revival rectory, like a temple with chimneys, also coal-black. It is really St. Margaret's, but Muncastrians always call it St. Austin Friars, in memory of the Augustinian canons who had their monastery there in the Middle Ages.

Then it stood in fair countryside, amid its own rich estate. Muncaster was no more than the houses of the monastic servants. But the Industrial Revolution came to Muncaster and it grew, covering all the green fields and hills with soot and sweat and money. By the time that the Reverend Martin Williams was appointed rector in 1970, the only traces of the monastery, apart from the church, were a mean street called Fishponds and another called Cloister Lane.

Martin Williams came when the Industrial Revolution

was departing, having had its way with Muncaster. The day after he moved into the rectory, the houses of Fishponds were being demolished. The dust from falling brick and the smoke from the scrap-wood fires were so engulfing that the demolition foreman, a decent man, came up to the rectory to apologize.

"You'll soon be shot of us," he said, sitting down to a mug of tea that Sheila, as a well-trained clergy wife, immediately laid before him. "Trouble is, you'll soon be shot o' your parish, too. It's all going, you know!"

"Yes, I know," said Martin, sticking his hands into the pockets of long thin trousers and staring out of the window. "It's a shame."

"Shame nothing!" said the foreman. "Seen a mort o' suffering, this place. Bringing up fo'teen bairns on a pound a week in a room no bigger nor your pantry. Beggin' yer pardon, missus. But me dad an' me grandad told me about it. Had an evil name, round here. Cholera—typhoid—afore they got the drains right. Four hundred dead in one week, they say; one long hot summer. Good riddance to bad rubbish, *I* say."

"Aren't they going to build multistory flats instead?" asked Sheila.

"Not that *I* heard," said the foreman. "Not that they tell the likes of us anything. Other parts, people are crying their hearts out 'cause they're having to leave—not in Fishponds. They can't wait to get out to the suburbs. What you aiming to do wi' yersel', then?"

Martin gave a violent start; he still could not get used to the sudden bluntness of the North, after his last curacy in Kent. Here, people asked you the most intimate questions the moment they'd shaken hands. This chap would be asking next when they were going to start a family.

"What am I going to do with myself? Well, it just so happens that the city center is also part of this parish. So I'll be down there a lot . . ."

"*They're* a right queer push an' all," opined the foreman, drinking deep into his mug and, to Sheila's fascination, actually wiping his mustache with the back of his hand. "Pimps, prostitutes, homosexuals, actors—what's the difference? Beggin' yer pardon, missus."

"Jesus mixed with prostitutes and sinners," said Martin, giving him a look of sharp blue charity that had the foreman on his feet in a second.

"Thank you for the tea, missus. And"—he gave Martin a sharp look in return—"best o' luck wi' the city center. Yer might just do something down *there*—wi' luck. All the best." And he wiped his hands on the seat of his trousers, shook both their hands, and departed. His boots crunching down the long drive left that peculiar silence which lay like the black dust all over the rectory, and which Martin and Sheila were to come to know so well.

"I don't like this place," said Sheila, washing up the mug to break the silence.

"I know you don't," said Martin. "But it's a good living, and a good city—think of all the concerts we can go to. And you'll be out teaching most of the time. And out in the evenings. We'll hardly be in the place—just camping out."

The kitchen was large and fully fitted. Equipped down to a Kenwood mixer, and not a thing in it was theirs. Pity the main areas of Formica were in a spirit-lowering shade of browny-purple . . .

All the many rooms were the same: beautifully decorated, beautifully furnished. The sitting room had leather settees and couches, hardly touched. The whole house was

recently wired, totally weatherproof, and structurally immaculate. There wasn't a bit of do-it-yourself for Martin
or Sheila to lay their fingers on.

"Canon Maitland must have been awfully well off, to
afford all this," said Sheila. "And no one to leave it all to
when he died."

"He was *very* old," said Martin. "Ninety-four."

"But they're supposed to retire at seventy."

"This place was special. Very little work, even before
the demolition. The Bishop told me." The Bishop had
told him many things.

The Bishop was an old-school-tie friend of Martin's
previous Bishop in Kent. The Bishop had wanted a bright
young man, willing to try unorthodox methods in a city-
center parish. And to be one of the Bishop's chaplains,
which mainly involved marking high-level clergy exam
papers. And to be a one-day-a-week lecturer in Christian
social work at the Church of England college. "Plenty of
interesting things to fill your week, young man. Don't you
worry your head about Fishponds and Cloister Lane," the
Bishop had said, hand on Martin's shoulder, when Martin
finally accepted the job, without consulting Sheila first (a
sore point).

But in spite of this, for a year they were happy. Sheila
enjoyed her school, and Martin his college. Three days a
week he worked his city-center parish, using the back
rooms of ornate Edwardian pubs such as the Grapes,
drinking half-pints of shandy carefully, and eating a lot
of curious pub grub. He knew enough to wear a sports
coat and cover his clergyman's collar with a polo-neck
sweater (except when a clergyman was actually required,
when he would roll down the neck of the sweater to reveal
all). By the time the pimps and prostitutes, actors and
homosexuals found out he was a clergyman, they'd also

found out that he was a good sort, a good listener, a good shoulder to cry on, and good for a bed for the night in a crisis. He was *quite* wise, but he was *very* nice; he helped a number of people to avoid committing suicide, simply because, in the moment of the act, they thought how upset he would be, how disappointed, if they really did it. A lot of the men kept his card and phone number in their pocket; a lot of the girls brought him home-knitted sweaters and jars of jam their mums had made. A certain number of the girls tried to persuade him into bed with them, in the cause of the New Theology, but he always got away by saying, "Not while on duty." He was always on duty. Sheila stored the sweaters (most of which didn't fit, but none of which he would throw away) in a large cupboard, and lined the shelves of the pantry with the jars of jam. They weren't for eating, Martin said; they were for looking at. Sheila was pretty philosophical; anybody who'd married Martin would have had to be philosophical.

They went to lots of concerts; threw lots of parties, full of drunken radical social workers, militant black leaders, manic-depressive pimps, and nymphomaniac Liberal debutantes. The isolated rectory kept their secrets; there was no complaint to the Bishop. But when the last of the guests had gone, the rectory returned to its own secrets.

Meanwhile, the demolition continued. Cloister Lane went, and Infirmary Street, and Boundary Road. Every time Martin looked out of the window, the battered gable ends of the houses, defiantly flaunting their tattered wallpaper through wind and rain, seemed to get farther away. Martin got the strange idea that the whole city was recoiling from St. Austin Friars, like the crowd at a circus when the tiger gets loose. He told himself not to be silly. Sheila told him not to be silly. They were living in clover.

The congregation at Sunday service was three: Sheila,

and the two churchwardens. One warden, Mr. Phillips, was also verger and caretaker. The other, Mr. Rubens, was said to be the city's last big pawnbroker. Dark, solid, formal, and sleek, he wasn't the kind of man you could ask that kind of question. The congregation on Wednesday morning was nil; Martin said the service alone in the great, dark, hollow church. He would have liked to sing it, but there were too many echoes answering, and he soon gave it up. He recognized this as his first defeat.

It was all defeats, as far as the church services were concerned. He went around the poor houses and corner shops that were left, beyond Fishponds and Cloister Lane. The people were respectful, sickeningly respectful. He tried to be friendly, but they treated him as if he were a pope, and not a jolly pope, either. If there was a crowd in a shop, they stood aside deferentially to let him buy his cigarettes, then listened silently, hushed, to his remarks about the weather or the football team. Waiting for him to go, so they could resume their whispering, scurrying, mouselike lives. If he called at a house, he was seated in the tiny, freezing front parlor, while the housewife sent out for expensive cakes and the children peeped around the door at him and fled when he spoke to them. They gave him horrifying amounts of money, "for the church." One pensioner gave him a five-pound note, though her stockings were darned and her shoes cracked. When he tried to refuse it, she burst into tears, pleading with him to take it, and would not be pacified until he did. He thought, bitterly, that they never saw *him* at all; they saw another Canon Maitland, or some other Victorian tyrant-priest. He was walking in another man's shoes. He hated that man; he would have strangled that man if he could. But that man was invisible; close to him as his own skin.

None of the local people came to church; they were paying him to go away and leave them in peace.

He had better luck with his city-center people; sometimes they came to church for love of him: a group of actors from the Library Theater, theatrically muffled in long scarves and wide-brimmed black hats; once, a bunch of the girls, in fun furs, miniskirts, and suede boots. They hadn't a clue how to take part in the service, and they caused an explosion at the churchwardens' meeting afterwards. Mr. Phillips, whose house now stood out of the flat, spreading clearances like a decaying Gothic tooth, said that the likes of them were not fit to be seen in church. His bitten gray mustache and his pendulous jowls wobbled in hideous indignation. But the smooth Mr. Rubens cut him short.

"Father Williams is entitled to have anyone he likes in his church. Your job is to keep it clean and ring the bell." Mr. Phillips came to heel like a whipped cur, which taught Martin a lot. Mr. Rubens cracked the whip. Mr. Rubens got things done.

Like the strange matter of the choir. Martin had discovered a mothballed oak wardrobe, full of red and white choir vestments. He said wistfully at one meeting that he *would* like to have a choir . . . The next Sunday, he was amazed to find he had a choir, of total strangers, complete with organist-and-choirmaster. They sang beautifully. But in conversation with one child in the vestry afterwards, he found they were a school choir, bused in from a distance at considerable expense, and quite obviously doing it for the money. When he pointed out to Mr. Rubens that this was not what he had meant at all, Mr. Rubens looked at him very sharply and said he wouldn't be bothered by them again. Just as long as he made up his mind what he wanted. Martin began to feel like somebody's pampered mistress. But he was growing a little afraid of Mr. Rubens. For one thing, Mr. Rubens had never given his address or phone number. He always rang Martin; he was the one that fixed the churchwardens' meetings.

Afterwards, Martin realized he should have got out of St. Austin's then. But the Bishop was pleased with all the work he was doing; and Mr. Rubens had told the Bishop that he was *delighted* with all the work Martin was doing. And everything but St. Austin's was going so well.

St. Austin's got worse and worse. Martin loved churches, but he couldn't love St. Austin's. It wasn't spooky exactly, just infinitely old and cold and dark. It rejected him. He had the vestry redecorated in contemporary style, installed a vinyl-topped desk and telephone, hung framed prints of the Turin shroud and Dali's modern Crucifixion on the wall. He would make that, at least, a place where people came, for coffee and a chat when they had a problem. Nobody came.

Still, Martin bravely persisted in his church, like an occupying army, for three hours every Wednesday morning. After the service, he drifted up the aisles reading the epitaphs of long-dead Muncastrians, engraved on Georgian and Regency marble on the walls.

Near this spot are buried the Mortal Remains of Jonathan Appleby Esq, who died on the 14th day of February, 1828, aetat 17 yeers.

For those who never knew him, no words can convey his Infinite Excellence of Character.

As for his grieving Friends, who had the Infinite Privilege of his Acquaintanceship, they are silenced by Greefe.

Therefore, no word Further is Uttered.

Tactful, that, thought Martin with a wry grin. But grave humor is thin gruel to feed the human heart, and on the whole the epitaphs did not console him. He did, however, notice a preponderance of odd names. *Canzo. Frederick Canzo, William Ewart Canzo, Joshua Canzo.* And *Betyl.* And *Morsk.* But especially the name *Drogo* cropped up. There must be more Drogos buried in the crypt under the church than all the rest put together. Funny, how these odd names had died out. He had never met a Canzo or a Betyl or a Morsk or a Drogo in his life.

One Wednesday morning, he was amazed to hear the phone ringing, at the far end of the church. He ran so eagerly he arrived quite out of breath. The only person who had ever rung him until now was Sheila, from the rectory, to tell him lunch was ready. But at this moment she would be hard at it, teaching.

"St. Margaret's Church. Can I help you?"

"That St. Austin Friars?"

"Yes."

"Why didn't you say so? We've got a funeral for you."

"Wait, let me find the diary and a pencil. Now, where did I—ah, good. Right." Martin was practically gabbling, at the idea of actually being useful for a change. "Who's speaking?"

"This is Bettle's, the undertakers. Deceased's name is William Henry Drogo. Yes, that's right, D-R-O-G-O. Friday morning, the 28th of March, at 10:30 a.m."

Martin glanced over his shoulder at the Mowbray's calendar on the wall. Today was Wednesday the 26th. "Fine," he said. "Will you want the bell rung?"

"Old Phillips knows how we like it. Leave it to him."

"And your telephone number?"

"Muncaster 213245." The voice sounded grudging.

"Phillips will fill you in." There was a click and the speaker was gone.

Martin looked down at the details in his diary. Strange, the name Drogo cropping up, just when he'd been telling himself that such names must be dead and gone. Usual kind of service, he supposed. No request for a special sermon.

It was then that he realized that today was not Wednesday the 26th of March.

It was only Wednesday the 26th of February. Somebody had booked a funeral a month in advance.

MARTIN RANG the number back.

"Excuse me, I think you've made some mistake. I think you want Mr. Drogo buried on the 28th of February. You said the 28th of March. It's a mistake that's easily made— I often make it—"

"When I say the 28th of March," said the voice, very Muncastrian, "I *mean* the 28th of March."

"But—"

"Ask old Phillips." The phone went down with an extra-loud click, and when Martin redialed, the other end didn't answer.

At first he was sure it was a practical joker. Especially as he went through the telephone directory and could find no undertaker called Bettle. Or Beddle. Or Bethel, for that matter. Nor Bettell, nor Bettall. So then he looked up Drogo.

To his surprise, there were quite a lot of Drogos—eight in all, including *Drogo's, Pharmaceutical Suppliers and Wholesalers*. And a *Drogo, William H.*, at a very lush address in Willington, out in the fresh air in the foothills of the Pennines.

Martin paced up and down the vestry in a rare state of agitation. Of course, he could always ask old Phillips, as he'd been told. But he had a certain reluctance to be laughed at by old Phillips. There must be other ways to check . . .

William H. Drogo was a man of importance—perhaps the chairman of Drogo's Pharmaceuticals? Heart pounding, he rang Drogo's Pharmaceuticals and asked for William H. Drogo. Yes, a very expensive female voice answered, Mr. William H. Drogo was chairman. Yes, Mr. William *Henry* Drogo. But unfortunately he was not available, being out all day at a meeting in London. If Mr. . . . ? —Mr. Williams would care to ring back tomorrow . . . ?

"Are there any other William Henry Drogos?"

No. The expensive voice allowed itself to sound faintly offended. There was only one Mr. William Henry Drogo. And she knew the *whole* family. There *was* only one Drogo family, at least in Britain. The voice curved upward, making the Drogos sound more distinctive than the Royal Family.

Martin rang off, before he was reduced to sounding a complete blithering idiot.

He took to pacing up and down again. That expensive voice . . . that imperturbable voice . . . would be quite calm enough to effect a cover-up. Why a cover-up? Perhaps for commercial reasons. Some firms were pretty vulnerable when the big boss man suddenly died. But you couldn't cover up a death for a month, for God's sake . . . Feeling even more of an idiot, but rather cross just the same, he rang the Drogo home number. This time a deep female voice answered, a voice so rich and exotic it made the other female voice sound plastic.

"I'm sorry, Mr. . . . Williams. My grandfather is away in

London all day today. If you rang his office in the morning, I'm sure he'd be delighted to speak to you."

He hung up. That was certainly no house of mourning, no house shaken to the roots by a death. That house was smug, rich, utterly certain of itself, full of the careless decency that comes from years without pain. It was a hoax. He wouldn't ask old Phillips. It was probably old Phillips who had made the hoax call. Who else knew all about the Drogos lining the aisles of his church with their memorials? Drogos and Canzos and Morsks and Betyls.

Betyl. Not Bettle the undertaker, but Betyl the undertaker.

Oh, don't be crazy. Whoever heard of anyone called Betyl?

Whoever heard of anyone called Drogo? He reached for the telephone directory.

No Betyl.

Then he realized that the current directory was held up by a pile of other directories, well nibbled by the church mice and rather damp toward the bottom of the heap.

In the rotting, falling-apart 1953 directory, he found it. *Betyl, Georg & Son, Funeral Directors, 4 Albert St., Hathershaw, Muncaster 213245.* Hathershaw was the next inner suburb, only two miles away.

Feeling slightly unreal, he got out the car and drove over.

HATHERSHAW WAS IN the throes of demolition, too. It was like fleeing through a doomed city. Houses first slateless, then roofless, then windowless. Streets that were only pavements and cobbles and solitary lampposts on corners; streets pressed flat like wildflowers in a book. Streets with no names, just old Victorian manhole covers.

Fires on every mound of fallen brick. Bulldozers; sweating, filthy, rejoicing demolition men.

"Albert Street?" yelled Martin, winding down his window and trying to compete against another wall falling down.

"You'll be lucky, squire. If you're quick, you might just catch it before it goes. Third right, second left. Mind yer head."

He caught it. The slates were just coming off the roof of Number 4. The bulldozers were three houses away.

Georg Betyl and Son. Funeral Directors. Established 1832.

The shop window was still draped in faded ecclesiastical purple. There were three black urns, tastelessly arranged, and a squat marble box for flowers, labeled *From friends and neighbors.*

"Stop!" shouted Martin, leaping from his car. The demolition team was facetious, but not unsympathetic.

"Yeah," said the gaffer, to his request for admittance. "Why not? It won't be here by five o'clock." They smashed in the black, rather nice Georgian front door with a sledgehammer, while Martin winced.

Inside, the place felt odd already, with half the roof stripped. There was the phone; dead when Martin picked it up.

"Telephone company was here an hour ago, to cut it off," said the gaffer. "If you want that phone, you can have it," he added generously. "Cost you a quid—you don't get many like that, these days." There was also an ancient iron safe, door hanging open, some cremation urns in white plastic, and a tin wastebucket full of empty envelopes addressed to *Georg Betyl and Son, Funeral Directors, 4 Albert Street, Hathershaw,* and going back sixty years. Two old wooden chairs, and nothing else at all.

———

THE NEXT DAY, Martin rang the telephone company. They were unable to help; all communications and bills for Mr. Betyl had always been sent to 4 Albert Street. As far as they were concerned, Mr. Betyl had paid his terminal bill and ceased to exist. There had certainly been no application for a new telephone number at a new address. Muncaster Corporation also did their best; yes, they had purchased the shop from Mr. Betyl, and had sent all correspondence and the final purchase check to 4 Albert Street. No, he was on their rolls of electors only at the Albert Street address. Perhaps he had lived above the shop?

Feeling the boldness of despair, Martin rang Drogo's Pharmaceuticals again. The expensive voice (who knew something more about him than she had known the previous day) put him straight through to Mr. William Henry Drogo.

"I don't know how to start," said Martin, suddenly help-less.

"You sound rather upset." Drogo's voice had the same richness as his granddaughter's.

"I am a little upset. There's something I have to tell you."

"You are the new rector of St. Austin Friars."

"Yes. How did you know that?"

"I've always had an interest in St. Austin's," said Mr. Drogo. "Perhaps you would honor my granddaughter and me with your company at dinner tomorrow night."

Martin gasped audibly. Did anybody still talk like that?

"We have our own ways," said Mr. Drogo. Martin had the idea that he was gently laughing at him.

MARTIN DROVE OVER to Willington in a fair state of resentment; he had had to lie to Sheila; had made up a story of church business and the offer of funds. It was the first time he'd ever seriously lied to her. But the whole business was so crazy . . . He'd tell her everything once he'd cleared it up.

The Drogo house was large, modern, but rather ugly, standing well clear of its neighbors among mature decorative conifers. The granddaughter answered the door and took his coat.

"I'm the housekeeper tonight. It's the servants' night off." Her appearance went with her voice; she was tall, about thirty, very much the confident businesswoman. Her looks could only be described as opulent: a mass of blue-black hair, swept up on top of her head, a figure that curved richly, but with the utmost discretion, in a dark gray business suit with white lace at throat and wrists drawing attention to the plump, creamy beauty of her face and hands. No wedding ring. Her dark eyes surveyed him with a frank female interest that was disconcerting. It was the way certain rich men eyed a new woman . . . He flashed up in his mind a vision of Sheila, thin, red-haired, and freckled. Ashamedly, he thought she made the vision of Sheila seem very thin indeed. She walked ahead of him, the powerful hips and calves moving discreetly, expensively, arrogantly.

The man who rose from the dark red leather armchair could not possibly be the grandfather. He could be no more than fifty. The same blue-black hair and dark, amused eyes, the same somber and wealthy solidness that could never be described as fat.

"Oh," said Martin. "I'd hoped to speak to Mr. Drogo."

"I *am* Mr. Drogo."

"Mr. William Henry Drogo?"

"The same."

"But . . ."

"Let me get you a drink. What will you have?" He moved to a highly polished mahogany sideboard. Martin thought that, with its brass handles, it looked like the most expensive kind of coffin. Desperately, he fought to get hold of himself. But his hand still trembled, and the sherry ran down over his fingers. For some reason he began to worry because he hadn't told Sheila exactly where he was going.

"Do sit down, Mr. Williams. How can I help you?"

Martin glanced at the girl, sitting listening intently. She got up at once, saying, "I must see to the dinner." Fascinated, Martin watched her as she left the room. At his next confession, he was going to have to confess the sin of lechery. It was not a sin he had had to confess before.

"My granddaughter interests you." It was not a question, it was a statement. There was no disapproval in it. Blindly, Martin lunged into the reason he had come: the phone call from the vanishing undertaker, the funeral of William Henry Drogo, booked a month ahead. Mr. Drogo listened, nodding sympathetically, without a hint of surprise or disbelief.

Martin finished up, lamely, "I wouldn't have bothered you, only it's been preying on my mind. Is it just some ridiculous practical joke, or is it a—a threat of some kind? Against your life, or something? I mean, it sounds like something the Mafia would do—if we had anything like the Mafia in Muncaster." He forced himself to smile and shrug at his own childishness.

"Oh," said Mr. Drogo. "We *had* the Mafia in Muncaster, a couple of years ago. On a very small scale. They tried to take over an interest in one or two rather second-rate gambling clubs. Very small beer. We had a quiet word in the chief constable's ear, and they went away peacefully enough."

The muffled note of a small dinner gong echoed through the house. "Come and eat," said Mr. Drogo, putting a fatherly hand on Martin's shoulder.

The meal was good, though a little strange and spicy. So was the wine. The daughter—no, the granddaughter —whose name was Celicia, moved about serving it as silently as a cat on the thick red carpet. The rest of the time, from the side, she watched Martin as he talked. Or rather, listened.

Mr. Drogo talked. In between eating with the most exquisite manners, he talked about Muncaster; he talked about St. Austin's, right back to the time of the Augustinian Canons. He talked with the authority of an historian. Martin was fascinated, the way he showed one thing growing out of another. He made it sound as if he'd lived right through it. Martin stopped trembling eventually. But if he listened to the grandfather, he secretly watched the girl. The girl watched him, too, a slight smile playing about the corners of her mouth.

"About that phone call." Martin's voice, almost a shout, broke through the smooth flow of Mr. Drogo's talk. "Was I *meant* to come and tell you?"

"Yes, you were meant to come and tell me." Mr. Drogo pulled a grape from a bunch that lay on a dish near him and popped it into his mouth with evident enjoyment.

"But . . . *why?*"

"I am going to die—on March 26th." He helped himself, unhurriedly, to another grape.

"Oh, I see. The doctor's told you. I'm so sorry." Then reality broke in like a blizzard. "But . . . but he can't have told you the exact date!"

"I chose the date." Mr. Drogo extracted a grape pip from the back of his excellent teeth, with the delicacy of a cat. He looked as healthy as any man Martin had ever seen.

"But what—"

"Do you know how old I am?" asked Mr. Drogo. He might have been asking the right time. "I am one hundred and ninety-two years old, on March 26th. I thought that made it rather neat."

Drogo stared wildly at the girl, as if assessing how much help she would be against this madman.

"And I am eighty-four next birthday," said the girl. She smiled, showing all her perfect white teeth. Martin noticed that the canines were slightly, very slightly, longer than usual. But not more than many people's were . . .

Martin leaped to his feet, knocking over his chair behind him with a thud. "I came here in good faith," he cried. "I didn't come here to be made a fool of!"

"We are not making a fool of you. Have you got your birth certificate, my dear?"

The girl disappeared into the hall, returning moments later with the certificate in her hand. She passed it across to Martin. Even now, in his rage and fear, her perfume was soothing . . . Hands trembling again, he unfolded the paper roughly, tearing it along one fold. It was old and frail and yellow.

Celicia Margaret Drogo. Born July 8th, 1887, to William Canzo Drogo and Margaret Drogo, formerly Betyl.

"Do you want to see her parents' marriage certificate?" asked Mr. Drogo gently. "I want your mind to be absolutely satisfied."

"I'd like my coat!" shouted Martin, only half hoping he would be given it.

"As you wish," said Mr. Drogo. "But," he added, "it would be easier for you if you went with my granddaughter now. She could make everything perfectly clear to you. She helped Canon Maitland to see things clearly. We gave Canon Maitland a very contented life for many years. He was almost one of us."

"Get lost!" shouted Martin, most regrettably. "All I want from you is my coat!"

They did not try to stop him. Celicia came with him, but only to help him on with his coat. Her fingers were still gentle, pleading, on the nape of his neck. Then he was outside and running for the car. He roared out of the drive like a lunatic, narrowly avoiding a collision with a Rover that hooted at him angrily until it turned a corner. He made himself pull up, then, and sit till he had calmed down. Then he drove home shakily and painfully slowly. Sheila was just standing on the doorstep, pulling on her gloves before going to the pictures; she had a distaste for being in the rectory on her own at night and went to watch whatever film was on, however stupid.

"What's the matter with you?" She took him inside gently. After three whiskies, he plucked up the courage to tell her everything. It said a lot for her love for him that she believed him unquestioningly.

"I TRIED TO RING YOU on Tuesday," said the Bishop. "Tried all day."

"Tuesday's my day off," said Martin. "I was in London."

"That explains it," said the Bishop, who always had the last word, however pointless. He shuffled the papers on his desk, as if they were a squad of idle recruits. He had begun life as a major in the war, passed on to be an accountant, and only in later life been drawn to the Church. Some spiteful clergy said he remained a major first, an accountant second, and a bishop only third. His jutting nose and bristling mustache certainly sat oddly under his miter on high days and holy days. Every church in his diocese had its accounts scrutinized by his eagle eye, and paid the uttermost farthing. He was brave, honest, loving, and as unstoppable as one of his own old tanks when he'd made up his mind.

"I've taken up your complaint with Mr. Drogo," he announced. "He apologized handsomely, I must say. Said his granddaughter was a great one for practical jokes, and rather a one for the men. More than I'd care to admit about *my* granddaughter. Said he was a fool to go along with her, but he didn't know how far she was going. Damned decent apology, I call that. He's writing to you. Wants you to take your missus over for a meal—make things up."

Martin gaped. He had not complained about Mr. Drogo; he had sent the Bishop a long and detailed report marked *Personal and Confidential*. That Mr. Drogo now knew all about it filled him with a nameless dread.

"It wasn't a practical joke," he said. "I've been doing some investigating. That's why I went to London—Somerset House: births, deaths, and marriages. I spent the whole day checking. There has not been a single Drogo birth since 1887—that *was* Celicia. But from the electoral rolls, there are at the present time thirty-two Drogos living in Muncaster."

"Rubbish!" said the Bishop. "Stuff and nonsense. Of course they were born—I know a lot of them well. Michael Drogo is solicitor to the diocesan board, Giles Drogo was chairman of Rotary last year. Why, in a quiet way, the Drogos *are* Muncaster. Don't know what we'd do without them. Without their generosity, St. Austin's would have had to be demolished years ago. Your lectureship at the college is funded by Drogo money—"

"How long have *you* been in Muncaster?" shouted Martin. "Ever baptized any Drogo babies?"

"I've been here five long years, my lad. And no, I've never baptized a Drogo baby—it's not my line of business. And what's more, I won't have young clergymen who are no more than jacked-up curates havin' the vapors on *my* hearthrug. Go away, Martin, before I start revising my good opinion of you. You'll not prosper in Muncaster long if you get the Drogos' backs up. Though why anybody in their senses should want to . . . Stop waving those bits of paper in my face!" Color was showing in the Bishop's cheeks—what the cathedral clergy referred to as the red warning flags.

"There's something funny going on at St. Austin's . . . something against the will of God . . ."

"That," said the Bishop, "is my province to decide. If you don't agree with me, you can always resign. *Well?*"

Martin swallowed, and was silent, as the enormity of it hit him. If he resigned the living, Sheila and he had nowhere to go. They'd even sold off their own poor sticks of furniture, because they looked so pathetic in the opulence of the rectory. They could just about exist on Sheila's teaching salary, but if the Bishop passed the word he was an awkward hysterical character . . .

The Bishop pounced on his hesitation; he was never one to miss an opening. He came around the desk and put an arm on Martin's shoulder, in a way horribly reminiscent of Mr. Drogo. "This is racial prejudice, Martin, don't you see? There is foreign blood in the Drogos— touch of the tarbrush there, perhaps. Lot of people think they're Jews, but they're not. Good old Church of England—among our keenest supporters. They have their own funny ways in private, but they do a lot of damn good work in public. They don't do any *harm*—I happen to know their chemical workers are the highest-paid in the city. Live and let live, Martin, live and let live. Go home and think it over—I don't want to lose you now you're doing so well. Why, I've just had an invitation for you to give a talk on your city-center work to the social science department of the university . . ." He picked up a thick, expensive-looking envelope from his desk, with the university crest on the back flap. "Bless you, my boy." He shook Martin's hand warmly on the way out.

Martin opened the envelope in the car, his hands shaking with something that might have been anticipation. There was the invitation to give the James Drogo Memorial Lecture.

On the twenty-eighth. Friday, 28th March. At 10:30 a.m.

"THEY WANT ME out of the church on that morning," gabbled Martin. "Don't you see? They want me out of the way so they can . . ."

"Can what?" said Sheila, with a brave attempt at briskness. But her hand shook as she passed Martin another whisky.

"I don't know," said Martin. "That's the awful thing. It's only two weeks off and I don't *know*."

"Well, they can hardly bury him in the churchyard. It's been closed how long? A hundred years?"

"More than that."

"And it's so jam-packed it's practically standing room only. And people would notice . . ."

"What people?" said Martin, despondently. "Anyway, they wouldn't have to use the churchyard—St. Austin's has got a crypt. All those names on plaques on the church walls—*near this spot lie the Mortal Remains of*, etc. They're down under the floor in coffins on shelves, in a place probably as big as the church itself."

"Ugh," said Sheila. "I didn't know that."

"Most people don't, or they wouldn't go near some churches. It's a kind of clerical conspiracy of silence. What the eye doesn't see, the heart doesn't grieve over. Tastes have changed. Mind you, some crypts are just coke holes, even headquarters for Telephone Samaritans or tramps' shelters, like St. Martin-in-the-Fields. But a lot . . ."

Sheila glanced around the opulent kitchen and shuddered. "Where was old Canon Maitland buried?"

"It'll be in the church diary—in the church. Let's go and look."

Sheila glanced out of the kitchen window. Dusk was just starting to gather around the graceful spire of St. Austin Friars.

"We can be there and back in ten minutes," said Martin. "It's better than wondering. Better than not knowing."

The church door was locked, but Martin had his key. He banged his hand down across the massed banks of switches in the vestry and the whole church sprang out into light. Martin hoped the lights at this hour would not attract the eye of Mr. Phillips. Old Phillips who knew the ropes, old Phillips who would see to it. Old Phillips who spent a quite extraordinary amount in the betting shop for a poorly paid church verger.

They opened the church diary, holding their breath. The entry for the burial of William Henry Drogo, in Martin's own handwriting, mocked them.

"That was the *awful* thing," whispered Martin. "When he told me he was going to die, he smiled. As if he was looking forward to it, like his summer holidays."

Sheila firmly turned over the page in the book, because his own handwriting seemed to have paralyzed Martin, as a snake hypnotizes a rabbit. The previous entry, in old Phillips's hand, recorded the funeral of Canon Maitland,

conducted by a Rev. Leonard Canzo, fellow of a minor
Cambridge college. The body had been interred in . . .

. . . *the crypt of St Austin Friars, by special faculty, authorized
by the Bishop. Because of his long and faithful service to the church
of seventy years* . . .

"Where's the door down to the crypt?" whispered Sheila.

"I don't know. There are two I've never been down.
One's the boiler house for the central heating—I left all
that to old Phillips." They looked around nervously, expecting to see old Phillips coming up the aisle at any
moment, in his dull overcoat and checked muffler, which
he seemed to wear, winter and summer, as a uniform. But
he was nowhere in sight. And yet all that stood between
the brilliantly illuminated church and the verger's house
was a flat stretch of demolition site . . .

"Probably in the betting shop," said Sheila, and giggled,
then stopped herself abruptly.

They swiftly found the pair of doors; the door surrounds
were Gothic and crumbling, but the doors were Victorian,
oak and very solid. And the hasps and padlocks on them
were even newer and even more solid.

"Have you got keys?"

"Not for these locks."

"Old Phillips has got them," said Sheila, grimly. She
thought. "Look, most boiler rooms have another door to
the outside, for the coke deliveries in the old days—I
mean, they didn't want coke all over the aisle floors and
people crunching up to communion. That might be
open—it's worth a try."

Every fiber of his body said no. But some kind of frenetic
excitement had seized Sheila. She flew off down the aisle.
He didn't dare wait to switch the lights off; besides, they
would need them, shining out through the church win-

dows, if they were not to break a leg in the wilderness of tilted table tombs, leaning urns, and tangled brambles in the graveyard outside. He wished he'd thought to bring a torch . . . but he caught sight of Sheila's slim figure, in her white mackintosh, flitting through the tombscape ahead. Halfway around, he found her waiting for him, outside a low Gothic door.

"It's shut," she said. "Locked."

He felt suddenly flat, and yet glad. "It'll only be the coke hole," he said. In the semidark, they could hear the coke droppings of centuries crunching beneath their feet. Relief made him gabby. "It's funny about this churchyard; disused urban churchyards are usually a menace: vandals writing on the tombs with aerosols, or throwing the gravestones over—even black-magic cranks. But here, there isn't a trace of vandalism—"

A hand on his arm stopped him both talking and walking. She pointed ahead. There was a faint crunching of footsteps on the coky path. "Somebody's coming." They hid in a flurry behind a miniature Greek temple, black as coal.

It was old Phillips: shabby overcoat and checked muffler. He kept glancing up at the lighted windows of the church as he walked: a little uneasy, a little cautious. He passed, and went as far as the locked door. Without benefit of torch or light, he fitted a key neatly first time into the keyhole.

"That's not the first time he's done that in the dark," whispered Sheila.

"Shhh!"

Old Phillips swung the door open; the hinges did not creak.

"Well oiled," muttered Sheila.

"*Shhh!* What's he doing?"

But it was all too obvious what old Phillips was doing. He was returning, leaving the little door not only unlocked but ajar. He passed again, and faded into the dusk.

"What's he done that for?" whispered Sheila. "That's mad—*unlocking* a door at dusk. Shall we look inside?"

Just then the church window above their heads went dark. Old Phillips was busy putting off the church lights. Another light went off, and another. It was enough to panic them. They fled across the graveyard, and didn't stop running till they reached the rectory.

"Quick!" said Martin. "Let's get all the lights on—on the *far* side of the house. Not these. Phillips can see these from the church." Suddenly it was desperately important that Phillips should not know they'd been anywhere near the church.

They went and sat in the sitting room, which, fortunately, *was* on the side away from the church. The central heating was on, but low, and the room was too cold. Martin banged on all three bars of the electric fire and the telly. They sat shivering till the room began to warm up. "Get something to do," whispered Martin, savagely. "Get your knitting out. Take your coat off. Get your slippers on . . ." He was just taking off his own coat and hiding it behind the settee when there came a ring on the doorbell. "Relax!" screeched Martin, and made himself walk slowly to answer it.

Old Phillips's face was set in that look of joyful censoriousness beloved of caretakers the world over. He held up Martin's bunch of keys.

"Your keys, I believe, Mr. Williams. I found the church unlocked and *all* the lights on. Vestry open, *and* the church diary." He held that up in turn, still open at the page that recorded Canon Maitland's funeral. "I thought at first it was vandals."

"Sorry," said Martin, and his voice didn't shake. "I've been meaning to go back and lock up, but I got lost in the football on the telly. Won't you come in for a moment? The match is just over."

Phillips came in; his eyes did not miss the slippers and the knitting, the telly and the warmth of the room. They roamed over everything, making it dirty as if they were a pair of gray slugs. When he was satisfied, *barely* satisfied, he turned to them.

"You want to be careful, Mr. Williams. A lot more careful. And you, Mrs. Williams. Canon Maitland would never have made a mistake like that. Very happy and well settled here, Canon Maitland was."

They all knew he wasn't talking about the church keys.

THEY WERE CAREFUL. They hardly went near the church at all; Martin found he could no longer face his solo Wednesday service. If God was listening above, who was listening down below, beneath the black stone slabs of the nave floor? Martin found his thoughts going downward far more than they ever ascended upward. What was down there? Why did they need their door *opened* at dusk? What was Mr. Drogo looking forward to, more than his holidays? Anyway, old Phillips was now around the place practically every hour of the day and night, as the 28th of March approached. None of the crypt doors was ever found unlocked again.

But they planned carefully, too, for the 28th of March; and it worked out well. An actor friend called Larry Harper stayed in the rectory overnight (and they were very glad to have him). He was tall, thin, and fair like Martin, and by the time he had donned Martin's rector's garb and a huge pair of horn-rimmed spectacles, he even gave Sheila a fright. His walk was the living image of Martin's lope; he said he'd been practicing mimicking it for nearly a year, to get a laugh around the Grapes.

He left for the university at nine-thirty, Sheila with him in her best suit and hat, driving the car. He delivered Martin's talk (from the pages Martin had written out for him) far more convincingly than Martin would ever have done, and got a tremendous round of applause. He fumbled his impromptu question time rather badly, but everyone put that down to well-earned exhaustion. Nobody at the university ever dreamed they hadn't seen the real Martin Williams . . .

. . . who had been up the tower of St. Austin Friars since seven that morning, creeping in through the cobwebbed dewiness of the graveyard with a sergeant from Muncaster Constabulary, summoned by phone with some nasty hints of black-magic activity in the churchyard. They waited behind the uppermost parapet of the tower, well hidden, so that they saw it all.

At ten-twenty, the overcoated, mufflered figure of old Phillips walked leisurely through the churchyard and unlocked the main door. At ten twenty-five he began to toll the bell. At ten twenty-eight, five large black Rolls-Royce limousines started across the huge demolition plain, following a Rolls-Royce hearse. Thirty-one Drogos, men and women, emerged, sleek in black topcoats, black fur coats, and the flash of a black-nyloned leg. All the women were very handsome and looked about thirty, so it was impossible to pick Celicia out. There was the undertaker, Mr. Betyl, no doubt, proper in black tailcoat and top hat swathed in black muslin. The opulent coffin (which looked sickeningly like Mr. Drogo's sideboard) vanished into the church.

"Let's go and get a good view inside," Martin whispered to the sergeant. They went down through the bell chamber—the bell had stopped tolling but was still swaying in its bed—and down into the ringers' chamber, where a little window gave a good view into the body of the church, from just under the ancient rafters.

Martin looked down, and almost fainted.

Far from a scattering of thirty-one Drogos near the front, the church was full. The door to the crypt was gaping open. And as he looked down, every dark figure turned and looked up at him.

"Come on down, Mr. Williams," called Betyl, the undertaker, with sepulchral joviality. "We are so glad you could make it after all."

Martin turned desperately to the policeman.

"Time to go, sir," said the policeman gently. He got out his warrant card and held it up open for Martin to inspect.

Sergeant Harold Morsk, Muncaster CID.

Like a condemned man, Martin tottered down the stairs and was marched to the front of the congregation.

"We shall only require you to say amen," said Mr. Betyl. "We are a God-fearing race and have always supported your church. It is the least you can do for us." Then he began to declaim to the congregation in a harsh, strange tongue, and they replied in the same tongue. And when they all looked at Martin, with their smooth, handsome faces, he knew it was time to say "Amen." Twice they took black books from their pockets and broke out into a hymn. Old Phillips played the organ reasonably well. Then the body was reverently borne, on the shoulders of six pallbearers, down into the crypt. One corner, grating against the doorjamb, lost a sliver of wood and rich varnish, and some flakes of white limestone dropped on the black floor.

After all was over down there (strange sounds floated up in the silence above) a man who looked incredibly like the late William Henry Drogo came across to Martin and shook him firmly and warmly by the hand.

"I am glad you were here. If *they* are not blessed by the presence of a clergyman, they get out of hand and run wild, and then there is trouble. There are still people cruel enough to sharpen ashstakes for us—the world gets little better, except on the surface. Now we shall have no trouble in Muncaster . . . thank you." He paused, and said concernedly, "You do not look well . . . these things are troubling you . . . you may have had bad dreams. Here is my granddaughter—Celicia, come here, Celicia—she has an affection for you. Go with her now, and she will make all things well and clear for you. No, Celicia, *not* in the crypt—the vestry will do for Mr. Williams." He spoke to her quite sharply, as if he suddenly feared she might go too far.

As in a dream, Martin walked through the open vestry door, his hand in Celicia's.

When he woke up on the vestry floor, he could never quite remember anything that had happened the morning of the 28th of March, in the church of St. Austin Friars.

But it didn't matter, for shortly afterwards he and Sheila left the city, for a small rural living that had fallen vacant in Kent.

THE HAUNTING
OF CHAS MCGILL

THE DAY war broke out, Chas McGill went up in the world.

What a Sunday morning! Clustering around the radio at eleven o'clock, all hollow-bellied like at the end of an England–Australia cricket test match. Only this was the England–Germany test. He had his scorecards all ready, pinned on his bedroom wall: number of German tanks destroyed; number of German planes shot down; number of German ships sunk.

The Prime Minister's voice, finally crackling over the air, seemed to Chas a total disaster. Mr. Chamberlain *regretted* that a state of war now existed between England and Germany. Worse, he bleated like a sheep, or the sort of kid who, challenged in the playground, backs into a corner with his hands in front of his face and threatens to tell his dad on you. Why didn't he threaten to kick Hitler's teeth in? Chas hoped Hitler wasn't listening, or there'd soon be trouble . . .

Immediately, the air-raid sirens went.

German bombers. Chas closed his eyes and remembered

the cinema newsreels from Spain. Skies thick with black crosses, from which endless streams of tiny bombs fell. Endless as the streams of refugee women scurrying through the shattered houses, all wearing head scarves and ankle socks. Rows of dead kids laid out on the shattered brickwork like broken stick dolls with glass eyes. (He always shut his eyes at that point, but *had* to peep.) And the German bomber pilots, hardly human in tight black leather flying helmets, laughing and slapping each other on the back and busting open bottles of champagne and spraying each other . . .

He opened his eyes again. Through his bedroom window the grass of the Square still dreamed in sunlight. Happy ignorant sparrows, excused the war, were busy pecking their breakfast from the steaming pile of manure left by the Co-op milk horse. The sky remained clear and blue; not a Spitfire in sight.

Chas wondered what he ought to *do*. Turn off the gas and electric? With Mam in the middle of Sunday dinner, that'd be more dangerous than any air raid. His eye fell on his teddy bear, sitting on top of a pile of toys in the corner. He hadn't given Ted a glance in years. Now Ted stared at him appealingly. There'd been teddy bears in the Spanish newsreels, too; the newsreels were particularly keen on teddy bears split from chin to crotch, with all their stuffing spilling out. Headless teddy bears, legless teddy bears . . . Making sure no one was watching, he grabbed Ted and shoved him under the bed to safety.

Not a moment too soon. Mam came in, drying her sudsy hands.

"Anything happening out front? Nothing happening out the back." She made it sound as if they were waiting for a carnival with a brass band, or something. She peered intently out of the window.

"There's an air-raid warden."

"It's only old Jimmy Green."

"*Mr.* Green to you. Well, he wrote to the Air-Raid Precautions yesterday, offering his services, so I expect he thinks he's got to do his bit."

Jimmy was wearing his best blue suit; though whether in honor of the war, or only because it was Sunday, Chas couldn't tell. But he was wearing all his medals from the Great War, and his gas mask in a cardboard box, hanging on a piece of string across his chest. His chest was pushed well out, and he was marching around the Square, swinging his arms like the Coldstream guardsman he'd once been.

"I'll bet he's got Hitler scared stiff."

"If he sounds his rattle," said Mam, "put your gas mask on."

"He hasn't *got* a rattle."

"Well, that's what it says in the papers. An' if he blows his whistle, we have to go down the air-raid shelter."

Chas bleakly surveyed the Anderson shelter, lying in pieces all over the front lawn, where it had been dumped by council workmen yesterday. It might do the worms a bit of good . . .

"Who's that?"

Jimmy had been joined by a more important air-raid warden. So important he actually had a black steel helmet with a white "W" on the front. Jimmy pointed to a mad, happy dog who, finding the empty world much to his liking, was chasing its tail all over the Square. The important warden consulted a little brown book, and obviously decided the dog was a threat to National Security. They made a prolonged and hopeless attempt to catch the dog, who loved it.

"The Germans are dropping them Alsatians by parachute," said Chas. "To annoy the wardens."

That earned a clout. "Stop spreading rumors and causing despondency. They can put you in prison for that!"

Chas wondered about prison; prisons had thick walls
and concrete ceilings, at least in the movies. Definitely
bombproof . . .

But a third figure had emerged into the Square: an
immensely stocky lady in flowered hat. A cigarette thrust
from her mouth and two laden shopping bags hung from
each hand. She was moving fast, and panting through her
cigarette; the effect was of a small but powerful steam
locomotive. The very sight of her convinced Chas that the
newsreels from Spain were no more real than Marlene
Dietrich in *Destry Rides Again*. Bloody ridiculous.

She made the wardens look pretty ridiculous, too, as
they ran one each side of her, gesticulating fiercely.

"Get out of me way, Arthur Dunhill, an' tek that bloody
silly hat off. Ye look like something out of a fancy-dress
ball. Aah divvent care if they hev made ye Chief Warden.
Aah remember ye as a snotty-nosed kid being dragged up
twelve-in-two-rooms in over Hudson Street. If ye think
that sniveling gyet Hilter can stop me performin' me
natural functions on a Sunday morning ye're very much
mistaken . . ."

"It's your nana," said Mam, superfluously but with much
relief. Next minute, Nana was sitting in the kitchen,
sweating cobs and securely entrenched among her many
shopping bags.

"Let me get me breath. Well, she's done it now. Tempy.
She's *really* done it."

"It wasn't Tempy," said Chas. "It was Hitler."

"Aah'll cross his bridge when Aah come to it. You know
what Tempy's done? Evaccyated all her school to Keswick,
and we've all got to go and live at the Elms as caretakers."

Chas gave an inward screech of agony. Tempy gone to Keswick meant the loss of ten shillings a term. Thirty bob a year. How many Dinky Toys would that buy?

War might be hell, but thirty shillings was serious.

The siren suddenly sounded the all-clear.

MAM LET Chas go out and watch for the taxi in the blackout. The blackout was a flop. It just wasn't black. True, the streetlamps weren't lit, and every house window was carefully curtained. But the longer he stood there, the brighter the sky grew, until it seemed as bright as day.

He'd hauled the two big suitcases out of the house, with a lot of sweat. He stood between them, ready to duck in case a low-flying Messerschmitt 109 took advantage of the lack of blackout to strafe the Square. Machine-gun bullets throwing up mounds of earth, like in *Hell's Angels*, starring Ben Lyon. He wondered if the suitcases would stop a bullet. They seemed full of insurance books and all fifteen pairs of Mam's apricot-colored knickers. Still, in war, one had to take risks . . .

The taxi jerked into the Square at ten miles an hour, and pulled up some distance away.

"Number eighteen?" shouted the driver querulously. "Can't see a bloody thing." No wonder. He had covered his windscreen with crosses of sticky tape to protect it against bomb blast, and peered through like a spider out of its web.

"Get on, ye daft bugger," shouted Nana from the back. "Aah cud drive better wi' me backside." Granda, totally buried beside her in a mound of blankets, traveling rugs, overcoats, and mufflers for his chest, coughed prolonged agreement.

It was a strange journey to the Elms. Chas had to sit on

the suitcases, with what felt like Nana's washday wringer sticking in his ribs.

"I shouldn't have left the house empty like that," wailed Mam. "There'll be burglars, an' who's going to water the tomatoes?"

"You coulda left a note asking the burglars to do it," said Chas. It was too dark and jam-packed in the taxi for any danger of a clout.

"Ye'll be safer at the Elms, hinny," said Nana. "Now ye haven't got a man to put a steadyin' hand to you."

"She's got *me*," said Chas.

"God love yer—a real grown man. 'Spect ye'll be j'ining up in the Army soon as ye're twelve."

"Aah j'ined up at fourteen," said Granda. "To fight the Boers. Fourteen years, seven months, six days. Aah gave a false birthday."

"Much good it's done you since," said Nana, "wi' that gassing they gave you at Wipers."

"That wasn't the Boers," said Chas helpfully. "That was the Germans."

Granda embarked on a bout of coughing, longer and more complicated than "God Save the King," that silenced all opposition for two miles.

"It'll be safer for the bairn," added Nana finally. "Good as evaccyating him. Hilter won't bomb Preston nor the Elms. He's got more respec' for his betters . . . Besides, ye had to come, hinny. I can't manage that great spooky place on my own—not wi' yer Granda an' his chest."

"Spooky?" asked Chas.

"Don't mind me," said Nana hastily. "That's just me manner of speakin'."

Just then the taxi turned a corner too sharply; outside, there was a thump, and the crunch of breaking glass. "Ah well," said Nana philosophically, "we won't be needing them streetlamps for the duration. Reckon it'll be all over by Christmas, once the Navy's cut off Hilter's vitals . . ."

"Painful," said Chas.

"Aah owe it to Tempy," concluded Nana. "Many a job she's pushed my way, ower the years, when yer Granda's had his chest . . ."

Chas pushed his nose against the steamed-up window of the taxi, feeling as caged as a budgie. He watched the outskirts of Garmouth fall away; a few fields, then the taxi turned wildly into the private road where the roofs of great houses peeped secretly over shrubbery and hedge and tree, and at the end was the Elms, Miss Temple's ancestral home and late private school and the biggest of them all.

SO BY BEDTIME, on the 3rd of September 1939, Chas had risen very high in the world indeed. A fourth-floor attic, with the wind humming in the wireless aerial that stretched between the great chimneys, and ivy leaves tapping on his window, so it sounded as if it was raining. Granda's old army greatcoat had been hung over the window for lack of curtains.

Chas didn't like it at all, even if he did have candle and matches, a rather dim torch, a book called *Deeds That Have Won the Victoria Cross*, and six toy pistols under his pillow. You couldn't shoot spooks with a toy pistol, he didn't feel like winning the VC, and he wanted the lav, bad.

There was a great cold white chamber pot under the narrow servant's bed, but he'd no intention of using it. Mam would be sure to inspect the contents in the morning, and tell everyone at breakfast how his kidneys were functioning. Mam feared malfunctioning kidneys more than Stuka dive bombers.

Finally he gathered his courage, a pistol, his torch, and

his too-short dressing gown around him, and set out to seek relief.

The dark was a trackless desert, beyond his dim torch. The wind, finding its way up through the floorboards, ballooned up the worn passage carpet like shifting sand dunes. The only oases were the light switches, and most of them didn't work, so they were, strictly speaking, mirages. Down one narrow stair . . .

The servants' lav was tall and gaunt, like a gallows; its rusting chain hung like a hangman's noose, swaying in the draft. The seat was icy and unfriendly.

Afterwards, reluctant to go back upstairs, Chas pressed on. A slightly open door, a shaft of golden light, the sweet smell of old age and illness. Granda's cough was like a blessing in the strangeness.

But he didn't go in. He didn't dislike Granda, but he didn't like him either. Granda's chest made him as strange as the pyramids of Egypt. Granda's chest was the center of the family, around which everything else revolved. As constant as the moon. He had his good spells and his bad. His good spells, when he turned over a bit of his garden, or hung a picture on the wall, grew no better. His bad spells grew no worse.

Chas passed on, noiselessly, down another flight of stairs.

He knew where he was, now. A great oak hall, with a landing running around three sides, and a broad open staircase leading down into a dim red light. Miss Temple's study was on the right.

Miss Temple, headmistress, magistrate, city councillor of Newcastle upon Tyne. He knew her highly polished shoes well; her legs, solid as table legs in their pale silk stockings, her black headmistress's gown, or her dark fur coat. He had never seen her face. It was always too high above him, too awesome. God must look like Miss Temple.

At the end of every term, ever since he had started school, Nana had taken him to see Miss Temple at the Elms. With his school report clutched in his hand. They were shown in by a housemaid called Claire, neat in black frock, white lace hat, and apron. Up to Miss Temple's study. There the polished black shoes would be waiting, standing foursquare on the Turkey carpet, the fat pale solid legs above them.

A sallow plump soft hand, with dark hairs on the back, would descend into his line of vision. He would put the school report into it. Hand and report would ascend out of sight. There would be a long silence, like the Last Judgment. Then Miss Temple's voice would come floating down, deep as an angel's trumpet.

"Excellent, Charles . . . excellent." Then she would ask him what he was going to be when he grew up; but he could never answer. The plump hand would descend again, with the report and something brown that crackled enticingly.

A ten-bob note. He would mumble thanks that didn't make sense even to himself. Then the tiny silver watch that slightly pinched the dark plump wrist would be consulted, and a gardener-chauffeur called Holmes would be summoned, to drive Miss Temple in state to Newcastle, for dinner, or a meeting of the full council, or some other godlike occasion.

It never varied. He never really breathed until he was outside again, and the air smelled of trees and grass, and not of polish and Miss Temple. Sometimes, hesitating, he would ask Nana why Miss Temple was not like anybody else. Nana always said it was because she had never married; because of something that had happened in the Great War.

And now there was another war, and Miss Temple fled

to Keswick with all her pupils, and her study door locked, and, outside, Hitler and a great wind were loose in the world.

He crept on, past the grandfather clock on the landing that ticked on, as indifferent to him as Holmes the chauffeur in his shiny leather gaiters. Prowled out to the back wing, where the girls' classrooms were. Searched their empty desks by torchlight, exulting spitefully over the spelling mistakes in an abandoned exercise book. There was a knicker-blue shoe bag hanging on the back of one classroom door. He put his hand inside with a guilty thrill, but it only contained one worn white gym shoe.

Downstairs, he got into a panic before he found the lightproof baize-covered kitchen door; thought he was cut off in the whole empty windy house, with only Granda above, immobilized and coughing.

He pushed the baize door open an inch. Cozy warmth streamed out. A roaring fire in the kitchen range. Nana, in flowered pinafore, pouring tea. Mam, still worrying on about burglars, peeling potatoes. Claire the housemaid, raffish without her lace hat, legs crossed, arms crossed, fag in her mouth, eyes squinting up against the smoke.

"Shan't be here to bother you much longer. Off to South Wales next week, working on munitions. They pay twice as much as *she* does. Holmes? Just waiting for his call-up papers for the Army. Reckons he'll spend a cushy war, driving Lord Gort about."

Chas was tempted to go in; he loved tea and gossip. Hated the idea of the long climb back to the moaning wireless aerial and ivy-tapping windows. But Mam would only be angry . . .

He climbed. At the turn of the last stair, a landing window gave him a view of the roof and the chimneys and the row of attic windows. Six attic windows. His was the fourth . . . no, the fifth, it must be, because the fifth was dimly candle-lit. Oh, God, he'd left his candle burning, and Granda's greatcoat was useless as blackout, and soon there'd be an air-raid warden shouting, "Put that bloody light out!"

He ran, suddenly panting. Burst into his room.

It was in darkness, of course. He'd never lit his candle. And his *was* the fourth room in the corridor, the fourth shabby white door.

He ran back to the landing window. There was candle-light in the fifth window, the room next to his own. It moved, as if someone was moving about, inside the room.

Who?

Holmes, of course. Snooty Holmes. Well, Holmes's flipping blackout was Holmes's flipping business . . . Chas got back into his ice-cold bed, keeping his dressing gown on for warmth. Put his ear to the wall. He could hear Holmes moving about, restlessly; big leather boots on uncarpeted floorboards, and a kind of continuous mournful low whistling. Miserable stuck-up bugger . . .

On that thought, he fell asleep.

NEXT MORNING, before going to the lav, he peered around his door in the direction of Holmes's. He dreaded the sneer that would cross Holmes's face, if he saw a tousle-haired kid running about in pajamas. Nana said Holmes had once been a gentleman's gentleman—a valet—and it showed.

But there was no sign of Holmes. In fact, the whole width of the corridor, just beyond Chas's room, was blocked off by a dirty white door, unnoticed in the blackout last night. It looked like a cupboard door, too, with a keyhole high up.

Chas investigated. It *was* a cupboard; contained nothing

but a worn-out broom and a battered blue tin dustpan. Then Chas forgot all about Holmes: because the whole inside of the cupboard was papered over with old newspapers. Adverts for ladies' corsets, stiffened with the finest whalebone and fitted with the latest all-rubber suspenders. All for three shillings and elevenpence three-farthings! Better, photographs of soldiers, mud, and great howitzers. And headlines:

NEW OFFENSIVE MOUNTED AT CAMBRAI
MILE OF GERMAN FIRST-LINE TRENCH TAKEN
NEW "TANKS" IN ACTION?

Chas read on, enthralled and shivering, until Nana shouted up the stairs to ask if they were all dead up there.

As he was hurling himself into his clothes, a new thought struck him. All those old newspapers seemed to be from 1917 . . . If the cupboard had been there since then, how on earth did Holmes get into his room? He went back and rapped violently all over the inside of the cupboard. The sides were solid plaster, the plaster of the corridor walls. The back boomed hollowly, as if the corridor went on beyond it. But there was no secret door at the back; the pasted-on newspapers were intact, not a torn place anywhere.

"Are ye doing an impersonation o' a deathwatch beetle? 'Cos they only eat wood, an' in that case Aah'm going to throw your breakfast away."

Even though he knew it was Nana's voice, he still nearly jumped a yard in the air.

"There's newspapers, here, with pictures of the Great War."

"Ye've got war on the bleddy brain," said Nana. "Isn't

one war enough for ye? Ye'll have a war on yer hands in the kitchen, too, if you don't come down for breakfast. Yer mam's just heard on the radio that school's been abolished for the duration, an' it's raining. Aah don't know what we're going to do wi' you. Wi' all the bairns driving their mams mad, getting under their feet, Hilter's goin' to have a walkover."

But Chas was surprisingly good, all day. He did demand his mac and welly boots, and walk around the house no less than fourteen times, staring up at the windows and counting compulsively, and getting himself soaked.

"He'll catch his death out there," wailed Mam.

"He'll catch my hand on his lug if he comes bothering us in here. Let him bide while we're busy," said Nana, her mouth full of pins from the blackout curtains she was sewing.

Then he came in and had his hair rubbed with a towel by Nana, until he thought his ears were being screwed off. Then he scrounged a baking board and four drawing pins, a sheet of shelf-lining paper, and Mam's tape measure, and did a carefully measured plan of the whole kitchen, which everyone agreed was very fine.

"What's that great fat round thing by the kitchen sink?" asked Nana.

"You, doing the washing up," said Chas, already ducking so her hand missed his head by inches; she'd a heavy hand, Nana. Then, sitting up, he announced, "I'm going to do something to help the war effort."

"Aye," said Nana. "Ye're running down to the shop for another packet of pins for me."

"No, besides that. I'm going to make a plan of the whole house, to help the Fire Brigade in case we get hit by an incendiary bomb . . ."

"Ye're a proper little ray o' sunshine . . ."

"Can I go into all the rooms and measure them?"

"No," said Mam. "Miss Temple wouldn't like it."

"Can I, Nana?" said Chas, blatantly.

"What Tempy's eyes doesn't see, her heart won't grieve. Let the bairn be, while he's good," said Nana, reaching for her bunch of keys from her pocket.

So, in between running down to the shop for pins, and running back to the kitchen every time there was a news broadcast, Chas roamed the veriest depths of the house.

Looking for the back stair leading up to Holmes's room.

Looking for the hidden stair leading up to Holmes's room.

Looking for the secret stair leading up to Holmes's room . . .

He searched and measured until he was blue in the face. Went outside and counted windows over and over and got himself soaked again.

No way was there a secret stair up to Holmes's room. He was pretty hungry when he came back in for tea.

Nana switched off the radio with a sniff. "The Archbishop of Canterbury has called for a National Day of Prayer for Poland. God help the bleddy Poles, if it's come to *that*."

"Nana," said Chas, "where does Holmes live?"

"*Mr.* Holmes, to you," said Mam in a desperate voice. At which Holmes himself, the sneaky sod, rose in all the glory of his chauffeur's uniform and shiny leggings from the depths of the wing chair by the fire, where he'd been downing a pint mug of tea. "And why do you want to know that, my little man?" he said, with a know-all smirk on his face. Chas blushed from head to foot.

"Because you're in the room next to mine, an' I can't see how you get up there." He wouldn't have blurted it out if he hadn't been so startled.

"Well, that's where you're wrong, my little man," said Holmes. "I have a spacious home above the stables, with my good wife and Nancy Jane, aged nine. You must come and have tea with Nancy Jane, before I go off to serve my King and Country. She'd like that. But why on earth did you think I had a room up in the attics?"

"Because someone was moving last night, an' whistling . . ."

Holmes looked merely baffled; so did young Claire. Mam was blushing for his manners, like a beetroot. But Chas thought Nana turned as white as a sheet.

"It's only the wind in that bleddy wireless aerial. Get on wi' yer tea and stop annoying your elders an' betters . . ."

NEXT EVENING, Chas pushed open the door of Granda's room, cautiously. The old man lay still, propped up on pillows, arms lying parallel, on top of the bedclothes. He looked as if he was staring out of the window, but he might be asleep. That was one of the strange things about Granda, the amount of staring out of windows he did, when he was having one of his bad spells; and the way you could never tell if he was staring or asleep. Also the fact that his hair didn't look like hair, and his whiskers didn't look like whiskers. They looked like strange gray plants, growing out of his purply-gray skin. Or the thin roots that grow out of a turnip . . .

"Granda?"

The head turned; the eyes came back from somewhere. They tried to summon up a smile, but Chas's eyes ducked down before they managed it.

"Granda—can I borrow your brace-and-bit?"

"Aye, lad, if ye tek care of it . . . it's in the bottom drawer there, wi' the rest o' my gear . . ." The old head turned away again, eyes on a red sunset. Chas pulled out the drawer, and there was Granda's gear. Granda's gear was the only thing Chas really loved about Granda; the old man could never bear to throw anything away. Everything might come in useful . . . The drawer was full of odd brass taps, bundles of wire neatly tied up, tin toffee boxes full of rusty screws and nails, a huge bayonet in its scabbard that Granda used only for cutting his endless supplies of hairy white string. There was the brace-and-bit, huge and lightly oiled, sweet-smelling. He pulled it out, and a hank of wire came with it, and, leaping from the wire onto the floor, a small silver badge he hadn't seen before.

"What's that, Granda?"

"That's me honorable-discharge medal, that Aah got after Aah was gassed. Ye had to hev one o' those, or you got no peace back home in Blighty, if you weren't in uniform. Women giving ye the white feather, making out ye were a coward, not being at the front. The military after ye, for being a deserter. Ye had to wear that, an' carry yer discharge papers, or ye didn't get a moment's peace, worse nor being at the front, fightin' Jerry . . . Put it back safe, there's a good lad . . ." Granda's voice, vivid with memory for a moment, faded somewhere else again. Chas took the brace-and-bit, and fled.

Up to the corridor cupboard by his bedroom. Soon the brace-and-bit were turning in his hands, tearing the pasted newspapers (in a boring item, advocating Senna Pods for Constipation). Then came the curling shavings of yellow pine, smelling sweetly. After a long while, he felt the tip of the bit crunch through the last of the pine, and out into the open air behind the cupboard. He withdrew it, twisting the bit in reverse as Dad had once shown him, and put his eye to the hole.

He saw more corridor, just like the corridor he was

standing in. Ending in a blank wall, ten yards away. A green, blistered door on the left, but no secret stair. No possible place the top of a secret stair could be. The green door was slightly ajar, inward, but he could see nothing. The only window, in the right-hand wall, was thick with cobwebs, years of cobwebs. There was a little mat on the floor of the corridor, kicked up as if somebody had rushed past heedlessly and not bothered to replace it. Many, many years ago. The air in that corridor, the kicked mat, were the air and the mat of 1917. It was like opening a box full of 1917 . . .

Then a bedspring creaked; footsteps moved on boards, more footsteps returning, a sigh, and then the bedspring creaked again. Then came the sound of tuneless, doleful whistling, and a squeaking, like cloth polishing metal . . .

Chas slammed the cupboard door and ran through the gathering gloom for the kitchen. He didn't realize he still had Granda's brace-and-bit in his hands until he burst in on the family, gathered around the tea table.

There were toasted tea cakes for tea, dripping melted butter. And on the news, the announcer said the Navy had boarded and captured ten more German merchant ships; they were being brought under escort into Allied ports. Slowly, Chas shook off the memory of the noises in the attic. Bedtime was far off yet. He dug into another tea cake to console himself, and Nana loudly admired his appetite.

"Got a job for you after tea, our Chas. We've finished all the blackout curtains. When it's *really* dark, ye can go all around the outside o' the house, an' if ye spot a chink of light, ye can shout 'Put that light out' just like a real air-raid warden."

"That was no chink you saw in my bedroom last night,"

said Holmes in a girlish simpering voice, "that was an officer of the Imperial Japanese Navy . . ."

Mam didn't half give him a look, for talking smut in front of a child. Which was a laugh, because Chas had told Holmes that joke just an hour ago; he was working hard, softening Holmes up; know your enemy!

CHAS WAS really enjoying himself, out there in the dark garden. He was again half-soaked, through walking into dripping bushes; he had trodden in something left behind by Miss Temple's dog, but such were the fortunes of war.

A little light glowed in the drawing-room window, where the blackout had sagged away from its frame. He banged on the window sharply, indicating where the light leak was, and inside, invisible, Nana's hand pressed the curtain into place. The little glow vanished.

"O.K.," shouted Chas, "that's all the ground floor."

"Let me draw breath and climb upstairs." Nana's voice came back faintly.

Chas paced back across the wet lawn; the grass squeaked under his wellies, and he practiced making the squeaking louder. Then he glanced up at the towering bulk of the Elms. The blackouts on the first floor looked pretty good, though he wasn't going to let Nana get away with *anything*; it was a matter of National Security . . .

Reluctantly, his eyes flicked upward . . . Granda's room was O.K. There was no point in looking at the attics. There was only his own room, and there was no electric light in there, and his candle wasn't lit . . .

He looked up at the attics, and moaned.

The fifth window from the right was gently lit with candlelight. And there was the distinct outline of a man's head and shoulders, looking out of that window. He could see only the close-cropped hair, and the ears sticking out.

But he knew the man was looking at him; he *felt* him looking, felt the caressing of his eyes. Then the man raised a hand and waved it in shy greeting. It was not the way Holmes would have waved a hand . . . or was Holmes taking the mickey out of him?

Suddenly, beside himself with rage, Chas shouted at the almost invisible face, "Put that bloody light out! Put that bloody light out!"

He was still shouting hysterically when Nana came out and fetched him in.

"There's a face in that window next to mine!" shouted Chas. "There *is*. Look!" He pointed a trembling finger.

But when he dared to look again himself, there was nothing but the faint reflection of drifting clouds, moving across the dim shine of the glass.

Nevertheless, when Nana picked him up bodily and carried him inside, as she often had when he was a little boy (she was a strong woman), Chas thought that she was trembling, too.

He was given an extra drink, and set by the fire. "Drink your tea as hot as you can," said Nana. It was her remedy for all ills, from lumbago to Monday misery. Nana and Mam went on with the washing up. They kept their voices low, but Chas still caught phrases: "highly strung" and "overactive brain." Then Nana said, "We'll move him down next to his Granda afore tomorrow night." When Mam objected, Nana said sharply, "Don't you *remember*? It was in all the papers. Course, you'd only be a young lass at the time . . ." The whispering went on, but now they had lowered their voices so much Chas couldn't hear a thing.

HE WAKENED again in the dark. The luminous hands on his Mickey Mouse clock said only two o'clock. That meant he'd wakened up four times in four hours. It had never

happened to him in his life before. He listened. Horrible
bloody total silence; not even the wind sighing in the
wireless aerial. Then, glad as a beacon on a headland to a
lost ship, came the racking sound of Granda's cough
downstairs.

It gave Chas courage, enough courage to put his ear to
the wall of the room next door. And again he heard it:
the creak of bedsprings, the endless tuneless whistling.
Did he never bloody stop? Granda's cough again. Then
bloody whistle, whistle, whistle. Fury seized Chas. He
hammered on the wall with his fist, like Dad at home when
the neighbors played the wireless too loud.

Then he wished he hadn't. Because the wall did not
sound solid brick like most walls. It trembled like cardboard
under his fist, and gave off a hollow sound. And at the
same time, there was a noise of little things falling under
his bed; little things like stones. He bent under the bed
with his torch, without getting outside the bedclothes. A
lump of the wall had cracked and fallen out. Plaster lay
all over the bare floorboards, leaving exposed what looked
like thin wooden slats. Perhaps there was a hole he could
peep through . . . He put on his dressing gown and crawled
under the bed, and squinted at the place where the plaster
had fallen off.

There seemed to be a thin glim of golden candlelight
. . . Suddenly Chas knew there was no more sleep for him.
He had a choice: the indignity of running down to Mam's
room, like a baby with toothache—or finding out just what
the hell was going on behind that wall.

Downstairs, Granda coughed again.

Chas took hold of the first slat, and pulled it toward
him. There was a sharp crack of dry wood, and the stick
came out, pulling more plaster with it.

After that, he made a big hole, quite quickly. But the wall had *two* thin skins of slats and plaster. And the far one was still intact except for a long thin crack of golden light he couldn't see through. He'd just make a peephole, no bigger than a mousehole . . .

He waited again, for the support of Granda's cough, then he pushed the far slats.

Horror of horrors, they resisted stoutly for a moment, then gave way with a rush. The hole on the far side was as big as the hole this side. He could put his head and shoulders through it, if he dared. He just lay paralyzed, listening. The man next door *must* have heard him; couldn't *not* have heard him.

Silence. Then a voice said, "Come on in, if you're coming." A Tyneside voice with a hint of a laugh in it. Not a voice to be afraid of.

He wriggled through, only embarrassed now, as if Granda had caught him playing with his watch.

It was a soldier, sitting on a bed very like his own. A sergeant, for his tunic with three white stripes hung on a nail by his head. He was at ease, with his boots off and his braces dangling, polishing the badge of his peaked cap with a yellow duster. A tin of Brasso stood open on a wooden chair beside him; the sharp smell came clearly to Chas's nostrils. He was a ginger man with close-cropped ginger hair, the ends of which glinted in the candlelight. And a long sad ginger mustache. Chas thought he looked a bit old to be a soldier . . . or old-fashioned, somehow. Maybe that was because he was a sergeant.

"What you doing here?" he asked, then felt terribly rude.

But the sergeant went on gently polishing his cap badge. "Aah'm on leave. From the front."

"Oh," said Chas. "I mean, what you doing *here*?"

"Aah knaa the girl downstairs. She knew Aah needed a billet, so she fetched me up here."

"Oh, Claire?"

The man didn't answer, merely went on polishing, whistling gently that same old tune.

"Do you stay up here all the time? Must be a bit boring, when you're on leave?"

The man sighed, and held his badge up to the candle, to see if it was polished enough. Then, still with his head on one side, he said mildly, "You can do wi' a bit o' boredom, after what we've been through."

"At the front?"

"Aye, at the front."

"With the British Expeditionary Force?"

"Aye, wi' the British Expeditionary Force."

"But the B.E.F.'s not done anything yet. The war's just started."

"They'll tell you people on the home front anything. Aah've just started to realize that. Wey, we've marched up to Mons, and we fought the Germans at Mons, and beat 'em. Then we had to retreat from Mons, shelled all the way, and didn't even have time to bury our mates . . ."

"What's the worst thing? The German tanks?"

"Aah hevvn't seen no German tanks, though Aah've seen a few of ours lately. No, the worst things is mud and rats and trench foot."

"What's trench foot?"

The man beckoned him over, and took off his gray woollen sock. Up between his toes grew a blue mold like the mold on cheese. The stink was appalling. Chas wrinkled his nose.

"It comes from standing all day in muddy water. First

your boots gan rotten, then your feet. Aah'm lucky—they caught mine in time. Aah've know fellers lose a whole foot, wi' gangrene." He put back his sock, and the smell stopped.

"Is that why you're up here, all day—'cos you got trench foot? You ought to be going out with girls—enjoying yourself. After all, you are home on leave . . . aren't you?"

The man turned and looked straight at him. His eyes . . . his eyes were sunk right back in his head. There were terrible, unmentionable things in those eyes. Then he said, "Can yer keep a secret, Sunny Jim? Aah came home on leave, all right. That was my big mistake. Aah knew Aah shuddn't. Aah didn't for three whole years . . . got a medal for my devotion to duty. Got made sergeant. Then they offered me a fortnight in Blighty, an' Aah was tempted. The moment Aah got home, an' saw the bonny-faced lasses, an' the green fields an' trees an' the rabbits playing, Aah knew Aah cud never gan back. So when me leave was up, the girl here, she's a bit sweet on me . . . she hid me up here. She feeds me what scraps she can . . ." He kicked an enamel plate on the floor, with a few crusts on it. "Ye can get used to being in hell, when you've forgotten there's owt else in the world, but when ye come home, an' realize that heaven's still there . . . well, ye cannot bring yerself to go back to hell."

"You've got no guts," said Chas angrily. "You're a *deserter*."

"Aye, Aah'm a deserter all right. They'll probably shoot me if they catch me . . . but Aah tell ye, Aah had plenty of guts at the start. We used to be gamekeepers afore the war, Manny Craggs an' me. They found us very useful at the front. We could creep out into no-man's-land wi'out making a sound, and bring back a brace of young Jerries, alive an' kicking an' ready for interrogation afore breakfast. It was good fun, at first. Till Manny copped it, on the Marne. It wes a bad time that, wi' the mud, an' Jerry so close we could hear him whispering in his own trench, and their big guns shelling our communication trench. We couldn't get Manny's body clear, so in the end we buried him respectful as we could, in the front wall o' our trench. Only the rain beat us. We got awake next morning, an' the trench wall had part collapsed, and there was his hand sticking out, only his hand. An' no way could we get the earth to cover it again. Can ye think what that was like, passing that hand twenty times a day? But every time the lads came past, they would shake hands wi' old Manny, an' wish him good morning like a gentleman. It kept you sane. Till the rats got to the hand; it was bare bone by the next morning, and gone the morning after. Aah didn't have much *guts* left after that . . . but Aah cudda hung on, till Aah made the mistake o' coming on leave . . . now Aah'm stuck here, and there's neither forward nor backward for me . . . just polishin' me brasses to look forward to. You won't turn me in, mate? Promise?"

"Oh, it's nothing to do with me," said Chas haughtily. The man was a coward, and nothing to be afraid of. He must have run away the moment he got to France; if he'd ever been to France at all . . . the war had only been on three days. Making up these stupid stories to fool me 'cos he thinks I'm just an ignorant kid . . . "I won't give you away."

And with that, he wriggled back through the hole, and pushed his trunkful of toys against the hole in the wall, and went to bed and fast asleep: to show how much he despised a common deserter.

———

THE FOLLOWING MORNING, when he wakened up, he was quite sure he'd dreamed the whole thing. Until he peeped under his bed and saw the trunk pushed against the wall, and plaster all over the floor. He pulled the trunk back, and shouted "Hello" through the hole. There was no reply, or any other sound. Puzzled, he shoved his head through the hole. The room next door was empty. Except for the bed with its mattress, and the wooden chair lying on its side in a corner. Something made him look up to the ceiling above where the chair lay; there was a big rusty hook up there, driven into the main roof beam. The hook fascinated him; he couldn't seem to take his eyes off it. You could hang big things from that, like sides of bacon. He didn't stay long, though; the room felt so very *sad*. Maybe it was just the dimness of the light from the cobwebbed windows. He wriggled back through the hole, pushed back the trunk to cover it, and cleaned up the fallen plaster into the chamber pot and took it outside before Mam could spot it.

Anyway, the whole business was over; either the man had scarpered, or he'd dreamed the whole thing. People could walk in their sleep; why couldn't they knock holes in walls in their sleep, too? He giggled at the thought. Just then Mam came in, looking very brisk for business. He was to be moved downstairs immediately, next to Granda.

Suddenly, perversely, he didn't *want* to be moved. But Mam was adamant, almost hit him.

"What's the matter? What's got into you?"

But Mam, tight-lipped and pale-faced, just said, "The very idea of putting you up here . . . get that map off the wall, quick!"

It was his war map of Europe, with all the fronts marked with little Union Jacks and Swastikas and Hammer-and-

Sickles. He began pulling the Union Jack pins out of the Belgian border with France. Then he paused. There, in the middle of neutral Belgium, where no British soldier could possibly be, was the town of Mons. And down there was a river called the Marne . . .

"GRANDA?"

The old, faded gray eyes turned from the window, from the scenes he would never talk about.

"Aye, son?"

"In the last war, was there a Battle of Mons?"

"Aye, and a Retreat from Mons, an' that was a bleddy sight worse. Shelled all the way, and no time to stop an' bury your mates . . ."

"And there was a Battle of the Marne . . . very rainy and muddy?"

"Aye. Never seen such mud till the Somme."

Then Chas knew he'd been talking to a ghost. Oddly enough, he wasn't at all scared; instead, he was both excited and indignant. With hardly a moment's hesitation, he said, "Thanks, Granda," and turned and left the room and walked up the stairs. Though he began to go faster and faster, in case his courage should run out before he got there. He wasn't sure about this courage he suddenly had; it wasn't the kind of courage you needed for a fight in the playground. It might leave him as suddenly as it had come. He pulled aside the trunk of toys, and went through the hole like a minor avalanche of plaster.

The sergeant was there, looking up from where he sat on the bed, still cleaning his cap badge, as he'd been last night. The pair of them looked at each other.

"You're a ghost," said Chas abruptly.

"Aah am *not*," said the sergeant. "Aah'm living flesh and

blood. Though for how much longer, Aah don't know, if Aah have to go on sitting in this place, with nothing to do but polish this bloody cap badge."

His eyes strayed upward, to the big rusty hook in the ceiling. Then flinched away, with a sour grimace of the mouth. "Aah am flesh and blood, and that's a fact. Feel me." And he held out a large hand, with little ginger hairs and freckles all over the back. His expression was so harmless and friendly that, after a long hesitation, Chas shook hands with him. The freckled hand indeed was warm, solid, and human.

"I don't understand this," said Chas, outraged. "I don't understand this at *all*."

"No more do Aah," said the sergeant. "Aah'd ha' thought Aah imagined you, if it hadn't been for that bloody great hole in the wall. Wi' your funny cap an' funny short trousers an' socks an' shoes. An' your not giving me away to the folks down below. Where are you from?"

"I think it's rather a case of *when* am I from," said Chas, wrinkling his brow. "My date is the 6th of September 1939."

"Aah *am* dreamin'," said the sergeant. "Today's the 6th of September 1917. Unless Aah'm out in me reckoning . . ." He nodded at the wall, where marks had been scrawled on the plaster with a stub of pencil. Six upright marks, each time, then a diagonal mark across them, making the whole group look like a gate or a fence. "Eight weeks Aah been in this hole . . ."

"Why don't you get out of it?"

"Aye," said the sergeant. "That'd be nice. Down into Shropshire, somewhere, where me old Da sent me to be a good gamekeeper. They'll be wantin' help wi' the harvest, now, wi' all the lads bein' away. Then lose meself into the green woods. Hole up in some cave in Wenlock Edge for winter, an' watch the rabbits an' foxes, and start to forget . . ." He screwed his eyes up tightly, as if shutting something out. "That is, if God gave a man the power to forget. Aah don't need me sins forgiven; Aah needs me memories forgiven." He opened his blue eyes again. "A nice dream, Sunny Jim, but it wouldn't work. Wi'out civvy clothes an' discharge papers, I wouldn't get as far as Newcastle . . ." Again, that glance up at the hook in the ceiling . . .

"I'll try and help," said Chas.

"How?" The sergeant looked at him, nearly as trusting as a little kid.

"Well, look," said Chas. He took off his school cap and gave it to the man. "Put it on!"

The sergeant put it on with a laugh, and made himself go cross-eyed and put out his tongue. "Thanks for the offer, but Aah'd not get far in a bairn's cap . . ."

Chas snatched it back, satisfied. "Wait and see."

HE HAD TO WAIT a long time, before Nana was busy hanging out the washing, and Mam holding the peg basket, and Granda was asleep. Then he moved in quick, to the drawer where Granda kept his treasures. The honorable-discharge badge and the discharge papers were easy enough to find. Though he made a noise shutting the drawer, Granda didn't waken. The wardrobe door creaked, too, but his luck held. He dug deep into the smelly dark, full of the scents of Granda, tobacco, Nana, fox furs, dust, and old age. He took Granda's oldest overcoat, the tweed one he'd used when he last worked as a stevedore, with the long oilstains and two buttons missing. And an oily old cap. They would have to do. He pushed the wardrobe door to, getting a glimpse of sleeping Granda in the mirror. Then he was off, upstairs. He had a job getting the overcoat through the hole. When he finally managed it, he found the room was bare, cold, and empty. The chair was back in the corner, kicked away from under the rusty iron hook. The sight filled him with despair; the whole room filled him with despair. But he laid the overcoat neatly on the bare mattress, and the cap on top, and the badge, and the discharge papers. Then, with a last look around, and a shudder at the cold despair of the place, he wriggled out. At least he had kept his word . . .

He haunted that room for a fortnight, more faithfully than any ghost. Perhaps *I* have become the ghost, he thought, with a shudder. The coat and cap remained exactly where they were. He tried to imagine that the papers had moved a little, but he knew he was kidding himself.

Then came the night of the raid. The siren went at ten, while they were still eating their supper. Rather disbelievingly, they took cover in the cellars. Perhaps it was as well they did. The lone German bomber, faced with more searchlights and guns on the river than took its fancy, jettisoned its bombs on Preston. Three of the great houses fell in bitter ruin. A stick of incendiaries fell into the conservatory at the Elms, turning it into a stinking ruin of magnesium smoke and frying green things.

Nan surveyed it in the dawn, and pronounced, "That won't suit Tempy. And it's back home for you, my lad. This place is more dangerous than the bleddy docks, and yer Mam's still worrying about those bleddy tomato plants . . ."

Chas packed, slowly and tiredly. Folded up his war map

of Europe. Thought he might as well get back Granda's badge and coat from upstairs.

But when he wriggled through, they weren't on the bed . . .

Who'd moved them, Nana or Mam? Why hadn't they *said* anything?

And the chair was upright by the empty bed, not kicked away in the corner. And on it, shining bright, something winked at Chas.

A soldier's cap badge, as bright as if polished that very day. And on the plaster by the chair was scrawled a message, with a stub of pencil:

Thanks, lad. They fit a treat. Shan't want badge no more—fair exchange no robbery. Your grandfather's a brave man—kept right on to the end of the road—more than I will do, now. Respectfully yours, 1001923 Melbourne, W. J., Sgt.

Chas stood hugging himself, and the cap badge, with glee. He had played a trick on time itself . . .

But time, once interfered with, had a few tricks up its sleeve too. The next few minutes were the weirdest he'd ever known.

BRISK FOOTSTEPS banged along the corridor. Stopped outside his room next door, looked in, saw he wasn't there, swept on . . .

Swept on straight through where the corridor cupboard was . . . or should be. The door of the soldier's room began to open. Chas could have screamed. The door had no right to open. It was fastened away, inaccessible behind the corridor cupboard . . .

But there was no point in screaming, because it was only

Nana standing there, large as life. "There you are, you little monkey. Aah knew ye'd be here, when Aah saw that bleddy great hole in the wall . . . ye shouldn't be in this room."

"Why not?"

"Because a poor feller hanged himself in this room—a soldier who couldn't face the trenches. Hanged himself from that very hook in the ceiling, standing on this very chair . . ." She looked up; Chas looked up.

There was no longer any hook in the beam. There had been one, but it had been neatly sawn off with a hacksaw. Years ago, because the sawn edge was red with rust.

Nana passed a hand over her pale weary face. "At least . . . Aah *think* Aah heard that poor feller hanged himself . . . they blocked off this room wi' a broom cupboard."

She peered around the door, puzzled. So did Chas. There was no broom cupboard now. Nor any mark where a broom cupboard might have been. The corridor ran sheer and uninterrupted, from one end to the other.

"Eeh," said Nana, "your memory plays you some funny tricks when you get to my age. Aah could ha sworn . . . Anyway, what's Melly going to say when Aah tell her ye made a bleddy great hole in her wall? Aah expect you want me to blame it on Hilter and the Jarmans?"

"Who's Melly? You mean Tempy?" said Chas, grasping at straws in his enormous confusion.

"What d'you mean, who's Melly? Only Mrs. Melbourne, who owns this house, and runs the school, and has given ye more ten-bob notes than Aah care to remember."

Chas wrinkled up his face. Was it Miss Temple, shoes, legs, and gown, who gave him ten-bob notes . . . or was it Mrs. Melbourne, who sat kindly in a chair and smiled at him? Who, when he was smaller, had sometimes taken him down to the kitchen for a dish of jelly and ice cream from her wonderful newfangled refrigerator? He had a funny idea they were one and the same person, only different. Then time itself, with a last whisk of its tail, whipped all memory of Miss Temple from his mind; and his mind was the last place on earth in which Miss Temple had ever existed.

"Aah don't know what the hell you made that hole in the wall for," said Nana. "You could just as easily have walked in through the door; it's never been locked."

Chas could no longer remember himself, as he tucked the shining cap badge in his pocket, and gave Nana a hand to take his belongings down to the taxi.

"Why did Aah think a feller hanged himself in that room?" muttered Nana. "Must be getting morbid in me old age . . ."

"Yeah," said Chas, squinting at the cap badge surreptitiously.

IN CAMERA

I FIRST MET Phil Marsden when he reported a burglary. The superintendent sent me. Only routine, we thought, but the people who live on Birkbeck Common are rich and can turn nasty if not handled diplomatically.

I rang his chimes and saw him swimming toward me through the pebble glass of his front door. My first thought was that he was quite little.

His first thought . . . he looked crushed as people do when they've just been burgled. Then his little face lit up and he said, "Hellooooooh!"

As if I was the Easter Bunny and a Christmas hamper all rolled into one. I have that effect on men: it makes life as a policewoman very difficult. I showed him my warrant card to take the smile off his face. He read it with great care, then made the remark I'd learned to dread.

"It's a fair cop!"

I suppose it was funny the first time somebody said it.

"If we can get on, sir?" I said it as severely as I could. I work hard at being severe, even scraping back my hair into the severest bun possible, so tight I give myself a headache. But that only draws attention to my ears, which I have been told are shell-like more often than I care to remember . . .

I sat down briskly with my notebook out. He sat with that stupid look on his face, admiring my legs. But I eventually got out of him that there was no sign of a break-in and that he had a very expensive burglar alarm, which he was sure he'd left switched on that morning, as he never forgot things like that.

"They must've nobbled it," he said.

"That type are very hard to nobble. Have you checked to see if it's still working?"

It was working perfectly; *that* took the look off his face.

"Not nobbled," I said. "Just switched off. By somebody who knew the code. And by the look of your front door, they had a key, too."

"Impossible. I've only got three keys: one with my neighbor and two on my key ring."

I established that the helpful neighbor was a famous barrister who had no need to resort to part-time burglary to keep the wolf from the door. Then Phil fetched his key ring and found one of his keys missing.

"It's somebody you know," I said. He spent the next half hour telling me his friends weren't *like* that. Meanwhile, I found out what was missing. Usual dreary round, hi-fi, video, TV, gold cuff links. But the thing he was most upset about was three antique cameras, God help us. I didn't know people collected antique cameras; I thought they just threw them away when they stopped working.

"Show me."

He led me to a room quite unlike the others. No designer furniture, just plain shelves filled with old cameras. Things in mahogany and brass, big as briefcases. Tatty little

Bakelite Kodaks from the fifties, prewar things with bellows, Brownie boxes.

The room was also a darkroom, with big black-and-white prints hung up to dry. Off-beat views of the world, taken from funny angles. That was what first intrigued me about him.

"Which cameras have gone?"

He showed me three sad gaps. "Two Leica IIc's and a very old Hasselblad. The only ones worth anything."

That made me prick my shell-like ears. Few burglars are experts on antique cameras.

"Do you show your friends this lot?"

He looked pained. "They're not the sort to be interested."

I betted not; this place was where his funny little heart and soul were; very few of his lovely friends would be shown this.

"But you showed *somebody*? Recently?"

"Only Rodney. Rodney Smith. But he wouldn't . . . I was at school with him."

"Were you and Mr. Smith *alone*?"

"There was his girlfriend. Big dishy brunette. Madeleine Something. But she wasn't interested. She was half-pissed. Kept stroking his back and giggling. Wanted bed. Not that Rodney would be my cup of tea . . ."

Well, it transpired that they'd all gone out to the pub before dinner. And Rodney and Madeleine had watched while he tapped in the code on the burglar alarm. And Phil had left his keys in the pocket of his raincoat, hanging up in the pub . . .

"But," he kept on saying stupidly, "but . . ."

To cut a long story short, his mate Rodney didn't have any criminal record, beyond drunk driving. But Madeleine

Something had a record as long as your arm, as well as a little friend we knew very well called Spike Malone. And the Metropolitan Police were just about to raid Spike's mum's tower-block flat . . .

Two days later, I laid the cameras at Phil's feet. At least metaphorically, for they were still required as evidence.

"Hey, you're bright, sergeant," he said. "Sherlock Holmes rides again, eh?"

I could've hit him, except I was on duty. But he got his act together in time and asked me out to dinner. Which I accepted, as I like good food but a sergeant's pay doesn't run to it. And we sort of went on from there. Though I never took him seriously, because he was an inch shorter than me. But he was fun. An innocent, really. And I had a maternal urge to tidy up his little life for him.

At the first of his parties that I went to, somebody lit up a reefer. I got my coat and left before you could say "New Scotland Yard" and we had the mother and father of a row over the phone afterwards. He promised to get rid of certain people from his life, and he must've done, because I never spotted anything dicey again.

The most interesting friends he had left were John Malpas the painter and his wife, Melanie. John wasn't your typical artist. Looked like a worried banker and worked at his paintings like a stevedore, all the hours God sent. He was always so busy talking at table that you had to throw out his glass of wine afterwards. Melanie was pain-fully thin but very elegant, with the most enormous gray eyes. I approved of the fact that, unlike most of Phil's friends, they were actually married. Terminally married. They really needed each other, like my mum and dad do. So I felt comfortable with them.

That Saturday morning, Phil and I'd been up the Portobello Market and Phil had acquired yet another camera. A 1930s Zeiss Ikon. He had three Zeiss Ikons already, but you know what collectors are. But what had really turned him on was that this Zeiss had a roll of exposed film still inside it. A random slice of somebody else's life, Phil called it, and vanished into his precious darkroom to develop it, leaving me to finish getting dinner ready, because John and Melanie were coming. Ambitious cook, Phil. Always does the main dishes, soaking them overnight in wine or oil, till you can't tell whether you're eating beef or lamb. But he's not keen on doing all the fiddly bits.

He was in the darkroom so long I had to lay the table as well. And give John and Melanie their first drink and dips. When he finally emerged for dinner, after much screaming and hammering on the darkroom door, he was still in his oldest jeans and a T-shirt that stank of developer. He was as high as a kite; you would almost have thought he was on a trip. He held a handful of big ten-by-eight enlargements that dripped fixer on the carpet he'd paid thirty-five pounds a yard for.

He shoved one print at John, saying, "What do you make of that?" and then sat with the other prints in his lap, where they made a spreading damp patch on his jeans.

Now, John had one little vanity: his powers of observation. He could never see a picture postcard, or a photo on a calendar, or even a half-finished jigsaw puzzle, without sitting down to work out what the picture was of, what time of day it had been taken, and even what month of the year it was—shouting, "Don't you *dare* give me a clue!" I think he saw me as a rival. He was always saying that artists had greater powers of observation than any detective.

Determined not to be left out, I took my drink and went

to sit beside him. The photograph, needle-sharp, was of a village green, with the parish church in the background.

That would tell him where east lay . . .

"Taken in the evening," he said. "Look at the length of those shadows."

"October," I said. "Leaves still on the trees, but quite a lot fallen."

"Taken after 1937," he said. "There's the last sort of prewar Austin Seven."

"But before the war," I said, cock-a-hoop. "There's one of those Wall's ice-cream tricycles—you know, 'Stop Me and Buy One.' They never came back, after the war."

"Sergeant, I take my hat off to you!" Then he shot in, "Pantile roofs—that means somewhere near the east coast."

"There's a flint wall—the southern part of the east coast. East Anglia . . ."

"Look at the size of the church. That's Suffolk or I'm a Dutchman."

"There's a white weatherboarded house—you don't get many of those north of Woodbridge." Then I played my trump card. "A Sunday evening—kids in their Sunday best, people coming out of church, women carrying prayer books . . ."

"Damn you, Sergeant. This country's turning into a police state." But his eyes were still scanning the photo, looking for the last word.

Phil laughed diabolically, pleased to have set us off against each other. He handed us another photograph.

"Try this, my children!"

It was the photograph of a woman, or perhaps only a girl, holding on to the door of the Austin Seven, looking shyly up into the camera.

"She's not married," I said. "No ring."

"A prim miss—no nail varnish. Ankle socks."

"But . . . in love, I think. Very much in love. With the man who took the picture."

"You sentimental old sergeant. I didn't know the Met had it in them."

I was silent. Weighing up the girl. She had a shy, self-effacing way of standing. And yet her eyes were huge and glowing, and her lips parted . . . a shy girl made bold by love, I thought. And no engagement ring either. I didn't like to see such vulnerability. Then I told myself not to be an imaginative fool . . . you could read too much into faces.

"Want to know what her fellow looked like?" asked Phil. He passed another photograph. This one was much less professional, with the camera held crookedly, and the man's head hard up against the top edge. He, too, was leaning against the Austin Seven. It was the kind of photo an inexperienced girl might have taken . . .

"He looks very pleased with himself," said John, rather crossly. Was he a little in love with the girl in the photo? Was he jealous of the man? "And old enough to be her father."

I wasn't so sure about that. The man's hair was cut short at the back and sides, as all men's was in those days. It made his ears stick out and look huge. It also made him look middle-aged, but then that hairstyle in old photographs could make schoolboys look middle-aged.

"Eyes too close together," said John. "I never trust a man whose eyes are too close together." Then he added, "A bit of a puritan, I would say. Look at that mouth, a real thin rat trap."

Phil gave another of his mock-sinister laughs. "Not so sure of that. Look at this one."

It was the girl again. Lying down in what seemed to be a woodland glade. On a tartan rug, with a straggle of items around her: thermos flask, picnic basket, raincoats. Her clothing was not at all disarranged, except for the skirt, which had ridden up over one knee. But her smile, the glow in her eyes, stronger now . . . every hallmark of a girl who has happily made love. A lock of her hair was falling over one eye . . .

"Yes," said John. He wriggled a little, on the sofa next to me. I think he was embarrassed because the same thought had come into his head. A very nice man, John.

"And this," said Phil triumphantly, handing us the last print with a flourish. "Talk about the wreck of the *Hesperus*."

The girl still lay in the forest glade, but she lay full length now, her head resting flat against the ground, her eyes nearly shut, the mouth drooping open in a most unpleasing way . . .

I froze. I had seen such photographs too often to be mistaken. The grace of the long limbs was gone; they were as untidy as a pile of dropped garbage.

"She's dead," I said. "I've seen too many like her. I *know*."

"God, I feel sick," said John. And the next second he was running for the bathroom.

WE SAT round in a huddled, excited heap.

"Can't *you* do something?" Phil asked me plaintively for the fifth time.

"Not if I value my job," I said, backing off vigorously. "We don't know when that picture was taken or where, or who they were. We only know it was well over fifty years ago. And that last photograph is *not* evidence. It could be a trick of the light, a trick of the camera. Maybe she was just in pain, or feeling sick. We have no evidence it was even taken in England."

"The other photo was—you said it was Suffolk."

"That was the other photograph. They might have taken the camera overseas . . ."

"It looks like an English glade."

"Don't you think they have glades like that in France or Germany? What the hell do you mean, an *English* glade? Are you an expert on English glades or something?" I was starting to get mad.

Poor Phil wilted and looked moodily at his expensive carpet. "We could try and find the place," he said feebly. "That wouldn't do any harm. We could drive over there and make inquiries . . ."

"Have you ever tried making inquiries?" I asked savagely, remembering how many doors I'd knocked on, and my aching feet. "If that girl was alive now, she'd be in her mid-seventies. Most of the people who knew her when she looked like that will be dead long since. Do you see yourself knocking on the door of every old granny in Suffolk saying do you remember this girl?"

"All the same," said John thoughtfully, "I think we ought to try. That girl's face will haunt me. I feel I owe it to her."

I glanced at Melanie, expecting the support of some common sense from the distaff side. But her face, very sad, was watching John's. Again, I felt how close the two of them were.

At last she said, "I think we must. It's so awful to think of him killing her, then photographing her when she was dead . . . as if he wanted to gloat over it. I don't think a man like that should be wandering about loose, however old he is, even if he's eighty. It's like those Nazi war criminals . . . it's never too late to bring them to justice."

"Let's go over and look next weekend," said Phil, a little smile of excitement lighting up his face, so I could have *kicked* him, for his heartlessness.

"A sort of murder holiday weekend," I said bitterly. "Like they lay on at hotels now. Only with an extra luxury, a real corpse."

"C'mon," he said. "I know a super pub we could stay at, at Felsbrough. The cooking is out of this world . . ."

I didn't go for the food. I went to keep him out of trouble.

I DIDN'T SEE him again until the next weekend, when I'd booked myself three days' leave; I had plenty of rest days in hand.

He seemed to have regained his high spirits by the time he rang my bell. Regained them indeed, considering he was wearing a ridiculous outfit of white flannels and a pink blazer with white stripes.

"What's this—a fancy-dress ball?" His little face fell, and I felt a bit of a brute.

"Just getting in the spirit of the thing—Albert Campion and all that . . . 1930s."

"I suppose I should give you a clip over the Lugg . . ."

Worse was to follow when I locked my flat and went downstairs. Parked next to my Metro was a huge green object with brass headlights and no roof.

"What's that supposed to be?"

"Bentley four-liter. 1936. Borrowed it off a mate—he owed me a favor."

From the back seat of the monstrosity, John and Melanie waved. They were wearing matching and tasteful tweed

suits and deerstalker hats. Melanie's outfit even had a
cape. They looked exceedingly chic, and I felt I was joining
a circus.

"Where do I put my luggage?" I said tightly. "Where's
the boot?"

"Hasn't got much of a boot," said Phil. "I'll strap it on
the back with the rest."

God, all that great length, which would be hell to park,
and no boot. Even the spare wheel was strapped on the
outside. That was the trouble with that monster. It was all
outside and no inside. Most of the inside appeared to be
occupied by the engine. The accommodation for passengers would've disgraced a First World War fighter plane.

"I hope it doesn't rain."

"There is a top. It takes about twenty minutes to put
up. My mate *has* done it occasionally. But the weather
forecast's good."

Needless to say, they'd found room for a food hamper
between John and Melanie. There was the expected clink
of champagne bottles as they shifted uncomfortably in
their leather seats.

"Hold on to your hats! We're off!"

I must say Phil seemed to know how to handle it—he
was always good at mechanical things. I never actually felt
in danger of my life, though the flashy way he showed off
his skill at double declutching was a little grating after a
while. And I suppose there is something in that old saying
about the joy of feeling the wind in your hair; fortunately,
I keep mine in a tight bun, as I said. But what with digging
flies out of my eye, and having to scream every remark at
the top of my voice over the *vroom* of the exhaust, and
worrying about the straps holding my luggage on the back
. . . it didn't improve my temper.

Nonetheless, it didn't stop the conversation.

"We've made a bit of progress since last week," said Phil. "I talked to a feller about that film in the camera. He said it was impossible for a roll of exposed undeveloped negatives to have lasted since the 1930s. Yet they *are* from the 1930s . . ."

"You call that making *progress*?" I snapped (if you can snap while screaming at the top of your voice).

Yet it spooked me, what he said. As a policewoman, I don't go for the inexplicable. I would like a world without the inexplicable. I felt a shiver run down my spine, as if somebody had walked over my grave.

And John and Melanie in the back didn't help any. John had spent the week going over the big prints with a magnifying glass. I began to realize that he had an obsessional personality, and he was obsessed.

"That bloke . . . his hand on the car door . . . he's wearing a wedding ring on the third finger of his left hand. He's got a ring, and she hasn't . . . that's a motive for his doing her in."

"What do you mean, a motive?"

"He might have got her pregnant . . . she might have been threatening to go to his wife and spill the beans. So he had to shut her up, hadn't he?"

"We haven't even proved she's dead yet." The whole thing began to disgust me. John and Melanie were high on what I suppose a bad novelist would call the thrill of the chase.

You don't get the police talking about the thrill of the chase. Or if you do, avoid them, because they're very bad police. If you talk about the thrill of the chase, it means you've decided who's guilty, before you can prove it. Oh, you have that temptation inside you all the time, but you sit on it and sit on it and never let it take you over . . .

"I've found something else," said John, not at all abashed. "There's a signpost on the village green in the first print —just in front of the church. You can't read the names on it, even with a magnifying glass. They're out of focus. But you can count the *letters* in the names, as blobs. There are five letters in the top name, and twelve in the bottom name."

"What good is that? Lots of place names have five letters."

"Yes, but not many have twelve, even in East Anglia, which is famous for long names. I've been over the road atlas, and I can only find four: Tattingstone, Wickham-brook and Grundisburgh in Suffolk, and Wethersfield in Essex. It gives us places to start. I suggest we eliminate Wickhambrook first—it's farthest from the sea, and the least likely to have pantiles on the roofs . . ."

"We'll take the M11," said Phil. "Show you what the old girl can do." He put his foot down.

The old girl showed us what she could do. Once, before I put *my* foot down and made Phil take his off, she did well over a hundred. It was very painful. The slipstream came around the tiny windscreen and hit us in the face like a mob throwing half-bricks. And the poor old thing was straining every sprocket; I thought she was going to blow up on us. And then, of course, the modern cars, the Jags and Mercs and big BMWs, began to want to show us what they were made of . . . and since I knew they could do a hundred and thirty without more than a whisper of a whistle . . . We were attracting more male attention than a bitch in heat.

I finally got Phil to cut it to eighty, and that was bad enough. I didn't fancy being pulled up by a jam-butty car for speeding, even as a passenger. They give you such a look . . .

Once we had turned off for Wickhambrook, and I had

breath to think, a nasty idea came floating into my mind out of my past. The medieval idea, from Chaucer's day, of the Ship of Fools. Wealthy fools voyaging to their own destruction.

Only we were a Car of Fools.

OF COURSE, Wickhambrook was nothing like the photograph. They hadn't expected it to be. You don't get a signpost saying "Wickhambrook" in Wickhambrook. You drive around Wickhambrook in ever-increasing circles, looking at church towers. A bit like a steeplechase, because the church in our photo certainly had a spectacular steeple. What John referred to as a broach spire . . .

It was quite fun at first. I had no idea there were so many kinds of church towers. Round ones, ones with octagonal tops, ones with four pinnacles and ones with eight, ones with spectacular gargoyles, and even ones with flat plain tops. Needle spires and broach spires. I owe all my extensive knowledge of church towers to that weekend.

And just about the time my head began to spin, they got discouraged and had lunch in a sweet meadow in the sunshine. With the champagne, which always improves my temper.

After lunch, we drove on to Tattingstone. After they had despaired of Tattingstone, we went on and they despaired of Grundisburgh.

It was when they had reached the point of total despair, when reality was at last breaking in on them, when they were talking about going on to the hotel and the whole thing might have collapsed into a harmless weekend, that I had to go and set them off again.

I don't like being beaten, you see. So I was still keeping my eyes open. And then I saw something. Nothing at all like a steeple, but it was a church just the same. Only this church didn't have a tower at all . . .

I saw a bus outside the church. A luxury touring bus, disgorging a stream of elegant and sprightly pensioners, who were hung about with cameras, binoculars, and clipboards. A cultural course on Suffolk churches, in full swing. And I simply got Phil to stop the car, walked over to them, picked out the course leader, who was the only one without camera, binoculars, and clipboard, and showed him our photograph.

"Bless me," he said, pushing up his bifocals onto his impressive forehead and squinting at the photo closely. "That's Bendham, before it lost its spire; in the great gale of 1976 . . ."

"But we've *been* to Bendham. It's nothing like. Just a tower peeping above great trees. And no village green."

He twinkled at me. "In the country, trees grow a lot in fifty years. And, sadly, developers move in . . ."

I must say, Albert Campion and the two Sherlock Holmeses were not as pleased as I thought they'd be. Downright peevish.

But it *was* Bendham. The post office was still the same.

By then it was time for a shower before dinner. Their stomachs took over and their brains went dead.

I BOUGHT a *Sunday Times* in the hotel next morning, and read right through it while they got on with their tomfoolery. The plan was to seek out old ladies within a ten-mile radius of Bendham.

I had pointed out that the best place to catch old ladies in the countryside on a Sunday morning was coming out of church. After that, the old ladies would sensibly go home, cook their roast lunch, and have an afternoon snooze till it was time to go to church for Evensong . . .

They'd agreed with this. But next morning, Phil had a hangover, and the breakfast was out of this world, and I couldn't get them moving before eleven. Perhaps it was as well. The vicars might have disapproved of a lunatic dressed as Albert Campion frightening their parishioners in their own churchyard. By the time we reached the first village, however, Matins was over and there wasn't a vicar or an old lady in sight.

What there was, was a lot of small boys, born after 1975, drawn by the sight of the car, and even more middle-aged men, born after 1945, on their way to the pub. I suppose that damned car did help in a way . . .

Through them, Phil tracked down some old ladies in their rose-covered lairs, and knocked on their pretty white doors. Most of the old ladies thought he was on a promotion campaign for a new sort of washing powder, and were avid for coupons, free samples, and chances to win £100,000 without committing themselves to buying anything.

But none of them knew the girl in the photograph, though some of them knew an Austin Seven from a Singer Ten.

As I said, I read the *Sunday Times* right down to the stock exchange news, and let Phil exhaust himself with his own deadly charm.

Again, it might have trailed off into a normal Sunday, with drinks and crisps in a pub and then a long expensive lunch.

But I had finished the *Sunday Times* and I was getting bored.

"Has it occurred to you," I said to Phil as he leaned exhausted against the bonnet, "that if your girl was murdered when you think, she didn't live around here very long? Whereas your murderer, if, as you think, he got away with it, may have lived around here very much longer?"

"You mean . . . show them *his* photograph?"

"Yes, my sweet love."

He almost vaulted the last old lady's gate, he was so filled with renewed inspiration.

And then he came back, looking very solemn and important, and my heart went down into my boots.

"Got 'im," he said. "He was the local doctor. Dr. Hargreaves. Lived in Berpesford till he retired in 1967."

"A doctor," said John, suddenly abandoning a lump of the *Sunday Times* he'd pinched off me. "Doctors have more ways of killing people than ordinary folk . . ."

"Doctors," said Melanie dreamily, "like Dr. Crippen and Dr. Buck Ruxton . . ." She reeled off a list of famous murdering doctors.

God, would you credit it? Bored farce to high drama in ten seconds. The atmosphere grew positively hysterical. I thought it was a good thing we had a police force. If it was left to the general public . . .

"Have you got his old address? Might as well see where he lived . . . and there's a very good pub in this guide, only about three miles from Berpesford," added John.

After an excellent lunch, we found the house. Phil knocked at the front door, asked after the good doctor, and came back looking very disgruntled.

"They haven't a clue where he went. They'd never even *heard* of him. They've only lived there for a year, and they bought the house off some Americans, who bought it off a civil engineer who worked in Ipswich."

"Honestly," said John, indignantly. "There's just no continuity in village life anymore. Rich outsiders moving in, not caring about the place, not staying five minutes . . . bloody *yuppies*."

They sat for a long time, glaring at the house, as if willing the pillared front door and Virginia creeper to give them a clue. After a while the people inside noticed us, and began glaring back.

"Let's go. Before they call the police," I said.

THEY PULLED UP in a lay-by, and sat and talked things over. The best they could come up with was that we should backtrack to all the old ladies we had already spoken to, to ask them if they knew where the good doctor had retired to.

It was not a good idea. It's hard to remember which old lady you've spoken to, in a village where you've only been once. And we'd been to so many villages that I never wanted to see a pretty Suffolk village again, as long as I lived. We slowly foundered in a mass of argument.

"I'm sure it's that street on the left; I remember turning by the pub with the green shutters."

"I don't think it's this village at all; the church was set back among trees and it had a smaller tower."

"That was *Tattersham*, you idiot."

"Fettersham, you mean!"

What old ladies we did find were grumpy at being disturbed again from their naps. They thought the good doctor had retired to Framlingham, Hedingham, Swannington, Walsingham, and Clacton, respectively. They all said he would be very old by now, well over eighty, and two thought they'd heard he'd died. The only thing they were agreed about was that he had been a wonderful doctor, whom they'd never forget as long as they lived.

Then it began to rain. John and Phil had a marvelous swearing match over putting up the folding top, which took much longer than twenty minutes. It reduced the interior of the car to a small dim rabbit hutch, with yellowing celluloid windows.

Phil said the top was genuine and authentic.

Melanie said it was leaking in at least three places.

It also obscured Phil's view to the rear, so that he crunched the precious love object slightly, getting out of a narrow parking space.

He was reduced to a sweating babbling wreck, thinking what the good mate who had loaned him the car would say, and how much the repair would cost him. I gathered he might be drummed out of his City bank, as the mate was considerably senior to him . . .

In the end, they slunk back to the hotel with their tails between their legs, and I went and had a hot shower and changed. I was idly lounging around, waiting for Phil to knock on my door for pre-dinner drinks, when I noticed my room had a telephone.

And, of course, a local telephone directory.

And, ever so casually, to satisfy my own curiosity, I picked it up and looked up the name Hargreaves.

There was only half a column of Hargreaveses; and a Dr. L. Hargreaves sat halfway down it. He lived in Framlingham.

I sat paralyzed.

I was a copper; and coppers become coppers because they believe strongly in law and order, and in making the punishment fit the crime; and as they tell you at training school, a copper is never off-duty.

But this man must be so old, and it was all so long ago, and the only evidence I had was one photographic negative that I'd been told couldn't possibly have survived for fifty years. And I wasn't even on my own patch. I thought of trying to explain it all to some grim, cynical, stolid local superintendent and I thought he'd give me a pitying look and tell me to run away and play. He'd have a word with my own super, and I'd be the divisional joke. It's hard enough to get any credence as a woman copper, and this could *destroy* me.

At that point, Phil walked in without knocking. He'd never done that before. I don't know if he was trying to catch me running about stark naked or what.

Instead, his hopeful little eye fell on the open telephone directory. And he got it in one. I mean, he's not stupid, just childish.

"You've *got* him!"

"There is a Dr. Hargreaves in the book," I said coldly.

We had another terrific conference over the crisps and drinks. That awful hunting look had come back into their eyes and I hated them. Talk about bloodlust . . . Their only problem was whether they should corner their fiend in human form before or after dinner.

I used all the arguments I could: that he was so old, that he might be the son, that he might be a different Dr. Hargreaves altogether. It was no use. They were set on their bit of fun.

"There'd be no harm in ringing him up," said Phil. "Find out if it *is* him."

"No," I said.

"Well, if you won't, I will."

That I couldn't allow. He'd go in like a bull in a china shop; he might give the old boy a fatal heart attack.

So I went back up to my room and rang the good doctor's number. They all clustered around to listen.

I knew it was him, the moment he answered. The voice was clear, but faint and a little wavering. His breathing was much louder than his talking. I knew he was not only old but sick.

"You won't know me, Dr. Hargreaves," I said, "but I've just come across a camera that I think used to belong to you. And there was a roll of film in it. I thought you might like to see the prints we got from it . . ."

After all, what else could I say?

I heard his sharp intake of breath. I was expecting him to put the phone down on me, or at least begin to bluster. But he only said, almost normally, "The Zeiss Ikon? I've been waiting for you a long, long time, my dear. I began to doubt that you'd ever come."

His voice was calm, resigned. As if he truly had been waiting for me. He was so calm and sure I grew a little afraid. Then he said, "Would you like to bring the photographs over? This evening?"

Because I was afraid, because I knew he *was* the one, I said, "I have three friends with me."

"Bring them. They will be quite welcome. Nine o'clock?"

I looked at the avid faces crowding around me, straining to listen to both sides of the conversation. All I could do was say yes.

He gave me directions on how to get there, and rang off.

HIS GARDEN was an old person's garden, small but as neat as a pin. The knocker was brass, a fox's face, and highly polished. There was a general air of quiet prosperity, and the smell of old age as he opened the door.

It was the man in the photograph all right. Wrinkles gather and gather, but bones don't change. His eyes were still too close together, and his mouth even more like a rat trap. He had been tall, but now he stooped over two sticks. His hands clenched on the sticks as an old tree's roots clench into the soil.

"Come in, come in." He looked at my friends one by one. Not one of them had the guts to look him in the face. I thought of juries, who will not look at the prisoner in the dock when they have found him guilty.

He asked us to sit down; offered us a drink, which we all declined. I could not tell if his hands were trembling from fear, or whether they always trembled like that.

When he had slowly settled himself and laid one stick carefully against each side of his chair, I gave him the first photograph.

He smiled, remotely. "Bendham. It's changed so much I wonder you were able to find it. And my old Austin Seven. I had it until 1950. Then I was able to afford something better . . ."

Then I handed him the photo of himself. And he smiled remotely again and said, "That's still how I imagine myself, in my mind's eye. These days the mirror is always rather a shock. You just can't believe you're getting old, and the older you get, the less you believe it. But there I stand, on the verge of middle age. Still hopeful . . . it's amazing how hopeful middle age can be."

He put it down beside him and gestured for the next print, with what seemed like eagerness. I somehow knew he hadn't forgotten the other pictures on that roll of film. He was expecting her . . .

When I handed it to him, he smiled a third time, and this time it was a *real* smile. A smile of joy; a smile so joyful that I gave a little shiver down my spine.

"Peggy," he said. "Peggy. She was so young. Young and hopeful, too. And very much in love. Dear Peggy."

I saw Phil's hand grip the arm of the sofa. Melanie kept giving little coughs, as if she was trying to dislodge something in her throat. John's face was white and sweating. I think it was starting to get too real for any of them to cope with. I've long known the feeling, from my job.

I handed him the fourth photograph.

"Bendham Woods," he said. "We had to be so very careful. I was a married man, with three children. And she was one of my patients. I tried to get her to go to another doctor, but she wouldn't. It would have meant her going into Ipswich by bus . . . She was a lovely girl, but unworldly. Never had a job, just looked after her aged parents till they died. They left her comfortably off, but what kind of life was that for a young woman?"

He looked up; looked at me.

"You're very *calm*, my dear! Are you a policewoman?"

I said, "Yes, but not from around here. I'm with the Met."

He said, "I'm glad." I couldn't make out whether he meant he was glad I was a policewoman, or whether he was glad I wasn't from around here.

I handed him the last photograph, and he shook his head sadly and said, "You spotted she was dead, then?"

"I've seen too many . . ."

"Yes," he said, "yes."

Then he looked at me very straight, with those eyes that were too close together.

"What do you want?"

"The truth."

"Yes, I can see that. But what do your *friends* want?"

He surveyed them calmly. None of them would look at him.

"I expect they want me punished," he said. "The world is full of people who want other people punished. I find it a little disgusting. Revenge I can understand. It's an honest emotion. But people who haven't been harmed themselves, who want people *punished* . . . What do you think they're up to, eh? I meet people who want the striking miners punished, or unmarried mothers, or drug addicts, or Pakistanis who dare speak up for their beliefs. It's not pretty, my dear. It's not pretty at all."

He let a long and unbearable silence develop, and watched them writhe.

"Such people never seem to think that life itself can be sufficient punishment. Life and the years that pile up. But no, your friends want me *arrested*. Put on trial. In all the papers, so that all the other people who want to punish can read about my punishment, and have their appetite for punishment satisfied. For a little while. Until they find a new victim." Then he added, with another straight look at me, "But I think you only want the truth, my dear. So you shall have it. It's all you will get, I think, because even being arrested would be enough to finish me off. I shouldn't last a week . . . I'm a doctor, and I *know*."

"Are you guilty?" I blurted out. Because the strangest thing was happening. He was separating me from my friends. It was them I saw as monsters now. I was on his side. Had he some strange magic, that still worked, behind those mottled deathly cheeks and weary burned-out eyes? Was it the strange magic that had lured Peggy to her death?

"I was guilty—of great heartlessness," he said. "And I have been punished for it."

"Heartlessness is not a crime," I said.

"Ah, but it should be. It was right that I was punished." There was no self-pity in his voice, no special pleading. Just . . . I hope when I am old, I can reach that kind of tranquillity.

"What happened?"

He shrugged. "We fell in love. With all our hearts. I had thought I knew what love was, with my own wife, for my wife and I were always comfortable together, and I loved her till the day she died. But this . . . It was springtime and . . . I don't think we cared if we died for it. We both knew it couldn't last, somehow. It was as if Peggy gathered all her careful life into a great bundle and threw it to me. My only concern was that my wife should not find out and be hurt. So we were very, very careful. We would meet in a quiet spot, and drive to places where nobody knew either of us. That's how we came to pass through Bendham that day."

"Yes," I said.

"It may sound very strange to you, my dear, but we never made love—not all the way. We were innocents in those days—not at all like now, when people hop into bed the first time they meet. I know I was an experienced married man, but half the time Peggy seemed more like a daughter. I sometimes think we got more out of holding hands than some of them today get from bed."

There was a strangled indecipherable grunt from Phil, and he stirred uneasily.

"What happened?" I asked.

Dr. Hargreaves gave me another of those straight looks from his faded eyes, ghostly eyes, and said, "She just died, there in the glade, as I was taking her photograph. We had been . . . extraordinarily passionate, for us. She had a weak heart. I saw her die through the camera viewfinder, as I was clicking the release. I ran to her, tried everything. There was nothing I could do. Except leave her where she lay."

"*Leave* her?" All John's suppressed rage boiled out in one terrible shout.

"What else could I do? There was nothing I could do for *her*. She was beyond my aid. And I was a married man and a doctor, with a reputation and a job to lose. My wife would have suffered terribly if the truth had got out. My children might have starved. Life wasn't a bed of roses in the 1930s, especially for a disgraced doctor who'd been struck off the register. I might never have worked again. And I was a *good* doctor."

He put his face quite suddenly into his hands. I thought he had been taken ill, and touched his arm, but he shook me off.

"It was a solitary spot. They didn't find her body for nearly a week . . . the animals had been at her . . . her face and hands."

"We've only got your word you didn't kill her," said John, with a savagery that made me shudder.

"Oh, no," said Dr. Hargreaves, looking up. "There was a postmortem. And an inquest, of course. She died of natural causes. She had an aneurysm. She couldn't have lasted six months more, the coroner said. I have often wondered if she knew that, instinctively, and that was what made her so desperate for love . . . Here's the details."

He handed me a brown newspaper clipping, and the same dark innocent face of Peggy stared out at me. But this was a formal studio photograph; she was wearing a silly little hat. The inquest did record a verdict of death from natural causes. There was a coroner's warning about young girls in poor health going for walks alone in lonely places.

"So you got away with it?" said John savagely.

Dr. Hargreaves eyed him long.

"I suppose you could say that. My name was never connected with hers. My wife never found out; my children got a good start in life, and still think highly of me."

John made a sound of disgust in his throat.

"But I don't think I got away with it," said Dr. Hargreaves. "I was the police surgeon for the area. I was called in to give my professional opinion. I had to help at the postmortem. There was no way I could get out of it."

"Oh, my God," said Melanie. "John, I feel sick."

"I should take your wife home, sir," said Dr. Hargreaves, "while you still have her."

Phil went too. Dr. Hargreaves and I stood up. He looked at me, as if from a great distance, as if from the doors of death itself.

"You are a good policewoman," he said. "You'll go far. Because you want the truth. God bless you." There were tears in his faded eyes now.

"One last question . . ." I said. Diffidently. Because I didn't want to upset him anymore, but I had to know the whole truth.

"Yes, my dear?"

"The camera. How did you come to lose the camera?"

He smiled, a little painfully. "I couldn't bear to touch it again, after what happened. Knowing what film it had inside it. I wanted to have it developed, so I could have a last photograph of her. But I couldn't risk sending it to any chemist for developing, could I? They look at the prints in the darkroom . . . So the camera hung unused in the cupboard in our bedroom for years. It irritated my wife greatly, that I couldn't bring myself to use it. She wanted photographs of the children as they grew up, like any mother, and she couldn't use it herself—she was frightened of it, it wasn't simple like a Brownie box. In the end, in a fit of rage, she sent it to the church jumble sale. I never knew a moment's peace after that . . . I didn't even dare to try and trace who'd bought it."

"Will you be all right?" I asked.

"Whether I live, or die tonight, I shall be all right now. It's such a relief to tell somebody at last. You were as good as a priest in the confessional, my dear."

I kissed him then, on both withered cheeks. He was so light and frail it was like kissing a ghost. But a good and faithful ghost.

I have no worries for him. Wherever he has gone.

But I still wonder Who preserved those negatives.

FIFTY-FAFTY

FRIDAY AFTERNOONS, my mother picked me up from school and we went shopping down the town. Out of our leafy suburb, down into the smoky jungle. Wondrous shops were there, full of Dinky Toys and pink ladies' corsets. But the poor were there, too. Beyond the shops, all down to the river, they got poorer and poorer. In the lower depths they Drank, and had no drains; emptied their soapy washing-up water and worse straight into the furrows of yellow-clay paths that trickled, in the end, into the black waters of the Tyne, iridescent with the sick beauty of oil and awash with broken fish boxes, where only the inedible blackjack swam, caught by boys who had no boots or shoes, and left lying to rot on the cobbled quays. Where dirty women hung out of windows and shouted incomprehensible things as you passed, and did incomprehensible things with sailors, then cut their throats as they slept and lifted their wallets and dropped their bodies straight into the river through trapdoors in their houses.

I don't remember how old I was. I know I had sadly abandoned hope of dragons. I had checked for wolves under the stairs and found only a sack of musty potatoes and a meter with the faint exciting whiff of gas. But there were still monsters. The lamplighter walking in front of us was a minor wizard. He put up his long pole to the gas lamps and created darkness. It was broad daylight till the gas lamps flared; instantly, night gathered around them like smoke. My own headmaster was a fabulous monster of sorts—tiny, bent, wizened, and silver-haired; we loved him. But the boys said that he had once been a six-foot sergeant major in the Welsh Guards, broad as a house, with a voice like a bull. Till the gas got him, in the Battle of the Somme. And down the town there were much more satisfying monsters, like Happy Ralph, who lurked at the bottom of Borough Road and rushed out at you with outstretched arms and incoherent cries, whether to embrace you or strangle you nobody ever lingered to find out. On Sundays, Happy Ralph went from church to church, roaming the aisles and terrifying the vicar in his pulpit and the spinsters in their pews.

A trackless safari into the dusk. But not without water holes. First my Aunt Rose's house, only a little way into the jungle, where people still scoured their doorsteps and polished their knockers daily. But Aunt Rose was definitely a denizen of the jungle, her living room long and dark as a dungeon, only a pale ghost of daylight trickling in past aspidistra and lace curtain, over the massive overstuffed three-piece suite crowded like cattle in a byre.

She gave us tea, which we balanced on our knees. She stayed on her feet, solid as a bullock in her flowered pinafore, hair in a tight black bun, and railed against God.

At home, God was the God of green grass and fresh air and Sunday best, the vicar in spotless black and white, missions to save the Africans from naked sinfulness, and roast beef for dinner after. But down where Aunt Rose lived, God prowled like a man-eating tiger, driving good men to drink by killing their young wives with TB, and slaughtering innocent babes in their cradles. And not one of His evil tricks escaped Aunt Rose's eagle eye.

"How could He do it?" she would thunder. "To a little innocent lamb who had done no wrong?"—as she stood against the oaken altar of her sideboard, arrayed with photographs of the dead of whom God had robbed her. I treasured her as I never treasured our vicar. The vicar had God on his side, was teacher's pet. My Aunt Rose stood and thundered, fearless and alone. She couldn't possibly win against God . . . could she? Still, I could imagine her smashing through the Pearly Gates, blazing out accusations like a medium tank.

My mother saw it differently. Pale, prim, and pious, she sat through Aunt Rose's sermons in silence, and walked silent down the street afterwards. Glancing up slyly, I would see a furtive tear trickle down her cheek. Often, afterwards, my father would shout at her, demanding to know why she bothered going to Rose's at all. All she would ever say, white as a stone, was "Blood is thicker than water."

Then I would see the dead sailors' blood, thick as Tate & Lyle syrup, red as Heinz tomato ketchup coiling up through the black oily waters of the Tyne.

NEXT STOP, the Co-op on Howdon Road. Sawdust on the floor, full of footprints where the bare floorboards showed through; sawdust that was carried by departing feet across the wet pavements for miles around. You could have tracked your way to the Co-op without ever raising your head, just by following the sawdust prints. There was a fat black-and-white cat, sitting on a sack of loose dog biscuits, licking sawdust off its fur; whole sides of smelly bacon, hanging from floor to ceiling; round blocks of dewy butter and cheese, big as barrels; gleaming brass weights; and Jack Sylph.

Jack Sylph was also a magic monster, more magic even than my aunt. I knew from poems that I'd learned that a "sylph" was a slender naked female. Jack, though undeniably thin, was also undeniably male, and clad in a long brown coat, with a yellow pencil behind his ear. And though his face was young he was as totally bald as a polished egg. Did he polish his head every morning with a duster, after he'd cleaned his teeth? Did he use furniture polish on it? As my aunt used polish on the photo frames of her Dead? My mother said he'd been bald ever since he was eighteen, yet he had courted and married and had four children. I thought of his wife, waking up in the dark, and feeling for that warm bald polished egg, as I still reached for my teddy bear.

Jack was a wizard, too. He could cut you a piece of cheese any weight you wanted. My mother always asked for odd weights, just for the pleasure of seeing him do it.

"Six and three-quarter ounces, please, Jack." He draws himself up to a great height, his eyes as keen as those of Don Bradman scoring a six for Australia in a test match. Down comes the cheese wire. Onto the scales . . . exactly right. My father says he should be on the music halls.

And he makes up her order without ever stopping asking about her family. "I'm glad her sciatica's better . . . and a pound of washing soda." His head talks and all the time his clever white hands are reducing whatever bags, tins, drums, or packets she has bought into an exact geometrical cube, wrapped in brown paper, and tied with string, with a double loop at the top for her to put her fingers through to carry it.

Next, to Tawse's the draper's, where my mother used to work before she married. Tawse's is a cliff, twelve foot high, of shelving behind the counter. There are ladders nearly as high as firemen's ladders, up which the assistants run to lift down enormous overwhelming boxes and rolls of cloth. My mother has a huge dent in her shin where she used to lean into the rung of the ladder when she raised both arms to lift something down. Sometimes, on evenings around the fire, I grow fascinated by it, press on it, ask her if it hurts. She doesn't wince. I ask her if she was scared, up the cliff; she says she got used to it.

My mother, after endless pursing of her mouth and feeling the material between finger and thumb, proving she is no fool and has been in the business to the young chits who are working there now, makes her purchase and hands over her ten-shilling note, for a pair of rayon stockings at one and elevenpence three-farthings.

Now is the big moment. The assistant screws the bill and the note into a round wooden cylinder a bit like a shell. She loads it into a cage . . . I look at the ceiling. There is a kind of miniature tramway screwed along the ceiling. The assistant pulls a lever and the wooden shell whizzes along the tramway like a rocket with a fearful rattle, just like a tram, and vanishes into a mysterious little wooden house marked CASHIER. After two minutes, the shell comes rocketing back, with the receipted bill and, magically, the correct change in it.

Why does that person hide inside that blank wooden box? Has he no legs, like the man who sings songs for money from a little trolley at the top of Saville Street? Or is he hideously deformed, like the midnight mechanics who empty the earth closets in the cart-rumbling lamplit dark and never show themselves by daylight, because their faces are eaten away by unmentionable mysterious diseases?

Out into the rainy street. My mother takes my arm in hers now. For the unemployed men were squatting in groups at every street corner, passing a smoldering fag end around between them, smoking it down to the last quarter-inch by impaling it on a pin they take from the lapels of their coats. You could see the heads of a row of pins, gleaming in each of their lapel tops, for they had turned up their collars against the drizzle. They pick up the pins from the ground, the way they pick up fag ends.

It is not that my mother is afraid of anything the men might do or say to her. They dwelt in a world of their own, their heads much nearer the ground, their cracked boots polished till they shone like diamonds, their white mufflers spotless, their caps as sharp-set as those of the brave soldiers they once were. Wearing their hopeless pride like a wall. No, we did not fear them; but we feared what had happened to them. As if unemployment was infectious, like diphtheria or scarlet fever that could pass through the air from their very breath. My father is employed: at the gasworks. His work muffler is filthy; he never has time to clean his boots. He is busy working.

Last stop, the chemist's. It glows through the dark like a jewel, huge globes with pointed stoppers, two feet high, full of mysterious liquid, red, blue, green, enough to poison the whole town. And inside, more huge jars with unreadable names. SOD BIC. AQUA FORTIS. CANT MEM. Rows of varnished drawers full of wickedness.

But the most terrifying thing about the chemist is the way he speaks. He speaks posh, posher than anyone I've ever heard. My mother wants some Sal Hepatica. I am always encouraging her to buy Sal Hepatica. Every time we set out for town I ask her whether she has enough. The medicine chest in the bathroom must be full of it; I don't even know what she uses it for. But I long to hear this chemist echo her, with his utterly eerie voice.

"Sal Hair-pair-teeh-caaah." It sounds like a spell; like the names of one of the Pharaohs in school, or of those volcanoes in Mexico.

In the street again, I chant it to the night. "Saaaal Heeeeep-eeeeeh-tiiiii-caaah. Saaaaal Heeeeep-eeeeeh-tiii-caaaaah." My mother tells me to stop; it is rude. So I chant "Tuuuutaaaankaaaamen" and "Coootooopaaaxi" instead.

And so to Nana's for tea. Her front door opening at a touch; my mother's timid "Yoohoo" echoing through the churchlike gloom of the cold front hall. Then the kitchen door opened, the red light, the blast of heat from the kitchen range, the sweet overpowering smell of baking bread, and Nana, up to her elbows in white flour, wiping her pink perspiring forehead with the back of her hand, and adding more white streaks to what was there already. Behind her, the kitchen range gleams black and silver in the red gloom, and on the mantelpiece all the horse brasses and ornaments, polished till they, too, gleam silver. Nana polishes things to within an inch of their life.

Half the table oilcloth is covered already with the plump white female shapes of finished bread, cooling on wire grids. Inside the gleaming brass fender, great cloth-covered bowls, where domes of white female dough rise inexorably every time you lift the cloth to peep. And yet more white dough, twisting between Nana's strong hands.

"Sit yourselves down," she says, with a gasp of exhausted glee. "Give the bairn a bun, while they're hot."

At home, I might be made to wait. Not here. Here I am a little king. I can have all the buns I can eat. Instantly. Till I am sick, though I never am. That is her way, that is part of her magic.

The smell of the opened bun, the smell of the running melting butter. The heat of the fire on my face, turning to pricks of perspiration on the back of my neck. The black horsehair sofa prickles against the backs of my knees, under my short trousers. My grandmother is a white bread-witch, solid and strong as her rising dough, and I am safe in her kingdom.

When I was born, my mother had a bad time. She often tells me and I feel dreadful guilt. Afterwards, she was too weak to carry me in her arms. But my grandmother carried me about everywhere, till I was three. My father often says, in a quietly glad voice, "Your nana's a strong woman."

Yet she's as quick to joke as a child. Once, when my grandfather was washing at the kitchen sink, stripped to the waist, after work, she held a handful of snow against his bare back. His mouth flew open with the shock. His false teeth fell out, and Nana still gets helpless with laughter when she remembers.

Sometimes, she still takes in stray men as lodgers. Lost dogs, down on their luck. An ex-Army major, full of wondrous stories about pig-sticking in India, but often still shell-shocked and shaking with black memories of the trenches. The first Oriental merchant in the town, a carpet seller called Ali Hassan. He is prospering greatly now, but he still calls every year to bring her a Christmas present. He sits at the table in a turban, with two turbaned grown-up sons standing respectfully behind him, waves his jeweled hands, and tells her stories and gives her huge drums of

Turkish Delight. The real stuff, not Cadbury's rubbish: wooden boxes with Turkish writing on the side, powdered white, which I share while he is still sitting there. He is more exciting than Charlie Chan in the movies.

MY MOTHER REALIZES she has forgotten to buy my father's cigarettes.

"Run along back, hinny. You've just got time, before he comes," says Nana.

I am alone with my magic woman.

She says, "Eeh, where've I put my oven cloth?" I giggle, because I can see it hanging over her shoulder. She follows my eyes, and finds it.

"Eeh, Aah'm daft. Aah'd forget me head if it was loose."

I say, "Fifty-fafty, you're a dafty." I wouldn't dare say that to my mother. She would say it was rude. Nana doesn't care. Instead, she says, "Do you know who Fifty-fafty was?"

"No. It's just something we shout to each other at school. I didn't know it was a person."

Her eyes grow thoughtful. "Oh, aye, he was a person all right. Poor bugger. But you don't want to hear about him . . ."

"I do." I know she is only teasing. There is a story coming up. There is a glint of excitement in her eye.

She draws herself together, like Jack Sylph cutting cheese.

"He was a poor boy. Born down by the river. Fishermen. Hadn't two pennies to bless themselves with."

I shiver deliciously; they put two pennies on the eyes of dead people.

"Anyway, Fifty-fafty was bright. He could see there wasn't any money in fishin', so he ran away to sea to make his fortune. Just like Bobby Shaftoe. An' when he went, he took his father's silver ring. The family heirloom, the only thing they had worth tuppence.

"Well, they cursed him an' forgot him. All except his sister—he'd been closest to her. An' they got poorer and poorer. Aah can't tell ye the things they had to do to make ends meet."

I shiver again; I know the things they do, down by the river.

"An' then, one day, years later, this grand rich man comes to the town—wearing a fur coat and so many rings on his fingers it was dazzlin'. He was buyin' drinks for everybody he met. He was the talk of the town. But he had a great beard coverin' his face, an' he wouldn't tell anybody his name. An' that night he wouldn't stay at the inn—he walked down to the river and sought out that family an' asked them if they could put him up for the night. An' they looked at his fur coat an' rings, an' the great bag he carried, an' they said they could. And at supper, and all the time till bedtime, he talks about the places he'd been an' the wonderful things he'd seen, an' of all the ships and land and houses he owned.

"An' just afore bedtime, he catches the sister outside, an' swears her to secrecy, an' tells her who he is. It was Fifty-fafty. He showed her the ring an' she believed him, even after all those years. He had come back, like he had promised all those years ago, to make them all rich, so they could live like lords. She begged him to tell everybody straightaway. But he wanted to give them the big surprise he'd worked an' slaved for all those years. An' it was Christmas Eve, an' his big bag was full of presents for them . . . An' she couldn't do nothing about it—'cos he'd sworn her to secrecy. So she went to bed, upstairs with her mam.

"And in the morning, when she came down, her father and brothers were all laughing and winking at each other, and there was no sign of Fifty-fafty. They said he'd had to leave early, to catch a boat on the tide.

"An' then she knew what had happened. They'd killed him in the night, when he was asleep, an' robbed him in the dark. It was his dead body that had sailed out on the tide, not a ship.

"An' then she burst out weeping, and told them about the ring. An' they took out the stuff they'd stolen, an' there was his father's ring they'd slipped off his finger in the dark, and never noticed.

"An' they fell to blaming and quarreling, and word got to the magistrate, an' they were all hanged . . . when they could've lived like lords.

"An' that's the story of Fifty-fafty."

She sighed. "If only he'd listened to his sister."

I was silent, and she was silent. Then she finished kneading the last of the dough and set it to rise. And I thought of Fifty-fafty, and all his work and all his hopes, and the way he died, his throat cut in the dark, like a beast, on Christmas Eve. And the way, for hundreds of years, he had haunted the school yards, with the boys shouting, "Fifty-fafty, you're a dafty."

Poor Fifty-fafty, would they never let him rest? Would his daftness live on, to the end of time, in the boot-stamping dead-fly toilets, in the rain-soaked school yards?

And then my mother came back with my father's cigarettes. And then my father came from work, all grinning and greasy and black with his job, with his three-pound pay packet in his pocket. And Nana made the fire up and we had a slap-up tea with bacon and eggs and new bread. And Nana drew her dark-red velvet curtains against the rain and the dark. And we were snug, as we always were.

But I listened to the wind and the rain, and thought how thin the glass of the window was, and out there was Fifty-fafty, at the bottom of the sea still, his blood that was thicker than water coiling up through the black depths, like the slime from a rotting cod's head. And Jack Sylph who lost all his hair at eighteen, and the unemployed men squatting on the corners when it was not their fault, and the man-eating God who killed good men's young wives with TB and drove them to drink, and my headmaster who had shrunk in the poison gas of the Somme . . .

And I cried for them all, quite suddenly.

My father was furious with me, saying I was going on like a wet girl. I had never seen him cry; I don't think he ever did. When I told him about Fifty-fafty, he said Nana had just told me the story of an old play she'd seen years ago at the old Theatre Royal. It wasn't true. But why should the boys call out about Fifty-fafty if he was just some old play?

My mother said, rather proudly, that I had too vivid an imagination, just like her.

But Nana marveled at the softness of my heart.

I was glad for once, that night, to get back up into the green suburb. It was some years still before I realized that God prowled up there as well.

THE CATS

TODAY THERE WAS a cat in the house.

There has been no cat even in the grounds for thirty years, since we bought it. My dogs have seen to that. I am a dog person.

I came in from the garden, stripping off my gardening gloves, my eyes full of sunlight, thinking about nothing in particular. I went upstairs to get changed for tea. And there it was, sitting at the head of the stairs, perfectly at home, looking down on me as if *I* were the intruder.

I hate cats. But I had to admit it was a prime specimen. A blotched tabby, with great thick gouts of pure black running down its coat. Almost, in the sunlight on the stair, a black cat with stripes of golden guard hairs, like networks of stars. Big. Fat. Silently purring: so hard it was rocking slightly with pleasure, the way cats do. As if it had got something it had waited for a long time. Certainly the purring was not for me; its eyes, staring into mine, were as cold as green ice. As cold as mine, I suppose. It looked at me as if it were my equal—as if it were my superior. Its claws were extending and retracting in time with its purring.

I waved my gloves in its face, shooed at it.

It did not move. It held its place. You may say it could not get past me, down the stairs . . . It did not even want to get past me. It wanted to keep me out of my own house.

I grew uneasy, as I stood there, on the sixth step down. I noticed again how big it was; how big the claws, extending and contracting. On the top step, it was nearly level with my face. It looked . . . a nasty beggar to tackle. Animals should know the rules. My dogs have always known the rules. This cat didn't. And when animals don't know the rules . . .

I backed down a few steps. Called to my dogs, knowing they wouldn't be far behind me, coming in from the garden, yawning and stretching.

They did not come; they did not answer, useless brutes. Nervous, I turned back quickly to face the cat, frightened it might spring.

It was gone from the stair head. It was not in the upstairs corridor. And all the doors were shut, except the one to my husband's study. I went in, in a bit of a temper. My husband used to be very fond of cats, when he was young. I had a feeling he might have encouraged this one . . .

But he was asleep, in the swivel chair at his desk, a big book on the Adriatic open on his knees. He was having his fallow time, as he calls it. He had finished this year's play for the West End. At the end of August, we were going off to the Adriatic, for this year's travel book. He spends his fallow time reading and dozing in the sun. When you're nearly seventy, I suppose it's permissible. He does work hard when he *is* working . . .

His face looked, somehow, different. A little . . . transparent. You watch them, when they get to that age. But he was breathing very softly, normally. So I just put it down to the late afternoon sun that was flooding the room with light. In any case, he awakened then; stretched and smiled. To himself, not at me. He hadn't even realized I was there.

"Nice dream?" I asked.

He closed his eyes again, instantly. The wrinkles around his closed mouth moved, resorting themselves into a new expression. Then he opened his eyes and looked at me, and said, "Can't remember it. But, yes, nice . . ."

Liar, I thought. Whatever your dream was, I wouldn't have been welcome in it. I was cross, so I said, "There was a damned cat on the stairs. Hasn't been in here, has it?"

"I've seen no cat. What color was it?" Once he's got his defensive wall up, there's no getting past it.

"Big tabby thing. Fat and cocky. Faced up to me, on my own staircase. Didn't give a damn."

"You should've set your dogs on it!"

"Damned dogs were nowhere to be seen."

He was laughing at me, inside himself. I can always tell.

Then he said, "The cat sounds a bit like old Mirabelle." He spoke as if Mirabelle were still around, not dead for nearly forty years. Then I knew he was really sticking his knife into me.

So I went and had a shower.

SHOWERS USUALLY SET ME UP; but not this one. I took the late Mirabelle in with me, and brought her out again. Mirabelle was the cat he had when I first met him. When he was plain Harry Tremblett, failed poet and pub crawler, not Sir Harold Tremblett, playwright, travel writer, and critic. Living in a three-room basement in King's Cross, with rows of dirty milk bottles at the door, and rows of empty wine bottles by the dustbins in the areaway. God knew how he kept himself in booze; God knew how he could bear to live in that slum of unmade bed and dirty plates with the cold tap dripping on them, and an old wind-up gramophone piled with scratched 78s of Bunk Johnson and Bessie Smith. And the queen of that slum was Mirabelle, with her knowledgeable eyes that had seen everything and told nothing.

I don't know how I ever brought myself to make love on that bed, with that cat watching, that first time. Afterwards, the cat came sliding over, fussing at him, licking his sweating face, trying to force herself between us, so that he accused her of being jealous, and laughed with delight.

She lasted a long time, did Mirabelle—longer than the unmade bed or the dirty plates or the rows of empties; longer even than all his revolting friends: the well-heeled amateur Communists, the duffel-coated anarchists, and the ex-girlfriends who thought they could absorb me into their complaisant ranks.

Mirabelle was the last thing to go. It was after my father got him that temporary lectureship at Leeds, the first step he made up the ladder. I'd arranged everything: the university flat where pets were forbidden, even the friends who would take Mirabelle off our hands.

Then, the day before we left, Mirabelle got ill. Suddenly she was uncontrollably messing all over the flat. It's lucky we were packed by that time.

I told him, "You can't expect my friends to have her now—messing all over the place. She'll have to *go*, Harry."

He gaped at me. "Go *where*?"

"Be put to sleep. She's over ten years old . . ."

"But the vet could make her better . . ."

"And how much would *that* cost? Treatment and drugs

and kennel bills. You've hardly got the train fare to Leeds . . ."

"Lend me the money . . ."

"No. I've lent you *enough*. I have to earn it, the hard way. I'm not wasting it on a damned *cat*."

He sat down and took her on his knee, a little gingerly. He glared at me and said, "I'm not going to Leeds. You can stuff your bloody Leeds and your stinking little bourgeois lectureship. I'm staying here with Mirabelle, and I'm going to make her well, and we're going to live here and be *happy*."

"You've given up the lease," I said. "The new people are moving in tomorrow, God help them."

"I'm not going . . ."

"Suit yourself. I'll tell my father you're resigning, that you don't want the flat up there. And you won't be seeing any more of me. Blow this chance, and we're *finished*."

He put his head down. I didn't realize he was crying till the drops of water began hitting Mirabelle's tangled fur. God, I can't stand men who cry; it just disgusts me. So I threw down a couple of pound notes onto the old washed-out mattress and said, "That's to pay for the vet—to put her down. And if you're not at the station by the time the train goes, it's bye-bye."

Then Mirabelle finished herself off. She gave a low mournful cry, and messed on the trousers of his only half-decent suit.

I didn't stay to be argued with. I picked up my suitcase and left. I will never forget the look the cat gave me as I walked out the door. It was as if she *knew*.

Harry was at the station on time.

Alone.

Back in the shower, I told myself I was being stupid,

and toweled myself dry too vigorously, so I broke out
sweating again.

By the time I'd dressed, I'd convinced myself the cat on
the stairs was nothing like Mirabelle. The world was full
of large, fat, arrogant blotched tabbies. The world was
also full of slightly dotty sixty-three-year-old women, so
I'd better pull myself together before I joined them.

THE LATTER PART of August is like a great tide going
out. The world is suddenly too full of trees and the trees
are too full of leaves and the leaves fade from green to
dark gray like an old photograph left too long in the
glaring sun. And even the quality of the sunlight fails—
not the quantity, but the quality. It is almost as if the eyes
have had too much sunlight and can't take it in anymore,
so that there is a sudden darkness in the midst of the
sunlight. And the heat is a dead heat: the dead heat of a
kiln just turned off because the final temperature has been
reached. And all your friends are away, and all the village
organizations are asleep. Even the vicar is away, and the
Sunday service is taken by some uncouth and nervous
stranger from the nearest town. And the Final Test drones
down to an endless hopeless draw. I listen to the sleepy
commentary, and I imagine the cricketers, lost in the dark
sunlight, moving slower and slower, and the commentator's
eyelids drooping. Someone, before the First World War,
wrote a novel in which the Germans invaded on August
Bank Holiday, and won because nobody on our side could
bother to mobilize. That writer knew August.

I am a doer. I have a horror of nothing to do. I have
been a doer all my life. If I cannot do, I begin to cease to
be. I grasped at tiny things, as at straws. I was glad that
Mrs. Temple, our housekeeper, had gone to Ibiza with

her husband, so that at least I had the cooking and dusting. I swept up the first errant autumn leaves when there were not enough to fill half a garden basket. I cut down plants long before their time. I made sudden despairing telephone calls to town, to people whom I had lost touch with for years, only to find they were away, too.

Harry does not seem to mind. He reads; he sleeps in the sun. He does not sprawl disgustingly in his sleep like some elderly men. He curls up gracefully, like a cat. He smiles in his sleep, like a cat. As with a cat, it is impossible to tell if he is *really* asleep when I come into the room, or just pretending. Even awake, he is oddly far away, further away than he has ever been. It makes me nervous. I try to coax him into doing things. But he knows they are needless. He will do them when autumn comes, after we are back from the Adriatic. Or we will get a man to do them . . .

I don't press him. We have always had this bargain. He has written his play for the year. Soon he will begin gathering stuff for his travel book. Fair's fair.

So why does it make me so afraid?

I HAVE SEEN another cat. A quite different cat. A long-haired white cat, playing in and out of the shrubbery, under the shadow of the dark rhododendron leaves, like a moth fluttering at a lamplit window after dark, coming and going.

I shouted at it when I came around the corner of the house. Waved my arms to scare it. It paused, looked at me with dark empty eyes from a head like a beautiful skull. Then went on flitting, in and out.

Harry was asleep on the lounger, under the french windows, which were open to cool the house. I gave him a too rough poke, because I was seized with the awful irrational fear that he might be dead. He came awake, smiling again, as if he'd had yet another pleasant dream.

"There was another cat," I said, crossly. "Didn't you see it?"

"Where?" he said.

And he looked straight at the shrubbery—when he could've looked anywhere.

"What color was it?"

"White," I said, flatly. "A white longhair. Playing in that shrubbery—where you were just looking."

"I can't see any cat." Was he laughing at me again?

"It's gone now," I said.

"Funny—it's always you who see them. It isn't as if you're a lover of them. A white longhair, you say? Sounds like Imogen's cat, Suki . . ."

IMOGEN.

Imogen Smallbridge. I first heard her name over the telephone, when Derek Pither phoned me from Rome. He said he wanted a quiet little word with me. Derek was famous for his quiet little words; few could have been as devastating as the one I got.

Harry had gone off the rails. In Rome. Right in the middle of a lecture tour for the British Council that I had worked heavens hard to get him. He had missed giving his talk in Florence, and the one in Venice was due that day and there was no sign of Harry. And Derek had a jolly good idea where Harry and Imogen Smallbridge had gone. A boat she had hired for the summer, tied up in Malta.

I flew straight out, cursing my own stupidity. It was the first time in five years I'd let Harry off the reins.

We reached Valetta harbor that evening in one of those ridiculous horse-drawn things. Upset as I was, I had to pause as I got down from that ridiculous smelly old open carriage.

Valetta harbor is grand theater. The huge stone quays; the nooks and crannies of water, leading out of sight; the houses peering one over the other, like people in the topmost balcony; the distant domes. It was a very fine sunset: all the western half of the harbor was already slipping into blue shadow, but the eastern half glowed as if freshly cast in gold. The air was like a soothing warm bath on my bare arms. I was bitterly entranced—what an evening to be happy, if the world had been different. The water of the harbor, filthy as it was, looked fresh and pale blue. There was an aircraft carrier at anchor; Britain still had carriers in those days. A three-funneled troopship full of troops returning from Egypt was just sliding in to anchor alongside. Rows of silent sailors watched from the carrier; rows of soldiers in khaki drill stared back silently from the troopship. I was caught up in that magic that can accompany the worst misery.

Then the troopship anchor rattled down; and a single voice of coarse jeering called to the carrier from the troopship.

"Get yer knees brown!"

And in a moment, there was a barrage of insults from both ships, and the magic was broken forever, and Derek Pither, little fat balding Derek with his bad breath, whom I could never stand, but whom I clung to now, pointed down to where a white boat lay against the quay, already overcome by blue shadow.

We went down an endless succession of worn sandy treacherous steps, and crept aboard like thieves. I remember the gap between the boat and the quay: oily water full of small oranges and the bloated body of a dog, with a swollen belly that the hair was starting to fray off. The gangway I crossed sagged as I stepped on it, and I nearly missed the handrail and fell into the water, and didn't really care.

All I remember about the boat was that it was big and white, and didn't seem in very good repair. Patches of white paint had flaked off, and the handrails were rusty. From the upraised ventilator of a skylight a scratchy gramophone record played. Bessie Smith's coarse voice yelling. I knew I had found him. Even before I saw the long-haired white cat sitting at the top of the companionway, almost like a schoolboy keeping watch for his friends.

The cat looked at me, and I looked at the cat. It was bold, bolder than any dog would dare to be. Stared me out, its only sign of anxiety a front paw raised in the air, as if about to strike me. Then its eyes faltered from left to right; it licked its lips and swallowed twice. I swung at it wildly with my bag, and with a spat it had wriggled through a gap of open door and run down inside.

I heard Harry's voice say languidly, "What's the matter, Suki? What's upset you?"

And then I stormed down out of the sunlight and air into the dark cabin.

The smell of booze; booze and bodies. Not dead bodies—living blatant bodies. The smell of frying and French cigarettes.

They were sitting on a padded couch with lockers underneath it. The padding of the leather was scuffed. Harry's white shirt, which two weeks ago I'd washed and ironed, was filthy and open at the neck. There were spots on his lightweight trousers, and he didn't seem to have bothered to comb his hair. None of which surprised me, any more than the row of empties stacked at the top of the companionway had.

What surprised me was Imogen Smallbridge. I had been expecting a tart; I would've welcomed a tart. I could have quickly dismissed a tart from my memories. Imogen Smallbridge was not a tart. She looked every inch the lady. Tall, slim, in clean white slacks and an open-necked shirt of white and green bands. Neat leather sandals on long neat clean feet. An enviably long neck, dark hair pulled tightly back in a bun. About thirty-five, and the knuckles of her long hands already enlarged with arthritis. Her spectacles gave her an intellectual look, but her cheekbones were beautiful, and her eyes the saddest I have ever seen. You can see why I would've welcomed a tart.

"Who is it?" asked Harry in a cheerful voice. "Do we know you?" I was in silhouette against the light of the companionway; he hadn't recognized me yet. So I had a long moment to savor their togetherness, the relaxedness of their bodies sitting side by side, the hands coiled together loosely because of the sweaty heat. It was the way he said "we" that hurt so much. Oh, yes, I remember them in their cozy paradise. And the cat at their feet, glaring at me as if it would like to kill me, paw uplifted to strike, ears back.

I won't go into all that passed between us. Suffice it to say that in the end I gave Harry the same old choice. He still wasn't established then. His job was better, but still the gift of my father. The man who was publishing Harry's first travel book was a friend of my father's; so was the magazine editor who gave Harry poetry books to review.

Harry came to the airport on time. I watched him say goodbye to Imogen Smallbridge at the gate to the airport. I never asked what he said to her.

Two weeks later, she got the engine of her boat going,

and sailed out into one of those savage little storms they get off Malta. Neither she nor her hired boat was ever seen again.

I suppose the white cat went with her.

I DON'T THINK he cared for any of them, after Imogen Smallbridge. I even think he went out of his way to choose girls who would not be hurt when they lost him. As far as I ever found out, none of them vanished in tragic circumstances. They smiled and forgot him. After all, it was the Swinging Sixties. He didn't try to hide them. I was always aware when a thing started. A strange smell on his clothes as I picked them up for the laundry basket. And the cat hairs on his trousers, of course, which I could stroke up into thick whorls with my hand. So I could tell what color of cat it was this time. I didn't try to break any more of his "things" up. I thought he was getting a taste for histrionic scenes, and in the Swinging Sixties, histrionic scenes were getting more and more ridiculous. It was a bad time to be a possessive wife. It was a good time to be a girl with a pet cat.

I never thought of leaving him. There was too much to do. He was having his great successes. *Hard Morning* at the Royal Court. *Sunderland Bay* at the Roundhouse, and then in the West End. As the sixties drew on, and Wesker faded out of sight, and Pinter stuck at a certain level, and Osborne went embarrassing, Harry turned a little more popular in his views. Tough plays for the softhearted. Provocative plays you could safely take your mother-in-law to. *Darkling Thrush* at the Duke of York's. *Ambuscade* at the Prince of Wales. Even that damned musical that ran and ran, *Midsummer Morning*. Then he was the royal choice: Sir Harold Tremblett, up there with

Sir Terence Rattigan, Sir Harold Hobson, and Sir John Gielgud. A knight of the theater, welcome on any TV discussion panel, putting the view of the intelligent decent common man.

I think he started to ease up in his private life by the beginning of the seventies. After all, he was over fifty, and success is *so* exhausting. But he made up for it with the cats, as he gave up going to bed with their owners. Any walk with him became a nightmare. He would spend hours crouched on his heels at some set of areaway railings, trying to coax the staring cat behind to come and be fondled. He kept a pocket full of those new cat biscuits, to make sure they would follow us home through the hot summer streets.

I don't think he ever thought of leaving me, either. He needed a tyrant to rebel against, a fascist dictatorship at home to make symbolic protests against, because it was too much bother to go and howl at the protest crowds in Trafalgar Square anymore. So cozy to have your own dictator handy.

I must stop writing. There is a large ginger cat sitting staring at me from the top of the garden wall. It has been there nearly half an hour, just staring. There are so many cats getting into the garden now. Every time I garden, I find their paw prints in the wet mud on the paths after a shower, their scrabblings amid my flowers, their hollowed-out resting places among my lavender bushes. The dogs do not deter them. It often seems to me the dogs are scared of them.

Why are they coming? I am afraid.

THIS AFTERNOON I got home and called out to Harry as I came in the front door.

There was no reply. Frankly, it terrified me. He is such a creature of habit, usually. He writes in the morning, until one. In the afternoon, he reads, or lounges, or goes for a little walk, no doubt to find cats to talk to. In the evening, we have people in, or go out ourselves, or watch television.

He could not be out for a walk today. It had been nice, earlier in the afternoon, but a hot wind had got up, and storm clouds had been gathering ominously. Anyone could tell there was going to be a storm, and Harry is as sharp about weather changes as a cat. And like cats, he hates wind and rain. Where was he? I ran upstairs to his study, thinking he might be asleep and might not have heard my calling.

He wasn't there. He wasn't in any of the upstairs rooms. I heard a door bang downstairs. Bang, bang. Then a tinkle of glass. The french windows . . .

The french windows were banging in the wind. There was glass on the living room carpet. And outside, in his lounger, Harry lay, asleep, the rising wind ruffling his silver hair, the first drops of rain from the storm falling on him. Around him sat four cats. And there was a gray cat lying on his chest. They were all staring at his face. Then they seemed to sense me, and turned to stare at me.

Have you ever been stared at by five cats together? With hate in their eyes? For a moment, I couldn't move. I could only watch the movements of the huge thin straggly gray cat that lay upon Harry's chest. Its paws were in constant movement, kneading at the wool of the gray sweater he wore, the claws going in and out, pounding at him just where his heart was.

I might have stood forever, caught in the web of those five sets of eyes, if the french windows hadn't banged again, breaking another pane of glass.

I ran at them, shouting. Screaming my head off, actually.

The french windows seemed to have slammed shut. I wrestled desperately with the handle, and then they were open again, and I fell through, tripping over the step and almost going full length across Harry and the lounger.

He opened his eyes sleepily, bewildered. "Helen! What . . . ?" I pushed myself up by my hands, and stared around. There wasn't a cat in sight. Just a scatter of yellow autumn leaves, blowing across the patio, lodging around the legs of Harry's lounger. And the increasing shilling-sized spots of rain.

I got him indoors by brute force, as the storm started in earnest. He seemed very sluggish, dazed. I took him into the kitchen, and made us both a strong cup of tea.

The tea seemed to revive him, though he still looked very pale and drawn. He said, almost to himself, "I've been asleep. I've been a long way away."

"You *have* been asleep. With that great cat on your chest . . ." I was too frightened and relieved to nag him.

"Which great cat?" He seemed genuinely surprised for once—not having me on.

"A great big gray scraggy thing. Longhair. Thin as a rake . . ."

"I don't like gray cats," he said, and shuddered. "I don't like thin cats. I like fat cats." He really did seem bewildered.

"It doesn't remind you of any lady's cat in particular, then?" I was getting back the courage to be spiteful.

He shook his head thoughtfully. "I never knew anyone with a thin gray cat. I don't like them." He shuddered again.

"You've got yourself chilled," I said. "What made you go outside with a storm brewing up?"

"It was sunny when I went out there. After lunch. I must have dozed off."

"You must have been asleep over an hour. What were you thinking of?"

"I must've been very tired. I didn't sleep well last night." Suddenly his face changed, and he said, "I am glad to see you."

"And I'm glad to see you. I leave you too much on your own . . ."

He smiled at me. "Perhaps you do."

For some reason, I held his hand, and he let me.

"I won't leave you alone so much in the future," I said.

"Good. I think I'll have a bath, to warm myself up." He got up stiffly. Suddenly, for the first time, I thought of him as old; someone to be looked after.

I LIT THE FIRE in the living room, though I didn't put on the central heating. It didn't seem cold enough for that, though with the storm it had got colder. We had our supper by the fire, and were cozy.

Just before I switched on the television he said to me, "We haven't been very nice to each other, have we, Helen?"

"It's not been bad, these last ten years. We've stopped hurting each other . . ."

"Yes, we've stopped hurting each other . . . like an old cat and an old dog who've got too old for the game."

"Would you rather we'd gone on hurting each other?"

He smiled oddly. "It was fun . . . in the old days."

"It wasn't fun for me," I said shortly. And switched on the television. I've regretted turning on that damned set ever since. I think he wanted to talk to me, for the first time, really, in years. But I was tired, and still shaken. I didn't want to be shaken anymore, that night. As you get older, you can't take it anymore. And yet, as I turned on the set, I thought wistfully of the nights we stayed up to have a row all night, when we were young. We meant that much to each other, then. We'd make up, make love, with the first of the dawn streaking through the bedroom curtains, and lie snuggled tight and warm till lunchtime and someone frantically ringing the doorbell.

TWO DAYS LATER, Harry went up to London to see his publisher and spend the night at his house. He disliked the long journey to London, and liked a night to recover before coming back. I smiled to myself as I made my hot-water bottle (for the weather had really turned cold, as it sometimes does toward the end of August, and electric blankets were not in the beds yet).

I had let Harry off the hook again. He was on his own in London. He might be doing anything . . . Just like old times. In a perverse way, I almost liked the thought. It made me feel younger, somehow. Especially as I knew my fancy was rubbish. Harry was too old, and Paul Deane much too thorough a host and raconteur. Still, some imp of fancy made me ring Paul Deane's house, playing some foolish charade of being the wronged and suspicious wife.

Of course, Paul Deane himself answered, and said he and Harry were in the library, having a last brandy and putting the world to bed. Did I want a word with him? Harry came on, a little baffled at such wifely concern, but mellow with brandy, and, I think, a little touched and sentimental. We said quite a fond good night.

I started up the stairs.

And the blotched tabby was there again. Staring down at me, with that infinite knowing air of superiority.

I was not frightened. I had just heard Harry's voice, warm and relaxed, two hundred miles away and quite safe.

I just went berserk, that a cat should dare to invade my newfound glow of happiness.

"The dogs will settle you," I said to it. "Just you wait and see." I went back down to the kitchen, where the dogs were already curled up sleepily in their beds.

They wagged their tails feebly, but refused to move. They seemed . . . apologetic. It wasn't typical. An invitation to come upstairs with me, last thing at night, is usually greeted with great enthusiasm. I'm afraid I lost my temper and grabbed their collars and began to haul them out to the hall. They fought me all the way, squirming and collapsing in a heap, whining and licking their lips. Cringing.

I got them as far as the foot of the stairs, dragging them across the shiny parquet. Golden Labradors are a fair weight, especially when they are starting to get a bit old and fat, but I did it, one hand through each collar. I realize now that I couldn't have been in a normal mood, even at that point.

At the foot of the stairs, they collapsed completely, just squirming trembling heaps of slack bone and muscle. Keening soft and low in their throats. I despaired, and let go of their collars. Immediately they fled back to the kitchen.

And still I was not afraid. The dogs' leads hang on the hallstand. One of them is a thing I've never liked: half a leash and half a whip—a kind of plaited sjambok thing from South Africa that could be used to beat a dog half to death. I had never dreamed of using it on poor Rory and Bruce; I would not use it on any animal, even as a leash. I hated it.

But now I picked it up. That thing on the stairs was not an animal; it was a fiend that was persecuting me; I would destroy it . . .

I ran up the stairs. It saw the whip; a quick glance, then its arrogant eyes were back on my face, rejecting, hating, taunting. I was crazed by its arrogance. I raised the whip, and brought it down with all my strength.

It missed, and hit the stair carpet with a force that stung my hand.

I could not understand how I could have missed. I could not understand how the beast had not moved or even flinched but continued to glare up at me, half-crouched, ears back, mouth open in a silent snarl. I struck again and again, each time harder than the last.

And each time I missed. Hit the top step instead, with a sound like a hollow drum.

The world was insane; the world was twisting under my mind into unbelievable shapes. I could *not* go on missing at this range. The cat could not still be there, snarling silent defiance.

And then I watched my next blow carefully, with what sanity I could still muster.

I was not missing. The whip passed straight through the cat and hit the carpet beneath it.

The next second, the blotched tabby cat was no longer there.

Not in the upper hall, with all its doors closed. Not in the lower hall, which was bare and well lit. And certainly not in the kitchen with the dogs.

Not in the house at all. I sat in the living room a long time, trembling and drinking whisky, over the revived remains of the log fire.

I finally went up to bed as dawn broke, and some kind of order returned to the world. I went up to bed without hope of sleeping. I think I hoped I might lie on my bed fully dressed and doze for a few hours, before facing another day.

But something made me stop at the closed door of Harry's study. I was a long time opening that door.

When I did, the blotched tabby was sitting on Harry's desk by the window. I could not see any detail of it, because it was hunched on his pile of foolscap paper, against the light.

But from the way it rocked, I knew that it was purring.

THE HOUSE IS FULL of cats now. They flick at the corners of my eye, and then when I look, they are gone—under a chair, behind a couch. But I know there is no point in searching for them. They are all ghosts. And yet, in the corner of my eye, I seem to see them quite clearly: a sort of detailed blur. It is often the long-haired white cat. Imogen's cat. Its fur is sleeked close to its skin, as if it has just emerged from water. There is a ginger cat with a white chest. There is a black cat that is no more than two green eyes, glaring out of the shadow beneath a chair.

I ignore them, as I ignore the cats in the garden. I think the cats in the garden are real, for they leave paw prints. I do not mind them; they only sit and stare at the house, as if waiting for something.

They are waiting for Harry. He is ill. The doctor does not know what is the matter. They have done tests, and can find nothing wrong. The doctor talks of overwork, of Harry needing to rest. But he has been resting for three weeks now. He never needed so much rest any other August. And the more he rests, the more he sleeps, the wearier he is. He hardly bothers to read, now. He picks up a book listlessly, and then I come back in ten minutes, and he is dozing over it. I think the cats are draining his life away; and he is letting them.

When he is awake, he is very affectionate. He kisses my

hand. He says I have looked after him very well. He says I have done my best, according to my lights. He forgives me for everything I have ever done to him . . .

I would rather that he hated me. Then there would be some hope. Then there would be something to hold him to this world.

Tonight, he said, "I'm sorry, Helen. I went too far away. I can't get back."

Before I could ask him what he meant, he had fallen asleep again.

My one consolation is that the cats mean him no harm. I know that in their own way they love him.

It is me they hate.

I have put the dogs into kennels. Left here, they did nothing but cower in their beds. They would not eat, and their toilet training was breaking down. I rang the kennels this morning. They are quite happy there, and recovering rapidly.

I HAVE JUST COME DOWN from Harry's study. I was going to his bedroom, to see if he wanted anything, when something made me open the study door. He was sitting in his desk chair, with his back turned to the desk and the window, the way he always sits when he is stuck in his writing, and thinking. He had his head up; he looked better than he had done for weeks. He was actually *dressed*, in a baggy old pair of trousers and sloppy old sweater I thought I'd thrown out years ago. I could not see him well against the light, but I saw his cheek curve out in silhouette as he smiled at me, that old lazy smile.

"You're better!" I said, amazed and glad.

"Yes," he said, "I'm all right now. It was a worrying time, but it's over. I'm fine now."

I began to weep, from sheer relief.

He said kindly, affectionately, "Don't cry. I'm sorry you've been so worried. I've been a burden to you. I've made your life wretched . . ."

"That doesn't matter. It doesn't matter at all. We've got to look to the future. There's so much still to do."

"Yes," he said, and smiled again. "There's still so much to do." He sounded glad.

I took a step toward him, a step into the room. It gave me a clearer look at him, because the swivel chair is big and enclosing, with high back and arms, like half an egg on a swivel.

I saw there was a cat sitting in his lap.

A blotched tabby. Not snarling at me now, but rocking, purring, triumphant.

And I watched his hand go down to caress her. I expected to see his hand pass straight through her.

It didn't. It rested gently on her back. I saw her fur bend beneath it. They were together, as they had been so long ago, in that wretched flat in King's Cross.

"Goodbye, Helen," he said. "Goodbye and thanks and sorry. I am me, and you are you. Who am I to cast the first stone?"

And then the chair was empty.

I did not go to the bedroom. I knew what I should find. The house is empty. No more ghosts. How I wish there could be ghosts, now. The real cats are still sitting in the garden, front paws together, and tails wrapped around. They are so still they might be statues. They look ceremonial, like mourners. They are paying their respects to Harry.

I must ring the doctor; or the ambulance or the police. I only wish I could move from this chair.

THE BOYS' TOILETS

THE JANUARY TERM started with a scene of sheer disaster. A muddy backhoe was chewing its way across the netball court, breakfasting on the tarmac with sinuous lunges and terrifying swings of its long yellow neck. One of the stone balls had been knocked off the gateposts, and lay in crushed fragments, like a malted milk ball trodden on by a giant. The entrance to the science wing was blocked with a pile of ochreous clay, and curved glazed drainpipes were heaped like school-dinner macaroni.

The girls hung around in groups. One girl came back from the indoor toilets saying Miss Bowker was phoning County Hall, and using words that Liza Bottom had nearly been expelled for last term. She was greeted with snorts of disbelief . . .

The next girl came back from the toilet saying that Miss Bowker was nearly crying.

Which was definitely a lie, because here was Miss Bowker now, come out to address them in her best sheepskin coat. Though she *was* wearing fresh makeup, and her eyes were suspiciously bright, her famous chin was up. She was brief,

and to the point. There was an underground leak in the
central heating; till it was mended, they would be using
the old Harvest Road Boys' School. They would march
across now, by classes, in good order, in the charge of the
prefects. She knew they would behave immaculately, and
that the spirit of Spilsby Girls' High School would overcome
all difficulties . . .

"Take more than school spirit," said Wendy Falstaff.

"More than a bottle of whisky," said Jennifer Mount,
and shuddered.

Rebeccah, who was a vicar's daughter, thought of Sodom
and Gomorrah—both respectable suburbs by comparison
with Harvest Road. Harvest Road was literally on the
wrong side of the tracks. But obediently they marched.
They passed through the streets where they lived, gay
with yellow front doors, picture windows, new carports,
and wrought-iron gates. It was quite an adventure at first.
Staff cars kept passing them, their rear windows packed
with whole classrooms. Miss Rossiter, with her brass mi-
croscopes and stuffed ducks; Mam'selle, full of tape re-
corders and posters of the French wine-growing districts.
Piles of *The Merchant of Venice* and Van Gogh's *Sunflowers*.

The first time they passed, the teachers hooted cheerfully. But coming back, they were silent, just their winkers
winking, and frozen faces behind the wheel.

Then the marching columns came to a miserable little
humpbacked bridge over a solitary railway line, empty and
rusting. Beyond were the same kind of houses, but afflicted
by some dreadful disease, of which the symptoms were a
rash of small windowpanes, flaking paint, overgrown fu-
nereal privet hedges, and sagging gates that would never
shut again. And then it seemed to grow colder still, as the
slum clearances started, a great empty plain of broken

brick, and the wind hit them full, sandpapering faces and sending gray berets cartwheeling into the wilderness.

And there, in the midst of the desolation, like a dead sooty dinosaur, like a blackened, marooned, many-chimneyed Victorian battleship, lay Harvest Road school.

"Abandon hope, all ye who enter here," said Jennifer Mount.

"We who are about to die salute you," said Victoria.

Rebeccah thought there were some advantages to having a classical education, after all.

THEY GATHERED, awed, in the hall. The windows, too high up to see out of, were stained brown around the edges; the walls were dark green. There was a carved oak board, a list of prizewinners from 1879 to 1923. Victoria peered at it. "It's B.C., not A.D.," she announced. "The first name's Tutankhamen." There were posters sagging off the walls, on the extreme ends of long hairy strands of sticky tape; things like "Tea-Picking in India" and "The Meaning of Empire Day." It all felt rather like drowning in a very dirty goldfish tank.

A lot of them wanted the toilet, badly. Nervousness and the walk through the cold. But nobody felt like asking till Rebeccah did. Last door at the end of the corridor and across the yard; they walked down, six strong.

They were boys' toilets. They crept past the male mystery of the urinals, tall, white, and rust-streaked as tombs, looking absurd, inhuman, like elderly invalid carriages or artificial limbs. In the bottom gulley, fag ends lay squashed and dried out, like dead flies.

And the graffiti . . . Even Liza Bottom didn't know what some words meant. But they were huge, and hating; the whole wall screamed with them, from top to bottom. Most of the hate seemed directed at someone called "Barney Boko."

Rebeccah shuddered; that was the first shudder. But Vicky only said practically, "Bet there's no toilet paper!" and got out her French exercise book . . . She was always the pessimist, but on this occasion she hadn't been pessimistic enough. Not only was there no toilet paper, but there were no wooden seats, either; and the chains from the old-fashioned overhead tanks had been replaced by loops of hairy thick white string, like hangman's nooses. And in the green paint of the wooden partitions the hatred of Barney Boko had been gouged half an inch deep. And the locks had been busted off all the doors except the far-end one . . .

Rebeccah, ever public-spirited and with a lesser need, stood guard stoutly without.

"Boys," she heard Victoria snort in disgust. "It's a nunnery for me. At least in nunneries they'll have soft toilet paper."

"Don't you believe it," said Joanne, their Roman Catholic correspondent. "They wear hair shirts, nuns. Probably the toilets have *scrubbing brushes* instead of paper."

Lively squeaks, all down the line, as the implications struck home.

"Some boys aren't bad," said Liza, "if you can get them away from their friends."

"Why bother?" said Vicky. "I'll settle for my poster of James Dean . . ."

"It's funny," said Tracy, as they were combing their hair in the solitary cracked, fly-spotted, pocket-handkerchief-sized mirror. "You know there's six of us? Well, I heard seven toilets flush. Did anybody pull the chain twice?"

They all looked at each other, and shook their heads. They looked back down the long shadowy loo, with its tiny high-up pebbled windows, toward the toilets. They shouted, wanting to know who was there, because nobody had passed them, nobody had come in.

No answer, except the sound of dripping.

THE BIG ATTRACTION at break was the school boiler house. They stood around on the immense coke heaps, some new, some so old and mixed with the fallen leaves of many autumns they were hardly recognizable as coke at all. One actually had weeds growing on it . . .

Inside the boiler house, in a red hissing glow, two men fought to get Harvest Road up to a reasonable temperature, somewhere above that of Dracula's crypt. One was young, cheerful, cocky, with curly brown hair; they said he was from County. The other was tall and thin, in a long gray overall coat and cap so old the pattern had worn off. They said he was the caretaker of the old school, brought out of retirement because only he knew the ropes; he had such an expression on his face that they immediately called him Crippen, after the murderer. Occasionally, the cocky one would stop shoveling coke into the gaping red maw of the furnace and wipe his brow; that, and the occasional draft of warm air, immediately swept away by the biting wind, was the only hint of heat they had that morning.

The lesson after break was math, with Miss Hogg. Miss Hogg was one of the old school: gray hair in a tight bun, tweeds, gold-rimmed spectacles. A brilliant mathematician who had once unbent far enough, at the end of the summer term, to tell the joke about the square on the hypotenuse. Feared but not loved, Miss Hogg made it quite clear to all that she had no time for men. Not so much a Female Libber as a Male Oppressor . . .

They ground away steadily at quadratic equations until

the dreary cold, seeping out of the tiled walls into their
bones, claimed Rebeccah as its first victim. Her hand shot
up.

"You should have gone at break," said Miss Hogg.

"I did, Miss Hogg."

Miss Hogg's gesture gave permission, while despairing
of all the fatal weaknesses of femininity.

REBECCAH HESITATED just inside the doorway of the loo.
The length of the low dark room, vanishing into shadow;
the little green windows high up that lit nothing; the
alienness of it all made her hesitant, as in some old dark
church. The graffiti plucked at the corners of her eyes,
dimly, like memorials on a church wall. But no "dearly
beloveds" here.

JACKO IS A SLIMER

F—— OFF HIGGINS

Where were they now? How many years ago? She told
herself they must be grown men, balding, with wives and
families and little paunches under cardigans their wives
had lovingly knitted for them. But she couldn't believe it.
They were still here somewhere, fighting, snorting bubbles
of blood from streaming noses, angry. Especially angry
with Barney Boko. She went down the long room on
tiptoe, and went into the far-end toilet because it was the
only one with a lock. Snapped home the bolt so hard it
echoed up and down the concrete ceiling. Only then,
panting a little, did she settle . . .

But no sooner had she settled than she heard someone
come in. Not a girl; Rebeccah had quick ears. No, big

boots, with steel heel plates. Walking authoritatively toward her. From the liveliness of the feet she knew it wasn't even a man. A boy. She heard him pause, as if he sensed her, as if looking around. Then a boy's voice, quiet.

"O.K., Stebbo, all clear!"

More stamping heel-capped feet tramping in. She knew she had made a terrible mistake. There must still be a boys' school here, occupying only part of the buildings. And she was in the *boys'* loo. She blushed. An enormous blush that seemed to start behind her ears, and went down her neck over her whole body . . .

But she was a sensible child. She told herself to be calm. Just sit, quiet as a mouse, till they'd gone. She sat, breathing softly into her handkerchief, held across her mouth.

But supposing they tried the door, shouted to know who was in there? Suppose they put their hands on the top of the wooden partition and hauled themselves up and looked over the top. There were some awful *girls* who did that . . .

But they seemed to have no interest in her locked cubicle. There was a lot of scuffling, a scraping of steel heel plates, and a panting. As if they were dragging somebody . . .

The somebody was dragged into the cubicle next door. Elbows thumped against the wooden partition, making her jump.

"Get his head down," ordered a sharp voice.

"No, Stebbo. *No!* Let me go, you bastards . . ."

"Ouch!"

"What's up?"

"Little sod bit me . . ."

"Get his head down, then!"

The sounds of heaving, scraping, panting, and finally a

sort of high-pitched whining, got worse. Then suddenly the toilet next door flushed, the whining stopped, then resumed as a series of half-drowned gasps for breath. There was a yip of triumph, laughter, and the noise of many boots running away.

"Bastards," said a bitter, choking voice. "And you've broken my pen an' all." Then a last weary pair of boots trailed away.

She got herself ready, listening, waiting, tensed. Then undid the bolt with a rush and ran down the empty echoing place. Her own footsteps sounded frail and tiny, after the boys'. Suppose she met one, coming in?

But she didn't. And there wasn't a boy in sight in the gray high-walled yard. Bolder, she looked back at the entrance of the loo; it was the same one they'd used earlier, the one they'd been told to use. Miss Bowker must have made a mistake; someone should be told . . .

But when she got back to the classroom, and Miss Hogg and all the class looked up, she lost her nerve.

"You took your time, Rebeccah," said Miss Hogg suspiciously.

"We thought you'd pulled the chain too soon and gone down to the seaside," said Liza Bottom, playing for a vulgar laugh and getting it.

"Let me see your work so far, Liza," said Miss Hogg frostily, killing the laughter like a partridge shot on the wing.

"What's up?" whispered Vicky. "You met a feller or something—all blushing and eyes shining . . ." Vicky was much harder to fool than Miss Hogg.

"Tell you at lunch . . ."

"The next girl I see talking . . ." said Miss Hogg ominously.

But they didn't have to wait till lunch. Liza had twigged that something was up. Her hand shot up; she squirmed in her seat almost too convincingly.

"Very well, Liza. I suppose I must brace myself for an epidemic of weak bladders . . ."

Liza returned like a bomb about to explode, her ginger hair standing out from her head as if she'd back-combed it for Saturday night, a deep blush under her freckles, and green eyes wide as saucers. She opened her mouth to speak—but Miss Hogg had an eagle eye for incipient hysteria, and a gift for nipping it in the bud.

"Shut the door, Liza; we'll keep the drafts we have."

Liza sat down demurely; but even the Hogg's frost couldn't stop the idea flaring across the class that something was excitingly amiss in the loos.

It was droopy Margie Trawson who blew it. She went next; and came back and bleated, with the air of a victimized sheep that only she could achieve: "Miss, there's boys in the toilet . . ."

"Boys?" boomed Miss Hogg. *"Boys?"* She swept out of the classroom door with all the speed her strongly muscled legs could give her. From the classroom windows they watched as she entered the toilets. Rebeccah, who was rather keen on naval warfare in the Second World War, thought she looked like an angry little frigate, just itching to depth-charge any boy out of existence. But when she emerged, her frown told that she'd been cheated of her prey. She scouted on for boys lurking behind the coke heaps, behind the dustbins, behind the sagging fence of the caretaker's house. Nothing. She looked back toward her classroom windows, making every girlish head duck simultaneously, then headed for the headmistress's office.

They saw the tall stately figure of the headmistress

inspect, in turn, the loo, the coke heaps, fence, and dustbins, Miss Hogg circling her on convoy duty. But without success. Finally, after a word, they parted. Miss Hogg returned with a face like thunder.

"Someone," she announced, "has been silly. Very, *very* silly." She made *silly* sound as evil as running a concentration camp. "The head has assured me that this school has been disused for many years, and there cannot possibly be a single boy on the premises. The only . . . males . . . are the caretakers. Now, Margie, what have you got to say to *that*? Well, Margie . . . *well*?"

There was only one end to Miss Hogg's well-Margie-well routine: Margie gruesomely dissolving into tears.

"There was boys, miss, I heard them, miss, hon-e-est . . ." She pushed back a tear with the cuff of her cardigan.

Liza was on her feet, flaming. "I heard them, too, miss." That didn't worry Miss Hogg. Liza was the form trouble-maker. But then Rebeccah was on her feet. "I heard them as well."

"*Rebeccah*. You are a clergyman's daughter. I'm ashamed of you."

"I *heard* them." Rebeccah clenched her teeth; there would be no shifting her. Miss Hogg looked thoughtful.

"They don't come when you're in a crowd, miss," bleated Margie. "They only come when you're there by yourself. They put another boy's head down the toilet an' pull the chain. They were in the place next to me."

"And to me," said Liza.

"And to me," said Rebeccah.

A sort of shiver went around the class; the humming and buzzing stopped, and it was very quiet.

"Very well," said Miss Hogg. "We will test Margie's theory. *Come*, Rebeccah!"

At the entrance to the toilet, Rebeccah suddenly felt very silly.

"Just go in and behave normally," said Miss Hogg. "I shall be just outside."

Rebeccah entered the toilet, bolted the door, and sat down.

"Do exactly what you would normally do," boomed Miss Hogg suddenly, scarily, down the long dark space. Rebeccah blushed again, and did as she was told.

"There," boomed Miss Hogg, after a lengthy pause. "Nothing, you see. Nothing at all. You girls are *ridiculous*!" Rebeccah wasn't so sure. There was something—you couldn't call it a sound—a sort of vibration in the air, like boys giggling in hiding.

"Nothing," boomed Miss Hogg again. "Come along—we've wasted enough lesson time. Such nonsense."

Suddenly a toilet flushed at the far end of the row.

"Was that you, Rebeccah?"

"No, Miss Hogg."

"Rubbish. Of course it was."

"No, miss."

Another toilet flushed, and another, getting nearer. That convinced Miss Hogg. Rebeccah heard her stout brogues come in at a run, heard her banging back the toilet doors, shouting, "Come out, whoever you are. You can't get away. I know you're there."

Rebeccah came out with a rush to meet her.

"Did you pull your chain, Rebeccah?"

"Didn't need to, miss."

And, indeed, all the toilet doors were now open, and all the toilets manifestly empty, and every cistern busy refilling; except Rebeccah's.

"There must be a scientific explanation," said Miss Hogg. "A fault in the plumbing."

But Rebeccah thought she heard a quiver in her voice, as she stared suspiciously at the small inaccessible ventilation grids.

THEY ALL WENT together at lunchtime, and nothing happened. They all went together at afternoon break, and nothing happened. Then it was time for Miss Hogg again. Black Monday was called Black Monday because they had Miss Hogg twice for math.

And still the cold worked upon their systems . . .

Margie Trawson again.

"Please miss, I *got* to."

Only . . . there was a secret in Margie's voice, a little gloaty secret. They all heard it; but if Miss Hogg did, she only raised a grizzled eyebrow. "Hurry, then. If only your *mind* were so active, Margie . . ."

She was gone a long time; a very long time. Even Miss Hogg shifted her brogued feet restlessly, as she got on with marking the other third-year class's quadratic equations.

And then Margie was standing in the doorway, and behind her the looming gray-coated figure of Crippen, with his mouth set so hard and cruel another poisoning was obviously imminent. He had Margie by the elbow in a grip that made her writhe. He whispered to Miss Hogg . . .

"Appalling," boomed Miss Hogg. "I don't know what these children think they are coming to. Thank you for telling me so quickly, caretaker. It won't happen again. I assure you, it won't happen again. That will be all!"

Crippen, robbed of his moment of public triumph and infant-humiliation, stalked out without another word.

"Margie," announced Miss Hogg, "has attempted to use

the caretaker's outside toilet. The toilet set aside for his own personal use. A *man's* toilet . . ."

"Obviously a hanging offense," muttered Victoria, sotto voce, causing a wild but limited explosion of giggles, cut off, as by a knife, by Miss Hogg's glint-spectacled *look*. "How would you like it, Margie, if some strange men came into your back yard at home and used *your* toilet?"

"It'd really turn her on," muttered Victoria. Liza choked down on a giggle so hard she nearly gave herself a slipped disk.

"No girl will ever do such a thing again," said Miss Hogg in her most dreadful voice, clutching Margie's elbow as cruelly as Crippen had. A voice so dreadful and so seldom heard that the whole class froze into thoughtfulness. Not since that joke with the chewing gum in the first year had they heard *that* voice.

"Now, Margie, will you go and do what you have to do, in the place where you are meant to do it?"

"Don't want to go no more, miss. It's gone off . . ."

Liar, thought Rebeccah; Margie needed to go so badly she was squirming from foot to foot.

"Go!" said Miss Hogg, in the voice that brooked no argument. "I shall watch you from the window."

They all watched her go in; and they all watched her come out.

"Sit down quickly, Margie," said Miss Hogg. "There seems to be some difficulty with question twelve. It's quite simple really." She turned away to the blackboard, chalk in hand. "X squared, plus $2y$ . . ." The chalk squeaked abominably, getting on everyone's nerves; there was a slight but growing disturbance at the back of the class, which Miss Hogg couldn't hear for the squeaking of the chalk. "$3x$ plus $5y$ . . ."

"Oh, *miss!*" wailed Margie. "I'm sorry, miss . . . I didn't mean to . . ." Then she was flying to the classroom door, babbling and sobbing incoherently. She scrabbled for the doorknob and finally got the door open. Miss Hogg moved across swiftly and tried to grab her, but she was just too slow: Margie was gone, with Miss Hogg in hot pursuit, hysterical sobs and angry shouts echoing around the whole school from the pair of them.

"What . . . ?" asked Rebeccah, turning. Vicky pointed silently, at a wide spreading pool of liquid under Margie's desk.

"She never went at all," said Vicky grimly. "She must have hidden just inside the loo doorway. She was too scared . . ."

It was then that Rebeccah began to hate the ghosts in the boys' toilets.

SHE TAPPED on Dad's study door as soon as she got in from school. Pushed it open. He was sitting, a tall thin boyish figure, at his desk with the desk light on. From his dejectedly drooping shoulders, and his spectacles pushed up on his forehead, she knew he was writing next Sunday's sermon. He was bashing between his eyes with a balled fist as well; Epiphany was never his favorite topic for a sermon.

"Dad?"

He came back from far away, pulled down his spectacles, blinked at her, and smiled.

"It's the Person from Porlock!" This was a very ancient joke between them that only got better with time. The real Person from Porlock had interrupted the famous poet Coleridge, when he was in the middle of composing his greatest poem, "Kubla Khan."

"Sit down, Person," said Dad, removing a precarious

tower of books from his second wooden armchair. "Want a coffee?" She glanced at his percolator, shiny and new from Mum last Christmas, but now varnished over with dribbles, from constant use.

"Yes, please," she said, just to be matey; he made his coffee as strong as poison.

"How's Porlock?" He gave her a sharp sideways glance through his horn-rimmed spectacles. "Trouble?"

Somehow, he always knew.

She was glad she could start at the beginning, with ordinary things like the central heating and the march to Harvest Road . . .

When she had finished, he said, "Ghosts. Ghosts in the toilet. Pulling chains and frightening people." He was the only adult she knew who wouldn't have laughed or made some stupid remark. But all he said was "Something funny happened at that school. It was closed down. A few years before Mum and I came to live here. It had an evil name, but I never knew for what."

"But what can we *do*? The girls are terrified."

"Go at lunchtime—go at break—go before you leave home."

"We do. But it's so cold. Somebody'll get caught out sooner or later."

"You won't be at Harvest Road long; even central heating leaks don't go on forever. Shall I try to find out how long? I know the chairman of the board of governors."

"Wouldn't do any harm," said Rebeccah grudgingly.

"But you don't want to wait to go that long?" It was meant to be a joke, but it died halfway between them.

"Look," said Rebeccah, "if you'd seen Margie . . . she . . . she won't dare come back. Somebody could be . . . terrified for life."

"I'll talk to your headmistress . . ." He reached for the phone.

"*No!*" It came out as nearly a shout. Dad put the phone back, looking puzzled. Rebeccah said, in a low voice: "The teachers think we're nuts. They'll . . . think you're nuts as well. You . . . can't afford to have people think *you're* nuts. Can you?"

"*Touché*," he said ruefully. "So what do you want, Person?"

"Tell me how to get rid of them. How to frighten them away, so they leave people *alone*."

"I'm not in the frightening business, Person."

"But the Church . . ."

"You mean bell, book, and candle? No can do. The Church doesn't like that kind of thing anymore . . . doesn't believe in it, I suppose . . ."

"But it's *real*." It was almost a wail.

"The only man I know who touches that sort of thing has a parish in London. He's considered a crank."

"*Tell me what to do!*"

They looked at each other in silence, a very long time. They were so much alike, with their blond hair, long faces, straight noses, spectacles. Even their hair was the same length: he wore his long; she wore hers shortish.

Finally he said, "There's no other way?"

"No."

"I don't know much. You're supposed to ask its name. It has to tell you—that's in the Bible. That's supposed to give you power over it. Then, like Shakespeare, you can ask it whether it's a spirit of health or goblin damned. Then . . . you can try commanding it to go to the place prepared for it . . ." He jumped up, running his fingers through his hair. "No, you mustn't do any of this, Rebeccah. I can't have you doing things like this. I'll ring the head—"

"You will *not!*"

"Leave it alone, then!"

"If it lets me alone." But she had her fingers crossed.

THE HEADMISTRESS CAME in to address the class next morning, after assembly. She braced her long elegant legs wide apart, put her hands together behind her back, rocked a little, head down, then looked at them with a smile that was 100 percent caring and about 90 percent honest.

"Toilets," she said doubtfully, then with an effort, more briskly, "Toilets." She nodded gently. "I can understand you are upset about the toilets. Of all the things about this dreadful place that County's put us in, those toilets are the worst. I want you to know that I have had the strongest possible words with County, and that those toilets will be repainted and repaired by next Monday morning. I have told them that if they fail me in this I will close the school." She lowered her head in deep thought again, then looked up, more sympathetic than ever.

"You have reached an age when you are—quite rightly—beginning to be interested in boys. There *have* been boys here—they have left their mark—and I am sad they have left the worst possible kind of mark. Most boys are not like that—not like that at all, thank God. But these boys have been *gone* for over twenty years. Let me stress that. For twenty years, this building has been used to store unwanted school furniture. You may say that there are always boys everywhere—like mice, or beetles! But with all this slum clearance around us . . . I went out yesterday actually *looking* for a boy." She looked around with a smile, expecting a laugh. She got a few titters. "The first boy I saw was a full mile away—and he was working for a butcher in the High Street." Again, she expected a laugh, and it did not come. So she went serious again. "You have been upset by the toilets—understandably. But that is no excuse for making things up, for—and I must say it— getting hysterical. Nobody else has noticed anything in these toilets. The prefects report nothing. I have watched first and second years using them quite happily. *It is just this class*. Or, rather, three excitable girls in this class . . ." She looked around. At Liza Bottom, who blushed and wriggled. At the empty desk where Margie should have been sitting. And at Rebeccah, who stared straight back at her, as firmly as she could. "Two of those girls do not surprise me—the third girl does." Rebeccah did not flinch, which worried the headmistress, who was rather fond of her. So the headmistress finished in rather a rush. "I want you to stop acting as feather-brained females—and act instead as the sensible hard-headed young women you are going to become. This business . . . is the sort of business that gets us despised by men . . . and there are plenty of men only too ready to despise us."

The headmistress swept out. A sort of deadly coldness settled over the sensible young women. It hadn't happened to the prefects, or to the first-years. The headmistress had just proved there were ghosts, and proved they were only after people in 3A . . .

IT WAS FIONA MOWBRAY who bought it. It happened so swiftly, after break. They'd all gone together at break. They never realized they'd left her there, helpless with diarrhea, and too shy to call out. She was always the shyest, Fiona . . .

Suddenly she appeared in the doorway, interrupting the beginning of French.

"Sit down, Feeownah," said Mam'selle gently.

But Fiona just stood there, pale and stiff as a scarecrow, swaying. There were strange twists of toilet paper all around her arms . . .

"Feeownah," said Mam'selle again, with a strange panicky quiver in her voice. Fiona opened and closed her mouth to speak four times, without a single sound coming out. Then she fainted full-length, hitting the floorboards like a sack of potatoes.

Then someone ran for the headmistress, and everyone was crowding around, and the headmistress was calling, "Stand back, give her air," and sending Liza for Miss Hogg's smelling salts. And Fiona coming around and starting to scream and flail out. And fainting again. And talk of sending for a doctor . . .

Right, you sod, thought Rebeccah. That's *it*! And she slipped around the back of the clustering crowd, and nobody saw her go, for all eyes were on Fiona.

Fiona must have been in the second-to-last toilet: the toilet-roll holder was empty, and the yellow paper, swath on swath of it, covered the floor and almost buried the lavatory bowl. It was wildly torn in places, as if Fiona had had to claw her way out of it. Had it . . . been trying to smother her? Rebeccah pulled the chain automatically. Then, with a wildly beating heart, locked herself in next door, and sat down with her jaw clenched and her knickers around her knees.

It was hard to stay calm. The noise of the refilling cistern next door hid all other noises. Then, as next door dropped to a trickle, she heard another toilet being pulled. Had someone else come in, unheard? Was she wasting her time? But there'd been no footsteps. Then another toilet flushed, and another and another. Then the doors of the empty toilets began banging, over and over, so hard and savagely that she thought they must splinter.

Boom, boom, boom. Nearer and nearer.

Come on, bastard, thought Rebeccah, with the hard center of her mind; the rest of her felt like screaming.

Then the toilet pulled over her own head—so violently it showered her with water. She looked up, and the hairy string was swinging, with no one holding it . . . like a hangman's noose. Nobody could possibly have touched it.

The cistern lever was pulled above her, again and again. Her nerve broke, and she rushed for the door. But the bolt wouldn't unbolt. Too stiff—too stiff for her terrified fingers. She flung herself around wildly, trying to climb over the top, but she was so terrified she couldn't manage that, either. She ended up cowering down against the door, head on her knees and hands over her ears, like an unborn baby.

Silence. Stillness. But she knew that, whatever it was, it was still there.

"What . . . is . . . your . . . name?" she whispered, from a creaky throat. Then a shout: *"What is your name?"*

As if in answer, the toilet roll began to unroll itself, rearing over her in swirling yellow coils, as if it wanted to smother her.

"Are you a spirit of health or goblin damned?" That reminded her of Dad, and gave her a little chip of courage. But the folds of paper went on rearing up, till all the cubicle was filled with the yellow, rustling mass. As if you had to *breathe* toilet paper.

"Begone . . . to the place . . . prepared for you," she stammered, without hope. The coils of paper moved nearer, touching her face softly.

"What do you want?" She was screaming.

There was a change. The whirling folds of paper seemed to coalesce. Into a figure, taller than herself, as tall as a very thin boy might be, wrapped in yellow bands like a mummy, with two dark gaps where eyes might have been.

If it had touched her, her mind would have splintered into a thousand pieces.

But it didn't. It just looked at her, with its hole eyes, and swung a yellow-swathed scarecrow arm to point to the brickwork above the cistern.

Three times. Till she dumbly nodded.

Then it collapsed into a mass of paper around her feet.

After a long time, she got up and tried the door bolt. It opened easily, and her fear changed to embarrassment as she grabbed for her pants.

It hadn't wanted to harm her at all—it had only wanted to show her something.

Emboldened, she waded back through the yellow mass. Where had it been pointing?

There could be no mistake: a tiny strand of toilet paper still clung to the brickwork, caught in a crack. She pulled it out, and the white paintwork crumbled a little and came with it, leaving a tiny hole. She touched the part near the hole, and more paint and cement crumbled; she scrabbled, and a whole half-brick seemed to fall out into her hand. Only it wasn't all brick, but crumbly dried mud, which broke and fell in crumbs all over the yellow paper.

What a mess! But left exposed was a square black hole, and there was something stuck inside. She reached in, and lifted down a thick bundle of papers . . .

Something made her lock the door, sit down on the toilet, and pull them out of their elastic band, which snapped with age as she touched it. Good heavens . . . Her mouth dropped open, appalled.

There was a dusty passport, and a wallet. The wallet was full of money, notes. Pound notes and French thousand-franc notes. And a driving license, made out in the name of a Mr. Alfred Barnett. And letters to Mr. Barnett. And tickets for trains and a cross-Channel ferry . . . and the passport, dated to expire on the first of April 1958, was also made out in the names of Alfred and Ada Barnett . . .

She sat there, and, church child that she was, she cried a little with relief and the pity of it. The ghost was a boy who had stolen and hidden the loot, so well concealed, all those years ago. And after he was dead, he was sorry, and wanted to make amends. But the school was abandoned by then; no one to listen to him; old Crippen would never listen to a poor lost ghost . . . Well, she would make amends for him, and then he would be at rest, poor lonely thing.

She looked at the address in the passport. Briardene, Millbrook Gardens, Spilsby. Why, it was only ten minutes' walk; she could do it on her way home tonight, and they wouldn't even worry about her getting home a bit late.

She was still sitting there, in a happy and pious daze at the virtue of the universe, when faithful Vicky came looking for her. Only faithful Vicky had noticed she was gone. So she told her, and Vicky said she would come as well . . .

"They've taken Fiona to the hospital . . ."

Perhaps that should have been a warning; but Rebeccah was too happy. "She'll get over it; and once we've taken this, it won't hurt anybody else again."

It all seemed so simple.

LIZA CAME, too, out of sheer nosiness, but Rebeccah was feeling charitable to all the world. It was that kind of blessed evening you sometimes get in January, lovely and bright, that makes you think of spring before the next snow falls.

Millbrook Gardens was in an older, solider district than their own; posher in its funny old way. Walls of brick that glowed a deep rich red in the setting sun, and showed their walking blue girlish shadows, where there wasn't any ivy or the bare strands of Virginia creeper. So it seemed that dim ghosts walked with them, among the houses with their white iron conservatories and old trees with home-made swings, and garden seats still damp from winter. And funny stuffy names like Lynfield and Spring Lodge and Nevsky Villa. It was hard to find Briardene because there were no numbers on the houses. But they found it at last, looked over the gate, and saw a snowy-haired, rosy-cheeked old man turning over the rose beds in the big front garden.

He was quite a way from the gate; but he turned and looked at them. It wasn't a nice look; a long examining unfriendly look. They felt he didn't like children; they felt he would have liked to stop them coming in. But when Rebeccah called, in a too shrill voice, "Do the Barnetts live here?" he abruptly waved them through to the front door, and went back to his digging. Rebeccah thought he must be the gardener; his clothes were quite old and shabby.

They trooped up to the front door and rang. There was no answer for quite a long time, then the image of a plump white-haired woman swam up the dark hall, all broken up by the stained glass in the door.

She looked a bit friendlier than the gardener, but not much; full of an ancient suspicion and wariness.

"Yes, children?" she said, in an old-fashioned bossy way.

Rebeccah held out her dusty package proudly. "We found this. I think it's yours . . ."

The woman took it from her briskly enough; the way

you take a parcel off a postman. But when she began to take off Rebeccah's new elastic band she suddenly looked so . . . as if she'd like to drop the packet and slam the door.

"It's a passport and money and tickets and things," said Rebeccah helpfully.

The woman put a hand to her eyes, to shield them as if the sunlight was too strong; she nearly fell, leaning against the doorpost just in time. "Alfred," she called, "Alfred!" to the man in the garden. Then Rebeccah knew the man was her husband, and she thought the cry was almost a call for help. As if they'd been attacking the woman . . .

The old man came hurrying up, full of petty anger at being disturbed. Until his wife handed him the packet. Then he, too, seemed to shrink, shrivel. The healthy high color fled his cheeks, leaving only a pattern of bright broken veins, as if they'd been drawn on wrinkled fish skin with a red ball-point.

"They're . . ." said the woman.

"Yes," said the man. Then he turned on the girls so fiercely that they nearly ran away. His eyes were little and black and so full of hate that they, who had never been hit in their lives, grew afraid of being hit.

"Where did you get these?" There was authority in the voice, an ancient cruel utter authority . . .

"At Harvest Road Boys' School . . . I found them in the boys' toilets . . . hidden behind a whitewashed brick . . ."

"Which toilet?" The old man had grabbed Rebeccah with a terrible strength, by the shoulders; his fingers were savage. He began to shake her.

"Eh, watch it," said Liza aggressively. "There's a law against that kind of thing."

"I think we'll go now," said Vicky frostily.

"Which toilet?"

"The far-end one," Rebeccah managed to gasp out. Staring into the old man's hot mad eyes, she was really frightened. This was not the way she'd meant things to go at all.

"How did you find it?" And: "What were *you* doing there?"

"We're using the school . . . till ours is mended . . . We have to use the boys' toilets . . ."

"Who showed you?" Under his eyes, Rebeccah thought she was starting to fall to bits. Was he a lost member of the Gestapo, the Waffen SS? So she cried out, which she hadn't meant to, "A *ghost* showed me—the ghost of a boy. It pointed to it . . ."

"That's right," said Liza, "there *was* a ghost." Stubbornly, loyally.

It worked; another terrible change came over the old man. All the cruel strength flowed out of his fingers. His face went whiter than ever. He staggered, and clutched at the windowsill to support himself. He began to breathe in a rather terrifying loud unnatural way.

"Help me get him in!" cried the woman. "Help me get him in quick."

Heaving and straining and panting and slithering on the dark polished floor, they got him through the hall and into a chintz armchair by the fire. He seemed to go unconscious. The woman went out, and came back with a tablet that she slipped into his mouth. He managed to swallow it. At first his breathing did not alter; then slowly it became more normal.

The woman seemed to come to herself, become aware of the little crowd, watching wide-eyed and gape-mouthed what they knew was a struggle between life and death.

"He'll be all right now," she said, doubtfully. "You'd better be off home, children, before your mothers start to worry." At the door she said, "Thank you for bringing the things; I'm sure you thought you were doing your best." She did not sound at all thankful, really.

"We thought you'd better have them," said Rebeccah politely. "Even though they were so old . . ."

The woman looked sharply at her, as she heard the question in her voice. "I suppose you'll want to tell your headmistress what happened? You should have handed in the stuff to her, really. Well, Mr. Barnett was the last headmaster of Harvest Road—when it was boys, I mean —a secondary modern. It happened—those things were stolen on the last day of the summer term. We were going on holiday in France next day; we never went, we couldn't. My husband knew the boy who had stolen them, but he couldn't prove it. He had the school searched from top to bottom; the boy would admit nothing. It broke my husband's health. He resigned soon after, when the school had to close. Good night, children. Thank you."

She went as if to close the door on them, but Liza said sharply, "Did the boys call your husband Barney Boko?"

The woman gave a slight but distinct shudder, though it could have been the cold January evening. "Yes . . . They were cruel days, those, cruel."

Then she closed the door quickly, leaving them standing there.

THEY HADN'T GONE fifty yards when Liza stopped them, grabbing each of them frantically by the arm, as if she was having a fit or something.

"Don't have it here," said Vicky sharply. "Wait till we get you to the hospital!"

But Liza didn't laugh. "I remember now," she said. "Listen. My dad went to that school; it was a terrible place. Barney Boko—Dad said he caned the kids for everything, even for spelling mistakes. The kids really hated him; some parents tried to go to the governors an' the council, but it didn't do them any good. There was a boy called Stebbing—Barney Boko caned him once too often—he was found dead. I think it might have been in them toilets. The verdict was he fell; he had one of those thin skulls or something. They said he fell and banged his head."

They stared at each other in horror.

"Do you think Stebbing's . . . what's in the toilets now?" asked Vicky.

They glanced around the empty streets; the lovely sun had vanished, and it had got dark awfully suddenly. There was a sudden rush coming at them around the corner—a ghostly rustling rush—but it was only long-dead autumn leaves, driven by the wind.

"Yes," said Rebeccah, as calmly as she could. "I think it was Stebbing. But he hasn't got anything against *us*—we did what he wanted."

"What *did* he want?" asked Vicky.

"For me to take back what he'd stolen—to make up for the wrong he did."

"You're too good for this world, Rebeccah!"

"What do you mean?"

"Did Stebbing *feel* like he was sorry?" asked Vicky. "Making Margie wet herself? Frightening Fiona into a fit? What he did to *you*?"

Rebeccah shuddered. "He was angry . . ."

"What we have just seen," said Vicky, "is Stebbing's revenge . . ."

"How horrible. I don't believe that—it's too horrible . . ."

"He used you, ducky. Boys will, if you let them." Vicky sounded suddenly bitter.

"Oh, I'm not going to listen. I'm going home."

They parted in a bad silent mood with each other, though they stayed together as long as they could, through the windy streets, where the pools of light from the streetlights swayed. Rebeccah had the worst journey. She took her usual shortcut through the churchyard; before she realized what she'd done, she was halfway across and there was no point in turning back. She stood paralyzed, staring at the teethlike ranks of the tombstones that grinned at her in the faintest light of the last street-lamp.

Somewhere among them, Stebbing must be buried. And the worst of it was, the oldest, Victorian, gravestones were behind her, and the newer ones in front. She could just make out the date on the nearest white one.

It was 1956.

Stebbing must be very close.

She whimpered. Then she thought of God, whom she really believed in. God wouldn't let Stebbing hurt her. She sort of reached out in her mind, to make sure God was there. In the windy night, He seemed very far away, but He *was* watching. Whimpering softly to herself, she walked on, trying not to look at the names on the tombstones, but not able to stop herself.

Stebbing was right by the path, third from the edge.

TO THE BELOVED MEMORY OF
BARRY STEBBING
BORN 11 MARCH 1944
DIED 22 JULY 1957
WITH GOD, WHICH IS MUCH BETTER

But Stebbing had nothing to say to her, here. Except, perhaps, a feeling it was all over, and his quarrel had never been with her. Really.

And then she was running, and the lights of home were in front of her, and Stebbing far behind.

She burst into the front hall like a hurricane. Daddy always kept the outside front door open, and a welcoming light glowing through the inner one, even in the middle of winter.

Daddy was standing by the hallstand, looking at her. Wearing his dark gray overcoat, and carrying a little bag like a doctor's. Instinctively, as the child of the vicarage, she knew he was going to somebody who was dying.

"Oh," she said. "I wanted to talk to you." All breathless.

He smiled, but from far away, as God had. He always seemed far away when he was going to somebody who was dying.

"You'll have to wait, Person, I'm afraid. But I expect I'll be home for tea. And all the evening. The Church Aid meeting's been canceled."

"Oh, *good*." Toast made at the fire, and Daddy, and a long warm evening with the curtains drawn against the dark . . .

"I wonder," he said vaguely, "can you help? Is Millbrook Gardens the second or third turning off Windsor Road? I can never remember . . ."

"Second from the bottom." Then, in a rush, "Who's dying?"

He smiled, puzzled. They never talked about such things. "Just an old man called Barnett . . . heart giving out. But his wife says he's very troubled . . . wants to talk about something he did years ago that's on his mind. I'd better be off, Rebeccah. See you soon." He went out. She heard his footsteps fading down the path.

She clutched the hallstand desperately, her eyes screwed tight shut, so she wouldn't see her face in the mirror.

"Come home soon, Daddy," she prayed. "Come home soon."

THE RED
HOUSE CLOCK

I WAS BORN into poverty. Poverty of mind.

My father taught himself to read after he married. By slowly deciphering the tombstones in the churchyard in his dinner hour. He would sit with a hunk of bread and cheese in one hand, slowly tracing the carved letters with the other. Because the tombstones were of men he'd known, he managed in the end. Well enough to print a short note, or read the *Daily Sketch*.

He did it out of desperation. Because he'd married the schoolmaster's daughter, and my mother's unspoken contempt grieved him.

My mother married beneath her. She married a farm laborer for his looks. For long, my father was the handsomest man in the village, with his tall upright figure, jet-black hair, and pale blue eyes. She made a bad mistake. Not only was he the handsomest, he was the hardest. In a village of hard men.

I must make this clear. He wasn't a cruel man. Not a sadist. Nor a drunkard that beat his wife, like some. But he was unforgiving, like the flint the plows turned up in the fields of Suffolk.

They said my mother's father died of shame at the marriage. Leaving them his house and furniture, the luxury of tapped cold water, and his books. It was as well he did, for we would have lived poorly on what a cowman earned, in the 1920s. My father was lucky to have a job at all. Lots of farm laborers were idle. Empire Preference, New Zealand lamb, New Zealand cheese and butter, Australian wool saw to that. They were cheaper, and at home the farms were left to rot. My father survived because he was a good cowman. And besides, he was good at mending things that seemed beyond repair: worn-out harness, buckets with holes in them, the village pump.

So we lived in our genteel poverty. Everything in the house was so polished and dusted you could see your face in it. But nothing changed. Nothing new was bought. My father and I walked around in our stockinged feet, for fear of wearing out the carpets.

At five, I went to school. Learned to read quickly, as my mother had.

The first time I brought home a book to read, my father threw it out of the window into the forest of bean plants and marigolds that was our garden. My poor mother ran out to rescue it, cleaned the wet soil off it with a look of horror on her face. It went back to school the following day cleaner and more highly polished than it had ever been. But I never dared bring home another.

Two weeks later, my grandfather's books were sold to the dealer in the village. My father got five pounds for them; he spent the money on a gift for my mother. A secondhand chicken coop and a dozen Rhode Island Red pullets. They laid abundantly. (Just as well for them, or my father would've wrung their necks.) We were glad of the eggs, and the little money they brought in, which my mother spent mainly, I think, on furniture polish. But she never forgave him for what he'd done, though only the tightness of her lips whenever he came home told me so.

Even the *Daily Sketch* was denied me, as I grew older. If I was caught with it, I was clouted and sent outside to play "in God's good fresh air." Each edition was carried off to the old shed where my father mended things. Only to reappear when a fire was being lit; or wrapped around some broad beans to be taken to the Red House, where the produce of my father's large garden was famous. Even my mother dared not ask to read it. Reading was for idle dreamers. The only thing that mattered was what a man could do with his hands.

I read everything I could lay my hands on at school. But there was no library in a village school in those days. Enough that farm laborers' children could read and write at all, before they went into service at the big house, or to work on the land.

My mind starved. Or would have starved, but for Tip. Tip was the dealer my father sold my grandfather's books to. He was often at our house, for a cup of tea. But only in the evenings, of course, when my father was home.

For some reason, the one soft spot in my father's heart was kept for Tip. Yet they couldn't have been more opposite. Where my father was tall, Tip was little. Where my father was brown and muscular from the fields, Tip was pale and plump. Where my father strode, Tip limped. Where my father was handsome, Tip was as ugly as a frog with his gold-rimmed spectacles and balding head. And where my father was silent, but for grunts, Tip could talk the hind leg off a donkey, as my father said. But he was always welcome. What he saw in us, I have long wondered. Perhaps he was sweet on my mother. Perhaps she was a little sweet on him. Though she never spoke, getting on with her ironing while Tip and my father sat on rockers each side of the kitchen fire, she often smiled at his stories. Secretly, down toward the smell of hot cotton on the ironing board.

And what stories they were! Tip and my father had both been in the Great War, and both had been wounded. But whereas my father had somehow survived the Battle of the Somme, Tip had served in Egypt and the Far East. He was full of yarns of Egyptian mummies and bazaars, and Chinese pirates in their junks. How much of his stories was just made up, none of us had any way of knowing. But he fed my young soul.

It was natural that as I grew older, I should be drawn to Tip's shop. For I will say this for my father; he would let neither my mother nor me go out stone-picking for a pound a cartful. The stones were picked from the fields, and used to mend the farm roads.

Most farm laborers' wives were expected to do it, were even glad to do it. But my father said if a man could not support a wife and family without their aid, he was not fit to be called a man. So I had plenty of spare time, and I spent it with Tip.

He was a kind of dealer you don't get today. Bluntly, he auctioned off the belongings of the dead. And of people who were desperately emigrating to Australia or Canada, hoping to change their luck. And of people who went bankrupt (I'll come to that later). But mainly, the furniture and possessions of the dead who had no relatives. The undertaker came for the body, and Tip dealt with the rest. Usually by a house sale, held in the house the Saturday morning after the funeral. Half the neighborhood turned up for the sales; they were as good as a party; he made people laugh. Not in a nasty city-slicker way, but with sympathy.

"How much for George's old frying pan," he'd say, "that's cooked many a borrowed egg!" And everyone would laugh, remembering George's little ways. Or, "How about Miss Letty's wedding dress? She died at eighty, but she never gave up hoping!" It was all a bit like the funeral tea: remembering the deceased and the funny things that had once happened to them. Tip was well liked, all around the village, though he'd only lived there since the war, and lived in Staffordshire as a young lad.

Of course, there was the other side to the laughter. The night before the sale, when he went up to the dead person's house, to sort and label the stuff into lots. He often took me with him, even when I was only eleven or twelve. It was not that he was *scared*; but he felt things deeply. And so did I. Walking into a house after a funeral is like walking into a dead person's life. The cups and plates from the funeral tea, sometimes washed up in the sink, and some-times just left lying, all crumbs. The chair the dead person had sat in by the fire, still showing the hollows left by his body. His wilting potted plants, or dying flowers in vases. The clocks he had wound up still ticking. The bundles of staring brown photographs that fell out of cupboards; the darned vests and socks.

"The secrets of all hearts shall be revealed," Tip used to say. "The secrets of all hearts."

And sometimes I thought you could feel the people still there, watching us; watching to see what we did with their life. Some felt happy, like Granny Burscombe, with her Bible open for its daily reading, at Matthew 13, and a bundle of receipts from the cripples' home, for the half crowns she'd sent them every month for thirty years.

"She had a soul like a bird," said Tip, "these last few weeks. A joyous bird waiting to fly out of her earthly cage and up to her Maker."

Or the poor empty hovel of Charlie Fairbrother, who had played the piano around the village pubs for thirty years, for the drinks people gave him, and lived on very little else. We found his music diploma, and a faded photograph of him with his massed choirboys, standing at the door of some great church.

"What a waste of a life," said Tip. "There was a Great Fall there, somewhere. But he wasn't unhappy in the end. Not really unhappy. He lived the way he wanted."

But sometimes the dead people felt angry, as if they *hadn't* lived the way they'd wanted. We found things that Tip read and whistled over, and quickly burned in the grate. "We don't want to cause trouble, do we, lad?"

He trusted me to keep my mouth shut. And I never let him down. But the fascination of the job grew on me. The things of the dead became my books; my knowledge was all inside my head, where my father could not reach it.

There were other perks, too. I helped Tip a lot: enough to be paid a wage. But money was short then; Tip only managed to get by, like all the rest of us. So he let me take things from the houses that weren't worth selling. Hanks of old wire. Collections of old string. (My God, how we collected knotted old string in those days. My mother had an apple crate full of it, all colors and thicknesses.) Part-used tins of boot polish; part-used bottles of Brasso. At first, I took these things home for my mother. But she refused them with a slight shudder, and said I didn't know where they'd been. Then I understood she feared the dead. Which seemed strange to me; for I had no fear of them at all. And I stored all these things in a tea chest in

the corner of my bedroom. It became a safe place to hide
things, for I knew my mother would never touch it.

Tip kept things, too. Things that didn't fetch enough
in the auctions he would buy himself. And then they would
appear in the window of his shop, and gather dust from
year to year. That was how I got my first bicycle. I had
yearned over it for months, poor rusted, tireless thing,
until he gave it to me for a Christmas present. My father
helped me get it back to working order in his workshop.
That was the closest we ever got, that world of prizing
rusted cogs apart, and soaking them in oil and paraffin,
and sorting through the bunches of part-worn tires that
festooned the ceiling of Tip's shop like dusty black trop-
ical fruit. I think my father sensed in me a desire to
mend, a cleverness at mending, that was the first thing he
ever approved of. Almost the only thing about me he ever
approved of. We were in the world of things, not the
world of books, and he did not mind my cleverness at all.

After that, the desire to mend and renew seized me. It
seemed to me that dead men's things had a right to life,
to live again. They became, if you like, my pets. You will
ask, did I never as a child have any pets? My mother had
a yellow canary, which sang beautifully, to her delight, on
sunlit mornings: though my father grumbled often about
the cost of seed for it, and she fed it mainly on groundsel
and rattails and other seeding plants that she gathered in
the fields and garden. But I soon learned the foolishness
of loving animals. I tried loving our family pig when I was
very little, till the day I heard it squealing when my father
cut its throat. I learned that kittens were quickly drowned,
and that sheepdogs too old to work were shot. Oh, yes, I
learned the hard way not to love animals.

But that old brass alarm clock in Tip's window . . . Black

with verdigris and never a tick to be got out of it, no matter how hard people shook it. I handled it so often that, with a sigh of exasperation, Tip finally gave me it to get some peace.

I ran home with it. That night, my father helped me to turn the screws that held it together. (Oh, the trained sinewy power of his wrists.) We found, to our mutual delight, that the works were only thick with gray fluff. It had wakened an old couple called Johnson all their married lives, and afterwards, every morning, the wife must have made her bed, tossing the blankets with vigor, filling the air with gray particles of wool that crept into the crevices of the clock and finally choked it. My father left the works soaking for an hour in a battered bucket of paraffin, then rinsed them vigorously, and they came up in his hand gleaming and burst into ticking life. It was like the Resurrection.

I kept the brass case soaking for a week in a bowl of vinegar (a nearly full pint bottle left behind by Mrs. Springs, who loved vinegar all her life) and then polished it with the Brasso Mr. Parsons had once used to clean his candlesticks, and we put it back together, gleaming and ticking and ringing like new. And I put it in Tip's window, with a price tag of two shillings, and old Simmins, who had sharp eyes, bought it on the second day, and it gave him good service, and I never passed him standing at his garden gate without he said, "Your clock's still going a treat, boy!"

It was then that I realized where old Tip was going wrong. He had a good eye for a bargain. He had a good eye for faults and flaws in anything. I have known him stand for twenty minutes just holding a thing lovingly and looking at it close, as if he was a balding, shortsighted squirrel. He had an eye for beauty. Looking back now, I realize that the grease-blackened chair he sat in at the shop every day was a priceless Chippendale. That he kept his unpaid bills behind a Staffordshire "Nelson" that would fetch several hundred pounds at modern prices. He dwelt in beauty, did Tip.

But he never cleaned or polished or even dusted anything. Let alone mended it. He was always a scruffy little beggar . . .

Now, I'd say, "Let me have a go at it, Tip!" And he'd smile and nod, and I'd bear the object away home and use up all my love and oil, Brasso and shoe polish on it, and bring it back gleaming. And it would sell straightaway. Off to a new life. I saved things from decay as the Salvation Army saved souls from hell. With the same fire in my belly.

But my great love was clocks. Nothing lives like a clock. Nothing can be your friend on a lonely dark evening like a clock. Its tick greets you as you walk in through your door. Its chime reminds you when it's time to make your supper. Each has a personality. American clocks limp their way through the world like a weary man. German clocks are exact and precise. When I was all het up, the slow tick of an English long-case would soothe me. When I was dreary, French clocks would brisk me up with their sharp tick and bright "ting."

I loved nothing better than to discover a clock in a house we were selling up. In some cupboard, long abandoned. Thick with cobwebs as a haunted house; blistered all down one side by the sun; stained white with the creeping blight of damp. Clocks like little houses, little haunted churches, little ruined black temples, from which all life had gone and only memory remained. And I would say, as Jesus

said of Jairus' daughter, "She is not dead, but sleepeth."
And set to work.

Of course, the village people, and even I myself, had
no idea of antiques in those days. When I remember the
clocks I bought off Tip for a shilling, and sold again for
five, I could weep now. But people just needed a good
clock to tell the time by. Even in the 1930s, most village
people had no radio to keep time by. People began calling
at the shop, asking if the boy had a good sound clock to
sell.

On my fourteenth birthday, I left school. No waiting till
the end of the summer term. I was suddenly a man, with
my living to make. There had been talk of my going on
the farm where my father worked, for a pound a week
wages. The farmer offered, and my father saw it as a great
favor. God knows what might have happened to me, if I'd
gone. I might be shoveling cow muck with an aching back
yet.

But Tip, bless him, asked for me. Offering the same
wage. And my father, comforting himself that there was
no book learning involved, let me go to him. He admired
my mending of things by then: said I was as good as he
was. I think he almost envied me my new job, when his
back was bad after harvest.

OF COURSE, once I was Tip's employee, he could no longer
protect me from the unpleasant side of the job. It wasn't
selling up the goods of those who were emigrating to
Canada and Australia I minded. They were sad occasions,
for people were leaving their whole families behind forever. But Tip could cheer even those up.

"Fine pair of wellies—lots of wear in them yet. Tommy
won't need those when he's chasing kangaroos in the
Outback!"

And everyone would laugh, and cough up what they could.

No. It was the bankruptcy sales. I suppose bankruptcy isn't so bad now. You think of posh businessmen selling up their business from the comfort of the bungalow they're allowed to keep, before they start making their fortune again.

But ours were different. It meant a family losing everything they had. Wife and kids going into the workhouse, while the husband set off tramping around England to look for work that wasn't there.

And we only had one cause of bankruptcy. A Scotsman called MacClintock. That most hated of men, a money-lender. He lived next door to us. But my mother and father never mentioned him by name. He was always "him next door" with an angry jerk of the head. They never spoke to him. Nobody in the village ever spoke to him.

I used to watch him with fascinated horror as he got into his black Austin Ten every morning, to drive to his pawnshops in Ipswich. A thin pale man, with Brylcreemed hair. My mother said you could tell he was dishonest, because his eyes were too close together. (I used to stare at myself in the mirror in my bedroom, to make sure that my eyes weren't too close together.) He had the prim correctness of a bank clerk, but there was a darkness about him, a sense of secrets, like you get with some undertakers. I don't know why he chose to live in our village; except that the house he lived in had come to him from a man he'd made bankrupt.

Of course, he had no interest in the village people. He was after bigger fish than us. But he was there, you see. And every so often, somebody in the village would get so desperate for money they'd go to him, in spite of all the warnings. Maybe to get the money to give their old dad a proper funeral. Or for medical treatment for a sick child. And once they were in his clutches, they'd never get out. It was just a matter of time before his bailiffs were removing their furniture to sell.

It was the interest he charged, see. Suppose he loaned somebody five pounds. He'd give them only four—the other pound would be the first month's interest. And a pound interest every month after that. And if they couldn't pay, he'd offer to lend them more . . . And he ate up our little fish just as hungrily as the big fish in Ipswich.

Tip didn't like doing business with him. But business was business. And money was short.

And so we'd end up auctioning children's dolls and prams, and men's medals, that they'd won in the war. I had to hold the things up, and I felt filthy afterwards. Nobody in the village came to those sales: there weren't any jokes to cheer you on. But plenty of other people did come. MacClintock's horrible little dealer mates from all the towns and villages around. A pack of shabby ill-tempered men who squabbled over the lots like vultures over a carcass, Tip said, and having been out East, he should know.

IT WAS BROAD-BEAN TIME, August, when the trouble at the Red House started. The first I heard of it was my father complaining that they hadn't sent down for any of his broad beans this year. He was proud of selling them his broad beans. And besides, every sixpence counted. And Dad liked his little chats with the Major, because they'd both been through the war in France.

"They must've forgotten," he said. "I've a mind to walk up with some, on the off-chance."

"Don't," said my mother. "There's something funny

going on. They've given the cook her notice. No trouble, either. People reckon they can't afford to keep her."

"That's daft," said my father. "Keeping a maid and letting the cook go."

"Little you know," said my mother. "What do you men talk about? Maid got her notice three months ago."

"Come to think of it, I haven't seen the Major's car around for a bit. Last time I saw him, he was pushing Miss Gwendoline in her wheelchair. I thought it was funny at the time . . ."

"It's awful," said my mother. "It doesn't bear thinking of. Miss Gwendoline's getting worse, and now with all the servants going, he'll be having to see to her all by himself . . ."

It was a terrible shock for me. The Major was the nearest thing we had to a squire in the village. His family had lived in the Red House for a hundred years. Not that it was a very big house. My mother, who'd had friends in service there, said it only had six bedrooms. But that seemed big to me then.

And the Major was a sort of hero of mine, though I would never have dared to speak to him. He had won the Military Cross in the war, for knocking out a German machine-gun post that was pinning down his company on the Hindenburg Line. He often saved people from MacClintock, with a little money and a lot of advice. I used to watch him stumping around the village on his wounded leg, chewing his gray mustache as if to hide the pain, and whistling softly, almost under his breath, a little tune that nobody in the village had ever heard before. I mean, everybody whistled in those days, rent collectors and butchers' boys delivering. But they whistled songs from the West End shows. And nobody could put a name to the Major's song. Maybe he picked it up overseas in the war . . .

And his daughter, Miss Gwendoline, I loved from a distance. Even in her wheelchair, she was such a beautiful lady, with huge gray eyes and long slender hands, and a lovely pale smile for everybody. She came to the village school to give out the prizes. And always opened the Church Fete and Flower Show. The village men would jostle for the privilege of lifting her and her chair onto the platform, ever so gently.

We knew the family had fallen on hard times. They'd had to sell off the farms they owned before the war, and not got much for them. But they still gave to all the good causes; nobody ever asked in vain. They were one of the pillars of my young universe, and when they began to fall, the world never seemed quite the same again to me.

IT WAS NEARLY the following Easter—Maundy Thursday —when the trouble at the Big House ended. Both Tip and I had been to Miss Gwendoline's funeral that morning, me in my first grown-up suit with long trousers, and Tip in a suit so shiny with age you could almost see your face in it. Tip had gone out to the pub at lunchtime, and not come back by three o'clock. That wasn't like him—he wasn't a great drinker. But I supposed he was drowning his sorrow over Miss Gwendoline, like so many of the village men. And I had a good fire roaring up our stove, and was fiddling with an old clock that refused to chime —an American Gilbert, I think it was.

When he finally came in, he just stood, with his hands on the counter. He stood so long silent I thought he was ill, and got up to him with a rush. I helped him into his chair and he said, "The Major's dead an' all, Billy."

"Dead?"

"Hanged hisself in the scullery at the Red House. Tommy Hargreaves was worried about him and went up to see if he was all right, and found him hanging. In the scullery."

"But . . . *why?*"

"He left a note—apologizing to the one that found him—and saying that MacClintock had taken him for every penny he had. MacClintock's got everything—the house, the land, the furniture."

"But . . . how?"

"Medical bills for Miss Gwendoline, they reckon. Best o' the Harley Street specialists, and they cost money. MacClintock was putting in the bailiffs, day after the funeral."

We were both silent a long time. I was used to life being hard in our village. But I had never dreamed there could be such evil in the world.

Then Tip said, "I saw MacClintock in the village on the way home. Bold as brass, as if nothing had happened. The wicked shall flourish as the green bay tree. He wants me to auction off the Major's stuff—week come Saturday."

"You'll not do it?"

He sighed. "I've got to, Billy. I've got to see the stuff's handled with respect. For the Major and Miss Gwendoline's sake. You don't want them mauling her stuff about, do you? And mebbe there's things people shouldn't see. It's the least I can do for the Major . . . I'll not ask you to come with me, Billy. It's too much to ask a young lad."

I looked at him then, sitting little and fat and defeated in his chair. And I loved him, as I'd never loved my father, or even my mother. He was the most decent, feeling little soul I ever knew.

"I'll come with you, Tip," I said. "It's not a job for one feller on his own."

"God bless you, son," he said, and gripped my hand tight.

WELL, WE DID IT. Together. I soon saw what Tip meant, about taking care of the Major. There was a diary, full of despair he'd never shown in public. There was his Military Cross, which Tip put in his pocket, to send to his old regiment. There were photographs: of Miss Gwendoline, when she was young and well and laughing; of another beautiful lady, who must have been her mother. Signed "To my beloved husband." Family letters. Photographs of dogs he had loved. Tip put them all into an old Gladstone bag, to be burned, or sent to those who cared.

I'm afraid I kept glancing toward the dreadful scullery, where it had happened. Till in the end Tip took me by the hand, and led me straight into it. Made me look at the rusty iron hook in the ceiling.

"He was a good man," said Tip, with a quaver in his voice. "He was a good man who looked after people in this village, the best he could. Who never did any harm to no one. Life was very cruel to him, Billy. Took away his wife, his daughter, his money, his house. But he wouldn't be a burden to anyone. They couldn't take away his pride. God bless you, Major, wherever you are. Well done, old lad."

I cried then; and it must have done me good. Because I was never afraid of the Major, or that scullery, or that whole house again.

We got on with labeling the stuff for auction. There wasn't much left. You could see the big dark patches on the wallpaper, where family portraits and such had once hung. Marks on the carpet, where furniture had once stood. Tip said the Major had had some lovely stuff, especially just after the war, before his wife died. "A picture, the house was, then. But all gone to pay the doctor's bills, Billy. Bit by bit. Till he only had MacClintock left to turn to. May he rot in hell."

All that was left were the things in two bedrooms, a couch Miss Gwendoline had lain on, and, on the marble mantelpiece . . .

A great clock. The greatest clock I had ever seen. I almost tiptoed up to it, it was so great.

It was in mahogany, in the shape of a castle, nearly two feet high. There were turrets and spires and windows and doors under the clock face, with its Gothic numerals painted on little shields made of ivory. The intricate hands were of gilded brass. It was stopped, of course. Long stopped from the look of it. Thick with dust and cobwebs, blistered down one side by the sun, and with white streaks from damp. A ruin of a great clock. A haunted castle of a clock. I lifted a trembling finger to move the minute hand around to twelve.

The clock stirred to life, with a deep-down ghostly whirring. And then it struck: a great gong-like sound that echoed through the whole house. Nine, it struck, so loud I wanted to stop it, but couldn't. And then the doors at the bottom, below the great dial, flicked open one by one, and wooden trumpeters emerged with stiff jerks, and raised jerky trumpets to their carved lips. And inside the clock, trumpets sounded; a tune. Slow, jerky, stopping in the middle. But a tune nonetheless.

"That's the Major's tune," said Tip, awed. "The one he used to whistle around the village. Musta been a German tune. The Major musta brought the clock back from Germany, after the war."

The tune began again; then ground to a jerky halt and died. It was as if the Major had died again.

"Let's get on with the labeling," said Tip.

TIP DROPPED ME at home. He leaned across and shouted through the old van's window, "Take four days off, Billy. I'm not opening the shop, Saturday. Have a good rest, son. You done well. Thanks a lot."

As he drove away, I knew he was going to get drunker than he'd ever been in his life.

It was only when I walked through our kitchen door that I felt something in my pocket, banging against my leg.

I'd forgotten to give him back the keys to the Red House.

I'LL NOT ASK you to believe the rest. But I'll tell it to you just the same. I dreamed that night that the Major came back to see me. He had a red groove around his neck, where the rope had marked him, but he smiled at me pleasantly. In every way, he was his same old self.

"Mend my clock, laddo," he said. "It's all that's left of me now. And I've still got a job I want to do." Then he went stumping off, in his old way, with a casual wave of the hand. He was so nice and ordinary I didn't even wake up in a cold sweat. I slept well, and woke up feeling fine.

That was Good Friday. I left home as if I was going to the shop. My mother was a bit put out, as she wanted me to go to church with her on Good Friday as usual. People went to church on Good Friday in those days; nearly all the village shops stayed closed. But I said Tip had a big job he wanted doing. And I gathered together all my bottles of oil and tins of polish and bits and pieces in an old brown-paper carrier bag and took them as well.

I must say, I suffered a few tremors as I opened the front door on that silent house. But it was all right. The sun was shining in through the great high sash windows, lighting up the walls and ceilings. Even all faded, they were gentle and beautiful. I suppose it sounds daft, but I felt all the love there'd been in that house, over all the years. And on the sitting room's faded Persian carpet, I saw a square of white, face down. It was a photo of Miss Gwendoline, when she was young and well and happy. I suppose Tip must have dropped it, out of his bag. But I set her on the old table, beside the clock, which I lifted down carefully from the mantelpiece. And she smiled up at me as I set to work. It was going to be O.K. I was doing what the Major wanted; I was doing what she wanted. I have never felt so calm in my life. Calm, and sunshine. I have never felt happier, those four days.

For four days it took me. The clock was very intricate: the hardest I'd ever tried. I should have despaired often, but something bore me up. I eased and I oiled. And by the end of the third day, it ticked and chimed and blew on its tiny bellows that made the trumpet noise, faultlessly. The noise filled the whole house, and made it glad, with the Major's old tune. I left it ticking that night, and I found it still ticking on the fourth morning.

So that last day I spent polishing. The wood came up like new, and the brass bezel and little brass decorations shone almost like silver. And so I left it, glowing like a jewel in that shabby faded house. It lived. And while it lived, there was something of the Major and Miss Gwendoline left in the world. It would find its way to someone who loved it, someone whom it would keep safe.

BUT ON THE MORNING of the auction, it was gone. There was only the dark place on the wall above the mantelpiece, where it had been.

"Where's the clock?" I hissed at Tip.

"MacClintock," he hissed back. "He took one look at it, and took it for hisself. Said it was the only decent thing left in the house and swore he'd have it. Reckoned the Major had cheated him, selling off the last of his pictures. He put the clock in his car and drove straight home. I doubt we'll see him again today."

It was as well we didn't. I felt like murdering MacClintock with my bare hands, small though I was, and him a grown man. I felt that I'd brought the Major back to life only to deliver him back into prison, at the hands of his worst enemy.

I was still lying awake in bed that night, writhing with rage, when I heard the sound from next door. (My bedroom window faced MacClintock's house, across the narrow alleyway between.)

The clock was chiming. Nine, ten, eleven, twelve, thirteen, on and on. And the trumpets blowing the Major's tune fit to wake the whole village. Fit to wake the dead.

And then a crash, at last. And silence.

LATE THE NEXT DAY, Tubby Pinns, the foreman of our council dustmen, came into the shop. He was quite useful to us, Tubby. And we were quite useful to him. Sometimes people put the most amazing things in their dustbins, like bundles of brass stair rods, or encyclopedias, or books about the Great War in very good condition. And of course, Tubby came round to us, and flogged them for a shilling, to share among the lads.

That day, he came in with his arms full of something that looked like a small suitcase, with funny knobs on top.

It wasn't till he put it down that I saw it was the Major's clock. He'd found it chucked down in the back lane by MacClintock's dustbin, with other rubbish.

It had taken a battering. The case was split from top to bottom, as if someone had struck it a dreadful blow. The glass of the dial was smashed, too, and the hands bent.

"Any use to you? I'll take a bob for it. I know you like clocks."

Tip gave him a shilling out of his waistcoat pocket, and he went. I hurried across to the clock, like a mother to a hurt child. It was not as bad as I feared. The case was split, but it had split down the glued joints. The old glue had given way instead of the wood, and that had saved it. The brass bezel was bent; the knobs had fallen off (Tubby had produced a lot from the pockets of his faded blue jacket). But it was all there. I could repair it. I heaved a sigh of relief.

"The bastard," said Tip. "The rotten Scottish bastard. How low can you get? Taking it home just to break it like that. He must have really *hated* the Major."

Somehow, even then, I didn't think it was quite like that. But I didn't say anything to him. I was too busy fussing over the clock. Working out how to get it back and going again. So that the Major and Miss Gwendoline could go on living.

I got it back and going perfectly in exactly a week. Polished off the white spots where it had been rained on, overnight, beside the dustbins. I put it in Tip's shop window, where everyone could see it and admire it, and hear it strike and trumpet. Somehow, my latest repairs seemed to have strengthened it. It now chimed and blew so loud it seemed as loud as the church clock, echoing from one end of our little village street to the other. Even lying in bed at night, I'd hear it faintly, and know that all was well with it.

TWO DAYS LATER, I came back from getting my dinner to find Tip and MacClintock both in the shop going hammer and tongs. Tip was shouting, "I'll not sell it to you, you Scottish loony. You just want to break it again, don't you? Like you broke it before? Well, you're not going to get the chance."

"Just name your price," said MacClintock, in a low strained voice. "How much do you want? Fifty? A hundred?"

I heard Tip gasp. A hundred pounds was a year's wages for a farm laborer in those days. But still he shook his head.

"It's a fine clock. The lad's slaved over it. I'll *not* do that to him!"

"Two hundred," yelled MacClintock. "Two hundred, ye stupid little loon." He seized Tip's lapels with both his hands.

That was a mistake.

"Take your hands off me," said Tip in a hating, icy voice. "I'll not sell that clock to you for any amount."

"Four hundred," said MacClintock, letting go of him.

I saw Tip hesitate. He was the dearest man under the sun, but he was also a dealer. And four hundred pounds was the price of a good farmhouse then.

MacClintock saw the hesitation, too. "Five hundred," he said, snatching out his wallet, so it dropped on the floor and white banknotes spilled out. It is terrible the effect the sight of banknotes has on people, even people as good as Tip.

"Done," he said, sharp and keen, just thinking about the money.

MacClintock counted out the notes into Tip's silent hand; twice one fell on the floor. Then he snatched up the clock with a terrible jangle, and was gone, clutching it to his chest.

"Tip!" I screamed. *"Tip!"*

He came out of his money daze, and his face was all concern for me. "Lad, lad, don't fret. I'll give you half. It'll set you up for life . . ."

But I didn't stop to listen. I ran out after MacClintock. Even though it was raining, I didn't stop for my coat. I saw MacClintock's car vanishing up the street. He didn't turn for home, he turned the other way.

I ran after him; I ran and ran, thinking only of the clock and the Major and Miss Gwendoline. I ran till my lungs felt they were bursting, till I got a stitch in my side. And still I staggered on. Even though I knew it was hopeless.

I caught up with him at Tom Pickering's little garage at the far end of the village. Tom only had one petrol pump in those days, and he had just finished filling a gallon can of petrol. He gave it to MacClintock, and MacClintock gave him money and got back into his car with the full can.

I knew then that he was going to burn the clock, after he'd smashed it. He saw me leaning exhausted against the garage fence as he passed, and he laughed at me, and I saw the clock through the car window for the last time . . .

I nearly gave up. I could run no farther. And Mac-

Clintock's house was half a mile away. And yet I could not give up. Something wouldn't let me. I ran and walked, ran and walked, as the Boy Scouts taught you then.

By the time I got home, and peeped over our garden fence, into the back lane, he had smashed the clock to a pile of smithereens, and was just pouring the petrol over it. He got a match out of his pocket, lit it, and threw it on the broken pile, and it went up *whoomf* with a blue flame.

And then the heavens really opened. Whole rods of rain. Drenching rain. How different all our lives would have been since, if the heavens had not opened up then. How different everything would have been . . .

MacClintock gave a glance at the burning pile, to make sure it was still alight, then ran indoors, his gray raincoat turning black at the shoulders with the rain.

And I ran out into the lane. Kicked the burning pile apart. Beat out the flames with the cap snatched from my head, with my bare hands, not even feeling the pain till afterwards, though my mother had to dress my blisters that night before bed. The rain helped a lot . . .

The back of the clock was still intact. It formed a shallow broken box, and into it, weeping, I piled all the broken fragments, then ran into my father's shed with it.

My father was there, mending a mousetrap. They sent farmhands home when it rained, in those days.

I said to him, "MacClintock's smashed the clock again!"

And my father said, picking up odd bits and looking at them hopelessly, "He's really done it this time. The feller's *bonkers*. That clock was worth *real* money."

"I'll take it up to my bedroom," I said, trying hard not to cry in front of him. It didn't do you any good to cry in front of my father; he called it going on like a wet girl.

I carried it up. My mother complained about having

such rubbish in the house, but I wasn't in any mood to heed her. Alone in my bedroom, I wept buckets again, for the sheer hopelessness of life.

But then . . . the wreckage seemed to call to me. Eyes still full of tears, I picked up the bottom half of a smashed pinnacle. Of course, then I had to find the other half, and saw by the way it had snapped, with the grain, that the two halves could be glued together again. I reached for the glue; and the glue dried my tears. *Bits* of the clock could still be saved. I could keep the bits to remember the Major by.

At some point, MacClintock must have come back to check his wreckage. I heard him and my father shouting at each other across the garden wall. My father was at his most bloody-minded. I think he had always hated Mac-Clintock, for what he'd done to the village people. He'd often threatened to break his neck. I think he hated him much more, after the Major died. And now he despised him for breaking the clock and wasting his own money. My father had a feeling for objects, and for money, that he never had for living things.

Anyway, over a long weary time MacClintock feverishly demanded his bits back, and my father told him to get lost. My father called him a Scots loony. MacClintock threatened to send for the police, and my father offered to knock MacClintock's teeth down his throat. They both knew the village bobby hated MacClintock as much as everybody else. In the end, MacClintock shut up and went away.

And then Tip turned up, and I was summoned down-stairs. Tip was waving white five-pound notes about, and having a terrible fit of conscience about the whole thing. He insisted on giving me half, and my mother took it from him to put in the savings bank for me. My father looked dazed at the sight of all that money, but he made no objection. Hard man he might have been, but too proud to steal off his only son . . .

After Tip had gone, I went back upstairs. Oddly enough, the money made no difference. Didn't cheer me up at all, though my mother said I could have five pounds to buy a brand-new bike. I just got on with rescuing tiny bits of the clock and fitting them together, like I was crazy, too.

And then my father came in, and saw what I was doing. He didn't call me a fool. He just squatted down on his haunches, and began picking up bits as well. After a long time, he said grimly, "Reckon we can mend it. It'll take months, though."

I really loved him then.

It takes a lot to stop a young lad from loving.

EVEN MY INDEFATIGABLE FATHER despaired many times. Repairing the wooden case was easy enough, just tedious. Again, it was the glued joints mainly that had given way, and saved the wood. He left that to me, and in the end, I managed it. Close to, the mended splits showed, under however many layers of polish I put on it, so it looked a bit like a jigsaw puzzle. But from a distance of four feet, it looked its old self. I straightened the enameled face, and repainted the places where the enamel had chipped. The bezel and glass were a total write-off, but my father scoured the junk shops till he found an exact replacement from another German clock lying without works. I spent a week straightening the hands millimeter by millimeter, with a tiny pair of pliers.

Meanwhile, my father had to sort out the scattered and

twisted cogs, like an archaeologist. Even when he got each straightened and in its right place, the thing wouldn't go. He had to hand it over to the clockmaker in Wivenby, and it cost him a whole week's wages. It was then I began to wonder at the extremity of his love for me.

But when that was done, and the clock ticked and struck and chimed again, and my father had cut up my mother's best pair of kid gloves to make anew the little bellows that sounded the trumpet noises, we put it together one evening . . . And it worked. It struck and chimed and blew the old tune, somehow more loudly than ever.

I hugged him, and thanked him, and we set it up on a table in my room. He gave a strange grin, and said, "Now let's wait and see!"

I didn't know what he was talking about. But I hadn't all that long to wait. We'd scarcely sat down to a celebration supper of sausages when there came a thunderous knocking at the door.

MacClintock burst into the room, pushing my mother aside, so she fell against the wall. His eyes were wild; his face was even paler than usual, showing up the five o'clock shadow on his chin as if it was painted on.

"I've been expecting you," said my father, putting a forkful of sausage in his mouth, as calm as anything. "How much will ye pay for the clock this time, MacClintock?"

MacClintock's eyes went to thin slits. "I'll see ye in hell first," he said.

"No," said my father. "I'll see *you* in hell first. That clock may be hell to you. But it rings like a cash register to me. How much?"

"A hundred," said MacClintock sulkily.

"I want a thousand pounds," said my father.

"Be damned to you!"

"You're the one that's damned, MacClintock. Go an' get a good night's sleep. If you can."

I DON'T KNOW how much sleep MacClintock got that night, but I got none. The clock chimed and trumpeted every quarter-hour, and the sound seemed to fill the world. I tossed and turned, thinking of the heartlessness of the universe. In the sea, as I knew from biology lessons, the fish ate each other to live. And on the land, lions ate antelopes and foxes ate rabbits. But I never realized before that men ate men. MacClintock gobbled up the poor and the foolish, and now my father was gobbling up MacClintock.

It was not love that made the world go round, as a popular song of the time said on the radio. It was money. All the world was reduced to how much will you give me, MacClintock?

As I imagined him tossing in his bed, I lost my hate of him, and began to feel pity. I felt pity for the three days and nights that followed. Pity and a mounting despair.

On the first day, he went to the village bobby. But the village bobby, when he came with him to our door, shook his head and would do nothing. MacClintock had smashed and abandoned the clock in the public domain, i.e., the back alley, and anyone could keep the bits . . .

On the second day, MacClintock turned up with two of his big debt-collecting men, who made the mistake of threatening my father. My father went berserk, and laid the two of them flat. And bloodied MacClintock's nose right in the middle of the street, in front of half the village.

And all the time, things screwed up tighter and tighter, like a clock spring overwound. And I knew what blood could be spilled when a clock spring broke.

The third evening, MacClintock came brandishing a

shotgun—one that his bailiffs had taken from Tom More-
ton, in payment of a debt. I don't think he meant to shoot
anybody; I think by that time he didn't know what he was
doing. I think he was crazed with guilt, and lack of sleep,
and the clock never stopping chiming and trumpeting
outside his windows.

At the height of the yelling, the gun went off. Somehow,
my father got the front door shut nearly in time; he only
got a few pellets in his hand. After that, MacClintock
seemed to go berserk, firing at all our windows. I remember
lying across my mother to protect her, as the glass showered
over both of us.

The noise fetched the village bobby. MacClintock took
one look at the approaching uniform, and fled back into
his house. The bobby demanded he come out and face
the music; for the first time in his dreadful life, Mac-
Clintock found himself on the wrong side of the law.

It was the last straw. He fired at the bobby. And even
though he missed, he knew then he would go to prison.

There were more policemen, all over the place, after
that. They threatened MacClintock, then they pleaded
with him. After about three hours (and still my father, in
his white rage, kept the clock chiming and sounding),
there was a dull bang inside MacClintock's house.

People said it was justice, that he killed himself with one
of the last debts he ever collected.

Afterwards, I think I lived in a daze for a year. Though
nobody in the village was sorry, everyone was very sub-
dued. Hardly anybody understood the awful thing my
father had done, except Tip. And Tip kept his mouth
shut, and was very kind to me.

He had to be. I was in turmoil. How could a thing that
I rebuilt for love have killed a man? Was that what the

Major had meant, when he came to me in that dream, and said he had something else still to do? And was it really the Major, or only a dream? Nobody on earth could *ever* tell me.

But none of this ever bothered my father. Nothing interfered with the swing in his stride, the way he whistled as he set about mending a bridle, or banking up his potatoes. I could see no difference in him at all; except he would sometimes say regretfully that he wished he'd taken MacClintock's hundred pounds . . . He had no more regret in him than a fox that kills a rabbit, than a woodworm that makes a house fall. Than life itself.

In the end, I found I could live with him no longer. He destroyed all hope in me. So that when Tip got me an apprenticeship with an old clockmaker friend of his in Huddersfield, I left home thankfully and never returned. For all I know, my father may be living yet. And losing sleep over nothing. He was always a good sleeper.

When I left home, I took the clock with me. My father raised no objection. With MacClintock dead, he said, it was only a valueless curiosity. I have it still, in my shop. I have prospered, but never married. All the love I have to give is for my clocks: that they are rescued, and go back into the world, and give good service.

That, and the picture of Miss Gwendoline, which still sits, framed, on my mantelpiece. Beside the Red House clock.

THE CALL

I'M ROTA SECRETARY of our local Samaritans. My job's to see our office is staffed twenty-four hours a day, 365 days a year. It's a load of headaches, I can tell you. And the worst headache for any branch is overnight on Christmas Eve.

Christmas night's easy: plenty have had enough of family junketings by then; nice to go on duty and give your stomach a rest. And New Year's Eve's O.K., because we have Methodists and other teetotal types. But Christmas Eve . . .

Except we had Harry Lancaster.

In a way, Harry *was* the branch. Founder member in 1963. A marvelous director all through the sixties. Available on the phone, day or night. Always the same quiet, unflappable voice, asking the right questions, soothing overexcited volunteers.

But he paid the price.

When he took early retirement from his firm in '73, we were glad. We thought we'd see even more of him. But we didn't. He took a six-month break from Sams. When he came back, he didn't take up the reins again. He took a much lighter job, treasurer. He didn't look ill, but he looked *faded*. Too long as a Sam director can do that to you. But we were awfully glad just to have him back. No one was gladder than Maureen, the new director. Everybody cried on Maureen's shoulder, and Maureen cried on Harry's when it got rough.

Harry was the kind of guy you wish could go on forever. But every so often, over the years, we'd realize he wasn't going to. His hair went snow-white; he got thinner and thinner. Gave up the treasurership. From doing a duty once a week, he dropped to once a month. But we still *had* him. His presence was everywhere in the branch. The new directors, leaders, he'd trained them all. They still asked themselves in a tight spot, "What would Harry do?" And what he did do was as good as ever. But his birthday kept on coming around. People would say with horrified disbelief, "Harry'll be *seventy-four* next year!"

And yet, most of the time, we still had in our minds the fifty-year-old Harry, full of life, brimming with new ideas. We couldn't do without that dark-haired ghost.

And the one thing he never gave up was overnight duty on Christmas Eve. Rain, hail, or snow, he'd be there. Alone.

Now, alone is wrong; the rules say the office must be double-staffed at all times. There are two emergency phones. How could even Harry cope with both at once?

But Christmas Eve is hell to cover. Everyone's got children or grandchildren, or is going away. And Harry had always done it alone. He said it was a quiet shift; hardly anybody ever rang. Harry's empty logbook was there to prove it: never more than a couple of long-term

clients who only wanted to talk over old times and wish
Harry a Merry Christmas.

So I let it go on.

Until, two days before Christmas last year, Harry went
down with flu. Bad. He tried dosing himself with all kinds
of things; swore he was still coming. Was *desperate* to
come. But Mrs. Harry got in the doctor; and the doctor
was adamant. Harry argued; tried getting out of bed
and dressed to prove he was O.K. Then he fell and
cracked his head on the bedpost, and the doctor gave
him a shot meant to put him right out. But Harry,
raving by this time, kept trying to get up, saying he must
go . . .

But I only heard about that later. As rota secretary I
had my own troubles, finding his replacement. The rule
is that if the rota bloke can't get a replacement, he does
the duty himself. In our branch, anyway. But I was already
doing the seven-to-ten shift that night, then driving north
to my parents'.

Eighteen fruitless phone calls later, I got somebody.
Meg and Geoff Charlesworth. Just married; no kids.

When they came in at ten to relieve me, they were
happy. Maybe they'd had a couple of drinks in the course
of the evening. They were laughing; but they were certainly
fit to drive. It is wrong to accuse them, as some did, later,
of having had too many. Meg gave me a Christmas kiss.
She'd wound a bit of silver tinsel through her hair, as
some girls do at Christmas. They'd brought long red can-
dles to light, and mince pies to heat up in our kitchen and
eat at midnight. It was just happiness; and it *was* Christmas
Eve.

Then my wife tooted our car horn outside, and I passed
out of the story. The rest is hearsay: from the log they

kept, and the reports they wrote that were still lying in the in tray the following morning.

THEY HEARD the distant bells of the parish church, filtering through the falling snow, announcing midnight. Meg got the mince pies out of the oven, and Geoff was just kissing her, mouth full of flaky pastry, when the emergency phone went.

Being young and keen, they both grabbed for it. Meg won. Geoff shook his fist at her silently, and dutifully logged the call. Midnight exactly, according to his new watch. He heard Meg say what she'd been carefully coached to say, like Samaritans the world over.

"Samaritans—can I help you?"

She said it just right. Warm, but not gushing. Interested, but not *too* interested. That first phrase is all-important. Say it wrong, the client rings off without speaking.

Meg frowned. She said the phrase again. Geoff crouched close in support, trying to catch what he could from Meg's earpiece. He said afterwards the line was very bad. Crackly, very crackly. Nothing but crackles, coming and going.

Meg said her phrase the third time. She gestured to Geoff that she wanted a chair. He silently got one, pushed it in behind her knees. She began to wind her fingers into the coiled telephone cord, like all Samaritans do when they're anxious.

Meg said into the phone, "I'd like to help if I can." It was good to vary the phrase, otherwise clients began to think you were a tape recording. She added, "My name's Meg. What can I call *you*?" You never ask for their *real* name, at that stage; always what you can call them. Often they start off by giving a false name . . .

A voice spoke through the crackle. A female voice.

"He's going to kill me. I know he's going to kill me. When he comes back." Geoff, who caught it from a distance, said it wasn't the phrases that were so awful. It was the way they were said.

Cold; so cold. And certain. It left no doubt in your mind he *would* come back and kill her. It wasn't a wild voice you could hope to calm down. It wasn't a cunning hysterical voice, trying to upset you. It wasn't the voice of a hoaxer, which to the trained Samaritan ear always has that little wobble in it, which might break down into a giggle at any minute and yet, till it does, must be taken absolutely seriously. Geoff said it was a voice as cold, as real, as hopeless as a tombstone.

"Why do you think he's going to kill you?" Geoff said Meg's voice was shaking, but only a little. Still warm, still interested.

Silence. Crackle.

"Has he threatened you?"

When the voice came again, it wasn't an answer to her question. It was another chunk of lonely hell, being spat out automatically: as if the woman at the other end was really only talking to herself.

"He's gone to let a boat through the lock. When he comes back, he's going to kill me."

Meg's voice tried to go up an octave; she caught it just in time.

"Has he *threatened* you? What is he going to do?"

"He's goin' to push me in the river, so it looks like an accident."

"Can't you swim?"

"There's half an inch of ice on the water. Nobody could live a minute."

"Can't you get away . . . before he comes back?"

"Nobody lives within miles. And I'm lame."

"Can't I . . . you . . . ring the police?"

Geoff heard a click, as the line went dead. The dialing tone resumed. Meg put the phone down wearily, and suddenly shivered, though the office was overwarm, from the roaring gas fire.

"Christ, I'm so *cold*!"

Geoff brought her cardigan, and put it around her. "Shall I ring the duty director, or will you?"

"You. If you heard it all."

Tom Brett came down the line, brisk and cheerful. "I've not gone to bed yet. Been filling the little blighter's Christmas stocking . . ."

Geoff gave him the details. Tom Brett was everything a good duty director should be. Listened without interrupting; came back solid and reassuring as a house.

"Boats don't go through the locks this time of night. Haven't done for twenty years. The old alkali steamers used to, when the alkali trade was still going strong. The locks are only manned nine till five nowadays. Pleasure boats can wait till morning. As if anyone would be moving a pleasure boat this weather . . ."

"Are you *sure*?" asked Geoff doubtfully.

"Quite sure. Tell you something else—the river's nowhere near freezing over. Runs past my back fence. Been watching it all day, 'cos I bought the lad a fishing rod for Christmas, and it's not much fun if he can't try it out. You've been *had*, old son. Some Christmas joker having you on. Good night!"

"Hoax call," said Geoff heavily, putting the phone down. "No boats going through locks. No ice on the river. Look!" He pulled back the curtain from the office window. "It's still quite warm out—the snow's melting, not even lying."

Meg looked at the black wet road, and shivered again.

"That was no hoax. Did you think that voice was a hoax?"

"We'll do what the boss man says. Ours not to reason why . . ."

He was still waiting for the kettle to boil when the emergency phone went again.

The same voice.

"BUT HE *can't* just push you in the river and get away with it!" said Meg desperately.

"He can. I always take the dog for a walk last thing. And there's places where the bank is crumbling and the fence's rotting. And the fog's coming down. He'll break a bit of fence, then put the leash on the dog, and throw it in after me. Doesn't matter whether the dog drowns or is found wanderin'. Either'll suit *him*. Then he'll ring the police an' say I'm missin' . . ."

"But why should he *want* to? What've you *done*? To deserve it?"

"I'm gettin' old. I've got a bad leg. I'm not much use to him. He's got a new bit o' skirt down the village . . ."

"But can't we . . ."

"All you can do for me, love, is to keep me company till he comes. It's lonely . . . That's not much to ask, is it?"

"Where *are* you?"

Geoff heard the line go dead again. He thought Meg looked like a corpse herself. White as a sheet. Dull dead eyes, full of pain. Ugly, almost. How she would look as an old woman, if life was rough on her. He hovered, helpless, desperate, while the whistling kettle wailed from the warm Samaritan kitchen.

"Ring Tom again, for Christ's sake," said Meg, savagely.

TOM'S VOICE was a little less genial. He'd got into bed and turned the light off . . .

"Same joker, eh? Bloody persistent. But she's getting her facts wrong. No fog where I am. Any where you are?"

"No," said Geoff, pulling back the curtain again, feeling a nitwit.

"There were no fog warnings on the late-night weather forecast. Not even for low-lying districts . . ."

"No."

"Well, I'll try to get my head down again. But don't hesitate to ring if anything *serious* crops up. As for this other lady . . . if she comes on again, just try to humor her. Don't argue—just try to make a relationship."

In other words, thought Geoff miserably, don't bother me with *her* again.

But he turned back to a Meg still frantic with worry. Who would not be convinced. Even after she'd rung the local British Telecom weather summary, and was told quite clearly the night would be clear all over the Eastern Region.

"I want to know where she *is*. I want to know where she's ringing from . . ."

To placate her, Geoff got out the large-scale Ordnance Survey maps that some offices carry. It wasn't a great problem. The Ousam was a rarity: the only canalized river with locks for fifty miles around. And there were only eight sets of locks on it.

"These four," said Geoff, "are right in the middle of towns and villages. So it can't be *them*. And there's a whole row of Navigation cottages at Sutton's Lock, and I know they're occupied, so it can't be *there*. And this last one—Ousby Point—is right on the sea and it's all docks and stone quays—there's no riverbank to crumble. So it's either Yaxton Bridge, or Moresby Abbey locks . . ."

The emergency phone rang again. There is a myth among old Samaritans that you can tell the quality of the incoming call by the sound of the phone bell. Sometimes it's lonely, sometimes cheerful, sometimes downright frantic. Nonsense, of course. A bell is a bell is a bell . . .

But this ringing sounded so cold, so dreary, so dead, that for a second they both hesitated and looked at each other with dread. Then Meg slowly picked up the phone; like a bather hesitating on the bank of a cold gray river.

It was the voice again.

"The boat's gone through. He's just closing the lock gates. He'll be here in a minute . . ."

"What kind of boat is it?" asked Meg, with a desperate attempt at self-defense.

The voice sounded put out for a second, then said, "Oh, the usual. One of the big steamers. The *Lowestoft*, I think. Aye, the lock gates are closed. He's coming up the path. Stay with me, love. Stay with me . . ."

Geoff took one look at his wife's gray, frozen, horrified face and snatched the phone from her hand. He might be a Samaritan, but he was a husband, too. He wasn't sitting and watching his wife being screwed by some vicious hoaxer.

"Now, *look*!" he said. "Whoever you are! We want to help. We'd like to help. But stop feeding us lies. I know the *Lowestoft*. I've been aboard her. They gave her to the Sea Scouts, for a headquarters. She hasn't got an engine anymore. She's a hulk. She's never moved for years. Now let's cut the cackle—"

The line went dead.

"Oh, *Geoff*!" said Meg.

"Sorry. But the moment I called her bluff, she rang off. That *proves* she's a hoaxer. All those old steamers were broken up for scrap, except the *Lowestoft*. She's a *hoaxer*, I tell you!"

"Or an old lady who's living in the past. Some old lady who's muddled and lonely and frightened. And you shouted at her . . ."

He felt like a murderer. It showed in his face. And she made the most of it.

"Go out and find her, Geoff. Drive over and see if you can find her . . ."

"And leave you alone in the office? Tom'd have my guts for garters . . ."

"Harry Lancaster always did it alone. I'll lock the door. I'll be all right. Go on, Geoff. She's lonely. Terrified."

He'd never been so torn in his life. Between being a husband and being a Samaritan. That's why a lot of branches won't let husband and wife do duty together. We won't, now. We had a meeting about it; afterwards.

"Go *on*, Geoff. If she does anything silly, I'll never forgive myself. She might chuck herself in the river . . ."

They both knew. In our parts, the river or the drain is often the favorite way, rather than the usual overdose. The river seems to *call* to the locals, when life gets too much for them.

"Let's ring Tom again . . ."

She gave him a look that withered him and Tom together. In the silence that followed, they realized they were cut off from their duty director, from *all* the directors, from *all* help. The most fatal thing, for Samaritans. They were poised on the verge of the ultimate sin: going it alone.

He made a despairing noise in his throat, reached for his coat and the car keys. "I'll do Yaxton Bridge. But I'll not do Moresby Abbey. It's a mile along the towpath in the dark. It'd take me an hour . . ."

He didn't wait for her dissent. He heard her lock the

office door behind him. At least she'd be safe behind a locked door . . .

He never thought that telephones got past locked doors.

He made Yaxton Bridge in eight minutes flat, skidding and correcting his skids on the treacherous road. Lucky there wasn't much traffic about.

On his right, the river Ousam beckoned, flat, black, deep, and still. A slight steam hung over the water, because it was just a little warmer than the air.

IT WAS GETTING ON toward one by the time he reached the lock. But there was still a light in one of the pair of lockkeepers' cottages. And he knew at a glance that this wasn't the place. No ice on the river; no fog. He hovered, unwilling to disturb the occupants. Maybe they were in bed, the light left on to discourage burglars.

But when he crept up the garden path, he heard the sound of the TV, a laugh, coughing. He knocked.

An elderly man's voice called through the door, "Who's there?"

"Samaritans. I'm trying to find somebody's house. I'll push my card through your letter box."

He scrabbled frantically through his wallet in the dark. The door was opened. He passed through to a snug sitting room, a roaring fire. The old man turned down the sound of the TV. The wife said he looked perished, and the Samaritans did such good work, turning out at all hours, even at Christmas. Then she went to make a cup of tea.

He asked the old man about ice, and fog, and a lockkeeper who lived alone with a lame wife. The old man shook his head. "Couple who live next door's got three young kids . . ."

"Wife's not lame, is she?"

"Nay—a fine-lookin' lass wi' two grand legs on her . . ."

His wife, returning with the tea tray, gave him a *very* old-fashioned look. Then she said, "I've sort of got a memory of a lockkeeper wi' a lame wife—this was years ago, mind. Something not nice . . . but your memory goes, when you get old."

"We worked the lock at Ousby Point on the coast, all our married lives," said the old man apologetically. "They just let us retire here, 'cos the cottage was goin' empty . . ."

Geoff scalded his mouth, drinking their tea, he was so frantic to get back. He did the journey in seven minutes; he was getting used to the skidding, by that time.

HE PARKED THE CAR outside the Sam office, expecting her to hear his return and look out. But she didn't.

He knocked; he shouted to her through the door. No answer. Frantically he groped for his own key in the dark, and burst in.

She was sitting at the emergency phone, her face grayer than ever. Her eyes were far away, staring at the blank wall. They didn't swivel to greet him. He bent close to the phone in her hand and heard the same voice, the same cold hopeless tone, going on and on. It was sort of . . . hypnotic. He had to tear himself away, and grab a message pad. On it he scrawled, "WHAT'S HAPPENING? WHERE IS SHE?"

He shoved it under Meg's nose. She didn't respond in any way at all. She seemed frozen, just listening. He pushed her shoulder, half-angry, half-frantic. But she was wooden, like a statue, almost as if she was in a trance. In a wave of husbandly terror, he snatched the phone from her.

It immediately went dead.

He put it down and shook Meg. For a moment she

recognized him and smiled, sleepily. Then her face went rigid with fear.

"Her husband was in the house. He was just about to open the door where she was . . ."

"Did you find out where she was?"

"Moresby Abbey lock. She told me in the end. I got her confidence. Then *you* came and ruined it . . ."

She said it as if he was suddenly her enemy. An enemy, a fool, a bully, a murderer. Like all men. Then she said, "I must go to her . . ."

"And leave the office unattended? That's *mad*." He took off his coat with the car keys, and hung it on the office door. He came back and looked at her again. She still seemed a bit odd, trance-like. But she smiled at him and said, "Make me a quick cup of tea. I must go to the loo, before she rings again."

Glad they were friends again, he went and put the kettle on. Stood impatiently waiting for it to boil, tapping his fingers on the sink unit, trying to work out what they should do. He heard Meg's step in the hallway. Heard the toilet flush.

Then he heard a car start up outside.

His car.

He rushed out into the hall. The front door was swinging, letting in the snow. Where his car had been, there were only tire marks.

He was terrified now. Not for the woman. For Meg.

He rang Tom Brett, more frightened than any client Tom Brett had ever heard.

He told Tom what he knew.

"Moresby Locks," said Tom. "A lame woman. A murdering husband. Oh, my God. I'll be with you in five."

———

"THE EXCHANGE are putting emergency calls through to
Jimmy Henry," said Tom, peering through the whirling
wet flakes that were clogging his windscreen wipers. "Do
you know what way Meg was getting to Moresby Locks?"

"The only way," said Geoff. "Park at Wylop Bridge and
walk a mile up the towpath."

"There's a shortcut. Down through the woods by the
Abbey, and over the lock gates. Not a lot of people know
about it. I think we'll take that one. I want to get there
before she does . . ."

"What the hell do you think's going on?"

"I've got an *idea*. But if I told you, you'd think I was out
of my tiny shiny mind. So I won't. All I want is your Meg
safe and dry, back in the Sam office. And nothing in the
log that headquarters might see . . ."

He turned off the bypass, into a narrow track where
hawthorn bushes reached out thorny arms and scraped at
the paintwork of the car. After a long while, he grunted
with satisfaction, clapped on the brakes, and said, "Come
on."

They ran across the narrow wooden walkway that sat
precariously on top of the lock gates. The flakes of snow
whirled at them, in the light of Tom's torch. Behind the
gates, the water stacked up, black, smooth, slightly steaming
because it was warmer than the air. In an evil way, it called
to Geoff. So easy to slip in, let the icy arms embrace you,
slip away . . .

Then they were over, on the towpath. They looked left,
right, listened.

Footsteps, woman's footsteps, to the right. They ran that
way.

Geoff saw Meg's back, in its white raincoat . . .

And beyond Meg, leading Meg, another back, another
woman's back. The back of a woman who limped.

A woman with a dog. A little white dog . . .

For some reason, neither of the men called out to Meg. Fear of disturbing a Samaritan relationship, perhaps. Fear of breaking up something that neither of them understood. After all, they could afford to be patient now. They had found Meg safe. They were closing up quietly on her, only ten yards away. No danger . . .

Then, in the light of Tom's torch, a break in the white-painted fence on the river side.

And the figure of the limping woman turned through the gap in the fence and walked out over the still, black waters of the river.

And like a sleepwalker, Meg turned to follow . . .

THEY CAUGHT HER on the very brink. Each of them caught her violently by one arm, like policemen arresting a criminal. Tom cursed, as one of his feet slipped down the bank and into the water. But he held on to them, as they all swayed on the brink, and he only got one very wet foot.

"What the hell am I doing here?" asked Meg, as if waking from a dream. "She was talking to me. I'd got her confidence . . ."

"Did she tell you her name?"

"Agnes Todd."

"Well," said Tom, "here's where Agnes Todd used to live."

There were only low walls of stone, in the shape of a house. With stretches of concrete and old broken tile in between. There had been a phone, because there was still a telegraph pole, with a broken junction box from which two black wires flapped like flags in the wind.

"Twenty-one years ago, Reg Todd kept this lock. His lame wife, Agnes, lived with him. They didn't get on well—people passing the cottage heard them quarreling. Christmas Eve, 1964, he reported her missing to the police. She'd gone out for a walk with the dog, and not come back. The police searched. There was a bad fog down that night. They found a hole in the railing, just about where we saw one; and a hole in the ice, just glazing over. They found the dog's body next day; but they didn't find her for a month, till the ice on the river Ousam finally broke up.

"The police tried to make a case of it. Reg Todd *had* been carrying on with a girl in the village. But there were no marks of violence. In the end, she could have fallen, she could've been pushed, or she could've jumped. So they let Reg Todd go; and he left the district."

There was a long silence. Then Geoff said, "So you think . . . ?"

"I think nowt," said Tom Brett, suddenly very stubborn and solid. "I think nowt, and that's all I *know*. Now let's get your missus home."

NEARLY A YEAR PASSED. In November, after a short illness, Harry Lancaster died peacefully in his sleep. He had an enormous funeral. The church was full. Present Samaritans, past Samaritans from all over the country, more old clients than you could count, and even two of the top brass from Slough.

But it was not till everybody was leaving the house that Tom Brett stopped Geoff and Meg by the gate. More solid and stubborn than ever.

"I had a long chat wi' Harry," he said, "after he knew he was goin'. He told me. About Agnes Todd. She had rung him up on Christmas Eve. Every Christmas Eve for twenty years . . ."

"Did he know she was a . . . ?" Geoff still couldn't say it.

"Oh, aye. No flies on Harry. The second year—while he was still director—he persuaded the telephone company to get an engineer to trace the number. How he managed to get them to do it on Christmas Eve, God only knows. But he had a way with him, Harry, in his day."

"And . . ."

"The telephone company were baffled. It was the old number of the lock cottage all right. But the lock cottage was demolished a year after the . . . whatever it was. Nobody would live there, afterwards. All the telephone company found was a broken junction box and wires trailin'. Just like we saw that night."

"So he talked to her all those years . . . knowing?"

"Aye, but he wouldn't let anybody else do Christmas Eve. She was lonely, but he knew she was dangerous. Lonely an' dangerous. She wanted company."

Meg shuddered. "How could he bear it?"

"He was a Samaritan . . ."

"Why didn't he tell anybody?"

"Who'd have believed him?"

THERE WERE HALF A DOZEN of us in the office this Christmas Eve. Tom Brett, Maureen, Meg and Geoff, me. All waiting for . . .

It never came. Nobody called at all.

"Do you think . . . ?" asked Maureen, with an attempt at a smile, her hand to her throat in a nervous gesture, in the weak light of dawn.

"Aye," said Tom Brett. "I think we've heard the last of her. Mebbe Harry took her with him. Or came back for her. Harry was like that. The best Samaritan I ever knew."

His voice went funny on the last two words, and there was a shine on those stolid eyes. He said, "I'll be off, then." And was gone.

THE CAT, SPARTAN

I WAS ALMOST happy at Granda's funeral. It was his own church, see? Where he took the collection and counted it in the vestry afterwards, and let me help when I was little. Where he rang the bells and mowed the churchyard.

His mate the vicar told us what a good old boy he'd been, who would do anything for anybody. And the church was full of flowers from the village gardens, glowing against the gray stone. All except the awful wreath of lilies my parents had sent from the florist's in town.

And afterwards, at the church door, the whole village must've come and shaken me by the hand, and everybody said what a good old boy he'd been.

And Spartan was there all the time. He came in last, walking up the aisle as slow and solemn as a judge, and sat by the coffin right through the service. And the village people nodded, and gave each other fleeting funeral smiles.

And Spartan followed the coffin to the grave, which was on the warm south side of the churchyard. The place Granda had chosen, near the big yew that's been there since Cromwell's time. And Spartan followed us with his eyes as we each sprinkled soil on the coffin in the grave with a sandy rattle.

I just couldn't believe that Granda was down there in the horrible shiny dark coffin, with its vulgar shiny brass handles. He wasn't fastened up in there; he was *everywhere* now. Watching over his church and his friends around the grave, the sunlit trees and the cornfields all around. Watching, and pleased. Especially with Spartan.

We left Spartan carefully supervising the gravediggers filling in the grave, and straggled down toward the gate.

And then it went all wrong.

Batty Henty was talking to me, tears in his eyes, holding both my hands. He's not at all batty really, even if he does live alone, and can't read or write. He can tell tomorrow's weather, and he's never wrong. Any animal will come to him.

Batty was telling me what they *all* thought, "Yer Granda shoulda lain in his own house, where he belonged to be. Not in that there undertakers . . ." when my father came up tight-lipped and said we had to be going. He ignored Batty like he was the gatepost.

So we left in the Mercedes; and the village people followed us with their eyes, and did not wave. They knew we'd done wrong, not giving Granda a proper send-off after the funeral, back at his cottage. With ham sandwiches and a drop to drink, and lots of stories, like the hare that jumped over Granda's head in the harvest field . . .

ON THE WAY to the solicitor's my mother said, "How soon can we get his cottage on the market? People go off buying houses in winter."

My father said, "Oh, I don't know. The way house prices are rising, it might pay to hang on till spring . . ."

"And risk squatters?"

"It's not an area for squatters."

"But . . . what about all Granda's *things*?" I said. "What about Spartan?" It came out as a kind of feeble squeak from the back seat. I knew it was no good before I said it.

"Whately's have offered most for the house clearance," said my mother. "And I've rung the SPCA to come and deal with Spartan."

I might as well not have existed.

Granda might as well not have existed.

Soon Spartan would cease to exist. My mother was efficient. She already had the date of Granda's death in her Filofax so she could phone the papers to insert anniversary memories next year.

God, Granda, where *are* you? Why did you have to go and get yourself killed? And leave me with these two . . . *vultures*? What can I *do*? If I make a fuss, they'll call it teenage tantrums. If I make a big enough fuss, they'll probably send me to a shrink.

Granda's voice inside my head: "Patience, our Tim. Slow and steady wins the race!" But it was only a memory. What can a memory do against *vultures*?

"CAN WE HURRY it along, Mr. Makepeace?" asked my father. "I have another appointment at four."

Appointment? Playing squash with John Victor. Of Victor Enterprises PLC. A *very* important business client. And my mother would be itching to start chopping and blending in her wonderful fitted kitchen, because the horrible Southwarks were coming to dinner.

Mr. Makepeace looked up over his half-spectacles. Tapped Granda's will with the nail of his forefinger. He was an old mate of Granda's. They used to go shooting pigeons together. Mr. Makepeace should've looked sad. But he looked like a little boy about to light a firework. Was *nobody* sad about Granda?

Then he straightened his face, as became a family lawyer. "I'm afraid this will come as rather a shock . . ."

"Shock?" said my mother, very hard and quick. "What kind of shock?"

Mr. Makepeace was quietly enjoying himself. Kept on tapping the will, like he was Jimmy Connors about to serve an ace. Like he was a terrorist loading his gun.

"Everything has been left to the grandson." He nodded at me.

"The bloody old *fool*," said my father, savagely.

"We'll see about *that*," said my mother.

"The will is quite valid," said Mr. Makepeace. "He was of sound mind and testamentary disposition. It's not unusual for everything to be left to a *beloved* grandchild."

"He's not old enough," said my mother, as if she was swatting a bluebottle that had dared to enter her beloved fitted kitchen. "He can't be expected to take on such responsibilities."

"Surely we must hold it in trust for him?" said my father.

"The boy is, I think, eighteen?" said Mr. Makepeace.

"This is ridiculous," said my mother. "There *must* be a way . . ."

"No way," said Mr. Makepeace, "to dispossess your own son. The will is very frank. It gives reasons. Would you want those reasons made public?"

My mother flinched. Alpotton's a small town; people gossip. Clients might get to hear: very bad for business.

My parents turned and looked at me. You know that look? The start of World War III? I hope for your sake you don't. My parents knew they couldn't shake Makepeace. So they were about to start on me. All the way home in the car. All the rest of my life, till I gave in. They might even cancel a few appointments so they could go on chewing me over. Even John Victor. Even the horrible Southwarks . . .

"I should like a little time alone with the heir, now, please," said Mr. Makepeace. He really loved himself saying that.

So did I.

My parents blundered out. Like the Wicked Queen and her henchman, from a bad performance of *Snow White and the Seven Dwarfs.*

"Now, young man," said Mr. Makepeace, "how can I be of assistance?"

"Is there a back way out of here?" I said. It was half a joke, a bitter joke. I had no real hope of not being chewed up till the small hours of the morning. I might want to save Spartan. I might want to save Granda's house and things. But I was too weary and sick with misery. I hadn't even had time to say goodbye to Granda. Killed in a second by a hit-and-run driver outside his own cottage gate. Only sixty-seven. Full of life. He could've lived forever.

They'd yell and yell at me, and I'd do what they wanted. In the end. The bitter end.

"Yes, there's a back way out of here," said Mr. Makepeace. "It comes out on the Totton road."

Totton. Where Granda lives. Lived. Four winding country miles and you were there. Parking your bike at the white front gate. Walking up the brick path between the wallflowers. Granda opening the front door. Somehow he always spotted me coming. Spartan coiling around his legs . . .

Never again. Never ever again. Where *are* you, Granda?

"If I might suggest," said Mr. Makepeace respectfully,

"you should secure the cat, Spartan. A neighbor called Mrs. Spivey is feeding him twice a day but . . . arrangements may have been made to dispose of him . . ."

I shot upright. The SPCA might come at any moment. Black Spartan, sitting sunning himself on Granda's front doorstep, all trusting . . .

"Shall I phone for a taxi?" asked Mr. Makepeace.

I ran my hands hopelessly through the pockets of my best, my only suit. "I've got no money . . ."

"I am prepared to advance you something on account. I think that will be in order. Will a hundred pounds do? To be going on with?"

I looked at his nice old face. He twinkled at me; perhaps it was a trick he'd picked up from Granda. I reckoned he knew a lot about the way things were in our family. Granda must've talked to him.

He rang for the taxi, to wait on the Totton road. He got me to sign a few things, then unlocked an old tin box carefully and handed me a thin wad of new bluebacks, with the brown wrapper still around them. Then he gave me a thick stiff folded paper.

"Here's your copy of the will. You won't lose it, will you? And if there's any way I can help further, don't be afraid to give me a ring." He shook hands, in a way that made me feel important. "And remember, Master Tim, possession is nine points of the law . . ."

On the way downstairs, I took a quick look out of the staircase window, at the parental Merc parked outside. My mother and father were still yelling and waving their hands at each other, like two Great White Sharks saying grace before meat.

Then I ran all the way up the back lane. The taxi was waiting on the Totton road.

"Where to, Sunny Jim?" asked the elderly driver.

"Rose Cottage, Totton," I said. "I'm going to live with my grandfather. He's called Bill Wetherby."

I PAID OFF the taxi with the first of my wad of bluebacks, and just for a moment, it seemed true. His immaculate roses shone in the slanting sunlight. There was his spade, still stuck in the earth, at the end of a row of potatoes. His green watering hose was lying coiled on the brick path. And Spartan was sitting on the front doorstep, waiting. He rose, with the stately solemnity of a family butler, and came to greet me.

And then a voice behind me said, "Is this the cat?"

Oh, it was the SPCA all right. The official cap; the official van.

"This is *my* cat," I said.

"I have instructions," he said. "This is Rose Cottage, isn't it? A black cat, answers to 'Spartan'?"

I was glad to have the will, to shove in his face. I jabbed with my finger at the bit about Spartan. He didn't look very convinced, even when I'd finished.

"You look a bit young," he said, doubtfully. So I showed him my driving license, as proof of my identity. I told him to ring my lawyer, Mr. Makepeace. But I couldn't shake him off. I looked about desperately for something to hit him with. A garden rake?

But just then Mrs. Spivey came bustling over from across the road. I explained to her, and showed her the will.

"Put down *Spartan*?" she said in shocked tones. "Old Spartan? That would've broken the good old boy's heart. Who's ordered such wickedness?"

The man consulted his paper. "A Mrs. Wetherby, of Alpotton."

"That woman's a fool," I said. "A meddling trouble-maker. I know her well. A busybody. A troublemaking busybody."

Mrs. Spivey nodded emphatically to everything I said.

"She's not well liked in this village," she added. "Not at all well liked."

The SPCA man said, "Wills—there's always trouble about wills," and finally went off, shaking his head dubiously.

Mrs. Spivey looked at me. "You shouldn'ta said that about your own mother, boy . . ."

"It's true," I shouted a bit, still worked up.

"It's true enough," she said, stubbornly. "But you shouldn'ta *said* it, that's all. You gotta live with her . . ."

"I *haven't*," I shouted.

"What you goin' to do, then, boy?"

AFTER SHE HAD GIVEN ME the keys and gone, I let myself in, called Spartan in after me, and locked the front door and shot both the bolts. Then just stood in the hall, shivering violently.

The grandfather clock ticked on, soothingly. *He* must have wound that clock. The Sunday morning he died. Every Sunday morning in life he wound it, and set it right, because it lost three minutes a week. Soon it would stop, and that would be like another death in the house. I couldn't *bear* it to stop. I took down the key from the shelf at the side of the dial, and wound up the great weights right to the top again.

It seemed a very good thing to do. Were there *other* good things to do? I didn't seem able to think at all; it suddenly hits you like that. I just stood and trembled, trembled and stood, watching the spots of light from the window crawl across the well-polished lino.

I might have stood there forever if Spartan hadn't saved me. He came and asked for his dinner. He always gave that tiny miaow, so tiny in so huge a cat.

I went to the kitchen and fed him and watched him eat. Then it struck me it was time to feed the hens. The hens always got fed after Spartan. But it was a mucky job, and I was in my only decent suit.

A pair of Granda's bib-and-brace overalls were hanging on the back of the kitchen door. I took a deep breath, and took off my suit with a rush, and put on the overalls and his wellies and went and fed the hens. Then the pig. She's called Hettie; she's a breeding pig, and Granda's had her for ages. Granda sold her piglets for fattening, but he always swore Hettie would die in her stall, good old girl. And so she would! I scratched her back when she asked for it, and talked to her, as Granda did. She seemed glad to see me; she was lonely for him, like me.

There was a sense of peace and quiet in the fly-buzzing sunlight. I somehow knew Granda was there, watching. And that he was pleased with me, for feeding all his animals. I felt so much better; I even felt hungry for the first time in a week. I went and got some bacon rashers out of the fridge; a packet *he'd* opened. And a tin of beans off the shelf, and cooked them. Sat in his dungarees, and ate his food at his table. And it felt *great*. I felt so happy I burst out suddenly singing. One of his old songs. One by Sir Harry Lauder.

> *Keep right on to the end of the road, keep right*
> *   on to the end.*
> *Though the way be long, let your heart be strong,*
> *Keep right on round the bend.*
> *Though you're tired and weary, still journey on*

Till you come to your happy abode,
Where all you love and are dreaming of
Will be there at the end of the road.

Then I burst out crying. Jesus, it's terrible having somebody die. You feel you're flying a plane through a thunderstorm with a load of crazy lunatics for passengers.

But old Spartan came and jumped on my knee, and reached up and licked the tears off my nose, as calm as anything. Then settled his huge bulk, with great care for his personal comfort. I stroked him, and it was better again.

It came to me, then, what Granda really wanted me to do. Just keep things running, as they had always been run. So that he could walk in any time, and find everything in its place. That seemed a most perfect ambition.

Then the telephone rang in the hall.

IT WAS MY MOTHER.

"Oh, you're *there*. You've had us worried *sick*!"

"Sick enough for Dad to cancel his squash? Sick enough to cancel the Southwarks?" I really let her have it.

"Don't be offensive. We've canceled *everybody*."

"Tough shit!"

"When are you coming home? Daddy will come and fetch you."

"Tell him not to waste his time. I'm staying here. Looking after things for Granda."

"Don't be silly. You're going to university in six weeks' time!"

"I doubt it."

"Have you taken leave of your senses? What about your future?"

"*Stuff* my future."

"Don't be so silly. What're you going to live on?"

"Granda's money. He left me loads and loads and *loads*."

He hadn't actually. Only about ten thousand in the Building Society. But no need to tell *her* that. Don't miss a chance to really screw her. She screws easy, where money's concerned.

"Listen to me. I am your mother . . ."

"I doubt it . . ."

There was a long, evil silence. Then she said, "I think you've gone *mad*," and hung up.

I gloated for a bit. Then a chill thought struck me. It would be right in their interests to get people to think I *was* mad. Then they could have me certified, and get control of everything again . . . Well, two could play at that game. I looked at my watch. Seven o'clock.

I rang Dr. Marsden at his surgery. He'd been Granda's doctor. And another old mate of his. Got a gift of fresh eggs every week. Came to the funeral.

He told me to come straight down. I went. I knew I was safe for the night: my mother would be "letting me sweat," as she would put it.

Dr. Marsden was great. He let me pour it all out, without saying a word till I was finished.

Then he said, "I don't think you're mad, old chap. Considering what you're going through. Your granda had a saying; it helped him a lot when he lost your grandma. He used to say, 'You get a little stronger every day.' "

"Yeah," I said. "That's sense."

"Anyway," he said, getting to his feet, "make sure you eat all right, and keep busy around the garden. There's probably a lot to do, it's a big garden . . . and see you get your sleep. If you can't get to sleep, come back and I *might* give you something. Come back and see me in a week anyway. Enjoyed the chat with you."

He saw me to his gate. Sniffed the cooling air, and looked at the sunset. "Going to be a fine day tomorrow."

"Good night," I said, feeling a lot better.

"Perhaps I shouldn't say this," he added, and paused. Then he said, "Your grandfather worried a lot about your father. And he worried more after your father married your mother. And he worried a lot about *you*. But I don't think he had much cause to worry about you. Good night."

IT WAS FUNNY, when I got home. Spartan didn't come to meet me. I thought he'd gone out, because he didn't even come when I called. But when I blundered into the dusk of the kitchen, and banged the light on, he was sitting on the old rag rug in front of the hearth. Staring at Granda's chair. Staring and staring. It was so . . . intense . . . I became convinced that Granda was sitting there. To tell you the truth, I didn't like that much. It's one thing to wish for people to come back; it's something else when they do. I mean, I couldn't see him, or hear him. The smell of him was strong, but maybe that was just the things in the kitchen cooling down after a hot day.

It was . . . unbearable. I couldn't *move*. But I couldn't go on standing there forever, or I'd have gone crazy.

It came down to, do I love Granda, or don't I? Alive or dead?

I couldn't bear not to love him. So I took a huge shuddering breath, and went and sat down in his chair.

It was strange. It was like sitting on Granda; it was a bit like sitting on his knee, when I was small. It was a bit like Granda was a cool bath, and I was lowering myself into him. Or he was flooding into me, making us one.

I shuddered once more, and it was done. Maybe Granda and I became one.

Anyway, Spartan seemed pleased. He came and sat on my lap again, purring, the way he used to sit on Granda's lap, every evening.

I fell asleep with Spartan on my knee. And dreamed of Granda. He just walked in the door and I looked up and he grinned at me in his old way. And I said to him, "Hey, I thought you were dead?" And he said, "That's what they all think." And we both laughed, and then he walked out the door again, to see to Hettie, and that was the end of the dream, and I wakened up with a crick in my neck.

It was ten o'clock. Time to go to bed. In Granda's bed, because mine wasn't made up, and I was too tired to start doing it now.

Spartan came with me, and curled up on the counterpane, in his old place, and it was O.K.

I WOKE UP about six, like I always do at Granda's. Because that's when he always got on the move in summer. Dazed, I listened for his stockinged feet creaking downstairs to make a mug of tea. Listened for that little cough he always had in the mornings, because he smoked.

Then it drearily dawned on me that I could lie there forever and there would never be creaking footsteps or that little cough again, and I made myself get up.

But once I got washed I felt half-human and, as the doctor had forecast, it was the beginning of a smashing day, and there *was* a hell of a lot to do in the garden.

And, when Dracula and Mrs. Dracula arrived, it would be best to meet them in the front garden, with the cottage doors locked behind me, and the keys hidden in the place that only Granda and I knew. That way, if they started shouting at me, as they were bound to end up doing, it would be in public, with half the village staring out of their windows, and that would soon put *them* to flight.

So after washing up the breakfast things, and last night's, I went out to the front garden, wearing Granda's wellies and dungarees, his old collarless striped shirt, and his old panama hat with the hole in the crown for good measure.

I started to work out where the old boy had got up to, the day he died. He'd been lifting his potatoes, to store in the little barn. And he would be dealing with the last of his broad beans by now, blanching the end of the crop for his freezer, and piling the stalks onto the bonfire place for burning. I knew exactly what to do; I'd helped him enough as a kid.

I was well on, and sweating, when I heard the Merc draw up, near silently, and the hand brake go on. I went on working, as if I'd heard nothing. My head was down, as I pulled out a potato plant and shook the soil off it, when I heard the gate creak. And then a rather loud gasp, which made me look up.

My father was standing there, clutching the gate with both hands, his knuckles white. His mouth was open, like a fish's when you take it out of water. He was rather a nasty color.

"Hello," I said. "You look like you've seen a ghost . . ."

And then it struck me, of course, that he had. I'm exactly the same tall thin build as Granda, and head down . . .

"Do you mind if I sit down?" he got out at last.

I nodded to the old white garden seat, with the ornate cast-iron ends. He sat down, and I sat down with him, because I was a bit worried, he was such a color. And he didn't seem able to bring himself to say anything.

"Are you on your own?" I asked.

"Your mother's waiting in the car. I thought we might have a quiet word."

Same old trick. In a crisis, my mother plays the tough bullying policeman, and my father plays the kind reasonable policeman. She's very good at it; he's not.

"We can't go on like this, Tim. It's not natural."

"Yes it is. You walked out on Granda. I walked out on you."

He had the grace to flinch. "Your granda and your mother didn't see eye to eye."

"That makes two of us."

"Tim, you don't understand. I was in the middle . . ."

"You didn't stay in the middle long. You walked out on him. You never came to see him. He was your *father*."

"Tim, I couldn't stay here. I had my way to make in the world . . ."

"You made yours. I'll make mine."

"But not going to university . . ."

"It won't sound good at Sunday drinkies, will it?" I said bitterly. "It's one thing, saying your son's at university. Something else, saying your son's a farm laborer."

"You wouldn't . . ."

"Bloody would."

"You're *mad*. Your mother said it was no good trying to talk to you reasonably."

"Well, she was right, then. For once. Run away and tell her I'm not coming home. Not for you. Not for her."

He got up and stalked to the gate, all pseudo-dynamic. Then he sort of turned and crumpled, hanging on to the gate again. "Tim, can't we talk this out sensibly?"

I suppose I was sorry for him.

"Not with *her* hanging around," I said. "Try coming on your own, sometime."

He gave something between a grin and a flinch, and vanished behind my hedge. I didn't envy him, going back a failure.

I braced myself for the real onslaught. But it didn't come. In a few minutes, the Merc roared away, my mother driving. She shot me a look as she passed.

I was expecting the rage; I wasn't expecting the fear.

FOR THE NEXT FEW DAYS, I just fell into Granda's rhythm. I'd been to see him so often, over so many years, that I seemed to know by heart what he'd be doing at any one time. Gathering the last of his greenhouse tomatoes, tying up the leaves of the cauliflowers so the heads didn't go green, dead-heading the roses. He had an old-fashioned cottage garden, that lovely mixture of flowers and vege-tables. I even entered his stuff in the village show, and won quite a lot of prizes. All his doing; none of mine. But people got to know that I was staying on. People started calling, to buy his eggs, to leave him the fresh-shot rabbits and little gifts of fruit they'd always left him. And I gave them the gifts he would have given them, in return.

Nobody in the village thought it strange I was living there. As far as they were concerned, it was Bill Wetherby's place, and quite right that his big grandson should inherit it. What else?

All through that glorious September, my old life faded. I did have the sense to write to my Cambridge college, telling my new tutor that I had inherited my grandfather's house and land, and was too busy seeing to them to go up that year. The tutor wrote me a very civilized letter back, saying I could only mature through being a working landowner for a bit, and to reapply next year if I wanted to. He couldn't have realized that Granda only had an

acre of garden and an acre of orchard, and an acre of
field for Hettie. But he did congratulate me on my A-level
exam results . . .

That was less important than the blackfly on the Brussels
sprouts, which Arthur Digby pointed out, as he daily sat
on Granda's white seat and made sure I was doing things
right. All the old boys in the village seemed set on that. I
didn't mind. I wasn't lonely, I can tell you. I liked it,
because they told me tales about Granda. How in the war
he got dressed up in a white sheet and frightened the
American airmen silly as they lay in the hedgerows with
the village girls. And about Spartan in his youth, when he
bested the Alsatian guard dog from the airfield.

I was even invited to join the Young Farmers Club . . .

Mother never came. But Dad dropped in once or twice.
I took to keeping a few lagers in the fridge for him, and
we sat on the seat in the front garden and drank them,
and never found much to talk about, except how the
turnips were doing.

"See yer dad was up last night," old Arthur would say,
the following morning. "Us all said he'd never settle. Not
like you've done, boy. You'll be thinking o' gettin wed,
soon . . . ?"

I never got a chance to get as settled as that, though.

IT WAS ONE DUSK early in October. I was pulling out
couch grass and ground elder, keeping things tidy, working
by the light of the open front door and the parlor window.
Spartan was watching me closely, pouncing on the showers
of soil as I pulled the weeds up. Then he gave a strange
growl, and stared at the gate. Really, it made my hair
stand on end. I looked up, expecting to see Granda
standing there. You go on expecting things like that.

But there was nothing; only the sound of feet approaching down the village street. Female feet, and not village feet either. Quick nervous feet.

A tall woman looked over the gate; a stranger; I knew everybody now in the village.

I stood up and wiped the soil off my hands on Granda's dungarees. I was wearing my granda set as usual.

She said, "Oh, thank God, you're all right!"

"All right?" I was totally baffled.

"You're the man I nearly knocked down. In August. I just caught a glimpse of the dungarees and the hat as I passed you. Your hat fell off."

"I wasn't here last August," I said. "That must have been my grandfather . . ."

"Is he all right?"

"No. He's dead."

She gave a little cry, and clutched at the gate with both hands. I thought she was going to faint. So I said, "You'd better come in. I'll get you a glass of water."

I was half sorry for her; and half wanted to get her in so I could ask her a lot more questions.

She sat down in Granda's chair, and I got her a glass of water, and she sat holding it, sipping it, and in between, her teeth chattered. I'd never imagined that the hit-and-run driver could look like this. I had always imagined him to be some drunken young punk, somehow. Somebody whose teeth I could knock down his throat, if I ever caught up with him, which seemed unlikely.

"What happened?" she finally asked. "To your grandfather?"

"He was knocked down by somebody who didn't stop, on the 16th of August at about five o'clock. Outside this house."

"Oh, my God," she said, and closed her eyes and clenched her hands so hard around the glass I thought it was going to break.

"What happened," I asked, "to you?"

"I was driving with my window open. A fly got in my eye and I swerved, and I thought I'd just missed a man in dungarees and a white hat like yours. There wasn't a bump or anything. So I just drove on. Then when we got home, my little daughter who was in the back said, 'The man in the white hat fell down.' There was nothing in the news. Or in the papers. But it's been preying on my mind ever since. In the end, I had to come back to make sure. All the way from Birmingham."

"Well, you know now," I said. Really hating her.

I wish I hadn't. Have you ever seen anyone go to pieces? Really go to pieces? Crying so you just can't stop them, no matter what you say, what you do? Being sick? I started off thinking about her going to prison, and I ended up thinking about her going to hospital.

She was quiet after a long time, just dragging in shuddering sobs.

And then Spartan, who had been sitting on the rug beside me, did a damned funny thing. He made that odd growly noise again and leaped on her knee, and licked the tears off her nose. She clutched him, hugging him, her thin tense fingers chafing at his fur like she was almost strangling him. But he just purred and didn't seem to mind.

I knew it was Granda again. Granda forgiving her.

And if Granda forgave her, who was I to point the finger?

So I said, "You didn't hit him much. He only had a little bruise on one knee. But you knocked him off balance and his head hit the curb. The curb killed him. If there'd been no curb, he wouldn't have died."

Her eyes stared at me so. "I must go and tell the police."

Something made me say, "What's the point? He's dead now. That won't bring him back. It wasn't your fault the fly got in your eye. Could've happened to anybody." Anyway, I said it.

We sat a long time, after that. I told her all about Granda, and what a good old boy he'd been, and how everybody missed him. Then I told her a lot of stories about him, including the one where the hare jumped over his head in the harvest field.

And she cried for him. As my father hadn't cried. As my mother hadn't cried. That night was Granda's proper send-off, from the cottage; after the funeral.

Around ten, she rang up her husband, to say she would be staying the night, and we talked on till about two in the morning, making it a proper send-off. Then I showed her up to Granda's bed, and slept on the couch in the parlor.

In the morning, she gave me her address. If I ever changed my mind, she was willing to go to the police.

But I never changed my mind.

I SPENT THE WHOLE WINTER with my grandfather. Getting up in that dark and cold house; breaking the ice in the morning, in the kitchen sink. Reading late by the dying coals of the kitchen range. Feeding the chickens in the snow-covered field. Going up to bed with old Spartan.

And I spent the spring with him. Watching the stuff shooting up in his garden. He had planted some, and I'd planted some, and they came up together, and they were good.

And summer came in, and I began to worry about

Spartan. Nothing you could put your finger on; but he was slower. He slept more, and ate less. He grew thin. I took him to the vet, but the vet just looked at his teeth and asked how old he was.

I didn't know. Ever since I could remember, Spartan had been there.

"Nineteen's a good age for any cat," said the vet. "But keep him warm and give him these vitamins, and you might keep him a while longer yet."

I didn't even miss him, when he finally went. I was lifting the main crop of August potatoes again when Arthur Digby looked over my gate.

"Will you be acoming to look at old Spartan?" he said. "I've just seen the sexton, and sexton says that old Spartan's alyin' on yer grandfather's grave."

I hurried down with him, but I was too late. Spartan was dead, neatly curled up on the mounded turf. Gone, but still warm. I touched the dusty black fur, and cried as hard as I'd done for Granda.

"Sexton said he did often see old Spartan sitting on yer granda's grave. Every morn an' evenin', he said. Looks like yer granda called him home at last."

We got a spade, and buried him secretly with Granda. Though nobody would've minded.

When we got back to the cottage, somehow it was empty. Not just empty, but *empty*. As if Spartan had gone, and so had Granda. I gave Arthur a lager, and had one myself. Giving Spartan his send-off. Telling the old stories . . .

Suddenly Arthur said, out of the blue, "Be you agoing to college this year, boy? Yer granda was always atalking about you goin' on to the college. Powerful proud he was, of you agoing to the college."

It was as if Granda, losing Spartan as his voice, had used Arthur, instead.

It was time to go. I had lived with him for a year, seen the year round, and it was time to go.

And suddenly I was able to give away his things. Arthur was glad to have old Hettie, who he said had many a piglet in her yet. Mrs. Spivey was glad to have a gift of the hens. I gave Arthur his old suits, too. But Arthur brought back a big fat diary that had been in one of the older suit pockets.

I opened it. A diary for 1969, in Granda's small spidery hand. I looked inside, curiously, and saw the phrase, *Worried about the boy* . . .

But I hadn't been *born* in 1969!

Then I realized the boy was my father.

The pages were full of Granda's distress. The boy missed his mother. The boy was restless. The boy rode his motorbike too fast. Went into town too often. Mixed with the wrong kind of girl. Was he being too hard on the boy? Why couldn't he talk to him anymore?

And then the girl was pregnant. The boy must do the honorable thing. Must marry the girl. Must give up college and earn money to keep her. If a girl like that was *worth* keeping . . .

The last entry for the year said, *I have failed. I have failed with them both. The times have changed, and I have not changed with them* . . .

And that was the end.

Well, it was a last job he had given me. The "boy" seemed strangely keen to talk to me. Granda had got me out of the mess at home; now he was asking me to walk back into it.

But with my eyes wide open.

I locked the door of my cottage, and walked via the churchyard to see Granda.

And the cat, Spartan.

BLACKHAM'S
WIMPY

YES, I DO fly in bombers. What's it like, bombing Germany? Do you really want to know? O.K., brace yourself.

Two more pints, please, George.

Well, I expect you've been bombed by Jerry yourself. Plenty of bomb damage around. And there's you, sitting down in your shelter, behind your steel plate and three feet of earth, near wetting yourself and hoping the next bomb hasn't got your number on it. Well, being in a bomber's a bit like that, only the nasty bangs are coming up at you, instead of down.

But that's where any similarity stops. You see, a Wimpy—a Wellington bomber to you—isn't made of steel. It's made of cloth, stretched over a few aluminum tubes, a bit like a tent. If you try hard enough, and sometimes even when you're not trying, you can put your finger straight through the cloth and waggle it in the slipstream outside. So when a shell bursts near you, you can see the shell splinters going right through your fuselage, like a horizontal shower of rain, and out the other side. I suppose I'm lucky, being the wireless operator: I've got two big radio sets to duck behind. Though by the time you've ducked, it's too late anyway.

And suppose you, down your shelter, were sitting on about two tons of TNT just waiting for an excuse to blow up. And about a thousand gallons of petrol, in leaky tins that stink the place out, so you never dare light up a fag, however much you need one. And your air-raid shelter's in a bloody express lift that keeps going up and down without warning, so there's always a smell of spew about the place, even when your skipper's not taking violent evasive action. And you can't breathe properly without a dirty great mask over your face; and when you've got a head cold it's so bloody freezing you have to keep taking off your mask to knock an icicle off your nose.

No, it's not much like what you see in the movies.

And I think wireless ops have the worst job—because I am one. You can't see a thing that's going on, being sat right in the middle of the crate. There's bits of celluloid windows in the side, but they're brown with oil and smoke from the engines—they're never cleaned, not like the windscreen and gun turrets. My oppo, the navigator, even he's got a little astrodome over his head. It's supposed to be for taking directions from the stars—doesn't that sound romantic?—but if he's ever reduced to navigating that way, we're really in trouble. He just uses it for being nosy, so he can add his two pennyworth on the intercom.

Because it's the intercom that keeps us sane. You see, in a bomber, the only thing you can hear is the noise of the engines; it blots out even the racket of bursting flak. And you get so used to it, it gets to seem like silence—unless one of the engines starts to pack up; then you notice fast enough. But otherwise, when you're over target, you can see bomb bursts and shell bursts and flak trails and even another crate buy it, and it's just like a silent movie, especially with your ears muffled up inside your helmet. But there's always the good old intercom, and all the lads yakking down it and even cracking mad jokes and laughing till the skipper shuts them up, like a teacher with a rowdy class. And it makes you feel not alone. And a good skipper keeps asking you every few minutes if you're O.K. and that helps, too.

My job's all listening, not looking. I have my eyes shut most of the time; might as well be blind. That's an idea, isn't it: blind wireless ops—save the fit men for the Army? Anyway, as I said, my job's listening. I've got two radio sets: RT and WT. WT's for long distance; Morse code only. It gives us directions from the top brass, like old Butcher Harris sitting on his arse at High Wycombe. And the only thing he'll tell you is to pack up and come home, 'cause the cloud's too thick to see the target, or maybe Fatty Göring's not at home that night 'cause he's sleeping at his auntie's. Now, that's a little signal not to miss; if you do, you'll find yourself doing a solo raid on Berlin. Oh, I know that sounds great, like something out of the *Boy's Own Paper*, but actually it's not, 'cause all over Europe there are little Jerry night fighters sitting on their little nests of radar, just waiting for you to fly over slow as the morning milk cart. That's why we have these thousand-bomber raids: so Jerry'll have so many to think about, he'll run around in circles like a kid with presents on Christmas Morning. Safety in numbers—if they're chopping some other poor sod, they're not chopping you. So I listen carefully for that little WT signal, which is not easy when the skipper's taking evasive action and the engines are doing their best to take thirty-six hours' leave of absence from the wings, and our guns are going full blast, and everyone's talking on the intercom at once. They're not supposed to, but try and stop them when the balloon's going up.

That's all about the WT, except you never use it. Jerry would get a fix on you in a flash; then you'd have company. Only time you use it is if you ditch in the sea coming home. Then you send out Mayday on five hundred kilo-cycles and hold the Morse key down for thirty seconds to give them a fix on you. Trouble is, everybody's listening on five hundred kilocycles—air-sea rescue, German air-sea rescue, U-boats . . . take your pick. I've heard of lads freezing to death in the sea while two lots of silly buggers were fighting over them.

The RT—intercom in all your war movies—is a worry, too. You've got to keep the volume just right, see, so no one outside the crate hears a squeak. Turn the knob too far—easy enough done, wearing icy gloves—and Himmler can hear you fart. I'm not shooting a line, honest!

So what keeps us going? Actually, we get a lot of laughs. Remember the time you and me were outside Beaky's study waiting to be caned, and we couldn't stop laughing? Well, it's like that all the time, almost. And we've got Dadda. Dadda's a great guy for laughs. Who's Dadda? the child asks. Dadda's our skipper—the big boss man. Dadda's like God, only cleverer. Dadda has changed my life, the way God never did. I remember the first time we saw him.

WE ARRIVED at Lower Oadby one January dusk in '43. Flying Wimpy III's. Just the five of us, no Dadda then. The adjutant hadn't time to bother with us—there was an op on that night—so he just shoved us into a barracks room with the crew of L-Love. L-Love were a bloody good crew—done twenty-two ops, but they weren't big-headed about it. They taught us a lot while they were getting kitted up. Things like always flying dead in the middle of the bomber stream because the Jerry fighters always nibbled at the edges. They weren't much older than us and made us laugh a lot, though we did wonder a bit why they looked so pale and sweaty; the barracks wasn't all that warm. And their rear gunner was chewing gum so hard his muscles kept standing out in knots all along his jaw. Anyway, they barged out saying don't do anything in Lower Oadby they wouldn't do. If you've seen Lower Oadby that's a big joke.

"They're O.K.," said Matt, our only pilot, and we drifted across into their half of the barracks room, inspecting their pinups and the photos of their girlfriends stuck on their lockers and touching their spare lucky silk stockings and rabbits' feet. Not being nosy; just looking and touching so that a bit of their luck would rub off on us. They'd shot down a Messerschmitt 110, a twittish night fighter that had flown slowly past them in the dark without even noticing they were there. Apparently it had blown up like the Fourth of July, and one of its prop blades had lodged in L-Love's main spar without hurting anybody. Battered and rusting, it now hung over their skipper's bunk.

The hut was quiet and peaceful. We stoked up the stove till its stovepipe glowed cherry-red halfway to the ceiling, and we all snored off like babes.

The barracks room door banged open with a gust of snow at four in the morning. Somebody shoved on all the lights.

"Good shopping trip?" shouted Billy the Kid, our rear gunner, always first with a wisecrack. We all sat up.

It wasn't them. It was three stupid-looking RAF police with snow on their greatcoats. Carrying big canvas sacks in each hand. They didn't say a word to us, just started grabbing all L-Love's kit and golf clubs and spare rabbits' feet and stuffing them into the sacks. Ripping down the pinups off the lockers.

"Hey!" shouted Matt. "What the hell you doing?"

One of the police turned to him, his face blank as a Gestapo thug's just before he pulls the trigger. "They got the chop," he said. "Tried to land at Tuddenham and overshot the runway." He turned away and began throwing stuff into his bags with renewed vigor. None of them looked at us again. We sat up in bed in our striped pajamas, hating them. Until they tried to take the prop blade off the wall. Then Matt was out of bed in a flash.

"Leave that alone. That's ours."

The policeman reached for the blade.

"It's ours, I tell you!" screeched Matt. "They *gave* it to us."

"Yeah," we all yelled. "They *gave* it to us."

The policeman shrugged. He knew we were lying. But Matt's a big lad and he was mad as hell. They finished stuffing stuff into bags and left, jamming off the lights.

"Bastards," said Matt, getting back into bed.

"They're only doing their job," said Kit, the navigator. "I don't expect they like doing it, over and over again."

"Some guys enjoy being undertakers . . ."

Nobody said anything for some time. Then, in the dark, Kit said, "They were a good bunch. I'm glad they all went together." Which was a pretty bloody stupid thing to say, but what isn't bloody stupid on that kind of occasion?

Billy the Kid went out to the bogs and was very sick. We listened. In a way he was being sick for all of us; saved us getting out of bed.

We kept the prop blade a week, then threw it away. It

sort of filled the whole hut, like the evil eye of the little
yellow god. We never tried interfering with those policemen again, except once.

NEXT MORNING, they ran us down to the dispersals to see
our new crate, C-Charlie. She really was brand-new, which
was funny. They normally give green crews the clapped-
out old crates. Why waste a good bomber on a mob who
are five times more likely to get shot down than anybody
else?

It was bloody freezing, even wearing two sets of long
johns and a greatcoat. We mooched around her, kicking
things and grumbling; feeling totally unreal and farting
and belching all over the crate and giggling every time.
Does that shock you? It was partly, I suppose, to show
how we felt about everything, and partly to try and get
something hard and solid out of our guts which would
never go away again. You probably know, that's the way
fear feels. And Billy the Kid kept bleating plaintively about
who the other pilot would be.

"Me," said Matt. "There is no other pilot. They're trying
to *save* pilots."

"If they blew this bloody crate up now, they could save
a navigator as well. And a wireless op and two air gunners
and a lot of petrol." Kit was the real joker, even then. Life
and soul of the party. Only, his big blue eyes were starey
that morning, the whites showing all around like they
seldom have since.

We dropped back onto the tarmac.

"I always wanted to be a land girl," said Matt. Since he
was six foot two and the only one of us who had to shave
every day, it was *quite* funny.

We stood and talked and froze. We found out that a
year ago we'd all been in the sixth form. We found out

that Matt had been the top pilot of his course, and Kit top
navigator. Mad Paul, the front gunner, and Billy the Kid
were top stuff, too—reaction times like greased lightning.
(They played a stupid game involving slapping each other's
hands; anyone else who joined in always lost, and it really
hurt . . .) Only I was mediocre. I had passed out halfway
down the wireless ops' list.

Still we stood. Were we all there was? Was Matt's horrible
idea coming true? Did we have to take this thing to
Germany on our own?

Just then a thirty-hundredweight truck drove up. A pair
of long, thin legs emerged from the cab, stooped shoulders,
and a cap pushed back to display a wrinkled forehead and
balding nut. He didn't look at us; he walked across to
C-Charlie with the precarious dignity of a heron hunting
frogs. We gaped at the apparition. His uniform, which
carried wings and a flight lieutenant's rings, was thin and
gray as paper.

"Look at that uniform," said Matt, not bothering to
lower his voice. "He's got some time in."

"Probably in the pay office," said Kit.

"You can make blues look like that over a weekend,"
said Billy. "Bit of bleach in the water, and a razor blade
to scrape the fluff off . . ."

The apparition kicked the starboard tire violently,
stalked on, and began doing a Tarzan act on the starboard
flaps. The Wimpy is a pretty whippy, flexible sort of plane.
Some pilots compare flying one to lying in a hammock;
others, to making love to a woman. The steering column
keeps nudging your chest, the engines nod up and down
in a regular rhythm, and the wingtips actually flap in
flight. This guy had the whole plane rocking in motion,
the way he was thumping hell out of her.

"Shall I go and tell him it's government property?" asked

Matt. We all got those stupid giggles again. The apparition
ignored us, until he had given the tail wheel a final kick.
Then he walked over to us.

He knew we'd been taking the mickey. He found us
amusing.

"Let's get you into your bunny suits," he said, "and see
if this thing flies." We bundled into the back of his thirty-
hundredweight, all except Matt, who he kept with him in
the front. All I will say about the way he drove is that I
was sick halfway back to the billet. Of course, I was sitting
over the exhaust . . .

"If he flies like he drives," said Kit, "we won't make the
coast."

"The German coast?" I gasped, pulling my head back
in over the tailboard.

"The English coast," said Kit.

NEW FLYING KIT has a life of its own. It makes you feel
like a giant panda, trussed up for its journey to the zoo.
It trails things that wrap around any knob or lever available; it makes you a yard wide so you knock things off
shelves that you think are miles away. Passing anybody
else in the confines of a Wimpy is like dancing with a
stuffed bear. You feel sweaty and cut off from everything.

Dadda's gear wasn't like that. He had battered all the
life out of it; it fitted him like a second skin. In places it
was creased and wrinkled like rhinoceros hide; in other
places it was worn smooth and shiny. There were great
dirty patches near the most-used pockets. He looked more
like a decrepit heron than ever.

We took off smoothly and easily. Piece of cake, I thought.
Then he told me I had too much volume on the intercom,
though I don't know how the hell he knew. Then he told

Kit he talked too much. I was still laughing silently about that when the WT set hurled itself violently into my side; lots of painful knobs, too. Next second, I was dangling, helpless in the middle of the fuselage on the end of my safety harness. Next second, I got the distinct impression I was hanging upside down. Certainly three pencils and a map shot up in front of my face.

I was sick again, and now there was no tailboard to lean out over. Farther forward, the Elsan toilet broke loose with a terrific clatter and came sailing past my head. Thank God it was empty. First I thought my last moment had come, then I hoped it had. When I got myself together a bit, Dadda told me to turn the intercom up. I was just reaching for the knob when the world turned upside down again. I heard Kit say, in a dreamy voice, "He *can't* fly upside down at zero feet." Kit had somehow strapped and braced himself so he could look out of the astrodome. "I can see ducks sitting in mud over my head." His face was lit up like a child's at a fun fair. After that, all I did was to keep my eyes shut, play with the intercom knob, and try to keep my guts inside me. And listen to Kit's running commentary.

"I think we're strafing Spalding . . .

"Two cars have just crashed . . .

"He's knocked three bricks off a factory chimney . . .

"We're flying down a canal—below the level of the banks . . ."

Mind you, I wouldn't swear to the truth of any of it. Kit always shot a line, given the least chance. But it *felt* like it. And there was a lump of bracken caught in our closed bomb doors afterwards that even Kit couldn't have faked.

We finally reached the ground and crawled out. Dadda began belting hell out of the crate again, this time in the

company of the ground-crew sergeant, and not sounding
too pleased.

"He can fly," said Matt judiciously. "But only Spitfires."

"Can't you tell him this one's got two engines?" added
Billy plaintively.

"He's mad," said Mad Paul. That, from Mad Paul, was
approval.

"I don't know what he does to the enemy," said Kit,
"but by God he frightens me." He lit a Woodbine and did
his impersonation of an aircrew recruiting poster, a foot
nonchalantly on the Wimpy's undercart as if he'd shot it
himself.

I was sick again, over the undercart, and his foot. It was
the only comment I could make. All those silly buggers'
eyes were shining, as if it was Christmas. Already they
were calling the flight the Battle of Spalding.

I set my mind to finding out more about this nut of a
pilot. I wanted to know who was killing me.

HIS NAME WAS TOWNSEND. He was an Irishman, a
Dubliner. Spoke that lovely clear English that only a certain
type of Irishman speaks. When he said "the Castle" he
meant Dublin Castle. He was a Catholic; drove (like the
devil) every Sunday morning to an ugly little yellow-brick
Catholic church in Wisbech. It was the only thing he didn't
joke about. They said he'd spent two years at Maynooth,
intending to be a priest and then a monk. But he'd left,
saying it made the years too long. That's why they started
calling him Father Townsend, which got shortened to
Dadda. At least, that was the story. Maybe they only called
him Dadda because he was so much older than the rest of
us. Thirty-five if he was a day.

After Maynooth, he seemed to have drifted. He taught

English in some kind of left-wing free school in Germany,
till the Nazis closed it down. He'd seen Hitler before Hitler
became famous; talked about him with neighborly Irish
spite as a busy, worried little man in a crumpled, belted
raincoat. Somehow, that cut Hitler down to size for us.
Later, Kit started the "Paddy O'Hitler" craze that was
unique to C-Charlie, though other crews tried copying us.
Night fighters became Paddy O'Hitler's chickens. Bremen
docks, on fire, became Paddy O'Hitler's rickyard.

"Rickyard's well alight tonight, Dadda!"

"Maybe Paddy won't be able to pay this quarter's rent."

"Maybe the great landlord in the sky will evict him."

"Chicken dead astern, Dadda."

"Wring its bloody neck," said Dadda dreamily, as he fell
down the sky in his famous corkscrew, and the Elsan broke
loose again. Half-full this time, and everybody laughing
like drains. Over a silly childish game. But, op by op, the
game kept us laughing, kept us alive. And maybe Billy did
wring a couple of chicken's necks.

After he'd lost his German job, Dadda seemed to have
drifted on around the English Catholic schools, teaching
languages. Never staying long. Until the war came, and
he learned to fly. This was his third tour of ops. You only
had to fly one. Most crews didn't last half a tour before
they got the chop. People said Dadda'd survived because
he didn't care if he lived or died; that was the way things
went. People said that when the war was over, there'd still
be one Wimpy flying over Europe in the dark, with Dadda
at the controls, wondering where the war had gone to.
They said he was mad as a hatter, flew like a lunatic.

They didn't know him. Actually, he didn't miss a trick.
Every day we polished the perspex of our own turrets and
windscreens, and he inspected them. "A fingerprint's

bigger than a night fighter, acushla. We don't want chickens hiding behind fingerprints."

On a raid, he always flew dead in the middle of the bomber stream. But at his own chosen height, which never appeared in Air Ministry Regulations: 3,800 feet. That's a very healthy height. The light flak's lost its sting, and the heavy flak—the 88s and 102s—is unhappy and slow. And any night fighter has got the ground and church steeples on hills to worry about, as well as you. Especially if it tries to attack from underneath, which is a favorite stinking little trick.

Besides, 3,800 feet gave Mad Paul the chance to have a crack with his front guns at the light-flak gunners and the searchlight crews. I dare say it didn't do Jerry much harm, but it did Paul a lot of good. Gave him something to do; left him no time to think. Time to think you do not need; people die of it. Dadda kept everybody busy. He let Matt really fly the crate, once he knew how. Didn't just leave him sitting and sweating like a stuffed duck, which happens to some second pilots. Kit was kept busiest of all: new readings, new courses, hot coffee all round; it suited him. Dadda even found something for me.

"I've got you a new box of tricks, acushla. A little beauty called Tinsel." Tinsel was a third radio, which I could use to search out the Jerry fighter-control network. There was a crawling fascination in hearing the voices from Tomtit and Bullfinch, earnest German voices trying so hard to shoot us down. Then, at the crucial moment, I could black out their transmission by sending them the sound of our starboard engine, neatly recorded by a microphone in the engine nacelle. God, it made those Jerries hop and swear. I tell you, and I'm not shooting a line, I've got the best collection of German obscenities in the RAF.

"How did you know I spoke German, Dadda?"

"Read it up in your records, acushla, before you were a twinkle in Groupie's eye . . ."

We had a private joke, too—Dadda and I. Any time a night fighter got on our tail, I was to shout, "You stupid dummkopf, Otto, can't you see I'm a Heinkel in disguise?"

I think it was when he first suggested this, and I laughed till I was nearly sick, that Dadda became a kind of God, even to me.

THE BUSINESS about Blackham's Wimpy started the night we raided Krefeld, at ops tea. Ops tea is the special meal they give you before you go over Germany. Best meals we ever got. Usually a heap of bacon and fried bread and two whole precious fried eggs. Trouble is, even if you're in a good mood, you keep thinking, the condemned man ate a hearty meal; and if you're feeling rotten, you feel you're a pig being fattened up for slaughter. The fried bread turns to sawdust in your mouth, the fried eggs turn to glue, and the edges of the crispy bacon start burrowing into the lining of your stomach. But you get your ops tea down somehow. It may be the last thing you touch before you do your flaming-torch act; except for a face wash of lukewarm coffee, halfway across the North Sea.

Crews sit together at ops tea, always. Even if they hate each other the rest of the time. Everybody's life depends on everybody; there's no room for hate. Love, or you're a dead duck. Instant Christianity. Did you know, someone actually wrote a book for aircrews called *God Is My Co-Pilot?* You used to find copies in the bogs, with half the pages gone. Anyway, crews sit together. And they're either very noisy or very quiet. If they're quiet, people reckon they're on the chop list. We do a lot of wondering who's on the chop list. Certain barracks huts lose crew after crew. Falling in love is fatal. There was one gorgeous WAAF in the parachute store; none of us would even speak to her. Anybody who looked twice at her got the chop.

Anyway, this night we were sat next to Blackham's lot. We didn't like Blackham's lot, though, looking back, I can see that the only thing really wrong with them was Blackham. Colin Blackham, their skipper. Blackham the bastard. In Civvy Street, he was a Yorkshire hill farmer, a real Yorkshire tyke. Pig-ignorant and hard with it, with a hill farmer's attitude to life and death. Would send his granny to the knacker's yard, if the price was right. Bradford Grammar had dragged him through school certificate, and he never forgave them for it. Well over thirty, nearly as old as Dadda, he was still only a flight sergeant, and he made a loud-mouthed virtue of it. Always started arguments with "Well, I'm only a flight sergeant, but . . ." And every time you saw him he was arguing. Horrible sober and worse drunk. A long, bony jaw and a big nose and beady dark eyes, and a hill farmer's broken veins in his cheeks, and black hair that escaped the Brylcreem after five minutes and stood out all over his head in greasy spikes. He always wore a filthy white polo-neck sweater that not only showed under his BD top but came down nearly to his knees. The best thing about him was, he was pretty small. A little bullock who would always settle a logical argument with his fists, if he was losing. Even after what happened to him, I still hate him.

As I said before, Blackham's lot were next to us and making even more noise than usual. They all mimicked Blackham, like we all mimicked Dadda. They were discussing that stupid Air Ministry instruction about machine-gunning farm animals on the way back from raids. To undermine Adolf's war effort. Of course, most crews ignored the instruction. We all had a shrewd idea what we were doing to women and children in the German cities, but we didn't have to look at it, and we didn't talk about it either. But being told to kill horses and cows in broad daylight . . . Anyway, if it was light enough and you were low enough to shoot at farm animals, you'd better save your ammo for the fighters.

Dadda hated the idea, and, being Dadda, mocked it. He worked out it cost us more for the ammo than it cost Adolf for the cow, and Adolf got to eat the cow anyway. But Blackham's lot loved the idea; went in for it (if you could believe them) in a big way. Last time out, they said, they shot at a Belgian girl herding cows and not only killed the cows but her dog as well *and* made her dive into a ditch so fast, they saw the color of her knickers. By now Blackham's face was red and sweating. His noise was stirring up the whole mess hall. Some tables were giving him dirty looks, others were starting to tap out Morse code with their knives and forks, or gouging bloody great chunks out of the tabletops. It was unbearable.

So I said, "Aah, shut your face, Blackham." Loud enough for everyone to hear. Next second I wished to hell I hadn't.

There was a horrible silence. Blackham turned to me slowly.

"Did you say something to me, son?"

I couldn't open my mouth.

"No," said Dadda, "I did. I requested you to shut your face, Flight Sergeant Blackham."

Blackham looked from one to another of us, baffled. He wasn't stupid; he knew who'd said it. But he was frightened of a trap.

"Yes," said Kit. "I distinctly heard our honorable skipper

request you nicely to shut your face, *Sergeant* Blackham. Is that not so, gentlemen?" He turned to us.

"Yeah," said Billy.

"Beyond any reasonable doubt," said Matt.

"Indubitably," said Mad Paul.

Blackham got to his feet with a heave that sent his mob scattering. Dadda sat still, laughing at him. One poke at Dadda, and the squadron would have lost Blackham for good. The noise of drumming fists and knives and forks from the other tables was thunderous.

"Flight Lieutenant Townsend. A word with you!" And there was Groupie, smiling his smile of pure ice. Groupie was a hero; bagged four Jerries, they said, in World War I. Didn't use his single synchronized Vickers gun—*froze* them out of the sky with his famous smile. Anyway, he came across and put his arm around Dadda's shoulders and held a perfectly fatuous conversation about the stirrup pump and fire buckets in "B" flight office. Somebody down the mess hall gave a loud snore; but when Groupie looked up, the wise lad was finishing off his eggs.

KREFELD WAS NO WORSE than usual. The PFs—pathfinders—seemed to have stayed sober for once and had dropped a new kind of marker: a bright red ring of fires that even the incompetent were able to get their bombs into. There was a smell of burning silk and disturbed chemicals in our share of the atmosphere over the target. Better than the Sunday-lunch smell you get from burning city centers. Matt saw a Lancaster buy it overhead; a shell from a 102 blew its wing off. We were glad it was a Lanc, and not anybody we knew. Those toffee-nosed bastards actually cheer when they hear we're on a raid with them. We're sent in first, you see, and we fly slower and lower, so we're easier targets. I mean, a Lanc can carry five times our bomb load, so why do they send us at all, except as bait for the flak and fighters?

On the way home we met clouds, thank God. It had been a clear sky all the way to Krefeld, and a three-quarters moon, and we'd felt as if we were doing a striptease in Adolf's front garden.

Now, skippers react differently to clouds. Some get inside and stay inside, even when the clouds are cumulonimbus. The buffeting inside cu-nim can bash a damaged plane to bits, and all that static electricity doesn't exactly mix with a crate full of petrol fumes . . . And you might meet somebody you know inside. A Wimpy's wingtip can kill you just as dead as a cannon shell. And the fighters can still track you on their radar and jump you when you come out blind.

Other skippers fly up the cloud canyons, as visible as a black fly on a tablecloth. O.K., black night fighters are easily spotted, too, but who's biggest and most visible, and who's looking for whom?

Dadda sort of flirted with the clouds; up and down the slopes, around the pinnacles, in and out like a flipping skier. It was fascinating and almost *cleansing*, after the flames and smell at the target. A bit like having a cold shower after a rugby match. Not a soul in sight; might as well be flying over the North Pole.

But believe me, Dadda wasn't flirting with the clouds to refresh his soul. Unless we were getting a star fix, Dadda never flew in a straight line for ten seconds at a time. They said he'd once scrounged a ride with RAF Beaufighters and knew just what makes a night fighter careworn; besides, he said his constant stunting kept the crew awake. It's fatally easy to doze off, once you've left the target, and many a poor rear gunner has departed this life lost in a frozen dream of hot crumpet. Other idiots play dance music on their WT . . .

"Dadda, you're getting too far south—out of stream. Steer three-ten."

Dadda banked to starboard, and there was a twitchy silence on the intercom, apart from Billy muttering, "Nothing . . . nothing . . . nothing," to himself as he swung the rear turret from side to side.

"We bring nothing into this world," said Kit, making eyes at me over his oxygen mask. "And it is certain we shall take nothing out." Honestly, that kid would roller-skate around the jaws of hell, laughing.

"Shut up," said Dadda.

"Wimpy at three o'clock," said Billy. "Beneath you." It was lucky he said, "Wimpy," and not "crate" or "kite," because before he could have corrected his mistake Dadda would have corkscrewed down a thousand feet, and we'd have lost the Elsan again. I stuck my head up into the astrodome alongside Kit's. Dadda was banking the crate to get a good look, so we got a good look, too.

"S-Sugar," said Matt.

"Blackham," said Mad Paul. "Seven hundred bombers out tonight and we have to get Blackham."

"Anyone watching the rest of the sky?" asked Dadda sharply.

There *was* something compelling, eye-catching, about that black Wimpy stooging straight up the cloud canyon, its big squadron letters glinting in the moonlight, its blue moon shadow skating across the cumulus below.

"Looks like a ghost ship . . . like the *Mary Celeste*," I said out loud.

"What d'you expect them to be doing—holding a candlelight dance?" said my good and honored oppo.

On and on we flew, three hundred yards apart. It was protection of a sort. If a night fighter found us, he couldn't attack both at once. Raised the odds to fifty-fifty. I saw the other Wimpy's rear turret swing toward us once or twice, winking in the moonlight. Whether he was just keeping a good watch, or putting up the two fingers of scorn at us . . . Dadda was still dodging in and out of the clouds. We kept losing and finding Blackham. I had a terrible temptation to turn up the intercom and say something to them.

People have died for less.

But it was company in a way, in all that empty sky. If I'd been pilot, I'd have wanted to huddle close.

People have died for less.

"This astrodome makes your ears bloody cold," said Kit, and went back to his navigator's table, leaving me to it. We could fly on and on forever, under the moon, I thought. Across the Atlantic and breakfast in America. If the fuel held out . . . which it wouldn't.

It was a moment before I saw it; and another moment when I didn't believe my eyes; then a moment when the blood pounded into my head and I sweated all over. Blackham's Wimpy had *two* blue shadows now, flitting beneath it on the cloud floor. How could a Wimpy have two shadows, when there weren't two moons?

Then one of the two shadows, the smaller one, changed its angle and began to climb up beneath Blackham, rising like a ghostly shark out of the cloud depths. Then the cockpit of the shadow glinted, and I saw it for what it was: a Junkers 88. The one the Germans call "Owl": mottled blue-gray skin, the bristling nose whiskers of the Lichtenstein radar, the twin black muzzles of the upward-pointing *Schrage Musik* cannons behind the cockpit. Nearer and nearer it climbed, toward the soft underbelly of the Wimpy. I croaked. I whimpered.

I banged the intercom wide open and yelled, "Black-ham—corkscrew port—fighter below you!"

Blackham didn't need telling twice. His bomber turned into a great black cross as he banked before diving. Even then I thought he was too late. A sudden thread of golden fire tied Junkers and Wimpy together like an umbilical cord; from the tail of the Wimpy to the center section of the Junkers. But when the flames came, they blossomed from the Junkers. Blackham's twist to port must have brought the Junkers momentarily into the field of fire of his rear turret. The turret guns must have been pointing in the right direction by sheer chance, and the gunner touched his buttons as a nervous reflex to something so close. Pure fluke. But enough. Next second, Blackham was cartwheeling down the sky in his defensive corkscrew like an insane crow. And the Junkers was describing a beautiful parabola of flame upward.

I still don't understand what happened next. I don't think my opening up of our intercom alone could have caused it. I can only think it was some kind of electronic hiccup. But suddenly our intercom was full of alien voices.

"I got the bastard! I *got* him!" That was Geranium, Blackham's rear gunner.

"You sure?" Blackham's voice, tense and very Yorkshire-tyke.

"Sure I'm sure. See him burn!"

Wild cheers from Blackham's lot.

Then a German voice. "Bullfinch Three to Bullfinch. Abandoning aircraft. Port wing on fire. Get the hatch open, Meissner! Meissner, get the hatch open. Ritter, help him!"

We listened, appalled, as the Junkers continued to burn and continued to fly wildly across half the sky, somehow keeping pace with us, arching its beautiful parabolas of fire.

"Meissner, Ritter! What's holding you up? Are you dead?"

The Junkers, by some trick of fate, was now flying almost level with us, almost parallel. So we saw the flames from the wing creep up the fuselage, and the cockpit canopy shrivel away under its licking. And the orange-lit face of the pilot staring at us, out of the flames, aghast.

Then the Junkers was gone, falling, falling.

"Watch the rest of the sky," said Dadda automatically. But none of us could tear our eyes away from the Junkers below. Because that was when the flames must have reached him.

He screamed. It should have been his death scream. But then the flames must have let go of him again, as a cat lets go a half-dead mouse. We could hear him whimpering as the Junkers, incredibly—flying like a singed moth, a half-swatted fly—climbed slowly back to our level.

This time, he noticed us. Maybe he blamed us for all his troubles. He made a frenzied attempt to ram us, screaming, "*Heil Hitler! Sieg Heil, Sieg Heil, Sieg Heil.*" At least, I think it was that, among the bubblings from his burned nose and mouth and lungs. He sounded more like a half-slaughtered animal than a man; except nobody would ever do that kind of thing to an animal.

Dadda, half-paralyzed for once by the approach of that terrible apparition, took evasive action just in time. The Junkers' slipstream batted us down the sky; we felt his heat and smoke billowing in through every nook and cranny; and that awful smell, just a hint, or maybe I only imagined it. Over the intercom, Blackham's lot were still laughing—laughing at him, laughing at us.

"Burn, you bastard, burn!"

Unbelievably, the Junkers began to overtake us again. Christ, he might blow up at any moment, wrapping us in a shroud of red-hot gas that would be his fuel and his glycol and his ammo and his flesh. I pulled my chute to me and began clipping it on. We were always more afraid of fire than anything else in those old cloth bombers. Especially of our own chutes catching fire, so that when we baled out we flared up like comets. He still kept after us. He was rambling in his mind, now. Calling on his radar controller one minute, his mother the next.

"Mutti, Mutti." Telling his mother he didn't have a left hand anymore, that his charred fingers had broken off on the control column. Three times, in between the flames catching him, he gave his name, rank, and number, clear as clear: "73794 Leutnant Gehlen, Dieter Ernst."

Once he cried, "My eyes, my eyes!"

And all the time, in the background, Blackham's lot were laughing. (I heard afterwards that Dadda told me three times to turn down the intercom, and I never even heard him.)

He blew up at last, well below us and about a mile behind. Long trails of pink and white burning stuff shot in every direction, as if someone had set off a bundle of Guy Fawkes fireworks. Then the sky was black, till the moon returned to our senses.

"Get that intercom turned down, Gary. I'm tired of telling half Germany where I am."

"Yes, Dadda." We had been flying three minutes on a straight course, sending out radio signals clear as lighthouse beams. We were *dead*. Dadda went into the steepest dive I have ever been in. We fell like a stone. I thought we would never pull out; I thought we were mortally hit, though I hadn't heard a sound.

We came home at zero feet, and, until we cleared the Belgian coast, on petrol-guzzling full boost. Zero feet with Dadda meant just that; I saw at least three church steeples flick by overhead. It felt better that way. When you're high up, you feel big as a haystack and slow as a cow. At zero feet, you feel powerful, like a crazy, souped-up racing car. We were almost part of the ground. Smells of the earth wafted through the fuselage for a second, and were gone. You always get your share of the local atmosphere in a Wimpy. And the smells were a sort of sad comfort: the sharp tang as Dadda clipped the tips of a pine forest, then the rich smell of pig farm. Once, enough to make you cry, the safe, warm smell from an early-working Belgian bakery. We saw no more fighters; none saw us. Perhaps they were all chasing Blackham. Maybe there was still some justice in the world, ha-ha. Two miles beyond the coast, a flak ship opened up on us with tracer; red and green balls, very pretty, very slow-curving, then accelerating alarmingly. Here's ours, I thought. Here we go to join Gehlen at the gates of hell. But they'd misjudged our range or speed. The tracers passed miles behind us.

When we landed at Lower Oadby, S-Sugar was already standing in her dispersal pan. And the debriefing hut was swamped with the noise of Blackham's lot. You always get a horrible tot of RAF rum at debriefing; it smelled and sounded as if Blackham's lot had joined the rum queue several times each. They had simply flown home, without taking any evasive action. Four times they'd been attacked by fighters, but, according to Blackham, they'd been "waiting for the little bastards, just waiting for them." They were claiming two more kills, and were giving the little WAAF who was debriefing them a hell of a time.

"Here's a lovely lad'll confirm one," said Blackham, grabbing both my cheeks between his fingers and thumbs.

"He gave it to me, didn't you, me lovely lad? Ah was going to *nail* thee, but now us is quits. When tha tell the young lady Ah roasted one o' them bastards over a slow fire." I was sick all down his flying jacket; and I was never less sorry about anything in my life. I blundered out of the debriefing hut; the light and heat and the noise were like some Viking feast . . . I'd heard that all Yorkshire tykes were Vikings in the beginning.

Dawn was just starting to break; the runways, the parked Wimpys were like pencil scrawls on a lavatory wall: meaningless garbage. How ungrateful can you get, I thought. Dadda's brought us home by a miracle, and I'm not even glad. Because tomorrow night, or the next, or the next, we shall be going back to do it all over again. Anyway, I wasn't home on the airfield; I was still sitting in that burning cockpit with Gehlen. He had sounded about our age . . . I was back with Gehlen, over and over and over again. Life had stopped with Gehlen, like a faulty gramophone record that keeps the needle jumping back to the same place and repeating the same tune. Bugger the Germans and the British. There were just those who flew three miles high on a load of petrol and explosives, and those who didn't. That was the real difference: those who flew and those who sent them.

I realized the lads had gathered around me, silently in their soft flying boots. We looked at each other, then looked away. Gehlen was in Matt's eyes, in Kit's, in Billy's eyes that looked like burned holes in a white sheet. We'd had it. We were on the chop list and we knew it, just as we'd been before Dadda arrived.

"Let's go and hunt up some ham and eggs," said Dadda. It wasn't an invitation; it was an order. We piled listlessly into the thirty-hundredweight, and he drove off, slowly.

It was very quiet crossing the Fens; the trees were the faintest possible silhouettes, the sky was flushing a pale pink, nothing like Krefeld, and the birds were just starting to sing. We passed an old farmhand, who wobbled on his bike in our slipstream, but waved just the same. And, slowly, the miracle happened, as it had happened before. The birdsong began to seep into our minds, then the silhouettes of the trees, like water seeping into a leaky old boat. We were back in the here and now, in a beautiful little nowhere, content to be there, and not to think at all. Gehlen began to fade. Oh, he still came, played over and over again, but the birdsong and the trees diluted him. Slowly, gradually, he got weaker and weaker. Dadda didn't hurry; he wasn't doing twenty miles an hour: the thirty-hundredweight bumped its springs over the uneven Fenland roads as gently as a cradle. Matt's cocked-up leg relaxed and slid slowly across the metal bed of the truck. Paul sighed and wriggled his shoulders back and forward. Kit let his head bounce on his hand where it lay on the tailgate, obviously enjoying the feeling.

Dadda had found the ham-and-eggs farm after a hairy forced landing in a Whitley in 1941. He had left his rear gunner in charge of the wreck, and just walked into the farmhouse. I suppose the famous Dadda smile did the rest, though people would do anything for somebody in flying gear in those days just after the Battle of Britain. You could sit and watch the farmer's wife cutting slices of ham off the joint, which hung up on a beam when it wasn't in use. If you had the energy, you could go out to the hen coop with the farmer's kids, and push the hens off the nesting boxes, and take your own personal eggs straight from the straw, still warm. There was never ham and eggs like Dadda's ham and eggs. The eggs didn't turn to glue

in your throat and the edges of the ham left the lining of
your stomach alone. And after breakfast you could mooch
around the farmyard, watching the milk squirt into the
galvanized bucket as the farmer milked each cow by hand.
Kick the horse manure and smell the pong coming off it.
Or listen to the farmer's wife getting aerated about the
Ministry of Ag. and Fish. inspectors. Those farmers were
so caught up in their little world, they never thought to
ask about ours. Sometimes they asked us to lend a hand,
cleaning out a byre. If we had nothing better to do.
Because we had the day off, hadn't we? The *whole* day
off? they asked enviously.

God bless their ignorance; it washed us clean.

Before we left, I took a couple of leaves from a plant
that grew in the garden. When you rubbed them between
your finger and thumb, they gave off a minty, lemony
smell. The farmer's wife said a couple of leaves under
your pillow helped you sleep. I went back to the billet with
mine, and slept like a baby.

NEXT RAID, our flight was sent on a diversionary attack,
on the docks at Lorient. For once, Lorient was a soft job,
practically a milk run. Dadda took us in at zero feet all
the way. Lucky it was a calm night; we still came back with
a length of seaweed stuck on the cockpit canopy. But he
got past the flak ships without a murmur, and under the
German radar, and because we hadn't to waste time gaining
height we arrived ahead of the bomber stream. We had
Lorient to ourselves, dumped the bombs somewhere near
the harbor, and were on our way out before the flak
opened up. Dadda for God!

We went out to sea on the way home, to avoid the
fighters; heading for St. Mary's in the Scilly Isles, slowly

climbing. Dawn found us still at sea; a lovely morning, the waves an engraving on the brazen glow behind us and sunlight streaming into the cockpit. It was a bit like sailing; I'd once spent a holiday on the Scillies.

Just as we sighted St. Mary's, Billy said, "Junkers about three miles off, dead astern." And there it was, a little black thing shaped a bit like a tadpole. Such a little thing to spoil a lovely morning . . . But you don't muck about with a Junkers 88, even in daylight. It could overhaul you no faster than a family car, but it had a much tighter turning circle than we did. Luckily, there was a great patch of cumulus just off St. Mary's, and Dadda put us straight into it.

We flew around inside, waiting for the Junkers to need his breakfast. Trouble was, we had to keep turning, to avoid flying out of the cloud again. A certain brightening of the light gave us a bit of warning when to turn, but three times we pushed our nose out, which the wily old Junkers was expecting. But he couldn't outguess Dadda. The first time we came out, the Junkers was miles below us; the second time, he was flying away from us, and the third, he was just crossing our bows. Mad Paul gave him a burst and he could hardly miss. Bits flew off Jerry's port-engine cowling and he sprouted a long white plume of glycol smoke. *He* knew what it was all about—headed straight for the French coast in a shallow dive. Their rear gunner even had the nerve to stick up two fingers at us. Paul stuck his right back. Paul wanted to chase him, but Dadda said we'd used up a week's luck already, and headed for home, mumbling some uncouth Gaelic ditty under his breath. The Junkers, now far behind, seemed to be roughly holding height; we wished him nothing worse than a ditching, and a pickup by RAF Rescue.

We landed in high good humor, for once with a good story to tell. The other flight was back, from Osnabrück. S-Sugar was in its pan. We breezed into the debriefing room—and it was like walking into the Arctic. They just didn't want to know us at all.

It took some time to get anyone to explain what had happened, but apparently a kid called Reaper had been landing after Osnabrück. Now, Reaper had once seen some silly bugger overshoot a runway. The effect had been so awful that it had left Reaper with just one ambition in life: never to overshoot a runway himself. So Reaper had his flaps down quicker, his throttles back quicker, his brakes on faster than anybody ever known. They called him the Caterpillar, offered him spare lettuce leaves in the mess.

Anyway, there was old Caterpillar caterpillaring in when another Wimpy comes in to land straight over the top of him. Its slipstream knocked Caterpillar all over the shop, though luckily he was nearly stopped by then. Then the other Wimpy lands right in front of him, neatly enough, but totally blocking Caterpillar's way to the dispersals. It was S-Sugar. Typical bloody Blackham. He'd even cut his engines. Caterpillar leaped out, apparently, and ran up to S-Sugar as if he was going to give Blackham the hiding of his life.

But Groupie in his jeep beats him to it. Just as well. Because there's something funny about S-Sugar. Something odd. The escape hatches are open and missing, though there's not a speck of damage anywhere on her. Groupie sent Caterpillar away, straight off. Groupie's been flying thirty years; he's got a nose for trouble. So somebody fires a flare to summon the ambulance. Then Groupie goes inside. And the first thing he finds is one dead rear gunner with a hole in his chest. Poor old Geranium. And there's a .38 service revolver lying just beside him, with one cartridge fired. And not a single bullet hole in the fuselage . . .

Blackham was one of the few men I knew who carried a revolver on raids, to help his escape if he got shot down.

Of Coade, the front gunner, Spann, the wireless op, Brennan, the navigator, and Beales, the copilot, there was no sign. Groupie *umph*ed a bit at that. They thought Blackham was dead, too, at first. But he wasn't. Just rigid: hands still on the wheel, feet still on the rudder bar. Staring ahead of him, as if he was still flying. He wouldn't answer when they spoke to him, wouldn't turn his head to look at them. In the end they had to prize his hands off the controls and carry him out on a stretcher. Catatonic schizophrenia, they said later, when he went on sitting and flying S-Sugar in the hospital ward. He's never said a word to anybody from that day to this. And late in the afternoon they phoned to say they'd found the four missing aircrew, buried in a large turnip field near Chelmsford. It seems they'd jumped from too low a height; their parachutes had had no time to open.

Nobody was ever going to know exactly what happened to S-Sugar on the journey home. Her bombs were gone, every single part of her worked to perfection, there wasn't a bullet hole or a scratch on her. No reason in this world for bailing out. So they serviced her and put her back in her pan. Groupie said she could serve as a spare aircraft for any crew whose crate was undergoing repair.

What they should have done was to throw her onto the scrap heap, as we had once thrown away that Messerschmitt propeller blade. But no one—not even Butcher Harris himself—has the clout to write off a fairly new, totally undamaged plane. And people flew quite regularly—if not cheerfully; never cheerfully—in crates where men had died, where men had been scraped off the seats. But at least we knew what happened to them. Nobody knew what had happened in Blackham's Wimpy.

After that, S-Sugar began to dominate the whole station, as the prop blade had dominated our barracks room. Nobody went near her. Shadows seemed to gather inside her cockpit and turrets. She grew to twice the size of any Wimpy on the field. It was the time of the autumn spiders; they spun webs all over her, as they spun them in the hedgerows, as they spun them on the other Wimpys. Except that flight and servicing and polishing scrubbed the other Wimpys clean every day. The cobwebs just grew thicker on S-Sugar. The ground-crew sergeant had a strip torn off him by Groupie about it; he swore he cleaned Blackham's Wimpy daily, but nobody believed him. Erks —airmen—cycling past the pan at night were seen to steer away from it, in a half circle. There were all sorts of rumors in the erks' mess, too. Voices had been heard inside it, when there was no one about: crackly intercom voices. Then the WAAFs got hold of the story. Had anybody noticed, they asked, that no birds ever perched on Blackham's Wimpy? Actually, very few birds perched on anybody's Wimpy; they don't make desirable perches, not with so many trees around—but that was the kind of stupid rumor that went around. Not that the aircrews were any better, though they never mentioned it. Aircrews are more superstitious than sailors. They all have mascots: teddy bears, old raggy dolls, umbrellas; won't fly without them, or without peeing on the tail wheel before they go and after they come back. So it came out afterwards that people had gone to extraordinary lengths not to fly in

Blackham's crate. Pilots with defective crates didn't report them, just slipped their ground crew fivers to work overtime on their personal planes, until they were fit to fly again. More than once there were unexplained fights between crews over job priorities.

Finally the scandal reached Groupie's ears, and he put his foot down. With all the lack of sympathy that scrambled-egg wallahs are capable of, he picked Reaper to fly S-Sugar on the next op, to Tallinn. Reaper's crew immediately put themselves on the chop list. They sat in a tight little group at ops tea, silent, sweating, eyes down, not touching a scrap of their grub. They had spent two days writing letter after letter to say goodbye to their folks back home, giving away their tennis rackets and golf clubs, and altering their wills. Nobody could bear to look at them. Most people expected them to crash on takeoff, and they damned nearly did.

But they came back. Came back late, made a very wobbly landing, but came back without a scratch. There were a lot of us waiting for them outside the debriefing hut, waiting to break out a bottle of whisky some cheerful type had bought to drink either with them or to their memory. All of us wanted to slap them on the back . . . only, the first bloke who tried it got a punch in the teeth that laid him flat on his face. We left them alone after that.

They answered debriefing in monosyllables. Piece of cake, they said, no fighters, no flak, found the target, easy. But they looked far worse than before they went; more destined for the chop than ever. And as their skipper rose to go, he spat out at the wireless officer, "Get that bloody intercom seen to!"

Next raid, they had their own plane back, but even that made no difference. They walked out to the truck that took them to the dispersals like—I can't get my tongue around it—like walking corpses. And that time they didn't come back. Oh, and the wireless officer had S-Sugar's intercom checked. It worked perfectly.

Groupie sent out another crew in her. Exactly the same thing happened, with knobs on. Came back in S-Sugar without a mark on them, and crashed their own crate on takeoff the following op.

By this time the whole flaming squadron was going down the drain. Groupie had Dadda in for a private talk in his office. I'll say one thing for Dadda: he made a condition with Groupie—he volunteered himself to fly Blackham's Wimpy, he didn't volunteer us. He left us free. Asked for a scratch crew from around the squadron. Nobody volunteered. Not a single soul, and I don't blame them. So Dadda said he would go on his lonesome.

Matt said he would go with him. Then Mad Paul said you had to die sometime and he'd rather die with Dadda than anybody else. In the end, even I said I would go. The idea of them buying it and me starting all over again with a new crew was unthinkable. Human beings are sheep in the end, aren't they?

It was our twenty-third op.

WE GET THE WINK from the control tower, and Dadda takes off a bit savagely; a tight rein on a strange horse. Is his voice a shade sharper, or is it just the strange intercom? I fiddle with the dials a bit, making no difference, and settle down next to Kit in the black windy tube that's the whole, noisy world.

Only tonight it's the wrong tube; it creaks and flutters in the wrong places. Piercing drafts sneak in from the wrong angles. I stick the nozzle of the heating hose down my right flying boot, and it's a marvelous comfort; it's the only thing that's giving me anything; it's the only thing that loves me. I champ my way through a bar of chocolate, before we reach eight thousand feet and we put on oxygen masks. I am glad I can see Kit's face through a gap in his navigator's curtain. It looks calm and thoughtful as he scribbles steadily on his maps. I love that face more than I love any girl's or film star's. It's always there. I could never tell him how I feel, but sometimes he punches me, when we've landed, and I punch him back, and that's it. Still, he'll punch anybody he even vaguely likes. Does he really not give a damn? Does he really think it's all a giggle still, on the twenty-third time? Don't think like that; I need to think he's like that.

As if he senses my stare, even through all his gear, he turns and bats his eyebrows at me, mocking. Behind his mask, I know he's grinning.

"Have you heard the one about the constipated navigator?" He's only three feet away, but his voice on the intercom sounds as far away as the backside of the moon. "He had to work it out with a pencil."

Snort from Mad Paul in the front turret.

"Oh, ha-ha," groans Billy.

"Shut up, Kit." But even Dadda is sniggering.

After the war, Kit's going to Oxford, and I'm going back to the True Form shoe shop in Clitheroe. Maybe he'll ask me down for a weekend . . . if there is an after the war.

"Keep that RT down," says Dadda; his voice *is* sharper, edgier. I fiddle with the knobs. Yes, the glowing dials are a comfort, too: a little glowing city where ants live. Ant palaces, ant cinemas . . .

Blackham's Wimpy is newer than C-Charlie; the wireless

op's seat seems harder-edged and colder than my own. Every crate they send, there's some new modification.

Yes, Kit's jumpy, too; makes two course corrections on the way to our wave rendezvous over Cromer. Celebrates too noisily the fact that he's pinpointed Cromer Pier.

"Shut up, Kit!" snarls Dadda. Normally, Kit does us a lot of good on the run-in, but tonight his comedy act's not working. The engine note keeps changing, too; Matt's making heavy weather getting the engines synchronized. And out over the sea, Billy tests his guns; but so often, we think he's seen a night fighter.

"What the hell . . . ?"

"Sorry, Skip. It's this turret. I've got to get used to it." Blackham, and Blackham alone, blast him, managed to get a four-gun Frazer-Nash turret fitted to *his* Wimpy, like the ones the Lancs and Halley-bags have. What did he do? Blackmail the gunnery officer? Sleep with the gunnery officer's missus? Wouldn't put anything past Blackham. The rest of us had to put up with two-gun rear turrets. I think of Blackham, still flying his Wimpy, sitting up in a straight, hard chair in the asylum. They say he pulls all the right invisible levers, and sometimes his flights take twelve hours, from breakfast to supper, when he starts all over again—unless they shoot some drug into him. If they try to stop him flying, he cries. Otherwise, his eyes are like shiny black marbles, they say, staring out of the ward window. Even when he cries.

Stop *thinking* . . .

I stick the heating hose down my other boot, readjust the RT. What else is there to do? Kit pushes past me, on his way to the cockpit, big as an elephant in his flying gear. The sheepskin brushes the back of my head; then I feel lonely. Another quick, nervous burst from Billy. Blackham's guns. The guns that did for Gehlen. I remember them all laughing at Gehlen. Now they've gone where Gehlen went . . . God, I'm shaking more than I usually do over the target, and we haven't reached the Belgian coast yet.

Suddenly, light-flak tracer is Morse-coding past the windows. And then rods of pure white light, leaking in through every chink in the fabric. We're caught in a searchlight. Then a throbbing through the Wimpy's frame; a light, rhythmic throbbing: our front guns firing.

Blackness and onward. Paul's voice saying, "Well, that'll cost him his weekend's pocket money for a new bulb and battery." He's hit the searchlight, which you can do at 3,700 feet. Wild cheers all around.

"It was a flak ship," says Dadda. "Converted trawler."

"Let him go back to catching kippers," says Billy. Having the last word is a rear gunner's privilege.

We all feel a lot better.

"Enemy coast ahead," says Kit. Somehow, it's good to be back in the thick of it.

WE'D JUST CROSSED the Rhine, spot on course and with a lot of premature rejoicing from Kit, when I began to get a vibration on the RT. You know when you've got your wireless at home tuned in to the BBC Home Service and Reginald Foort is belting away on the theater organ, and he hits a big note and your set can't take it and gives a kind of blurting rattle? Well, my RT was acting just like that, but much softer at first.

"Tune the RT properly, Gary. Get rid of that mush." Dadda's voice was suddenly harsh again. I didn't blame him. We were all as twitchy as hell about the intercom, and this noise in it was like a fat fly buzzing inside your head. I moved the tuning knob, dutifully but without hope. I am never off station.

"Fault in the set, Dadda. Hope it's not going on the blink."

"I'll *strangle* that RT mechanic . . ."

"Reaper grumbled about this RT," said Kit, thoughtfully. So had the other crew that bought it. That was all either of them had said, before they got the chop: get the intercom fixed. There was a nasty silence. Everybody was remembering. Nobody had anything to say.

The buzz faded, to the edge of hope, then got slightly louder. I tell you, it was hypnotic; I couldn't pay attention to anything else. Inside, I was praying, pleading with it to go away. I had never heard anything quite like it before. And if the set really went on the blink, we would each of us be alone and helpless, in a howling blizzard of engine noise. Please go away. *Please* go away. Just for tonight. I was talking to the bloody thing; stroking the dials gently, as if the RT was an angry cat that needed placating.

The noise got louder. And not just louder—it was developing a definite rhythm. A bit like a human voice. Like somebody very tiny, shouting to be let out, somewhere deep inside the set. A voice that couldn't yet get out.

"Turn coming up, Dadda," said Kit. "Steer one-oh-five . . . now." His voice was too loud, making us jump. God, that infernal buzz *was* like a human voice. If it got any clearer, I'd be able to tell what it was saying . . .

Get a grip, Gary. Or they'll be writing you off as LMF —lacking in moral fiber. You'll end up in a bin, like Blackham. Or cleaning the bogs, like the poor ex-gunner who thinks he's a Dornier 217.

"Fifteen minutes to target," said Kit. "Hope the PF's aren't pissed again. I get tired of setting the Black Forest on fire."

For once, nobody laughed at that good old joke.

"Oh, frig off, you miserable lot," said Kit. "Where's the flaming funeral?"

He shouldn't have said that. In the stony silence that followed, the idea of a funeral wouldn't go away. Aircrew bodies fished out of burning crates have shrunk so much, they hardly need coffins bigger than shoe boxes.

"Watch the sky," said Dadda. "You won't be shot down by a buzz on the intercom."

"Right," said Mad Paul.

"Right," said Billy, a long time after him. Billy's reactions were usually as quick as greased lightning. Hell, this whole crew was falling apart.

There wasn't one tiny voice talking inside my RT now; there were two, talking to each other. Oh, electronic mush on the air . . . it was always happening. But not when your RT was properly tuned. I played with the knobs again, pointlessly.

"Five minutes to target," said Kit. A dim red light was stealing down the black tube of the Wimpy's fuselage from the cockpit windows. We began to bounce under the impact of flak and the slipstream of the other bombers. Berlin coming up.

As I played with the knobs, the voices suddenly became audible, just barely audible.

"Steer two-seven-five. The *Kurier* is five kilometers ahead of you and five hundred meters above." The voices were talking in German. A night fighter was being homed in on its courier, or target.

"Some bugger nattering in German," said Kit loudly.

"Well, he's not after us," said Dadda soothingly. "We're steering one-oh-five. Now keep your mind on the run-up."

So Kit started the old left-left, steady, right-a-bit routine, and for the next five minutes he swamped the German voices. We had other things to worry about.

THE DARKNESS after the target is the most beautiful darkness in the world. Dadda checked us one by one. Nobody hurt; no damage as far as we knew. The twin Bristol Hercules engines droned on blissfully. Take us home, Hercules, great god of antiquity.

But the German voices inside my RT set were still there, louder, quite clear now. If we could hear them, could they hear us? Radio's a funny thing.

"Can you see the *Kurier* yet? He should be a kilometer ahead and fifty meters above you. Still steering two-seven-five. You should see him against the clouds . . ."

"How dense are the clouds, Kit?" I asked.

"What frigging clouds?" said Kit, his head in the astro-dome. "Haven't seen no frigging clouds."

"It's nothing to do with us," said Dadda. "We're steering three hundred."

"I'll just test him out on Monica." Monica is another little bag of tricks that Dadda acquired for me. It has a bulb that lights up when a fighter's tracking you on radar. I switched Monica on, and off again quickly. Monica, lovely girl, said there was nobody on our tail.

But the noise in the RT grew steadily.

"Can you see the *Kurier* yet?"

"Yes, I can see his exhausts. A twin-motored aircraft."

That made me jump. Wimpys are the only twin-motors left in the skies over Germany, and there were only thirty or so on this raid.

"He is about half a kilometer ahead, and fifty meters above me. He has not seen me. I will come up under him and give him a tune on my *Schrage Musik*."

"Some poor soul's for the chop," said Dadda. The *Schrage Musik* can tear the guts out of a Wimpy before the Wimpy even knows it's being followed.

"Nothing behind *us*," said Billy. "It's as clear as day."

The German voice was now as loud as Billy's own on the intercom. If anything, louder. It might have been inside the plane with us.

"I am a hundred meters behind him now, and twenty meters beneath. My guns are cocked."

"Anything?" said Dadda.

"Nothing," said Billy. "Not a dickybird behind us." But the voice had infected us all. I tried Monica again, though I knew it was pointless.

Nothing.

Even Dadda banked the crate left and right, to get a look underneath.

Nothing. But we all shuddered, waiting for the death of the unknown Wimpy. Was it one of our lot? Probably we should never know.

And then a new voice broke in, loud, a shout, full of fear.

"Blackham—corkscrew port—fighter below you!"

"For God's sake, stop shouting, Gary!" said Dadda abruptly. I didn't answer. It *was* my voice; but I hadn't opened my mouth. It was my voice, a month old, coming out of the dark, out of the past. Calling to Blackham, who at this moment was lying in a bed in Colchester mental hospital. And no wonder the night fighter's voice seemed familiar. It wasn't just a German voice. It was Gehlen's voice. Burned Gehlen, whom we had seen blown in pieces all over Germany.

Then another voice, exultant: "I got the bastard! I *got* him!" Geranium, dead a month, with a hole in his chest.

"You sure?" Blackham, very Yorkshire-tyke.

"Sure I'm sure. See him burn!" Geranium.

Wild cheers. From Coade, Spann, Brennan, and Beales. Dead in a turnip field near Chelmsford.

"Bullfinch Three to Bullfinch. Abandoning aircraft. Port wing on fire. Get the hatch open, Meissner! . . ." Gehlen. Dead, burned Gehlen.

"Shut the bloody RT off, Gary!" Only slowly, I realized it was Dadda talking to me, in the present day. But it was Kit who reached over and turned off the intercom, plunging us into the blessed silence of the engines' roar. When he looked at me, his blue eyes above the oxygen mask were showing white all around. I was shaking from head to foot. My hand shook so much I couldn't undo my mask. Then I was sick, and the spew built up inside it and cascaded over the top. At least it was real and warm and alive.

The next thing I knew, and that, too, came to me very slowly, as in a dream, was that Dadda had put the Wimpy into a hell of a dive. Either that, or we'd been mortally hit. Frankly, I didn't care. I just hung on like a drowning man to a life belt. But we pulled out, and I could tell from the movement of the crate that Dadda was ground-hopping. What else could he do to stay alive, with the intercom gone and all his crew, gunners and all, sitting in a paralyzed funk? Any night fighter could have come up behind and stolen our suspenders and we wouldn't have noticed.

Kit recovered first, as he always did. Bundled past me with a new course for Dadda to fly. That kid was incredible. I sat huddled, cold and still shaking, over the end of the heating hose; I held it up my jacket, against my crotch. It was a help. I watched the odd trail of tracer flying past the triangular windows, with the innocent wonder of a small child on a railway journey. Nothing came very near. Dadda was giving Jerry very little chance, as usual. Kit came bundling back to his navigator's table and settled to a problem, face very serious. As usual, it was a comfort to watch him. How did people get to have guts like him and Dadda? I must have been at the back of the queue when they were handing out guts.

It was then that I noticed that my RT dials were starting to glow up again. Had I knocked the switch back on, without knowing what I was doing? I reached to switch it off again.

It was switched off.

But the dials continued to glow up. I gave a noiseless moan, as sound filtered into my earphones. Faint cheers.

"Burn, you bastard, burn!"

An incoherent scream from Gehlen. Kit shoved me aside and reached for the off switch. It was still off. His eyes creased up over his mask. He tried the switch the other way, and the sound of Gehlen's screams grew louder. He turned it to the off position again. Back and forward he twisted it, back and forward, faster and faster. But still the voice of Gehlen grew.

"Mutti, Mutti."

Kit went berserk then. He grabbed the heavy-duty cables that led to the radio set from the crate's main batteries. Tore them out of their housings on the airframe. Tried to pull them out of the radio with brute force. Then he reached for a pair of rescue shears.

God, he would go up in a blue light! We'd all go up in a blue light if the naked ends of the cut wires touched the airframe. Frantically I tried to wrestle the shears away from him. We were still fighting like maniacs when Dadda separated us. We stood in a triangle, mouthing soundless screams at each other.

Dadda took a rescue hammer and smashed the shut-off RT set. The sparks flew, I can tell you; lucky the hammer had a rubber handle. Silence. The soundless noise of the engines once again closed like a fleecy blanket over our ears. Dadda went back to the cockpit. Kit and I sat and stared at each other. I don't think either of us expected the world to make sense anymore. We had got accustomed to living in a nightmare. Kit even produced a flask of coffee and offered me a cup. Coffee in a nightmare. But it still tasted like real coffee—as real as wartime coffee ever is.

We looked at our watches. Kit mimed, "Half an hour to the Dutch coast." Then he turned his head to look at a section of the airframe, puzzled. It *was* vibrating oddly, under our backsides, under our ungloved hands. Had we been hit? Had the engines developed trouble, or gone out of synch?

No, it was more like the rhythms of speech. Voices talking. A voice . . .

Suddenly the voice burst out again, like fire from a hosed-down plane—a fire the firemen thought they had under control.

"Meissner, Ritter! What's holding you up? Are you dead?"

And then the screams, the god-awful, burning screams, drowning the noise of the engines, shaking the airframe, tearing at every joint in our bodies. Nothing, nothing left in the world but screaming.

"Heil Hitler! Sieg Heil, Sieg Heil, Sieg Heil."

Kit and I clung together, held on to each other in a barricade of arms, of living flesh and bones. There was nothing else to do. It was all that kept us in existence. That, and the slight sway of the airframe that told our legs that Dadda, somewhere—Dadda, a million miles away—was still flying her.

The screaming gave back a little, like an army preparing for a fresh assault. Fell to a sobbing.

"*Mutti, Mutti.*"

And we felt another movement in the airframe, toward the tail. Something was moving there, coming slowly toward us. Kit reached down and pulled aside the curtain around his navigator's table. I thought it odd that his little table light was still shining. I thought it odd that it still existed at all. It belonged to the real world. He swiveled it toward the tail, and we both looked.

A man hung there, crucified.

For a moment, for me, the universe rocked on its pivot. Then I saw it was only Billy the Kid, face mask, oxygen hose, and intercom wires dangling down his front like entrails. His face was that white sheet again, with three holes burned in it now: his eyes and his silently screaming mouth. His freckles stood out like blood splashes. And he wasn't crucified; his arms were braced against the airframe to hold himself up. As we watched, he drew in a shuddering breath and screamed, silently, again. He wasn't looking at us; he wasn't looking anywhere.

Somehow, Kit started toward him. Immediately Billy let go of one side of the airframe. He had a hatchet in his hand: the little hatchet many rear gunners carry to hack their way out of the turret, in case of a crash. I wanted to run away. But a world without Kit was unthinkable, and Kit was still advancing on Billy.

The hatchet came up; the hatchet came down, on Kit's head. Fortunately, it struck the upper airframe stringers in its descent and lost most of its force. Kit grabbed Billy's wrist, and the next second we were all three struggling on the Duralumin walkway, a mass of sheepskin and bony, painful knees, air hoses and radio cables. Then we had hold of one of his arms each, and the hatchet was lying at our feet. Kit kicked it from where he lay, and it vanished into the darkness. He grimaced at me; his face mask had worked loose. Then he nodded up the fuselage to where the rest bed was bolted. Rest bed, ha-ha. Lie-and-groan bed; bleed-your-life-away-and-your-mates-can't-stop-it bed. We got Billy there. He was no longer struggling very hard. His mouth was open and there were long strands of saliva festooning it.

"Hold him down," Kit mouthed.

I buried my head in Billy's shoulder, wrapped my arms and legs around his, and clung on. Now I sensed Dadda was bending over us; I felt better. God, was it Matt doing the ground-hopping? Could Matt really fly this crate like that? I saw the dim glow from the navigator's light glinting on the syringe in Dadda's hand, saw the needle jab into Billy's rounded, straining backside. His shirt and trousers had come apart, and I could see the pale, shining, girlish skin of his back. Billy stiffened at the pain of the needle, then almost immediately began to relax. Next second, there was an agonizing beesting in my own backside.

"Hey," I shouted, "that's not fair!"

"Sorry," mouthed Dadda. "Meant for him." He pointed at Billy.

I was getting all weak and warm and drowsy as the morphia took over. I was frightened I would be too weak to hold Billy, but he had had his jab first: he was even drowsier than me.

That was the last I knew. As the terrible screaming started again, I slipped away from it into warm darkness.

WHEN I CAME ROUND, there was no noise but the roar of the engines. Billy the Kid was still out cold, snoring gently. I wondered who had drawn the great big blue marks under his eyes with a pencil. Kit was sitting at his table, still wearily doing his sums. He had no need of his navigator's light now, because sunshine—early, horizontal sunshine—was streaming in through our dirty triangular windows. I made some kind of movement with my arm, and at the third time he saw and came over.

"That noise has stopped," I mouthed.

"Halfway across the North Sea. Got weaker and weaker. Then it . . . seemed to give up." He held up five fingers. "Five minutes to Oadby."

"Any damage?"

Kit tried to smile, and gave up. The guy with the blue pencil who'd been drawing on Billy's face had been drawing on Kit's, too. With a slightly shaky hand, he gave me a flask top of cold coffee and said, "No damage. Not a bullet hole. I've checked."

"We're going to get home, then?"

"Dadda says this crate will always get home."

"What d'you mean?"

But Kit got up and hurried away forward. I heard the note of the engines change, and felt the airframe tremble as the flaps went down.

Dadda's landing was a perfect three-pointer; never a bounce. We shook Billy awake, got out onto the tarmac, and stood around and peed on the tail wheel. I caught myself wishing our pee was pure sulfuric acid, and that the tail wheel would dissolve and all S-Sugar with it.

The ground-crew sergeant came up, glancing at wings, tail, everything.

"Good trip?"

"Piece of cake," said Dadda. He grinned; dried-up saliva wrinkled his lips into strange patterns. "But the RT needs seeing to. And there's no point in arguing this time—it's smashed to hell."

Kit actually laughed, even if he couldn't quite finish it.

The debriefing WAAF kept asking me what happened, and I kept on saying, "Nothing. Piece of cake."

I CAME UP slowly out of the depths of sleep. The barracks room was cold and empty. Waking up was a mistake. I'd been happy asleep.

I went to the window. Autumn Fenland mist. Boundary fence. Mud this side and mud beyond, fading away into infinity. Through the fence a few dirty, ragged sheep stared at me, chewing. I despised them for their keen desire to stay alive. Personally, for the first time, I wished to be dead. Oh, not your Pearly Gates opening and St. Peter waiting to pin a gong on you. I'd settle for lovely, black-velvety nothing. Not see, not feel, not think. I tried to remember Clitheroe Grammar School, Mum and Dad, and a girl called Betty who wrote to me every week. But the memory of them stayed gray and remote, like photographs in a tattered copy of the *Daily Mail*, blowing around the dispersals.

This, I thought, without much real interest, was the effect of flying in Blackham's Wimpy. This was the huddled, inert state that Reaper's crew had reached, and Edwards's, just before they got the chop. In this state, the chop was inevitable. Dieter Gehlen, dead, was claiming more victims than ever. He was deadlier in Blackham's

Wimpy than he had ever been in a Junkers 88. To the glory of the Fatherland. And there was no reason why he should not continue to claim victims. Blackham's Wimpy, as Dadda had observed, would always come home. Probably unmarked. It could fly two more whole tours. How Gehlen's ghost managed to keep flak away, and other Jerry night fighters, God alone knew. But obviously if Blackham's Wimpy bought it, Gehlen's ghost bought it, too. And that would not be in the scheme of things . . .

I realized that what I was thinking was quite insane. The only comfort was that we six could huddle in a group, sharing a common insanity. For a bit. Like Reaper's lot; like Edwards's . . . the names tolled in my head like a funeral bell that would not stop.

Why hadn't Reaper reported it? He had, the only way anyone would believe. He had told the ground-crew sergeant to see to the RT. Something was wrong with it. Oh, my, was something wrong with it! But what else could Reaper have done? Told Groupie his squadron contained a haunted bomber? That would have got him one of two rewards: either sitting flying a bomber in Colchester mental hospital, like Blackham, or else found to be LMF, reduced to the rank of AC2—Aircraftman, Second Class, the lowest rank of erk—and put on cleaning out the bogs on your own station, with all your mates either trying to look you in the face or trying not to look you in the face. That crafty bastard Gehlen had it all taped. My eyes filled with tears of helpless rage. I'd like to *kill* Gehlen, for what he was doing. But that wasn't possible, was it?

The barracks room door was flung open with a bang, making me jump a yard in the air. I hadn't realized I had that amount of life left in me. It was Kit. He didn't look as if he wished he was dead. Instead, he looked slightly and gleefully insane. I retired into my pit, and he sat on the end of it, swinging his flying boots.

"You look terrible," he said.

"I feel terrible."

"What you reckon to last night, then?"

"Ghost?" I said feebly.

"That bastard knew what he was doing." He spoke as if Gehlen was a living man. "He kept on playing himself different ways, for maximum possible effect. Like a dirty old man flashing himself to schoolgirls in the park."

"How did you *cope*?"

"Oh, we all got in a bunch. I stood behind Dadda's seat, with a hand on Matt's shoulder. Being three together wasn't so bad. It was being alone in the tail that did for poor old Billy."

"What about Paul in the front?"

"We kept kicking him up the backside. That kept him going. And he popped away at the light flak and searchlights. He didn't hit a thing, but he said it relieved his feelings. He's out there now, fiddling with his motorbike. Doing wheelies up the runway and driving the warrant officer mad."

"It must help to be mad," I said. "How's Billy?"

"No worse than you. He's still with us; just." He stared out of the window. Then he said, "That bloody thing didn't scare Dadda at all, you know. All Dadda said was 'Poor soul.' That's what kept me going. That, and the fact that the bastard went on too long. When he was starting to fade, at the end, he sounded like a worn-out gramophone record. I got up enough nerve to walk to the back of the crate after that. You and Billy were curled up like a pair of babes in the wood. I even took a spell in the back turret. Didn't see anything. After that *thing*, what's a Jerry fighter?"

"Well, Gehlen's done for me," I said. "Like he did for Reaper and Edwards . . ."

Kit gave me a long hard stare. "I've got news for you, son. Just had a report on C-Charlie. She's in need of two new engines. Next time we go out, we go out in Blackham's again."

My world fell in. I didn't think I could have felt worse, but I did. "I'm not going. It's LMF for me. How do you hold a bog brush?"

"I'll come with you," said Kit. "But d'you fancy helping me do something first? I scrounged this out of Paul's bike." He pulled a stubby, flat whisky bottle out of his sagging tunic pocket. It was full of clear liquid. He let me smell it. Petrol.

"You don't mean—"

"I bloody do! Burn the sod out. If S-Sugar burns up, Gehlen can waste his time haunting the aircraft knacker's yard."

"You wouldn't dare . . ."

"Try and stop me. What can they do to us, even if they can prove it wasn't a careless fag end? How about three years in a nice quiet cell?"

"Bliss," I said, feeling suddenly a whole lot better. "When?"

"Now," said Kit. "Before the ground crew get to work on her. Dadda brought her home on full boost; there's hardly a cupful of petrol in her. She won't blow up and kill anybody, not unless somebody tries to be a hero with the fire extinguisher—and *they* can go and hold old Gehlen's hand." His eyes still had that slightly mad shine, but I went with him. Except for Dadda, we all did, even Billy. Especially Billy.

There seemed not to be a soul about as we walked to the dispersals across the wet, misty field. But I suppose there are always mechanics working inside the crates, and cozy, nosy buggers looking out of office windows. Which probably accounts for what happened later. You don't normally get a complete aircrew walking out to a crate the morning after an op. S-Sugar loomed up suddenly, as if she was a ghost. From the outside, she looked just like any other Wimpy: that wedgy, faithful-doggy profile. For a moment my mind did a double take about damaging His Majesty's property. But Blackham's Wimpy didn't really belong to His Majesty anymore, though, of course, His Majesty didn't know it. Matt reached up and pulled down the hatch and ladder. For no particular reason, I climbed in first.

I'd never smelled a bomber the morning after a raid before. Normally, the ground crew hose the crates out with disinfectant before we see them again. But this morning S-Sugar smelled as we had left her: petrol, cordite from the guns, a stronger kind of cordite from the German flak, the stench of vomit, the greater stench of the cold, black Elsan, the stink of sweaty socks and another smell that smells like the smell of blue funk. Only a burning Wimpy smells worse, when the crew's still inside.

It was dark, too. Thick dark. Not much pale yellow light showed through the smeared windscreen.

The moment I began to move up the fuselage, I stopped. There was something alive in there. I always know when there's something alive in a place. We have an old gray cat which hangs round our barracks room. She's fond of lurking, invisible, among the gray blankets. I always know she's there, somehow, but she always gives me a fright when she jumps out, purring. Now there was something in S-Sugar, and it wasn't a cat. Much bigger than a cat. The hair rose on the back of my neck. I tingled all over.

There was a murmur from beyond the rear of the cockpit. The wind was blowing a bit, rocking the Wimpy on her wheels and keening through struts and aerials, but the murmuring was louder than the keening, though half-lost in it. It seemed to be coming from somewhere near the RT; softly, rhythmically. I strained to hear it, and the hair on my neck rose afresh. God, this couldn't be happening.

The murmuring was in German . . .

"You have done well, Dieter. You have done very well. Nobody could have asked for more courage and loyalty than you have shown. Now you—"

"What the hell . . . ?" Kit, coming up the ladder, bumped into my back. One look at my face silenced him. And Matt and Paul and Billy, as they ascended one by one. We all listened, painfully holding our breath.

"It is time to go now, Dieter. It was terrible, dying, but now you are free. You have done your duty. Go now where there is no more Führer, no more British terror fliers . . ."

A ghost talking to itself. No, I just couldn't believe it. My mind was giving way about once an hour these days; almost as regular as breathing.

"Oh, for God's sake, let's get it over with," said Billy savagely from the back. Bravely, from the back, he began to push Paul and Matt and Kit and me up the fuselage. He mightn't have been so keen if he'd been in front. I tell you, I was fighting like hell to get back and out of there. Kit was giggling in my ear, wildly.

But in spite of my struggles, I was pushed nearer and nearer the wrecked RT set. There was a too dark shadow behind the set. I couldn't quite see what it was, because Kit's navigator's curtain was in the way, but I knew damned well that that shadow wasn't shadow, that that shadow shouldn't be there. It looked . . . leathery. Like a crouched airman in leathers.

Then, starting with a near-imperceptible motion, it rose and rose, and looked at us, with a dead-white face under a rounded leather flying helmet.

I shut my eyes and screamed again. My throat was already sore with screaming. A very solid hand reached out toward me, grabbed my arm.

"Steady, Gary," said Dadda.

HE HAD BEEN THERE almost since we landed, seven hours before. Just got debriefed, then went to his billet to fetch a couple of things and straight back into the stinking bowels of S-Sugar. He clutched the few things against his flying jacket now, with one hand. A fair-sized black book, and what looked like a string of fat black beads, with a little black cross on one end. "Relics of Maynooth," he said, with a wry, weary grin.

"I thought you'd be back," he added. "And that will be petrol in the whisky bottle, young Kit? I knew I didn't have all that much time." Kit had the grace to gape.

"Give me that bottle, Kit."

"I'm going to bloody do it!" said Kit, very defiant.

"No, you're not," said Dadda. "I'm going to do it. I'm skipper." Kit was so shocked, he forgot to argue.

Dadda turned and looked at the smashed RT set. "I've tried to persuade him to go." He sighed. "But he's very young, and very proud, and very brave, and, sadly, very much in love with his beloved Führer. I don't think I've done any good, with all my talking."

"Has he said anything?" asked Billy, curious.

"No," said Dadda. "Nothing at all. It's been me doing all the talking. Now let me have one more go, like good

lads. Get outside and wait for me. And stand well back."
He began to kick and scrape together on the walkway the
debris of the night: greaseproof paper from the corned
beef sandwiches, discarded maps and navigational instructions, my own Morse-code pad. Then, thoughtfully, he
unscrewed the whisky bottle and poured out the clear
liquid.

The sharp, dangerous smell of petrol filled our nostrils.

WE BUNDLED OUT, suddenly chattering like schoolboys
on Bonfire Night, full of a sick sense of a treat to come.
There were a few erks cycling past through the thinning
mist, and some ground crew kicking their heels under A-
Able in the next pan. That sobered us. There were more
people about than we'd thought. We spotted Dadda's old
thirty-hundredweight parked to one side of the perimeter
track, and hung about there. A ground-crew warrant
officer approached with steady ringing tread.

"What are you lot on?"

We shuffled. Aircrew sergeant's stripes, to a ground-
crew warrant officer, are as thin as the toilet paper they're
printed on. And it *was* unusual for an aircrew to go out
to a Wimpy, the morning after an op. The ground crew
think they own the bloody crates; they only lend them to
us for ops, and they even make us feel guilty when we
bend them.

"Waiting for our skipper," said Kit humbly. "He's giving
us a lift."

"You lot get in our hair," grumbled the warrant officer.
"We've got work to do, you know." He kept looking at us;
he wasn't going to go away. He could sense the excitement
bubbling up inside us; suspected some sort of practical
joke.

"Flight Lieutenant Townsend's lot, are you?"

"Yeah," said Kit, so quiet you could hardly hear him.

Dadda emerged down the ladder, in a rush occasioned by the respect we all have for the effects of burning petrol. He spotted the warrant officer instantly, and walked across, long-boned and relaxed. He was smoking a fresh fag; tipped the ash onto the warrant officer's shining toe caps, as if he wanted him to notice. The warrant officer backed off, surreptitiously wiping each ash-covered toe cap in turn on the back of the other trouser leg.

"You shouldn't be smoking aboard an aircraft, sir," he said, half cringing, half bad-tempered. Still uneasy.

"I shouldn't be alive at all," said Dadda. A bit of the old aircrew boast, putting ground crew in its proper place. "Sorry. One forgets about the smoking. C'mon, gang, let's go and find some ham and eggs." He opened the door of the thirty-hundredweight so casually that I wondered whether he'd lost his nerve and scrubbed the whole thing. We turned, to pile in the back.

Behind us, the warrant officer called out, "Hey!" Softly, to himself.

We swung around, and saw the leaping red flicker in the Wimpy's cockpit. Saw the first bit of fabric crinkle and blister and peel back from the airframe. Saw the first red serpent of flame lick its way upward, eating into the mist overhead.

"Hey!" the warrant officer shouted again, and began to run toward S-Sugar. But doped fabric burns fast. Halfway there he changed his mind and stood stupidly, shielding his face with his hand against the heat. A few more seconds and the whole front end of the crate was going up.

People came running from all directions; it seemed like everybody on the whole airfield. In the distance, the warning sound of ambulance and fire engine. But some way off, the fire engine stalled; they said afterwards the plugs oiled up . . .

Everyone stood and gaped. Especially when the voice started. The German voice, right here in the middle of an English airfield. Leutnant Dieter Gehlen, having his last fine careless rapture. And he might have claimed his last victims then, because several erks made crazy attempts at rescue. But the Wimpy was too far gone, aflame from nose to tail. And the voice grew so loud, it echoed around the mist-filled airfield; more than human, essentially the voice from a radio, distorted and full of static crackle.

"Bullfinch Three to Bullfinch . . . port wing on fire. Get the hatch open, Meissner . . ."

They backed away as the crate turned into a torch in which nothing human could have lived. Yet the voice still grew louder and louder.

"Heil Hitler! Sieg Heil."

Then the screaming: terrible, familiar.

"What is it?" shouted the warrant officer, to no one in particular. "My God, what *is* it?"

An aircraft's fabric doesn't take long to burn through. Within another minute, S-Sugar was a blackened skeleton, filled with black blobs. There was no big bang. The front guns fired two rounds as the heat reached them; then the four guns in the tail—fortunately, aimed only at the earth bank of the dispersal pan—got off a long burst all on their own. There were individual flame-ups of flares and glycol; then, for a short time, the near-empty petrol tanks kept us lively.

And still the German voice bellowed on, out of the blackened skeleton. The ghost of Dieter Gehlen, born in flame, was consumed in flame. If the life of a happy man flickers like a candle for seventy years and gutters out, the short life of Dieter Gehlen burned out like a rocket. All that assembled crowd, the aircrew especially, knew then what had done for Blackham and Reaper and Edwards. But I don't think that ground-crew warrant officer knows to this day.

At last, silence. He was gone. All those guts, all that energy, all that faith in an evil, unworthy cause. All that hatred of the *britischen Terrorflieger*. I like to think he bailed out before the bitter end, and landed at the Pearly Gates, and got a halo for mistaken effort. But I doubt it.

"They shouldn't have laughed at him," said Dadda softly, to himself. "They shouldn't have laughed at him."

At this point old Groupie turned up in his jeep. He asked a few questions, didn't bother waiting for the answers, and had our whole crew placed under close arrest. There was a sort of low rumble from the assembled aircrews that suggested, even to Groupie, that he hadn't particularly improved the shining hour.

We were questioned closely. Dadda admitted to lighting a fresh fag from a butt inside the crate, and maybe being a bit careless when he disposed of the butt. But there was too much flak flying around the station for Groupie not to know that something was up. Over the next twelve hours we were frantically marched here and there, which was a bit rough, though nothing like as bad as doing an op. Especially as every time we went out, we got more cheers than the last time. And we heard that Groupie was having the same experience, only with boos and catcalls.

Then Groupie brought in all kinds of guys to ask us questions; the coldest-smiling top brass RAF police I'd ever seen. If they're *that* terrifying, why aren't they out in North Africa, scaring the Germans? There were also technical experts, pretty in well-pressed blues, and a couple of civvies who I think were psychiatrists. We stuck to our story: nothing. Dadda stuck to his: fag end. We spent a lot of time reading old comic books and polishing kit that hadn't been polished since we got there. Meanwhile, the cheering and jeering got worse, and the adjutant ill-advisedly uttered the word "mutiny."

Groupie had us in one last time, late that night, and began going on about LMF. Dadda looked at him in a way even Groupie found hard to take. They went on staring and staring at each other till the WAAF stenographer dropped her pencil. Then Dadda offered to prove that his crew did not lack moral fiber. In the morning, he said, we would do a solo raid up the Pas de Calais, strafing gun sites from zero feet. If Groupie would care to accompany us, he would have the chance to observe personally if the crew of C-Charlie lacked moral fiber. It would have been pure suicide, of course. But as Groupie fixed his gimlet eyes on each of us, we gazed right back and nodded in turn. I even managed to stop myself swallowing.

We had Groupie over a barrel. He hadn't been expecting this. And too many people were there to hear our offer, including the WAAF, whose eyes were standing out like chapel hat pegs. Threaten as he might, news of it would be all over the base by morning. Mind you, I wouldn't want to do Groupie an injustice. He'd have come up the Pas de Calais with us if it would have done the war effort any good. But I think he saw then that we were another kind of problem. He rubbed out *LMF* after our names, and put in *Crazy* instead. The Crazies do exist; we'd met them. There was one air engineer I came across in London on leave who'd done four tours in Lancs. He would lie on his bed and try to trim his toenails with a .38 revolver. Crazies are hooked on destruction. They're clean over the horizon, and never coming back.

Groupie went off into his private sanctum and closed

the door and got on the blower to somebody you could tell didn't welcome being woken up. Maybe it was Butcher Harris on his bath night. They say old Butcher plays with bombs in his bath, like admirals play with boats. We couldn't even hear Groupie's end of the conversation properly, but the tone was "How the hell do I get out of this one?" Then Butcher, or whoever it was, had a bright idea. You could tell that from the sudden change in Groupie's tone. A moment later he came out and told Dadda to take his crew, and every last bit of their kit and possessions, and load them into C-Charlie and depart at crack of dawn. Dadda asked what about C-Charlie's over-due engine overhaul? Dadda was told where he could stuff C-Charlie's overhaul. Or rather, it would be done after arrival at the new station. The expression on Groupie's face implied he wouldn't break his heart if C-Charlie crashed on the way.

Dadda asked where he was to fly us to. Groupie told him St. Mawgan, in Cornwall.

"Long-range attack on Tokyo via Mexico City," muttered Kit to me. Groupie froze him with a look, but said nothing. We were officially Crazies now, and no longer under his command. All he wanted was to see the back of us.

We reached our billet feeling slightly drunk, and began throwing stuff into our kitbags; throwing stuff at each other. Billy proved what a rotten shot he really was by heaving a boot through the window. We all thought that was an excellent idea, and joined in. When there were no barracks room windows left (thank God it was only September) and no mirror either (we'd all have liked seven years' bad luck, after months of the prospect of less than seven hours), we sat on our beds and talked.

"What's St. Mawgan?" asked Paul, taking a breather

from working out how to get his motorbike inside C-Charlie.

"Probably missions of an extra-hazardous nature," said Matt solemnly, and hiccuped.

"Like delivering milk to the *Tirpitz* and picking up the empties," said Kit.

Just then we heard the thirty-hundredweight pull up outside. We loaded up, including the motorbike. It was starting to get light and we espied an RAF policeman leading a dog on a bit of string toward the small-arms firing range. It was a little runt of an Alsatian thing, with ears that were still floppy. We all knew where it was going, and so did the dog. Its head was down and its tail drooped. Aircrew aren't supposed to keep pets, but they do. They ask their mates to take them over if they get the chop. But if their mates get the chop as well . . . The police were always taking dogs up to the firing range, with a shovel in the other hand. Anyway, Kit makes for this policeman with terrible speed, and we all take after him like the clappers. Including Dadda, who is quietly swearing to himself. The policeman pulls up, a look of amazement and then of acute distress on his face.

"I don't like you," says Kit. "I don't like you at all. I would not wish to have your company. I would rather have the company of that dog."

"I'm only obeying orders," said the policeman, licking his lips.

"So is Heinrich Himmler," says Kit, rather unreasonably, I thought. I mean, Himmler gets far more overtime pay than an RAF policeman. Kit holds out his hand. "That's *my* dog."

"Who says?"

"We do," we all chorused. He looked from one to the

other of us, bewildered. It's rather fun being an official
Crazy.

"Give him the dog, corporal," says Dadda, very crisp
and RAF.

"Yessir," says the policeman, standing to attention with
relief and giving a very fine salute. Oh, to be a single-
celled animal . . . We bundle back into the truck.

"What you going to call him, Kit?"

"Dieter. Leutnant Dieter Ernst Gehlen. But Dieter for
short. He's one of the crew now. He buys it, we all buy it.
He lives, we all live. He flies. Every damned op. What the
hell has he got to lose? If he wasn't here with us, he'd be
dead by now. Pure profit. He's gained five minutes' life
already." He fondled Dieter's ears affectionately, and Dieter licked his face with some enthusiasm. He'd lost his
chop-list look already.

At precisely 0435 hours, C-Charlie got clearance for
takeoff. With a bomb load of fifteen kitbags, one BSA
motorbike, and one happy dog. Nobody was supposed to
know we were going, but a lot turned out to see us off.

DADDA FLEW DOWN to St. Mawgan at a very moderate
height and a very moderate speed. I don't think he wanted
to risk straining the crate's engines. It was funny, starting
out with the sun coming up over our shoulders.

"We've gone west at last," said Kit. "So this is heaven?"

"Looks more like Slough," said Paul.

"Not the Slough of Despond?" Kit was in a daft mood.
He had nothing to do; navigationally, it was a trip around
the bay. We all gawped like trippers at a countryside of
mist and hill, cornfields turning pink in the sunrise, with
reaping machines and hay carts left any-old-how overnight.
A countryside we would never have to bomb, where early

farmhands looked up at us once and pedaled on. Where we weren't *Terrorflieger*.

Soon the pale blue of the Bristol Channel crawled over the horizon, to join the English Channel in sharpening the land to a pencil point. Devon and Cornwall narrowed and narrowed; the sea gathered in as if, if not to welcome us, at least to look us over. The slice of atmosphere spilling into the Wimpy smelled cleanly of ocean and seaweed. We took a crafty look at St. Mawgan from the air. It had the solid brick buildings of a permanent station; no more tents and Nissen huts. And even from up aloft you could see traces of RAF bullshit: whitewashed patterns of stones around a guardroom; what would be a flower bed again in the spring. I turned up the RT, so Dadda could speak to the control tower. Tower, a rich, fruity voice, finished up by saying, "You've chosen the right day to arrive. Mutton chops for lunch and the Saturday hop."

Silence. We were all knocked silly by the idea of a regular Saturday hop. Saturday night was the Butcher's favorite time for the Happy Valley, the Ruhr, that is.

"This place sounds like a bloody Butlin's holiday camp," Kit blurted out.

"Watch your tongue, sergeant," said Dadda, more RAF than I'd ever heard him.

"I heard that," said the fruity voice, not at all put out.

THAT SATURDAY HOP was quite a thing. A sea of floral dresses; the smell of face powder and the swish of silk stockings. Not a bad band, either: three corporals and three LACs—leading aircraftmen—and a nice semiprofessional touch, even if the music was a bit out of date; provincial. Most of us just sat and watched anyway, and breathed in the females, though Billy the Kid got involved

with a red-haired WAAF with an amazing pair of Bristols.
And Paul found a guy who owned a motorbike.

I just kept watching faces. There were a lot of steady
couples, staid, steady couples. Nobody living it up, kicking
the place apart, or twitching. The aircrew looked hard-
worked, but they had the ruddy look of fishermen or
shepherds. Many were quite solid around the middle; if
bombers make your guts screw up, the boredom of Coastal
Command makes you nibble. They looked middle-aged;
quite a number had balding heads. But none of them
looked as if he was on the chop list. It was so hot and
flowery-smelling I fell asleep twice. But I wouldn't go to
bed. I was too busy absorbing the possibility of having
some sort of future.

And that's the way it's been, the last ten months. It's
not a soft life in Coastal. Try crawling out of your bed in
a 5 a.m. blizzard and trying to keep your perspex frost-free
with your heating hose and fingernails. And our lot have
lost three crews in ten months. We often wonder what
happened to them. Maybe they met one of those Junkers
that get into the north end of the Bay; maybe they met a
wind that read 120 knots on their API. But that's the
point: we have time to sit and wonder what happened to
them, and that's quite a luxury. We sometimes stay in the
air for thirteen hours at a stretch with extra-load tanks,
and that's a lot of time to wonder, while you're watching
the radar screen for the tiny blip that means a U-boat
snorkeling.

Meanwhile, we, too, have turned into fishermen and
shepherds. We've dropped plenty of depth charges, of
course, but as far as we know killed nowt but blossoming
white circles of belly-up fish. We met a U-boat once, on
the surface off the Skelligs, when we were coming home

with no depth charges left. Paul exchanged a few words with it, and it left the scene of the crime rapidly. We weren't all that bothered.

Otherwise, we see a lot of sunrises and sunsets from high up, and study the flight of birds. A storm petrel came through the windscreen once, and wrapped itself around Dadda's neck. Paul reckoned it had been trained by the Japs in kamikaze tactics. We had it stuffed for the billet mantelpiece. And we fly around in big circles and little circles, just like herring gulls, but a bloody sight colder. But when we leave a convoy and their Aldis lamp winks "Thank you," we feel a bit warmer.

Everything says we're going to finish the war here; the forgotten army. They've taken away Tinsel, but Dadda wouldn't let them pinch Monica. They've covered our black paint with a lovely coat of Coastal white, with two black bands around the fuselage. And we haven't burned any more crates. Dieter is great; he's not grown much, but he's put on weight and got this glossy, all-black coat that makes him look a proper Nazi. Which is a laugh, because he'll lie down for anybody to tickle his belly. He likes riding in the front gun turret, slobbering over Paul with excitement. He flies every op: Coastal understand about mascots; they're nearly all ex-bomber anyway.

Oh, and we've got this new game. Dadda disclosed that his family have a ruined castle and estate at a place in Eire called Castletownsend. We're all going to live there after the war, as gamekeepers and illicit whiskey distillers and things. He did a zero-feet raid on the Republic last month, to show us the castle from the air. The Irish authorities complained, but Dadda just told the Wingco he had an Irish passport. I don't know if any of Dadda's story is true, but it helps to pass the time.

Yes, we get a lot of time to think, in Coastal. Think about the old squadron; all new faces by now, nobody left who remembers the end of Dieter Gehlen. Think about all the English ex-schoolgirls filling bombs till their backs ache, all the German ex-schoolgirls making shells. Think about the guts of German mothers in Hamburg, sheltering their kids with their own bodies from the fire typhoon we started. Think about the craftsmen's skill in a Rolls-Royce Merlin, and a German medieval cathedral. All those people with all those guts, and our top brass are just turning them all into one great big rubbish heap that's slowly covering Europe. While we watch sea gulls.

I sometimes think, toward the end of a thirteen-hour flight, that we died after all, that we're in some kind of peaceful gray Valhalla where good little aircrews go. But where are the rest? Blackham and Reaper and Edwards? And Dieter Gehlen?

Don't ask me. It's May 1944, and I think I've got the little WAAF in the radio stores interested.

Two more pints, please, George.

NOTES ON
FIRST PUBLICATION

"Woman and Home" first published in *The Call and Other Stories* (London & New York, 1989). Reprinted here by permission of Viking Children's Books /Penguin Books Ltd.

"St. Austin Friars" first published in *Break of Dark* (London & New York, 1982). Reprinted here by permission of Chatto & Windus / Random House UK Ltd.

"The Haunting of Chas McGill" first published in *Ghost After Ghost*, Aidan Chambers, comp. (London, 1982). Reprinted in *The Haunting of Chas McGill and Other Stories* (London & New York, 1983).

"In Camera" first published in *The Fearful Lovers*, which appeared in the U.S.A. as *In Camera and Other Stories* (London, 1992; New York, 1993).

"Fifty-fafty" first published in *Hidden Turnings*, Diana Wynne Jones, comp. (London, 1989; New York, 1990).

"The Cats" has not appeared previously.

"The Boys' Toilets" first published in *Cold Feet*, Jean Richardson, comp. (London, 1985). Reprinted in *Ghosts and Journeys* (London, 1988).

"The Red House Clock" first published in *The Call and Other Stories*. Reprinted here by permission of Viking Children's Books / Penguin Books Ltd.

"The Call" first published in *The Call and Other Stories*. Reprinted here by permission of Viking Children's Books / Penguin Books Ltd.

"The Cat, Spartan" first published in *A Walk on the Wild Side* (London, 1989). Reprinted here by permission of Methuen Children's Books / Reed Consumer Books Ltd.

"Blackham's Wimpy" first published in *Break of Dark*. Reprinted here by permission of Chatto & Windus / Random House UK Ltd.

nic